DEMONS

Selected Works by John Shirley

DEMONS

John Shirley

THE BALLANTINE PUBLISHING GROUP

NEW YORK

A Del Rey® Book
Published by The Ballantine Publishing Group
Copyright © 2000, 2002 by John Shirley

All rights reserved under International and Pan-American
Copyright Conventions. Published in the United States by
The Ballantine Publishing Group, a division of Random House, Inc.,
New York, and simultaneously in Canada by Random House of Canada
Limited, Toronto. A portion of this work was previously published as a
novella under the title *Demons* by Cemetery Dance Publications in 2000.

Del Rey is a registered trademark and the Del Rey colophon
is a trademark of Random House, Inc.

www.delreydigital.com

LIBRARY OF CONGRESS CATALOGING-IN-PUBLICATION DATA
Shirley, John, 1953–
Demons / John Shirley.—1st ed.
p.   cm.
ISBN 0-345-44647-X
1. Demonology—Fiction.   I. Title.
PS3569.H558 D46 2002
813'.54—dc21   2001043478

Text design Mary A. Wirth

Manufactured in the United States of America

First Edition: March 2002

10   9   8   7   6   5   4   3   2   1

For Richard Smoley

AUTHOR'S NOTE

This book is a novel in two parts and two separate novels, at once. The second novel is a sequel to the first. It was written some considerable time after the first, but it could not stand alone—*Demons* Book Two is dependent on *Demons* Book One.

The material on clandestine government and military projects, sent by Glyneth to Stephen in Chapter Four of Book Two, is all quite real.

Both parts of the novel were written before September 11, 2001, but—they are not without relevance. . . .

LEXICON

TAILPIPES Massive leviathans but varying in shape at will; often are more or less like a giant slug with nothing like a head. Skin may erupt with mouths that steam. They show no sentience and may be controlled or dominated by Gnashers.

SPIDERS Three-legged but spidcrish in shape, intelligent yet arachnoid/insectile in activity—airborne via sky-gliding parachutes of web.

SHARKADIANS Can fly via rows of smallish leather wings that shouldn't be big enough to carry them but can. Head is *all jaws*; body is ostensibly like a human female, but with clawed hands and feet. Pure savagery. May be dominated by Bugsys.

DISHRAGS Shaped like bunches of furry rags big as VW bugs; can contort so they resemble some sea creature—no definite shape. Wrap and slowly crush victims, often with psychic/ metaphysical/quantum continuum disruption.

GNASHERS Talkative; at times, appear to have an agenda; are verbally sadistic; telepathic. Humanoid but have four arms; jaws are like Sharkadians' though the mouth parts are a little smaller, and with the addition of upper head parts; have human eyes. They possibly function in a leadership capacity, but no one is quite certain.

GRINDUMS Giant grasshopper legs, insectile/human heads with curling horns, big grinding jaws that move sideways, at an angle, or revolve as they choose. They can generate great heat at will.

BUGSYS Parodies of humans; no two are alike but all are similar in style, complete with skin that resembles clothing but spotted with oozing sores. They can sometimes be stymied for a while by offering to play cards with them—they love gambling. Tend to chatter idiotically . . . Like the Gnashers, speak English or any language of Earth at will—or their own tongue.

TARTARAN Demon language.

Who is a holy person? The one who is
aware of others' suffering.

—KABIR

BOOK ONE

DEMONS

A PROLOGUE

*I*t's amazing what you can get used to. That was a platitude;
now it summarizes life for everyone. It means something
powerful now. People can get used to terrible privation, to
famine, to war, to vast and soulless discount stores. Some got
used to prison; some got used to living alone on mountaintops.
But now . . .

This morning I saw a choleric-looking, pop-eyed sort of a
middle-aged man in a threadbare suit stop his huffing old Volvo
at a street corner, look about for cross traffic, accelerate slowly
to creep across the intersection—the traffic lights, of course, not
having worked for a long time, not through the whole north of
the state. And one of the demons turned the street to soft hot
tar, the demon rising up, howling, from the stuff of the street itself, rows of fangs in the creature's absurdly big jaws gleaming

3

and dripping. The demon was one of the Grindum clan—giant grasshopper legs, insectile heads with just enough human about them to sicken: curling horns, big grinding jaws that move sideways or at an angle or revolve on their skulls like an owl's head on its shoulders. The Grindum swam in the hot asphalt with a conventional freestroke, humming some tune.

The Volvo began to sink in the steaming asphalt. The driver merely got a good grip on his briefcase, opened the car door, used the door handle for a ladder rung, ran along the roof of the car to the hood, and jumped to the curb. Landing rather neatly, he continued on his way, not even looking back, hurrying only a little. He didn't even turn around as the demon, chattering in Tartaran, snapped the door off the car and sailed it through the window of a bank. The bank was long closed, as most of them are now.

A woman came out of a bar, too drunk to heed the warnings of her friends, and the demon heaved the car atop her, his iridescent green-black scaly torso still half buried in the molten street. I wondered absently if he were standing on a pipe down there.

I had already turned away from the street corner and saw most of this by glancing over my shoulder, now and then, in a measured retreat. If you ran in panic, the demon was more likely to notice you and pursue, especially the Grindum clan. The Sharkadians, on the other hand, are more methodical: When they've selected a neighborhood, they'll stalk through it and cut you down as they find you—or toy with you and leave you sorrowfully alive, wishing they'd killed you—whether you're running or not.

I made it around the corner. I heard another scream but didn't go back to look. I had an appointment to teach art to children, and I was looking forward to it. Creating little per-

sonal works of art raises them, for a few minutes, out of the fear and depression that haunts the young now, though the art usually expresses fear of the demons. And when they're raised up a little, in that moment of self-expression, they raise me up with them.

So I was not going to risk being late. Or risk, for that matter, being torn limb from limb or sat upon and whispered to for hours before being dispatched. My heart was beating faster as I hurried away, but I was all right. I was . . .

Used to it? I suppose it isn't really true. You can't be *really* used to them. You can only adapt, more or less.

But not everyone has. Certainly more people than ever before go quite mad, utterly psychotic, daily; driven mad by the presence of hundreds of thousands of flesh-and-blood demons who appear randomly and all too frequently among us now. Those who were mad before the transfiguration of the world feel more at home.

Some of those who were the babbling neighborhood schizophrenics sport a rather annoying look of smug vindication these days.

People sometimes tell jokes about the demons. "How can you tell a Sharkadian from a Gnasher?"

"Easy. A Gnasher doesn't like a screw-top cap—he always uses real cork to stop up their necks after he pulls their heads off." (You had to be there. Gnashers put on aristocratic airs.)

For a brief while, some said it was all a hoax. In the first day or two of the demonic invasion you could dismiss even the television footage as staged, perhaps special effects, a government scam to necessitate martial law. Often those who made such a claim in the media met a demon within minutes. They were then reduced—in the butcher's sense of the term—or watched their loved ones reduced.

There are some who said, for a time, that the coming of the seven clans of demons—their random dominance of our world, in daylight as much as night—was a fulfillment of prophecy. If the commentator was Christian he said it fulfilled Revelations. The Jews, the Sikhs, the Muslims pointed to other prophecies. The Fundamentalist Christians, anyway, were easily refuted: The Second Coming part never came about. They waited and waited for the Judgment; for the angel with the flaming sword, for the Rapture, for the dead to rise (now and then the demons raise the dead, but not the way the Christians expected), for Jesus to come in his glory.

Jesus was a no-show. Naturally, the evangelists rationalized his conspicuous absence: The Sacred Timetable, don't you know, is a little off, that's all. But the most "righteous" of them were eaten alive, a limb at a time, in public, no differently than sinners. I remember when the demons rampaged through Oral Roberts University. The sniggering delight that some hipsters and cynics took in this brutal series of bloody atrocities was most embarrassing—for the rest of us cynics and hipsters.

People adapt; they have their little ways. Some adapted by giving the demons little classification nicknames, which later caught on—names like "Gnashers" and "Dishrags" somehow making the creatures seem less threatening—or by spinning theories about them, trying to evolve methods of avoiding or controlling them, none of which work. There were TV specials for a while, demands on Congress, the short-lived National Guard assaults, resulting in forty thousand dead soldiers. The TV series *The World in Crisis* came to a grinding halt when every reporter was slowly and lovingly masticated by giant Grindums.

There were those, of course, who asserted at first that the demons were space aliens or the confabulations of aliens or multiple races of space aliens come to invade, that the invaders resembled demons only because our past encounters with the

aliens left ancestral memories of their shapes, extraterrestrial shapes, remembered as "demons." You know the sort of thing. But anyone who has survived an encounter with one of the seven clans is left with no doubt that these are supernatural creatures. There's no question that they are quite specifically demonic, that not only are they not aliens, they distinctly belong here. How does one know this? It's another one of those intangibles that, ironically, define the creatures. Once you've encountered them—you simply know. You can *feel* their miraculous nature; you can feel they're somehow rooted in our world. And after having such encounters, Close Encounters of the Nearly Fatal Kind, the purveyors of ET explanations fall silent.

I'm writing this now because of Professor Paymenz's theory. I should say one of his theories—he has so many. This one is something like Paymenz theory number 1,347. Dr. Israel Paymenz believes that we can communicate with other times, other eras, through the medium of a sort of higher, ubiquitous ancestral mind that links all humanity. He believes that writers and poets and declaimers in the past sometimes "dictate" to writers of the later eras through this psychic link; that historians of the future communicate, unconsciously and with only partial accuracy, with the writers of the past—thus the more believable science fiction. So it is that much writing is, unknown to us, a kind of Ouija affair; only, the receiver is not hearing from the dead but from people of another time, from the living of the past and future.

Not very likely, that theory; I doubt he believes it either. But writing this, at a time when I feel resoundingly helpless, makes me feel better.

So I try to believe his theory . . . which leaves me writing this just eleven years into the twenty-first century, hoping to warn the previous century, or even earlier. Not warn them of some specific act or mistake. We don't yet know *why* the seven clans came. But I dream of warning that they will come, so that, perhaps, the people of the past can begin looking for the *why* in advance. The demons certainly have given us no whys nor hows nor wherefores. They delight in communicating only what confuses.

Though the demons will talk to us sometimes, they are, of course, notoriously unhelpful. When the President went with a delegation, including the Vice President, to see an apparent demon clan chieftain—we don't know for certain he was a chieftain; their hierarchy is arcane, if they have any at all—who was stalking the West Wing of the White House, they had a rather extensive conversation, nearly fifteen minutes, that was recorded and analyzed and that offers exchanges like this, transcribed from near its end:

THE PRESIDENT: And why is it, please, that you have come to—to us, now?

GNASHER CHIEFTAIN: Home is where the heart is. Boy Scouts have a salty sort of taste, with marshmallow overtones. I like your tie. Are those Gucci loafers?

THE PRESIDENT: Yes, yes, they are. So you're familiar with all our customs?

GNASHER: I've never killed a customs agent. Are they good to kill? Never mind. Where is your wife?

PRESIDENT: My—she's . . . in Florida.

GNASHER: Does the Vice President have sex with her? Which vices does he preside over? I'm just fucking with you about that. But seriously: Do you like sweet or salt best?

PRESIDENT: Could you tell me please why you have come here and if there's something we can give you . . . some arrangement we can make. . . .

GNASHER: I wonder what you'd look like inside out. Like a
Christmas tree?
PRESIDENT: We are willing to negotiate.
GNASHER: I can almost taste you now. You once had a dream
you cracked open the Moon like an egg, and a red yolk came
out and you fried it on the burning Earth, didn't you, once, eh?
Did you? Do speak plainly and tell me: Did you?
PRESIDENT: I don't believe so.
GNASHER: You did. You dreamt exactly that. People think
someone like me would delight in the carnage of a battlefield,
but I prefer a nice mall, don't you?
PRESIDENT: Yes, certainly. Perhaps in that spirit—
GNASHER: You wish to sell me cuff links? Can you breathe in
a cloud of iron filings? Let's find out. Let's discover a new jigsaw, a new 3-D puzzle, shall we? The human body, disassem-
bled, might be put back together in a way that makes sense.
You could make a fine buckyball out of the bones and a yurt
from the skin and a talk show host of the wet parts. What an
imaginative people you are. We stand in awe at the outskirts of
Buenos Aires in the summertime, each fly a musical note. Can
we send out for ice cream? For girls who work in ice cream par-
lors and their boyfriends in their electric Trans Ams? Taste this
part of my leg. It tastes differently from this part. You won't
taste? I have a penis. Would you prefer it? Do you like salty or
sweet? Seriously. Choose one. Would you like to see my penis? I
asked for it special. There's a catalog.

With that, a steaming green member pressed from a fold
on the Gnasher's lower parts, and as the President tried to back
away the Gnasher caught him in a long ropy sweep of its arm
and pulled him close and forced him to his knees. In front of
the TV cameras.

DEMONS

An eruption of gunshots from the Secret Service had no effect, of course, on the Gnasher. It was the Vice President—a decisive man, who'd been broodingly biding his time for two years—who took a pistol from the President's bodyguard and shot the President in the back of the head. It was obvious to everyone there, and to a sympathetic Congress the next day, that the Gnasher, after all, was choking the President to death with his engorged, steaming green penis. It was a question of restoring dignity to the President and the office. The Vice President fled the scene, sacrificing a number of Secret Service men ordered to delay the pursuing demon while he escaped.

"It's profoundly tragic," the Vice President said afterward, "but it's God's will. We must move on. I have certain announcements to make. . . ." He is reported more or less safe in a certain underground bunker.

But I should tell you how it began. It was months ago. Despite the usual outbreaks of savagery, the wet snow of the ordinary was blanketing the world. The miraculous rarely shows itself. When it does, it comes seamlessly, and for some reason, everyone is surprised.

1

*A*s for me . . . I was up in a high-rise in San Francisco, those months ago: the morning the demons came.

I had gone to see Professor Paymenz or, to be perfectly honest, to see his daughter under the auspices of seeing the professor. It was housing that San Francisco State had arranged for him—they had a program supplying subsidized housing to teaching staff—and as I arrived I saw another eviction notice from SFSU on the door. Paymenz had refused to teach comparative religion anymore, would lecture only about obscure occult practices and beliefs, and rarely showed up even for those classes. He hadn't ever had his tenure settled, so they simply fired him. But he'd refused to leave the university housing on the simple but contumacious grounds, as he explained, that he deserved this more than the teacher down the hall, who taught "existential themes in daytime television."

Vastly bearded, restless-eyed, in the grimy alchemist's robe that he wore as a nightgown, Paymenz looked over my shoulder into the hallway behind me. Expecting to see someone back there. He always did that, and he never met my eyes, no matter how earnestly he spoke to me.

He seemed almost happy to see me as he ushered me in. He even said, "Why, hello, Ira." He rarely troubled with social niceties.

I saw that Professor Shephard was there, small-brimmed fedora in hand. Shephard seemed poised between staying and going. Maybe that was why Paymenz was happy to see me: It gave him an excuse to get rid of an unwanted visitor.

Shephard was a short, fiftyish, bullet-shaped man in an immaculate gray suit, vest, tie that matched the season. He had a shaved head, eyes the color of aluminum, a perpetual pursed smile, and a jutting jaw.

He put his hat on his head but didn't go. Standing there in the exact middle of the small living room, with his arms by his sides, his small feet in shiny black shoes neatly together, Shephard looked out of place in Paymenz's untidy, jumbled apartment. He looked set up and painted like one of those Russian toys, the sort made of smooth wood containing ever-smaller copies. Shephard was an economics professor who believed in "returning economics to philosophy, as it was with our Founding Fathers, and, yes, with Marx"—but his philosophy had something to do with "pragmatic postmodernism." Today his tie was all coppery maple leaves against rusty orange, celebrating autumn.

I knew Shephard from the last conference on Spirituality and Economics he'd put together—he'd hired me to create the poster, with "appropriate imagery," and paid me three times for doing three versions, each version less definite, blander than the one before. At every poster-design discussion, he'd brought up Paymenz. "I understand you're his good friend. What is he up to? And his daughter? How is she?"

The questions always felt like non sequiturs. Now, recognizing me, he nodded pleasantly. "Ira. How are you?"

"Dr. Shephard," Paymenz said before I could reply, "thank you for dropping in—I have guests, as you see. . . ."

Shephard's head swiveled on his shoulders like a turret, first at me, then to Paymenz. "Of course. I am sorry to have precipitated myself upon you, as it were; perhaps certain matters are of some urgency. Perhaps not. I only wished to plant the seed of the idea, so to say, that, should the conference on Spiritual Philosophy and Economics not come about this weekend for any reason, I do wish to stay in touch—very closely in touch. Please feel free to call me." He handed Paymenz a business card and was moving toward the door. He startled me by *not* seeming to move on rollers; he walked as any man his size might. A normal walk seemed odd on him. "I will speak to the board about your housing issue, as promised, one more time. Au revoir!" He opened, passed through, and closed the door with hardly a sound, smooth as smoke up a chimney.

Paymenz irritably tossed the business card onto a lamp table heaped with cards, unopened letters, bills. "That man's arrogance, the way he just shows up unexpectedly . . . always as if he has no agenda . . . babbling about his conference not coming off—when there's no reason it shouldn't . . . I should never have agreed to go to his antiseptic-yet-strangely-septic conference, if he hadn't offered me a fee . . . but he knows perfectly well I need the money."

Hoping Paymenz remembered he actually had invited me

over for coffee, I looked around for some place to hang my leather jacket. But of course there was no place, really, to put it. The closet was crammed full with clothes no one wore; and with junk. The other apartments in the twenty-story high-rise were underdecorated minimalist-modern affairs, trying to echo the utilitarian, airy curviness that the architects of the building had borrowed from I. M. Pei or Frank Lloyd Wright. Paymenz, however, had covered the walls with an ethnically disconnected selection of tapestries and carpets—Persian and Chinese and a Southwestern design from Sears. He collected old lava lamps, and though the electricity had been turned off, they churned away, six of them crudely wired to car batteries, with lots of electrical tape around half-stripped connections. The lamps sat on the car batteries and on end tables and mantels, shape-shifting in waxen primary colors. A week previous, it was said, the entire SFSU board of tenure review had come out to the university parking lot to find their cars mysteriously inert.

Half a dozen more lava lamps were broken, used as book-ends for the many hundreds of books that took up most of the space that wasn't tapestry. Two candles were burning, and a fading battery lamp.

Cats darted behind chairs and moved sinuously up and down much-clawed cat trees. I counted four cats—no, five: They'd taken in a new one.

There were bits of breakfast toast in Paymenz's long, shovel-shaped gray-and-black beard; his eyes, red-rimmed gray under bristling brows, rested on me for only a flicker as he spoke. "Many the auguries this morning, Ira. Would you like to see?"

"You know how I feel about medieval techniques, especially any that involve damp, decaying guts," I said, looking about for Melissa. I was an aficionado of the arcane metaphysical, being the former art director for the now-defunct

Visions: The Magazine of Spiritual Life, but I drew the line at peering into rotting intestines.

"It's fresh pig bladder," he said, "none of that decaying stuff anymore. Melissa made me promise. I suppose the place is rank enough already."

The place wasn't quite rank, but it bore a distinct smell: pipe tobacco and cat boxes and cloying Middle Eastern incense, all vying for dominance.

"I see you have some new lava lamps."

"Yes. Look at this one—a confection of gold-flecked red ooze fighting its way into a feverish primeval swelling. Unconsciously, the designer was thinking of the philosopher's stone."

"I don't know if they bothered with a designer for these things after the first one."

"They don't need one, it's true—and that's the point. The lava lamp is protosociety's purely unconscious expression of the primeval ooze on one level, shaping itself into our most remote sea-slime ancestors; on another level, the lava lamp is the pleroma, the fundamental stuff that gives birth to the existential condition. Hank, down at the antique shop, tells me he likes to smoke pot and look into his lava lamps, and then he sees girls there, apparently, in all those sinuous lava-bubbling curves—like Moscoso drawings—but it's all quite unconscious . . . tabula rasa for the subconscious. . . . Freud not utterly discredited after all, if we consider Hank and his lamps . . ."

Paymenz noticed my attention wandering; my gaze must have drifted to Melissa's bedroom door. "Oh good lord. Typical young person today. Post-MTV generation. Internet-surfing brain damage. Attention span of a gnat. Melissa! Come in here, this young man is already weary of pretending he's here to see me! He's aquiver with desire for you!" He clutched his reeking alchemist's robe about himself—Melissa had made it for him, as a mother will make a Superman cape for her little boy—and stumped off to the kitchen to finish his breakfast. "He's sniffing the air for your pheromones!" he called to her as he went.

I grimaced, but I was used to the professor's indifference to social insulation of any kind whatsoever.

Melissa came in then, wearing a long black skirt, no shoes, a loose, low-cut Gypsy-type purple blouse. Her crooked smile was even more to one side of her triangular face than usual in wry deprecation of her father's vulgarity.

"Shephard is gone?" she asked.

"He is," I said, "unless he's somehow watching us through his business card."

"Wouldn't surprise me. He makes my skin contract on my body," she said, locking the front door. "He asked me if he could hear me sing for him sometime! Like to hear my songs, he said."

I was thinking that Shephard had always had an unhealthy interest in her but decided not to remark on it. My own interest in her, I told myself, was . . . earthy.

She was a few inches taller than me, a big girl with tiny feet; I don't know how she kept from teetering. Her forehead was high, this only mildly mitigated by the shiny black bangs; long raven wings of hair fell straight to her pale, stooped shoulders and coursed round them. Her large green eyes looked at me frankly; they seemed to coruscate. Her chin was just a little slight. Somehow the imperfections in her prettiness were sexy to me. I suspected, after long, covert inspections from various angles through various fabrics, that her right breast turned fractionally to one side while the other pointed straight ahead. Each small white toe of her small white feet had a ring on it, and her ankles jangled with Tibetan bells. She was thirty, worked in a health food store, and did endless research for her father's never-finished magnum opus, *The Hidden Reality*.

"Come into the kitchen with me," she said, "and help me make tea and toast. You can make it on the gas broiler. We've got the gas and water back on."

"I couldn't possibly let you take on a big job like making tea and toast alone."

She stacked up the wheat bread, and I found the old copper teapot and filled it with tap water. As it filled, I said, "I wonder what impurities and pollutants this particular tap water has in it. No doubt some future forensic archaeologist will analyze my body and find the stuff. Like, 'This skeleton shows residues of lead, pesticides, heavy metal contaminants—' "

"Which perhaps weighted down his consciousness so he became doleful all the time. Great Goddess! Ira, you can't even pour a cup of tea without seeing doom in the offing?"

I listened to her bells jangle as she got the margarine off the cooler shelf in the kitchen window. I washed out some cups. "I see you've painted your toenails silver." I thought of making a joke about how they might be little mirrors allowing me to see up her skirt but decided it would come off more puerile than cute. There were times when it was paradoxically almost sophisticated to be puerile, but this wasn't one of them.

"I mean, it must've occurred to you," she was saying, looking through a cluttered drawer for a butter knife, "that this prevailingly negative view of the world could attract negative consequences."

"The butter knife is in that peanut butter jar on top of the refrigerator. My negative view of the world—I would only believe it would attract negative consequences if I were superstitious." I painted on mystical themes, illustrated for magazines about the supernatural, meditated, and prayed—and I was a notorious skeptic. This irritated some believers; others found it refreshing. I was simply convinced that most of what was taken for the supernatural was the product of the imagination. Most but not all. Sufi masters sometimes say that one of the necessary skills for the seeker is the ability to discriminate between superstition working on the imagination and real spiritual contact. "There are plenty of pessimists who are quite successful in life—look at that old geezer who used to be a filmmaker . . . he was just in the news, saying that his application to be part of the rejuvenation experiments was turned down because of some old scandal . . . what's-his-name. Horn-rim glasses."

"Woody Allen, I think. But still, overall, Ira—hand me the bread—overall, people can think themselves into miserable lives."

"I'm not so miserable. I've got work for a month or two ahead, and I'm playing house at this moment with someone who . . ." Suddenly I didn't know how to finish. She glanced at me sidelong, and I saw her droop her head so that her hair would swing to hide her smile. *I'm an idiot when I try to express anything but bile*, I thought. "Anyway," I went on hastily, "the world needs no help from my bad vibes or whatever you call it. The enormity of the suffering in it . . . Should we use this Red Rose tea or . . . you don't have English Breakfast or something? Okay, fine, I like Red Rose, too . . . I mean, regarding the world's own negative vibes, simply look at the news."

"Oh no, don't do *that*."

"Seriously, Melissa—over the last decade or so this country has gotten so corrupt. There was a lot of it already but now we're becoming like Mexico City. I mean, they discovered that a certain pesticide was causing all these birth defects in the Central Valley—there was a big move to get it banned. But if it was banned the agribusiness and chemicals people would lose money on the poison they kept in reserves. Cut their profit margin. So the ban was killed. And everyone forgot all about it, and the stuff is still choking the ecology out there and no one gives a damn. Then the corruption thing gets worse and worse—the feds just found out that all this federal aid that was supposed to go to vaccinating and blood-testing ghetto kids was stolen by all these people appointed to give it out. They just raked it off and put it in other accounts—they stole millions intended for these kids. . . . And a lot of the people doing the stealing were the same ethnicity as the poor they were supposed to be helping. It wasn't racism—it was simple corruption. It was greed. It's like life is a big trough and we're all looking for a way to elbow in and get at the slops and nothing else matters."

"Ira, butter these for me."

"Sure. And did you see that thing on PBS about that country in Central America—the big shots running the country decided that the fast money would come from making it into a waste dump for all these other countries that ran out of room. The entire country is a waste dump! The whole thing, a landfill! The guys who run the country moved to these pristine little islands offshore, and the entire rest of the country works in waste dumps—either they work in them, burning and shoving stuff around with big machines, or they pick through them. Literally millions of people picking through a waste dump thousands of miles across . . ."

"Oh, you must be exaggerating. Surely not the whole country. Bring me that blue teapot."

"I'm not exaggerating. That country is *literally* one giant dump—there is no farmland, there are no wetlands, there are no forests, and there are only a few towns left. It's all dump. Barges come from North America, Mexico, Brazil . . . from the neighboring countries. And people will live and die in that dump. Can you imagine? It's like a great festering sore on the epidermis of the planet—and it's not alone. Why, in Asia—"

"Ira?" She touched my arm. Her fingernails alternated silver with black flecks and black with silver flecks. "The sick get better. The world will suffer, and this will make it see what it has done, and it will heal itself. It will."

I guess we both understood, she and I, that it was a sort of script we had together. The tacit script brought me to her, and I'd tell her that the world was in Hell for this reason or that, and she'd tell me there was hope, that it would someday be all right, and not to give up on life. I guess we both knew that I came to her for a sort of mothering—my own mother had died when I was fifteen, from the amphetamines her boyfriend shot into her. I guess we both knew that when Melissa said there was hope for the world that it really meant there was hope for me.

Melissa always plays along. She is all generosity. She doesn't seem to mind.

I wonder if she wouldn't mind if I made love to her.

"There'll be hard times," she was saying, "but the world will heal."

"Maybe," I said. "Maybe so."

She took her hand away. "Would you carry the toast plate? I'll get the teapot and the cups." Not an allocation of duty made at random: She took the most breakable stuff herself. I was notorious for my clumsiness.

"Sure. I'll get it."

———

We ate breakfast, Paymenz and his daughter and me, out on the molded balcony. Breakfast of a sort: We consumed a stack of margarine-slick toast and bloodred tea at the tilting glass-topped wrought-iron table on their concrete balcony, overlooking a mist-draped west San Francisco, under a lowering sky, listening to pigeons cooing from the roof and sirens sighing from the projects, and the thudding rise and fall, like armies passing, of hip-hop boxes booming in the asphalt plaza below.

I watched the traffic on the boulevard visible between the glassy buildings of the hospital complex. The traffic pulsed one way, then came to a stop; and the traffic from the cross street pulsed by; then the first artery would resume pumping. Cars and trucks and SUVs and vans; about 20 percent of them were electric now. Was the air cleaner with the electric cars? Not much—there were so many more people now, which meant many more cars of both kinds.

The professor spoke of his wrangles with the university personnel board, his demands for back pay; and despite his promise he asked me to look at the bladders and the entrails he had cut open and kept in an ice chest with some of that perma-ice stuff, so that he could scry the patterns that would become the future. And I said no, I would be content if Melissa would bring out her Tarot cards, for Tarot cards have no appreciable smell, and he had just said, "Ah, but that's where you're wrong." Just then, the mist that had been hanging in the air seemed to drift upward over the plaza, and the clouds overhead developed drippy places on their undersides, like the beginnings of tornadoes, but which expanded into thick globules of vitreous emulsion, like drops hanging from the ceiling of a steam bath, getting heavier and heavier. The birds had fallen silent; the air grew turgid with imminence. Dr. Paymenz and Melissa and I found ourselves as silent as the birds, gazing expectantly at the clouds, then at the city, and then again at the strangely shaped clouds, as if the sky had developed nipples that were giving out a strange effluvium. But now the clouds up above bulged and seemed to swarm within themselves. . . .

2

"*D*ad?" Melissa said in a voice that quavered only a little. He reached out and took her hand but kept watching the sky.

Then the droplets burst like fungus pods, and gave out black spores. And the specks of black took on more definite shapes, shapes that soared and dropped and called from the distance with hooting, anticipatory glee. And then we saw little black cones forming on the streets below and exuding not lava but inverted teardrops, mercuric and quivering, that burst in counterpoint to cloud drops, scattering nodes of black that took shape and joined their fellows above. And we saw some of them drifting closer, coming toward us and to the other buildings in the city, growing as they came not only in the change of perspective but in individual size; and one of them—with a row of leather wings like thistle leaves up and down its back—came to grip our building, five stories below, with long ropy arms and legs that ended in eagle's claws. It was what we later came to call a Sharkadian. Its body was theoretically female—with leathery green-black breasts, and a woman's hips, and even a vaginal slit. But gender is only a parody among the demons. The Sharkadian's head didn't maintain the mock femininity— it was jaws and only jaws, and it used them to bite off a chunk of concrete balcony. It chewed meditatively for a moment and then spat wet sand. A man came out on a nearby balcony to see what all the shouting from the street was, and got out half a scream before the Sharkadian leapt on him and snapped part of his skull away, not quite enough to kill him instantly. It's been noted many times that the demons rarely dispatch anyone quickly; they always play with their food.

In the square below there was deep-throated laughter and weeping, pursuit hither and thither.

On our balcony the professor began to intone, so rapidly he seemed to be thinking hysterically aloud, something like, "It was this morning that I reflected that science knows all and nothing at once; that they may assert the core of the atom is the nucleus, a hydrogen atom comprising a single stable, positively charged particle, the proton, say; electrons around other sorts of particles making a kind of shell of particle-wave charge, and they are entirely correct, yet all they're doing is labeling phenomena, just labeling, labeling. . . ."

Melissa came to cling to me, but I could not enjoy the contact. I was about to drag her inside to tentative safety, when a demon—one of the almost elegant Gnashers, clashing its teeth as it came—settled onto the balcony beside ours; and then we were petrified, unable to move. We watched as a terrified woman on the neighboring balcony—Mrs. Gurevitz, I think her name was—tried to flee back inside. The demon pulled her close and, typical of the Gnashers, simply forced her to sit and engaged her in conversation for a while, telling her unctuously that it saw in her mind that she hated her bullying husband but was afraid to leave him because of the money problem, because she had no skills; and why didn't she have skills—because she was basically a mistake perpetrated by her mother in a careless moment, not a real person who could develop skills, not like her sister, who was a lawyer, *there* was someone real. And the woman writhed in her chair as both the demon and the professor droned on. The professor saying sotto voce to no one in particular: "They may assert, for example, that the region in subatomic space in which an electron is most likely to be found is called an orbital, but it's just a label, a tag used in describing the behavior of certain forces under certain conditions, that description accurate but offering no real insight into the nature of that thing—they don't know *why* the atom is that way, even if they can describe the series of events that took it there. It's just as mysterious as if they'd never studied it at all."

I wasn't sure if he'd gone mad—or was stunned into a stream-of-consciousness volubility.

Finally, as I saw four demons coming toward us through the air, I began to struggle with my paralysis, with rigidity of fear so pronounced that wrenching loose from it seemed to tear something in my mind.

But there—I was moving, I could grab the professor's arm and Melissa's, and pull them toward the glass sliding doors to the kitchen as the four demons drifted closer, closer; these creatures, who were appetite personified, whom I'd later know as Spider clan, drifting with their wispy bodies toward us on parachutes of spun glass that they express from their loins, coming closer and very deliberately to our balcony and no other . . .

We stumbled through the open doorway, and I pushed the professor and his daughter behind me and fumblingly slid the glass door shut. I locked it, though the act seemed to mock me with its futility.

3

The spidery things that had drifted to the balcony were not eight legged, like actual spiders, but only three legged, tripodal, each leg long and thin, jointed, and feathery like certain spiders but big, about two and a half yards long. Their upper parts, as big as laundry baskets, were like oversized suction cups, with a single yellow eye that seemed to slide around the convex top at will, slitting the skin as it went to peer out where it would. There was a sucking mouthpart in the concave underside where the three legs met; a membrane on the rim exuded the web stuff, like ectoplasm that mimicked spider silk. The connection to the parachute of demon silk broke when the spider latched onto the balcony, and its sail drifted and fell to the ground far below—where cars were exploding and fires gushing up—like a flag cut from a pole.

The three-legged spider thing sucked itself closer to the balcony, one of its legs probing at the doorway.

I pushed the still-babbling professor to the apartment door, started to open it, and then fell silent—listening to the bubbling, breathing sound from the other side. From the hall. The low chuckle. The whimper. Someone's "Please . . . please don't—" suddenly cut off. "Ple—"

I put the door chain in place. Paymenz had his arms around Melissa, whose face had gone so gray I was afraid for her.

Paymenz's expression changed from second to second: one moment delighted wonder, then sorrow, then fear—fear for Melissa as he looked at her.

I stepped into the doorway to the kitchen and peered around the edge of the dead refrigerator—which Melissa had filled with racks of dirt and used to grow salad mushrooms. I peered at the glass balcony doors, expecting to see them shattering. But instead the spider creatures seemed to have settled down onto the balcony, draping themselves over it, extending their legs to grip the outer walls, the outdoor light fixture, the drainpipe, the doorframe, arranging themselves at odd angles to one another. They seemed to be in a languid state of waiting. Then someone was drawn up, thrashing, from below, snatched perhaps from a lower balcony: a Chinese gentleman in a powder-blue suit. *Perhaps he was from the Asian Studies department*, the thought echoed in my head, ludicrously irrelevant. Round face quivering with terror, arms pinioned to his sides by the demon silk that wound around him, he was hoisted by the silk to the Spider clan demons. The two nearest pulled him apart between them, with swift movements of their giant pipe-cleaner legs, and stuffed him into their suctioning maws. Their bodies expanded to encompass the gushing halves of him, and then rippled, squeezing and relaxing, squeezing and relaxing, pulping him inside. He lived long enough for a brief muffled scream. Then they spat out the empty skins like grape peels.

A moment later the demon who'd had the upper half of the Chinese gent began to convulse, to shudder—then to strain like a woman in labor, to exude from its nether membranes a finer ectoplasm that spun to form itself into shapes . . . shapes of Chinese children, a Chinese woman, a ghostly boy. . . . Members of the man's family? His memory of himself?

The other spiders toyed with these productions as they emerged, pulling them apart, sniffing at them with the ends of their legs, where there were things like nostrils near the grasping claws.

Then I felt the professor pull me back into the living room. He seemed to be swaying in front of me, far away and yet very near. But it was I who was swaying.

"You were about to faint, young man," he said. "Your knees were buckling."

"Yes." After a moment, sinking onto the edge of a sofa arm, I said, "It's not a dream, is it?"

"No."

"What do we do now?"

Paymenz sighed. He sat down heavily on a split-open ottoman. "First, I apologize. I . . . began to babble out there. I was useless. Useless as—as bosoms on a . . . whatever that expression is. That's always been my failure: Faced with the abyss— which, really, is just an infinity of possibilities—I crumble. Into drink, sometimes. And good Lord I need a drink . . . but as for what to do—this calls for, ah, emergency measures. And we must have . . . we must obtain . . . information—so we must do the unthinkable. Melissa . . ." He took a deep breath, and then he made the decision, and he spoke it aloud: *"Take the television out of the closet . . . and turn it on!"*

He said this the way another man would say, Get the shot-
guns out, and load them.

To Paymenz, a television was more dangerous than a
shotgun.

———

We'd hooked car batteries to the little TV cord.

"The phenomenon seems to be global," the newscaster was
saying. "And it seems to be genuine. Early reports of mass hallucinatory drugs introduced into the water system and an out-
break of rye-mold toxicity turn out to be wrong—as we here at
KTLU can attest. Our own Brian Smarman was brutally killed
this afternoon by the phenomenon." He was an almost card-
board cutout newscaster; his hair looked like it had been poured
into a cast, and, like many local newscasters, he was heavily
caked in makeup. His voice quavered only a little.

"Did you ever notice," I said hoarsely, "that the closer you
get to Los Angeles, where the anchormen want to be, the better
looking they are? We're halfway up the state from Los Angeles
so we get the offbrand-looking newscasters. Up around Red-
ding they're all goofy-looking ducks who're saving their money
to buy condos—"

"Have *you* ever noticed," Melissa interrupted, gesturing for
me to be quiet, "how you tend to toss out irrelevant remarks
when you're nervous?"

I had noticed it, actually, yes.

The newscaster was going on hesitantly. "We—" he looked
at the paper, seemed to doubt whether he should read it, and
went on "—we are calling it 'the phenomenon' because there is
such disagreement about the nature of the attacks. Alien invasion, invaders from another dimension, robots created by an
enemy nation, and the first signs of—of Judgment Day—we've

heard all these explanations. Observers from the station here—"
his voice broke a little "—seem to agree that—that the beings in
question are demonic or supernatural. However, a zoologist who
encountered the beings and lived—I do not seem to have his
name here—believes that they could be 'some other form of biological life.' "

"Now will scholarship's imbeciles have their day," Professor Paymenz muttered.

"Shh, Dad," Melissa chided him. She held on to his arm.
We were all three of us huddled on her bed in her bedroom, the
farthest from the front door and the balcony; the little satellite-
seeker TV was on her bed. How I'd longed, in better times, to be
in her bed.

"Oh, we have a brief interview with a—it just says a 'theorist from San Francisco State'—Dr. Laertes Shephard."

"Shephard!" Paymenz burst out. "A theorist, is he! Why
don't they mention why he's here instead of at Stanford—
kicked out of Stanford . . ."

Footage showed Shephard looking strangely calm and collected standing by a window, smoke rising from the skyline
behind him. "We will need to look at this phenomenon from
every angle, from fresh angles—from below if necessary, as it
were—and ask ourselves, could this be a part of the natural order, just coming into its own? Perhaps this is not their first time
here. Could they have visited Earth at the time of the dinosaurs
and contended with the great reptiles? Could they come along
to precipitate a jump in evolution? If we understand their natural function we will—"

"We lost that feed," the newscaster muttered, as he replaced Shephard. "We . . ." He seemed to stare into space for a
moment.

"Poor man," Melissa said, looking at the newscaster. "He so
wants to run and hide."

"Why did they interview Shephard?" I asked. "What's an economist got to do with all this?"

"Putting a finger in every intellectual pie is his specialty," Paymenz growled. "He insists that economics is natural selection and natural selection is economics—got a minor degree in biology so he could make the argument and not be laughed at. . . ."

"We . . . we'll go on now to . . ." The newscaster was shuffling through the paperwork on his desk as if it were something that newscasters actually used. "I have here somewhere . . ." The newscaster looked off camera. His lower lip quivered. A shadow fell over him. He lunged from his seat, leaving the frame, and the image dissolved into snow.

But the sound feed continued for a moment. "They—!" It sounded like the same newscaster, but his voice was attenuated by distance and terror. "—demons, just—my family—if you could—stay in your—*No!*"

Then came a voice speaking in some language I didn't recognize. A silky voice, but the silk ribbon stretched into an infinity of darkness.

The professor dived the length of the bed, nearly bouncing the little TV off it as he went, stabbing at the button on the built-in digital recorder.

"Dad—we *do* have a remote!" Melissa said.

"Quiet, girl."

The voice babbled from the static and snow in some unknown language. It rose and fell in painfully unfamiliar accents and rhythms.

When the silky, murderous voice finished its rant, the television went silent; there was not even the sound of static.

"It—it sounded sort of . . . well, sort of like Greek," Melissa ventured.

"No, I don't think so," the professor murmured, combing

crumbs out of his beard with his stubby fingers. "If we succeed in recording it, we shall make its translation one of our plans of campaign." He looked around. "So this is my daughter's room."

"You've been in here many times, Dad," she said, "bursting in on me to tell me something that could easily have waited."

"Been in here but never really looked," he said. "Not really."

The room contained raw wooden shelves with books on two sides; stacks of books functioned as bookends upholding more shelves. In one corner was a zigzag tower of old magazines: the entire print run of *Visions*. The third wall was dominated by an elaborate homemade shrine to the Sophia, the feminine spirit of wisdom: a dozen goddess figures—Hindu and Greek and others—surrounded a Black Madonna, an Africanized Mother Mary. The corners of the room hung with dusty violet and green scarves, and the table next to the bed was scarred by fallen sticks of incense. Opposite the shrine was a poster of a movie star, Jason Stoll, whom I hated the instant I saw him on Melissa's wall. He was young, muscular, sensitive eyed, confident, dressed in fashionable understatement. *Every girl needs one,* I thought.

The books, crammed in every which way, were mostly novels and old textbooks—she'd had three years of liberal arts—and obscure volumes of "forgotten lore" her father had given her.

Someone screamed, long and bubbling, from the hallway. There was a desperate pounding on the front door that stopped abruptly.

Our feelings had been frozen, looming over us like a stop-motion tsunami, until that instant. Now the film ran forward, and all those feelings crashed down on the three of us. People may react differently to the same stimulus. But we all felt the same thing and knew we felt it together. As if steel chains had been kept in some freezer somewhere and then clapped onto us all at once, we all shrank, at the same moment, from the icy shackles.

Melissa spoke in the coiled silence. "Dad . . ." Her voice was small. "Is it some sort of Armageddon?"

He hesitated only a moment. "I do not believe it is."

I looked at him in surprise. He nodded. "Yes, I mean that. I do not believe it is Armageddon, biblical or otherwise."

"But," I asked, "what do we do, then? I mean—if we don't just wait for . . ."

Paymenz reached into a stack of books, pulled out *The New Oxford Annotated Bible*, and flipped expertly to the passage he wanted. He read it aloud.

"Book of Job, chapter five, verses 17 and 18: 'How happy is he whom God reproves; therefore do not despise the discipline of the Almighty. For he wounds but he binds up; he strikes but his hands heal.' "

He put the book on the bed, laid his hand thoughtfully on it. "We go with the assumption that all this is happening for a reason. Whatever happens, there is an appropriate human response. A lawful response, along with the natural reactions— fear, anger, whatever you feel. Even during the Holocaust there was an appropriate response, when physically fighting back was not possible. Even then, seeing your children taken away and murdered, there was a spiritually appropriate response. Hard to enter into the state where that response is possible sometimes. But it can be done. We will find the appropriate response."

"And just now?" I asked.

"Now? Now the appropriate response is to search for the appropriate response. That means research. Scholarship is our sword."

I didn't believe a word of it, but it was good to hear him say it.

"But there's a more pressing concern," Melissa said.

"Yes?" her father said, looking at her.

"Should we try to help those who are being murdered out there?"

We all three turned and stared at the door.

———

We went to the kitchen. I climbed up on the sink and peered out a lower corner of the kitchen window, expecting a feathery spider leg to ram through the glass the moment I lifted my head into sight, picturing it plunging a hook into my eye, digging for my brain. But the creatures on the balcony were immobile, maybe dormant.

The city below was reeling from the invasion. It made me think of footage I'd seen of the bombing of Kabul in 2007: dim, smoke-shrouded canyons of streets lit only by random bonfires and burning cars and now and then a burning storefront.

Below, figures darted for cover. A car careened, something clinging to the roof, flailing at it; the car piling into a hydrant, water geysering, the door torn aside, a man scooped out like a sausage from a can.

Above . . . was that a passenger jet, just under the lowering cloud cover? Was it veering in the sky? Was there something that ravaged, aboard it?

I climbed down, my mouth gone paper dry again. Melissa looked the question at me. She was hugging herself to keep from wringing her hands.

"It's not good," I said. Meaning, it was still going on, out there—so it was going on in the building, in the hall.

She nodded, biting her lip.

The professor and I armed ourselves with a baseball bat and a long piece of old pipe left by some plumber behind the water heater. We went to the door to the corridor and bent near it to listen. There was a thrashing noise and then a steady

JOHN SHIRLEY

thumping that sounded to me like it was from the apartment across the hall. Someone shouting for Allah. *Pleading* for Allah. Then—just the thumping, the sound having developed a *wet* quality.

The professor said, "No. Come." He turned on his heel and, breathing hard, went back to Melissa's bedroom and switched on the TV. He changed channels until he found another report. We followed him in.

"We need to know—" he began. But someone on TV finished the remark for him:

"Can they be killed? We are about to find out."

You know from the reality programming shows how real-life action looks on television. It hasn't got the good camera angles or the impressive splashing of the squibs or the special-effects explosions or even great visual crispness—the image is washed out, badly lit. It looks herky-jerky and uncertain. Half the time a cop tackling a criminal looks like a guy playing football with one of his friends. It's a lot of off-balance fumbling, and it's over so quickly you can't make out what happened.

But there were at least a dozen in the SWAT team. The demons—five Sharkadians, that I could count, and a Grindum— were all over one of those small school buses they use for mentally handicapped kids; and the kids were in there, slow kids and Down's syndrome kids and deeply pathological kids, a yellow box of them on wheels. The SWAT advanced toward them, firing with something like gleeful esprit, perhaps because the demons had no guns and because they were feeling the impact of the rounds, the bullets knocking them back, skidding them off the bus. The commentator, sounding a bit drunk, was saying something about a game a lot of us had played in childhood, *Doom,* and how *Doom* might've been designed like some kind of premonition to prepare us for this—

And then a Grindum that had been knocked down by a

3 5

swarm of bullets simply stood up and advanced against a stream of gunfire, jerked a gun from a wilting cop's hand, melting the gun in its own claws, and, as the man turned, took him by the throat and forced the molten metal of his gun—bullets exploding—down his throat. The others were running or were being pulled apart, like flies in the hands of sadistic children. I could see no wounds on the demons though bullets hailed into them.

The Grindum bounded on its giant grasshopper's legs back to the bus, lunged inside, and began to snap little heads off in its jaws.

We switched the television off and put our pipe and our baseball bat aside.

No. They cannot be killed. They can be inconvenienced by weapons. They can be slowed down and forced to reconstitute themselves if you shatter them sufficiently, but they cannot be killed by any conventional means: more proof that they are supernatural creatures, if any more were needed.

———

One night in 1986: I'm ten years old and something has awakened me and I can't get back to sleep. I thrash in the bed. It's June, and neither warm nor cold, but the sheets seem to abrade my skin and the air seems heavy over my bed. I can feel it pressing on my eyelids. The noise from the living room woke me, I suppose. But it's not the noise that's keeping me awake, it's a kind of shiver that pulses through the house from down there. It's my mother. I can feel her down there, shaking with anguish, although—I know this from past experience—she's probably curled up in a chair staring at the TV, not visibly shaking at all. Now and then she'll uncoil, with a whiplash movement like an eel on a hook; I'd seen it many times already this year. But once more I get out of bed, and wearing only my briefs, I go to the second-floor landing in our half of the divided Victorian and look down the worn wooden stairs at Mom in the living room.

It's the amphetamines, I know, confirming it to myself as I see her sit very still, then thrash herself to another position in the chair, then sit very still again. She's staring at the television. She's flicking it with the remote. Channel. Another, another. Channel for five, ten seconds. Another.

Suddenly she stiffens and jerks her head around—I pull back but she's seen me. "Git on down here," she says. She grew up in a trailer park in Fresno; though she's a relatively educated woman she slides back into trailer park diction easily. "Come on, come on, come on, git down here."

I go down, trailing my hand on the banister. "I woke up. I couldn't get back to—"

"You think I'm weird, don't ya, baby?" she says as I come to the bottom of the stairs. I sit down there and hope she'll let me stay there. She doesn't usually get violent, but she scares me when she's drugged. I wonder where Boyfriend Thing is.

The high-ceilinged room is lit only by the TV; the shifting images make the shadows of the room jump like dancing gray-white flames. *Picture flames,* I think to myself.

I notice that except for the van Gogh posters—my Mom had a van Gogh fetish—the room is more barren than it was. Something's missing. The easy chair is there, the vinyl at the end of its arms partly peeled away; the TV and a thin metal TV tray with its handful of rattling pot seeds, all that is left of Boyfriend Thing's pot stash—there's no other furniture: The sofa is missing. A nice brown-leather sofa. She'd begun to sell things off about then.

"You didn't answer me. You think I'm weird. You do."

"No."

"You do. Because of . . . because I stay in the house so

much now; you told your sister that. When she called." My sister had moved out; she was fourteen and she lived with my aunt. Sometimes I wanted to leave, too. "Well. Well, well, well. The world is an evil place, Ira. The world is sick and dangerous. You know what they just had on the news? I just saw it. Little girl chained to her bed for five years. She was six years old. That's what kind of world it is."

The irony isn't lost on me even at the time. My mom a speed freak flipping out about someone else's child abuse. But I know now it was Jung's shadow, the shadow projection.

"In Southeast Asia, this one country, people are, like, just chopping each other, just hundreds and hundreds, and hiding the bodies. . . . Oh and in Cambodia not that long ago, okay . . ." She tells me in too much detail about the Killing Fields. "You know what it is?" she says, coming to the question without a pause. "There's demons loose on Earth pretending to be people. And I'll tell you what—I saw this thing just now, the astronauts can see. They can see from orbit whenever they're over the night side of Earth, they can see lightning somewhere every few seconds. Always lightning bashing around somewhere on Earth, every few seconds. You know what that is?"

I nod, but she's already gone on. I had gotten very skilled, the past few months, at not seeing her face when she was high. It was so puppetlike. Her eyes looked like those glass disks, like the flattened marbles they use for stuffed-animal eyes; her skin looked taut as polished wood; her mouth seemed to clack like a puppet's.

"Those flashes they see from orbit, it's lightning, is what it is, is all," she is saying. "I'm not crazy. I don't think it's anything else. But I'll tell you what it's *like*. It's like the astronauts are seeing the flash of someone doing something cruel, some big cruelty. An atrocity, like; there *should* be, if there was any fucking justice, some kinda ol' flash or something you could see from space. Maybe it is, maybe there's one lightning flash for every atrocity somewhere on Earth. Ought to be. You think I'm weird? You do. Go back to bed. Go on. I've gotta . . . go on, go on, get your ass up there, go, go. . . ."

—

I was thinking of that night, listening to my mother's speed rambling, when the professor turned the televangelist on. The tube preacher was gassing on and on. He was using all his skills. His face was puppetlike; his eyes like glass disks. And he was babbling, but he didn't have his usual confidence. This was Reverend Spencer. I'd seen him before, and he usually strutted with confidence.

Tonight Reverend Spencer looked scared.

"It's occurred to him," the professor said.

"What?" I asked. I sat on the end of the bed, sipping Tokay. It had grown quiet outside . . . some sort of lull. . . .

"All the crust he's built up to hide what he knows in his heart has been clawed away by what's happening around the world," the professor said.

"I'm hungry," Melissa said, her voice muffled under the pillow she was holding over her head. She was lying in an S shape on the bed behind us. "But if I eat I'll throw up."

Without looking at her, Paymenz reached out and patted her shoulder.

I said, speaking slowly, "You mean, Israel . . . that it occurred to him . . . that if this is Judgment Day then he's going to be among the first cast into his favorite lake of fire."

A news flash had said there was a flurry of televangelists giving away their money.

The professor nodded. He was half listening to the televangelist, but his mind was mostly somewhere else.

The professor shut off the television, stood up abruptly, and went into his bedroom-office next door. I could hear him pull a book off the shelf, and turning pages.

We slept only fitfully that long, static night.

I had a dream of a laughing man in a hooded cloak with a face like shifting, running sand—sand that sometimes shifted into the well-sculpted shape of a fairly ordinary human face and sometimes crumbled to re-form into the face of a chimpanzee.

He was laughing but laughing sadly, his voice echoing in the high school gymnasium where we sat in the bleachers, he and I. My echoes mingled with his, when I suddenly spoke up: "You're laughing, but really you're quite sad like one of those songs about being a clown when you really want to cry."

"Yes," he said, sobering suddenly. "I am the one who brings sleep and dreams. And what has happened to the world? Who has vomited their colors all over my canvas? Where is my art now? Where is my art now, I ask you?"

His tears eroded his head so that it sagged off his neck and crumbled into a stream of sand that slithered down over the wooden bleachers.

4

*N*ot long before dawn, as Melissa sank into a doze, I found a sketchbook and pastels I'd given her; she'd never used it, so I did. It kept my mind occupied in the taut, weary hours of the night. I tried drawing everything but the demons, but could find no rest in denial. So I tried drawing what would later be called a Sharkadian, and found myself sketching a sort of bas-relief pattern, or something like Morris wallpaper, around it, locking it in.

"That's not a bad thing to experiment with," the professor said, looking over my shoulder, his words slurring a little. He'd been at the vodka. "You're unconsciously, if it is unconscious, fitting them into some kind of pattern, making some kind of artistic sense of them. And who knows what such a process might divulge. . . ."

But I soon put the sketchbook aside, exhausted and irritated by his occasional critiques and perhaps troubled by the fear that he was clutching at straws in suggesting the drawing was something useful. Nothing seemed useful anymore, except a deep hole to hide in.

The first of the Lulls came about nine A.M. During Lulls the demons seemed to vanish, or to go into some kind of dormancy. They were not sleeping—those who could be seen seemed to be listening.

It was a global Lull. The riots and panicky surges of refugees stopped in their tracks, when the demonic attacks ceased for a time, the refugees wondering which way to jump. Wondering if angels were next, Michael wielding a fiery sword. The world sank onto its haunches and let its shoulders sag as it panted for breath and wiped its brow.

During the first Lull there was time for pundits to argue on television. Back then they were still babbling the tediously familiar polemic of denial, with their "not demons but anarchists in rubber suits, bulletproof vests, cyborg enhancement," their "hallucinations, and the hallucinating attacking people, some of them in costume and makeup . . . water poisoned by terrorists," their "mind-control projections combined with bombings."

Then there was the inevitable countersuggestion: The demons are indicators that the moment has come for complete resignation and submission to Jesus (or Allah or angry ancestral spirits or Yahweh or . . . Lord Satan). Long lines formed outside churches, synagogues, Buddhist temples, and outside both the Church of Satan and the First Church of Interstellar Contact—this latter an extraterrestrial contactee outfit run by channelers. It was a riot of metaphysical confusion.

Only Paymenz and a few others kept their heads.

"We will go to the Council for Global Interdependence,"

Paymenz said to me. "We need an objective. That will be our first one."

"What," I asked, eating bread and jam in the bedroom, "is the council for . . . ?" Most of my attention was bent on sounds from the drainpipes on the outer walls that might have been the clicking of large claws.

"CFGI. The Council for Global Interdependence. It's not much of anything yet—it's just a gleam in Mendel's eye, compared with his plans for it. But there are real contacts there, and I was preparing to go over there yesterday morning. It happens that the very day of the demonic coming, about seventy representatives from twenty countries came to town for a conference funded by the Council. Shephard's conference, actually. One that's not going to go on, but— Most of the conferees are here and may be in the convention center yet . . . and Shephard . . ." His voice trailed off. He looked at me but said nothing. I was thinking the same thing: Hadn't Shephard suggested perhaps that the conference wouldn't happen?

Paymenz seemed to shake himself and went on. "The council is sheer talk so far, but it represents those who've made other initiatives."

He sipped his tea. I saw his eyes wander to a vodka bottle leaning precariously on one of Melissa's stacks of magazines, but he looked resolutely away from it. Melissa was sleeping— twitching in her sleep. She would sleep for five minutes, till something unspeakable drove her out of the dream, and she would sit up and then sink slowly back.

"What sort of initiatives?" I asked.

"Hm?"

"You said 'those who've made other initiatives.' "

"The initiatives . . . well, it actually began in the middle of the last century. Or perhaps much earlier . . . but most notably, the formation of the League of Nations and then the United

Nations. Then came the U.N. Peacekeeping force—the NATO actions in Kosovo, the global peacekeeping forces in East Timor. A slow movement toward a real global society with real global policemen, with uniform human rights rules . . . and it was not all as spontaneous as it seemed. It was planned, as much as it could be. They didn't know that the Indonesians would do what they did in Timor—but they knew what to do if a situation like that arose. And they did. The Council is another project of those same planners. I was one of many consultants. It's something still in its infancy, still unformed and tentative. It could go very wrong—or it could be something wonderful. At any rate, my boy, that's what I'd have said a few days ago. Now, all considerations of the future are subject to redefinition. The future itself is problematic. All our paradigms are in ruins. Let us go, however. Wake my poor daughter, and let us go to the Council."

———

Late afternoon. The sky was lowering with smoke and haze; it looked as if the world was roofed in shale. We were in my converted Chevy—it had been converted to an electric car about ten years before and never seemed to have reconciled to the change. The body was a little too heavy for the electric engine, and it strained to reach forty. I was driving, the professor beside me, Melissa in the back, leaning forward between the seats.

A burning garbage truck careened around the corner—I pictured it as a leviathan leaping from the surface of a sea of trash, a burning metal-and-rubber whale thrashing in and out of the oceanic swells of debris and decay at one of those really enormous landfills. It curveted on two wheels into the middle of our street, streaming flaming trash, its driver a black man with a bottle in one hand, laughing and weeping—I had to

JOHN SHIRLEY

drive onto the broad sidewalk to avoid it. The truck was soon
out of sight behind us.

"We've got the wrong car for this," I said, as we swerved
around another drunken cadre of looters banging and bumping
shopping carts full of holo-set players. "You need one of those
hydrogen-powered SUVs—oh shit . . ."

This last as an Arab with a rage-contorted face slammed a
teenage boy onto the hood of our car. He'd backed him out of his
half-demolished liquor store, was digging his rigid fingers into
the boy's neck. I had to hit the brakes to keep from dragging
them down the street—Melissa yelling out the window, "Stop
that, stop that, let him go!" The frustrated Arab, seeing his shop
destroyed by looters, finally had one in his hands, and his face
was—oh yes—*demonic* as he slammed the boy's head on the
hood of my car. He was enraged, but was he possessed? No.

No, no one was possessed. Not exactly. There have been no
possessions.

Have I said that before? I say it again. It means something.

The boy flailing and the Arab smashing, the two rolled off
my car's hood.

"Help them!" Melissa yelled.

I looked at Paymenz. "No," he said. "Drive on. We must get
there."

Driving on, past a group of children throwing bricks through
the window of a store, I remembered the game HACKK, a first-
person computer game I'd been addicted to. In HACKK, a bio-
warfare virus that attacked the human brain had turned most
of the population into murderous zombies. The zombies were
controlled by Terrorist Overlords. You had to get through the
smoking ruins of the city to a sanctuary on the far side, killing
psychotic ax-wielding viral zombies as you went, with weapons
you picked up along the way, while outsmarting the Terrorist

Overlords. It had been superbly realistic 3-D, in which every adversary was a distinct, cunning individual, and yet it had been dreamlike, had the tantalizing familiarity of some half-remembered nightmare.

"Who was it," I wondered aloud, as we veered down a mostly empty street—smoking ruins on one side, shattered plastic boxes trailing from store windows on the other—"who said that some video games had the quality of the bardos? E. J. Gold, I think. . . ."

"You're doing that nervous, irrelevant commentary again," Melissa said, her voice tight with fear as we drove through gathering shadows.

"Let him say whatever gets him through here," Paymenz said.

I was driving as I was speaking—as if in a trance. I was so tired. "Remember Gold? One of the last century's grassroots, homegrown California gurus. He used the game *Quake* to induce a kind of paranoia-sharpened awareness in his followers, told them to think of the bardo states that would come after death as computer games set up by some mysterious programmer. Or something along those lines. Learn the rules of that bardo and you'd find your way out, pass the test into the next realm . . . the next level. . . ."

What were the rules for *this* game? Were we in an afterlife bardo, here?

It wasn't that, either. Demons or no, this was life in all its homely grit, its panoramas of blandness and grainy contrast. Still, there were rules we had yet to define in the new world erupting around us, rules as if from some mysterious programmer. And that had always been true—but now that truth was prominent, unhidden, demanding notice. *You're taking part in a game the rules of which you do not understand! Find out the rules! Now!*

We passed through streets, then, that seemed untouched, distinguished only by the lack of human activity. No moving cars, everyone still hiding.

But two blocks from the convention center, we saw something big and black and steaming from vents on its knobby head, crouched just within the shattered-glass cube of a gas station. Just caught a glimpse of it, dormant in the Lull, and then we were past it—driving those last two blocks at the best speed the whiny little car could muster—and reached the convention center, near the Yerba Buena Gardens. A chopper was landing on its helipad as we approached. I watched raptly as it came in, its movements professionally smooth, landing easily. The helicopter was civilization embodied for me in that moment: civilization intact, confident, almost graceful. It was so reassuring.

"That might be Mendel," Paymenz said, watching the chopper.

"Watch out, damnit, Ira!" Melissa yelled.

I slammed on the brakes, swerved, just managed not to rear-end a white limo pulling up at the police barriers ahead of us.

I sat with my foot still jammed down on the brake, panting, staring at the opaque windows of the limo. Gently, the professor reached over and put the car in park for me; he turned the key, switched the engine off.

The building was modern, highly designed—one of those buildings you imagined on its drawing board when you saw it—but on the whole it was shaped like a giant bunker with frills: a concoction of beveled concrete and big panes of frosted glass and angular assemblies of painted girders. There were fidgeting cops standing behind cement barriers around the building, many of them swaying where they stood, probably drunk.

Others seemed grateful they had something to do that they could understand: crowd control, though there was no crowd.

A cop approached us, his beefy face blotchy red, his mouth open, breathing hard. "You . . . you people—just turn around."

"Officer? It's okay," said a tall—*very* tall—black man getting out of the limo. He wore a gray three-piece suit cut so masterfully that it made this man, who must have been more than seven feet tall, seem to have normal proportions. His movements had a touch of the mantis about them, but his face was chiseled with quiet intelligence, and his every word emanated simple authority. The cop evidently knew who he was, and walked away without another word.

"Dr. Nyerza," Paymenz said.

"Professor Paymenz," said Nyerza, nodding. "It has been too long, sir." A soft equatorial accent.

They shook hands. I thought that Nyerza seemed a little amused, looking Paymenz over; but it was not a condescending amusement, it was affectionate.

"I have gotten old, as you see," Paymenz said, signaling for me and Melissa to get out of the car. "But you still seem—no, not the student I had, your maturity is evident—but still quite boyish."

"Boyish at seven foot four? I enjoy the concept, sir. This is your daughter, perhaps? I am charmed. And—this young man?"

"He is—his name is Ira. He is here as my assistant."

I was feeling numb. I was happy to be his assistant. He could have said, "This is my trained monkey—we're going to teach him to ride a tricycle on a high wire today," and I wouldn't have blinked. Maybe he *did* say that.

"You all look so tired," Nyerza said. "The emotions we have all had—it's very draining, is it not? There are refreshments.

Leave the car where it is, and I will have someone move it to safety. Come this way, please."

———

We were walking down a long hallway. We passed a glass door through which I could see an enormous auditorium where groups of querulous people argued with the man at the podium in flagrant disregard for protocol. I couldn't make out most of what they were saying. I caught only crusts and spatters of sentences. ". . . the Islamic Front claims . . . the result of prayers—who are we to say it's not. . . . Let each man seek out his own salvation . . . perhaps sacrifice . . . the collective unconscious . . . quantum creations. . . . We're fools . . . dead minutes from now, everyone here. . . . Hysteria won't . . . ."

"There's food in the private conference room," Nyerza was saying. "But I must prepare you: First, we will pass by a Gnasher. I have just come from observing another one with a Tailpipe at the university."

"These don't sound like scientific terms to me," Melissa said. Somehow, then, she had an air of speaking just to see if she still could.

And in fact Nyerza seemed surprised she'd spoken. "No—already a slang has arisen for the various demons. Reports indicate six kinds so far. One of the creatures has remarked that there are seven expected. The seven clans, he said."

"You call them creatures," Paymenz said. "Is this an evaluation on your part? Apart from 'creatures' as in the created of God, the word has implications of—"

"Of the confines of the biologically conventional, or perhaps extraterrestrial. So I use it wrongly. It is an incarnate spirit, in my opinion. A malevolent spirit, these."

"Demons."

"Quite. Here—I warn you, when we pass the Gnasher and the Tailpipe—in this room, the Lull may end, they may attack. . . ."

Outside the room were six young National Guardsmen, three of them black, two Hispanic, and one a chinless, spindly Caucasian. They looked as if they were debating between accepting a probable death, when the Lull was over, or deserting.

It was a large conference room, empty but for video screens filling one wall and an oval conference table. The room was windowless; a skylight threw an increasingly rusty light on everything. The table should have collapsed under the weight of the creature occupying most of its surface. The big demon was a Tailpipe, like the one we'd seen squatting in the gas station, something like a pilot whale out of water, but its body was even blunter, curled cobralike in on itself. Nestled in one of its coils was a Gnasher, using the bigger, duller demon as a sort of beanbag chair.

The Gnasher was the color of a red and black ant; its head exactly that red, almost like colored vinyl, its body exactly that black. Its head sat on its long thin neck like an ant's, but it had a man's jaws, although oversized and gnashing, clashing loudly between sentences, like some exotic metallic percussion instrument—and its eyes were those of a man, the pretty blue eyes of a movie star, and its corded arms were lean and there were four arms, and they were leathery black. The Gnasher lifted its head languidly as we looked in and, unexpectedly, began to speak. It spoke at length to us—Nyerza took a step back at this. We stood in the open doorway and listened to the demon as it spoke. Its hands were talons and only talons; impossibly prehensile claws that rippled delicately like a Balinese dancer's fingers to emphasize its words. It had an enormous phallus, armored in big, spurred scales. I couldn't see the rest of its lower parts.

"We should have a tape recorder going. This is the first time it has spoken," Nyerza murmured to Paymenz.

"I'll remember every word," I said, my voice sounding whispery, husky in my own ears.

"Ira has a photographic memory," Paymenz muttered.

The demon reverberated on.

"I am so delighted to see you. I feel the delight as a violet fire on the roof of my mouth as I look at you, and I stiffen with recognition."

Its voice was a languid purr, but every word stood out like billboard copy printed on the projection screen of the inside of my skull.

"This is the joy of homecoming! How long we waited, forgotten children in a forgotten nursery, weeping for our return to those who left us to ripen in the outer darkness, whose patented polymer members drove the seed into the soil of the in between. My dear dears, how we hungered for the taste of your light, the one spark that each of you carries, that each of you monstrously denies us; how you hoard your little sparks, her fallen sparks—hers, not yours, little dears, but it's all finders keepers with you!—and for a moment when we return to the source of our course, and we pluck the fruit, and we draw the root, and we consume the harvest in one sweet bite, or two at most, and we taste the spark, we have the spark, then, within us. Oh, for but a moment. Before it flickers out . . . before it flickers out, snuffing itself like a sniffing little sob. Before it goes, the spark of your inner light warms the infinite cold of our withins; for a moment the aching emptiness is abated, and we can pretend we are the created and not the residue, and the journey is fulfilled;

and then the spark flickers and is gone and we must search
again for another morsel. And how does the song go?"

As it paused to consider before reciting something like verse,
I thought: *This is stupid, I should be running, hiding, and the only rea-*
son I'm not is because Melissa is here, watching me. And she would not
run with me; she is so much braver than I am.

It seemed to savor, for a moment, the sound of one of the
National Guardsmen weeping to himself, before theatrically
clearing its throat to go on.

"Consider this:
> *His eyes are white-light ceiling bulbs,*
> *his teeth syringe needles;*
> *he's attended by a retinue of shiny scarab beetles.*
> *I stood a-teetering on the vacuum-breathing brink,*
> *where you fall with the weight of a single thought you*
think . . ."

It's very good, don't you think? But to continue . . .

> *"where laughing things rise to find they truly sink*
> *and white on white on white on white is the color of*
my ink.
> *I didn't pass through the tunnel; the tunnel passed*
through me;
> *death will not hesitate to come unseasonably. . . .*
> *It takes joy in coming unreasonably. . . .*
> *I remember death—I remember death, oh but yes:*
> *I've bargained with that smug old merchant of rest*
> *though that time is past, and I pretend we never met*
> *you know what hasn't happened—will, onward, hap-*
pen yet . . .

I no longer taunt the lion, nor will I walk the edge.
I withdrew from the void that shimmers past the ledge,
But every morning when I wake
I see the shadows smile
I know that it is but his whim to bide a while. . . ."

The demon's mouth split his head in something like a smile. It seemed to me the demon was looking at Melissa, as he spoke . . . it seemed to me . . . as it went on.

"What do you think? One of your minor poets? Almost doggerel, in fact. But I like it. Because the fear of death is the tenderest thought you have for such as us, your forlorn offspring. The only elegy we have is your fear, your anticipation of darkness, and so we savor it, out of sentiment, sheer sentiment. How like the fish you are, swimming in the sea but unaware of it; you are the fishy swimmers awash in a sea of suffering! Waves of suffering break over us—to me, like the fragrance of a meal as it is cooked—how we mimicked you in our stony world, making meals over campfires when we could and appointing chieftains and kings and holding pageants—if you could see the pageants of our world, and how you were celebrated there!"

"What is your mission here?" Paymenz demanded suddenly. "What brought you here? Speak plainly!"
The demon simply ignored him, continuing:

"And now you at last acknowledge us, haughty till we squeeze her spark from you, and we are for a moment more truly one and—how did it go—'what do I see, in the dusty mirror? Not a human being but a human error' . . . And so we rectify, we return what you have supposed to be excrescence, to make you whole again, to rejoin, to warm ourselves

with the singled-out sparks until the great spark, the tongue of flame that will not flicker out, is revealed to us. We shall turn our faces up to it. . . . No longer taking part in your world by proxy but a part of you as you become part of us."

Saying this last, its voice began to boom, to make the very walls recoil in shivers, and it stood up.

"A part of us, a part of us, the infinite loneliness brought to an end, the serpent with its tail in its mouth swallows, at long last! He swallows and swallows in infinite repercussion!"

And the Tailpipe began then to uncoil, to rear up, and its slick black skin opened pores, which oozed something like petroleum and something like sewage sludge. I saw then that the pores were something else: They were the mouths of little girls, pink and perfect, complete with teeth and tongues, hidden before and now exposed and expressing black rivulets . . . and then steam, steam in place of the black ooze, hissing and smelling of sea trenches and filling the room with a congealing cloud of hot mist.

One of the guardsmen screamed and fired his weapon twice at the Gnasher. The demon's mouth spread in a caricature of a grin as it turned toward the babbling soldier, and something blurry whipped out from the Tailpipe and encircled the young soldier, who was yanked instantly through the air to the Gnasher, who held him nose to noseless face, the soldier screaming as the Gnasher said,

"Look—it's magic! *It's* **your** bullets! *See them!"*

I could just make them out—the two rounds the soldier had fired were floating within the Gnasher's eyes, pointed at him, cartoonishly replacing its pupils. The Gnasher moved—its movements too fast to follow. Then the soldier had no head.

The other soldiers began to fire, and Nyerza was pulling the professor and me back from the demons, from that mist-choked room; I thought I heard the Gnasher call,

"Melissssssaaaa!"

Then we were running down the hall. I looked back to see one of the soldiers, the spindly one with hardly any chin, his mouth twisted up like a little boy trying not to cry, wanting to run after us but a lifetime of fantasized heroism held him back, quivering there in the dirty mist that rolled from the door into the hallway. Then he ran into the room and was instantly killed. In a split second, his blood, most of it, flew back out the door and onto the corridor wall, as if tossed from an offstage bucket. I heard his last cry, a cry for Mama though no word was articulated: the echo of a million, million cries of suffering that had been going on for thousands of years. And I felt like an adult who sees a small child caught by spreading fire in a room; and the adult, who is not uncaring, chooses between himself and the child and runs out the front door, knowing that the child will die.

All the guardsmen were dead, soon after, for the Lull was over. Then the Gnasher and the Tailpipe moved into the auditorium and managed to kill a good third of the conferees before the survivors fled beyond reach. Beyond reach, for the moment.

———

We were in a basement conference room. The demons might materialize here; but they didn't. There was a cafeteria buffet on a big military folding table, but none of us could eat, though the professor drank some wine.

Nyerza was wearily saying something about patterns, patterns, patterns noticed already, geographical patterns in the arrival of the demons. "It is not really at random, no not at all. It is around certain urban areas, like the rays from an impact crater on the moon, really, lines of them spreading out from a center, in which is . . . Do you remember the industrial accidents last year?"

Nyerza and Paymenz were near the barred door of the dull concrete room—a chilly room, with gray walls, pipes crisscrossing the ceiling; Nyerza standing, leaning against the wall, as most chairs were too small for him, Paymenz sitting cross-legged on a plastic chair that was hidden by his bulk so that he seemed to be seated on air, with a carafe in one hand and a plastic cup in the other, drinking and talking, one knee bobbing nervously. He looked sickly pale under the fluorescent lights. There was a chunky black SFPD cop standing guard at the door, staring wistfully at the wine bottles on the table, chewing his lip. Nyerza was lighting an oval cigarette. The cop almost said something to him about it, then I saw him shrug. Demons were tearing up the city—and he was going to give him shit about the no-smoking rule?

Mclissa and I were seated on two plastic chairs. I had my arm around her; she leaned against me. It was more need for mutual comfort than anything intimate.

I wanted to tell her something.

If the end is coming, we should be somewhere else, making love and enjoying each other and, perhaps, praising God for whatever good there has been in our lives; grateful for one another and the goodness of our last moments together. . . .

But I knew I probably wouldn't say it. And if I did, it would avail me not.

Suddenly she interrupted Nyerza and Paymenz, who stared at her as she said, "That poem he recited . . ."

"Yes, do you know the author? It might hold a clue," Paymenz said.

"Yes, I do. It's actually a song lyric. I'm the author."

"You!"

"Yes. It's a song I wrote two years ago, when I was in that folk group, The Lost." She was staring at her hands on her knees. "I was going through a depression when I wrote it, and I was sort of— I was almost as morbid as Ira. And then, the demon looked at me and recited it: A song I wrote . . . wrote thinking about how my mom died, and how death doesn't care if it comes at a, you know, reasonable time, and it just took my mom, and I . . ." She stared wonderingly into space and repeated, "That thing recited a song I wrote."

5

*T*hey'd brought two folding cafeteria tables down into the basement room, pushed them together, and spread taped-together printouts over their Formica tops. "Please forgive this hasty presentation," Nyerza said as he smoothed the printouts with his enormous hands. We were gathered around the tables, the professor and Melissa and Nyerza and me.

I was noticing Nyerza's frequent glances at Melissa. He was suddenly very interested in her. She seemed drawn to stand close beside him. She glanced up at him; her nostrils quivered; her lips parted; she leaned just half an inch closer to him.

Oh yeah. Like I could compete with a giant black intellectual power broker from Central Africa.

On the printouts, taped together with Scotch tape where

the images connected, was a map of the United States. There were six cities designated in black letters: New York; Portland, Oregon; San Francisco; Chicago; Miami; Detroit. Concentric circles in light red were drawn around each city, as if it were the epicenter of some outrippling force: each city the center of a bull's-eye. The circles overlapped. Yellow dots marked the map in rough lines from each city—almost like the impact lines extending from the center of a lunar meteor strike. The meteor hits the moon, there's a crater, and impact lines radiate from the crater in every direction. But the actual bull's-eyes seemed slightly off center from the city marks.

"The yellow dots," Paymenz said.

"Yes," said Nyerza. "The demons. Where they appeared. We have here . . ." He drew another long printout, like a laser-printed scroll, from a briefcase and unrolled it over the map. "San Francisco. You see the epicenter of the strike points is over here—an industrial area to the southeast across the bay."

"Where the accident happened," I blurted. "Hercules!"

"Yes, the little city of Hercules," Nyerza said, "all but wiped out a few years ago in an industrial accident. Very like what happened in Bhopal in the last century, I understand. Perhaps you lost friends or relatives there?"

"Nobody. But I have friends who lost relatives there." I thought of Jerry Ingram, whose brother had been killed. I remembered how Jerry had put it: "Wiped out like a bug by pesticides . . . his whole family wiped out like bugs, his wife and kid wiped out like bugs. . . ." One of my very few real friends, Jerry. A writer. He'd slipped back into drug use after that—was supposed to be somewhere in L.A. If the demons hadn't killed him—his own demons or ours.

"You know," I said, staring at the printout, "it's very like that artwork I did. I never showed anyone but Melissa. I used a map of Hercules . . . and the area around it . . . and . . ."

Melissa's mouth dropped open. "God yes, you're right! That is weird—it's so . . . there's something like that drawing . . ."

"I've got it, I think, in my palmer. . . . We could hook it up to your printer—" I broke off, feeling foolish. "I don't know what the relevance is."

Paymenz looked at me. "Relevance? The lines converge now. Serendipity and catastrophic coincidence, my boy, are the order of the day." He turned to Nyerza. "Now we see, Nyerza, that intuition is our only guide in the present situation. And perhaps scholarship . . . Which reminds me." He searched through a number of pockets till he found the little recording we'd made of the televised demon speaking in his own language. "If you could run this through your best translation programs . . . try Sumerian analogues."

———

In an adjoining room was a row of workstations. The power was still on, then, and they had no problem loading the contents of my palmer into their system. I did a search through my saved art, scanned drawings mostly. A sketchy portrait of the magician A. O. Spare flickered by, an image of a pregnant angel giving birth to a demon . . .

"Interesting," Nyerza muttered, at that.

. . . A painting of the planets in alignment and a planet-sized being of electrical energies leaping from one to the next; a sketch of Melissa sunning herself nude on a rooftop.

I scrolled past that one as hastily as possible, but Paymenz said, "Remarkable accuracy." And put a hand in front of his mouth to hide a smile we couldn't see anyway, under the beard.

And then the drawing: a scan of a map of the town of Hercules, including the refineries. And superimposed, using streets for part of its diagramming and other parts drawn in, was . . .

"A pentagram!" Nyerza said wonderingly. "Turned upside down."

"Yes—horns upward," Paymenz muttered. "Indefatigable, the conjunctions . . . synchronicities more meaningful than ever . . . the atmosphere sensitive . . . very sensitive . . ."

I spread my hands, trying to remember how the image had come about. "I had this—this sort of vision of the area of the industrial accident as a kind of . . . like a sacrificial altar with a pentagram drawn on it. You see the blood around the edges. I felt the people who died in that area had been sacrificed to . . . I don't know."

"To Mammon," Melissa suggested.

"Perhaps not quite literally Mammon as such," Paymenz murmured. "I wish I had that son of a bitch Shephard here."

Nyerza tapped at the keyboard, and soon had my image superimposed over the map of Hercules with its demon manifestations.

Which lined up perfectly with the pentagram.

———

We passed the night in the rooms beneath the conference center. Army cots were brought to us, and Melissa and I lay down near one another, falling asleep almost immediately. There was just time for Melissa, lying huddled under a green blanket, turned away from me, to say, "You're in trouble, you know, you sneaky brat. That one drawing of me on the roof . . . You've got that birthmark on my ass—a naked ass you're not supposed to have had the chance to see. . . . You had to've spied on me when I was up there."

"One time I was looking for you and you were asleep up there. . . . It was purely by accident. . . . I left immediately."

"Immediately . . . my ass. You got the goddamn scene awfully detailed . . . you . . ."

"I can't help having a photographic memory."

But she was already snoring; I was asleep moments later.

———

Nyerza and Paymenz conferred with colleagues by Internet and phone, though some of the lines were down and power came and went. The next morning, in the little room with the printouts, we ate something an unnatural yellow, dry and glutinous and salty, we were told was reconstituted scrambled eggs.

"We have been working, developing a theory," Nyerza said, hunched in a bass clef over his plate.

"Last night?" Melissa said. "You need rest, too, don't you, Dr. Nyerza?"

He smiled shyly at her concern. I tried not to stare at her; I ground my teeth.

"I had a few hours, thank you," he said. "Anyway, we theorize that this industrial accident in Hercules was not an accident, that its parameters were quite calculated. Here, in Detroit—another accident, some years back. In Miami, no accident but there were, instead, what are called, I believe, 'cancer corridors,' extending from the industrial site here. . . . Dr. Mendel believes—"

"I believe they are also not accident," said a short bald stocky man with an accent that might have been Dutch. He came in, pulling off his overcoat, tossing it on a chair, which fell over with the weight of it. He didn't even glance that way. He was carrying a package, something long and narrow wrapped in brown paper. I thought of a sword in a scabbard, and then I thought, *That's silly, it's not a sword*. He put the package on the table.

Nyerza introduced Dr. Mendel. He had an ageless face that

seemed to have some kind of Oriental cast to it, as if he were perhaps a quarter Asian and partly—what?—Dutch? German? I guessed he was something like fifty, but it was hard to tell. His eyes were fathomless black. He wore a rumpled gray suit and simple athletic shoes, and he moved with a strange springiness as he crossed the room and shook our hands. He seemed tired yet fed by some relentless spring of inner energy. There was an indefinable resilience about everything he did. "Yes," he said, looking at the printouts. "I believe that none of this is an accident. Some happened before others—but each was timed. Some were greater pulsations, some lesser; that is, some events required sudden, widespread loss of life in a small area; in others, slow deaths, even suffering, was preferable. It was planned over a forty-year span. Maybe even more. Perhaps Bhopal was the beginning, really. For the demons are in other countries, too. But we have focused on this country as a sort of experimental subject in the study."

"Planned by who?" Melissa asked.

"Now, that is the question. I prefer to wait before speculating too openly. . . . More information is needed."

Who was this man? I wondered. *And where was he taking us with all this?*

He had an odd smell about him—not unpleasant. Rather exotic. Was it incense?

"If they were not accidents . . . these industrial horrors," I said slowly, "and if—if the demons are the by-product, please tell us what you think. Speculate. Who planned it? How? What sort of ritual?"

I was beginning to speak faster and faster, with a growing excitement that fed on hope. Real hope—for if what was happening had an explanation, then it might have a solution. An explanation meant that the universe, life itself, was not some manic absurdity where any random god of chaos could inflict his demons on us. There was hope for an underlying meaning after all.

"I mean—if someone planned it, then there are rules, there are—"

Mendel stopped me with a raised hand, as someone entered. I took it that he didn't want these things discussed in front of the new visitor. Paymenz laid some printouts facedown atop those taped to the tables to hide them.

The visitor was Professor Laertes Shephard, looking exactly as I'd last seen him, though there was a quality in his eyes like a candle just after it's been snuffed—a glow fading to ash. He came to where we stood at the tables, glanced at them and away.

"Gentlemen," he said. He looked at Melissa, a disheveled gamin, with what seemed to me like masked longing. "Melissa, I'm glad to see you're . . . well."

"Alive, you mean," she said.

"Just so." He turned like a turret to Mendel and said, "I will not mince words. I have come to ask you to take part in the appeasement program."

"And that would be exactly what, Shephard," Paymenz growled, "and proposed by exactly whom?"

"The Committee on Social Economics would be the who of it," said Shephard, unruffled.

"Who's that?" Melissa asked.

"Why, my dear," Shephard said, not quite looking at her, "it is a committee of economists and business people who have long been concerned about the world."

"It's an influential think tank made up of people highly placed in multinationals and conservative theorists. New Right, that sort of thing," Paymenz said impatiently.

Mendel nodded, adding: "I hope this appeasement is not what I think it is. . . . The demons cannot be appeased."

"We don't know they cannot be appeased," Shephard said,

64

inclining a stiff little bow toward Mendel. "We hypothesize that perhaps they can. That they can be conceded territory, a certain amount of . . . sustenance, and if it's offered up in a, shall we say, old-fashioned spirit of the sacrificial rite, we may hope to connect with whatever it was that pleased such entities in ancient times."

I looked at Melissa. At Paymenz. He nodded wearily to me. I asked Shephard, "Are you talking about going to the demons with people—offering them as sacrifices? Abasing ourselves? Facilitating the murder of human beings?"

"Do you have a better method, young man, for even so much as slowing them down?"

"It's too soon to say—but I think we'd all be better off dead than doing that. We have our souls to think of."

"Hear him," Mendel said, nodding. "He has gone to the quick of the matter. Shephard, it is unthinkable."

"It is already under way." And he turned and walked out.

"I suspect," Mendel said, "we should have killed him on the spot."

But no one went after Shephard.

———

I sat slumped in a plastic chair and stared up at the dusty metal pipes tangling the ceiling like a freeway interchange. I was beginning to feel a real hunger to see the sky. Nyerza and Mendel came over, carrying chairs, a bottle of wine, and plastic cups, to sit beside me. I sat up, looking from one to the other, feeling, as they looked at me, like a small animal about to be radio tagged by two zoologists.

"Uh—yes, gentlemen?"

Mendel said, "When you spoke of the origin of that image— the one that collated so interestingly with the appearances of the demons in that area—you said you had a sort of vision of it?"

"Yes."

"When you say 'vision,' Ira," Nyerza said, "do you mean, exactly, a— How do you describe . . . ?"

I thought about it. "No, not like Ezekiel. I mean, I envisioned it as an artist, that's all. But it was a very strong visual, um, inspiration, so . . . I almost think of it as a vision. But it's not like I heard a voice from heaven saying, 'Why do you persecute me?' "

"Quite," Mendel said, nodding. He looked at Nyerza. "Even so. And the synchronicities."

"We must make the leap," Nyerza said. "What he and the girl bring us cannot be brought by accident. Their higher selves collaborate with the higher design."

"I . . . wish to make a leap, too," I said. They looked at me, both with eyebrows raised. Nyerza's eyebrows a couple of feet higher than Mendel's. "Israel—Professor Paymenz—spoke of an organization. I take it you both belong to it. I took it to be a political organization. Progressive organization of some kind, but— You both seem to be involved in something, um . . . esoteric? I mean in the sense of the three circles—exoteric, mesoteric, esoteric." I thought I saw Mendel suppress a smile and I added hastily, "I don't mean that I *know* these things deeply. But I have some sense of them. I helped the professor edit his book at one point, and I worked at, well, it's just a magazine, but—"

"No, the magazine *Visions* was sometimes on the right track," Mendel said. "I occasionally contributed to it under a pen name."

"Which name?" I asked in surprise.

He shook his head, smiling. "Some things you know . . . I will tell you this much more, which will be some things you have guessed and heard and maybe a little more, but, if you trust me, this will serve as a confirmation: In ancient times, well before the birth of Christ, certain people struggled to became *conscious*—conscious, and not identified with what the Buddhists call samsara, with the false self, the shadows on the wall of the cave . . . and a few became truly conscious, more or less at the same time. Some were in what we now call Egypt, some in India, some in China, some in what is now Nepal, some in Africa, one in North America—a few others. You've studied enough to know there are degrees of consciousness, of being awake and mindful, of being aware of oneself and the subtler aspects of one's surroundings and of being aware of the cosmos itself. You have felt a little of this awareness yourself—almost anyone has had the feeling of being much more awake at some times than at others: things being more vivid, life lived more in the moment, some greater sense of connectedness. It passes quickly for most people, and they forget it. But there are those who know it can be cultivated and sustained and refined and taken to a very high level. When a certain degree of competence is achieved in this practice, one passes a threshold and becomes truly conscious—as much as one can be as a mortal person, embodied—and when that happens one becomes *psychically* aware of other truly conscious people, though they may be thousands of miles away. Aware of one another, they came together and formed a . . . what people call a secret society or secret lodge. One name for it is the Conscious Circle of Humanity."

"Mendel," Nycrza interrupted. "Are you sure? He has earned no such initiation."

"True, but it is only words, dear colleague, and in these extreme circumstances, perhaps everyone with a fertile soul must be initiated to the degree they can be. We need all the help we can get. And there are indications, do not forget, about these two young people . . . and he is a friend to the Urn . . ."

"Yes, true, true, go on then, please."

"So, the Conscious Circle continued in various forms. Sometimes its members were murdered by enemies, diabolic forces in various guises. But we continued as best we could. And we evolved a—a sort of plan, an overall scheme. We formed sublodges, lesser lodges, which not every member of the sublodge understood. For example, we created the original Masonic lodge and the Knights Templar and the original Rosicrucians and certain circles in the East . . . but few of the members of those lodges—even their highest initiates—were aware of the Conscious Circle or the real reason for the formation of those lodges. The *real* secret lodge was a circle that kept the other, better-known lodges as satellites of a sort. And these lodges were used to promote, for example, the Magna Carta, the Renaissance, the Enlightenment, and the development of the idea of the republic. The work of Lao-tzu. The Buddha was one of ours. Christ was, yes, the incarnation of God. But his teaching was of course co-opted and muddied. Thomas Jefferson was one of us. A few others you would know. But most kept to the shadows. There have been experiments, failed experiments. For example, we introduced LSD . . . and LSD was not supposed to become a street drug and what it led to—ah, we have our failures, you see. We yet hope to guide humanity to a global unity, a democratic unity, a United States of Earth."

"But not a unity controlled by the USA," Nyerza hastened to add. "Controlled by representatives of all the nations. Yet far more powerful than the United Nations."

Mendel nodded and continued, "In our awkward way, and with many false starts, we slowly guide humanity to, we hope, an attitude of tolerance, of social justice, of respect for human rights, and, yes, to the end of war. Ultimately, to a condition that makes for a greater probability of Becoming Conscious on the part of more people. And, therefore, a condition of service to the Higher, which men often call God. . . . Now, have a glass

of this regrettable chablis, and chew that over. You have answered our questions, and we have some work to do. God bless
you, young man. Pray for us all."

———

As I write this now, it occurs to me that had anyone else told
me the things that Mendel told me, any other time, the skeptic
in me—the skeptic shielding the man who deeply yearns to
believe—would have nodded politely but inwardly doubted
every word. Despite my association with *Visions* magazine and
my inner certainty that *some* kind of spiritual world is real, I
have always been skeptical of most of what people claimed to
be the manifestations of that world in our own. The Conscious
Circle of Humanity? Another supposedly ancient, supposedly
secret society? With anyone else, I'd have thought the man was
trying to set me up for induction into a cult, or that he'd become delusional and sucked others, like Nyerza, into his delu-
sions, as can happen with the charismatically mad.

But there was a recognition in me, when he told me of the
Conscious Circle—and implied his own part in it. There was a
certitude in the very air, an understanding in me, a resonance
with what he'd said that somehow transcended all doubts—
though others had made similar, rather convincing claims in my
presence about their own esoteric connections, and those others
I had not believed. Here was the real thing, and it was the force
of his being, the presence of the very consciousness that he described, that confirmed it to me. I felt it in the air as a man feels
a powerful electric field around a hydroelectric generator. I felt it
only when he chose to show it to me. But it was quite real.

Later, I drew Paymenz aside. "You know what Mendel told
me—about the Conscious Circle?"

"I heard."

"Do they . . . take students?"

DEMONS

"You would not have been told were you not a serious candidate."

"And—and you, Dr. Paymenz?"

He heaved a great sigh. "Once, Nyerza was my student. Now, I am his student. I was truly conscious, or nearly, for a time. But I—I *fell*. I re-experienced the Fall of Man. I—do not wish to discuss how it came about. My own frailty. Complete consciousness is a burden as well as a kind of enthronement. I now . . . struggle to return to the kind of consciousness they have—Nyerza and Mendel. And I warn you, to waken, to really waken, is as painful as a birth. And some die in childbirth."

He would say nothing more.

That night, I woke from a nightmare of a Sharkadian raging through an elementary school, and found Melissa gone from her cot. I got up and went down a hallway where only every second light was lit and even these flickered fitfully. I heard a cry from a room to the side and thought a demon had dragged her away to torture her to death there. I looked in, opening my mouth to shout, and saw Nyerza rearing naked over her on his cot, and it was he who cried out, and her face, turned to him, was like the Madonna. I hastened away, feeling shattered but hoping they hadn't seen me. No one should transgress on rapture.

6

I'd have laid odds that Mendel—who had, at Nyerza's side, been involved in saving tens of thousands of African refugees from tribal genocide a few years before, who had seemed unafraid, centered in the face of a relentless and immeasurable invasion of apparently indestructible supernatural predators—

That this man could not be shaken, could not be cowed. But he seemed pale, unnerved, the next morning, as he brought us a report from the translator programs and the industrial-accident investigation.

Before he came . . . waiting for Mendel, we sat around the cafeteria tables, drinking acrid coffee.

I was heartily sick of this place but afraid to go anywhere else, for we had news from the outside world sometimes: The demons seemed to move in fronts across the land, and whoever survived to remain behind the wave was safe for a time, until another demonic sweep through that area. People had begun to adapt already, adopting strategies for going on with some semblance of their lives around the demons, behind them, and during the Lulls, taking comfort in government announcements of research, of experimental relocations of population to less infested areas—that soon became diabolically infested.

Confrontations and sometimes gun battles came about between streams of refugees and people housed in the areas used, willy-nilly, as refuge—until refugee camps were established.

There were accusations in the fragmentary media, where the cables and fiber optic lines still remained, that attempts had been made by experimental governmental teams to sacrifice to the demons, as Shephard had suggested, offering up lifers from prison, volunteers, people whose status was murkily defined— even, according to some stories, homeless children. The demons, it was rumored, took the sacrifices but gave nothing in return. There were official denials that any of this had taken place. Meantime, the slaughter continued; cults formed and were dissolved; militias formed and were dissolved; National Guardsmen roamed in both fanatical order and anarchic melees.

In our underground lair, I sipped my vile coffee; I looked at Nyerza sidelong, now and then, and at Melissa. Though they weren't holding hands, I thought, with a stabbing pang: *They are lovers. She is his.*

And I told myself: *He's a great man, he deserves her. I don't.*

It didn't help.

That's when Mendel came in carrying a sheaf of printouts. He laid them with trembling hands in front of Paymenz, who seemed surprised himself at Mendel's state.

"Are you quite all right, Monsignor Mendel?" Paymenz asked.

This was the first and only time I heard him called monsignor, and it was news to me.

"I . . . have seen something . . . a bit of personal precognition . . . how things will end with me, at least, with my embodiment, and it is—it is not something I wish to discuss. But we have much else to discuss: The demonic declamation that you recorded from the television appears to be in a language related both to proto-Sumerian and the most ancient language associated with Egypt." He turned to his notes and went on, "It translates, to the extent it is translatable, as follows: 'Now at last is the long-delayed feast commenced; the sheep have been driven to the'—possible translation—'temple, and the slaughter is'—unintelligible. 'How richly run the'—possible translation— 'gutters, of jade and adamantine. The circle closes; the circle for which this world was created . . .'—untranslatable— 'cleave to my'—untranslatable—'Our fast is at an end . . . What astounding pretensions are theirs; how the'—unintelligible—'roll their eyes, how they'—possible translation—'bleat and try to rise on hind legs like men . . . How few the men'—or: 'true humanity'—'and how'—possible translation—'transient . . . Come now, attendants and brethren and'—untranslatable."

Mendel laid the text aside, took a long, slow breath, and looked at the others. "This business about the circle closing, the apparently foreordained foreplanning of it . . ."

Nyerza shivered visibly. "Perhaps it is . . . demonic hubris."

"It could be that they knew someone would translate and they sought to demoralize us," Paymenz said.

"It could be," Mendel said. "But deep in my soul there is a dread as never before. . . ."

"What was that line from Dickens," Melissa said. "Something about, are these the shadows of what will be, or what may be, if the way to the future is unaltered . . ."

Mendel smiled fondly at her. "Do you know, I believe that something speaks through you, my dear, something precious."

She looked at him in openmouthed surprise. Then managed, "Sure—Dickens."

Mendel chuckled.

Paymenz shook his head at Mendel. "Do not speak of it yet. Now, as to the industrial accidents?"

Mendel nodded. "It seems that recently two to three thousand men and women associated with manufacturing, especially in the chemicals and petroleum fields, have just . . . disappeared. Indeed: They vanished the night before the demonic attack. And, my friends, each one of them was an executive or key person associated with a company that had either had a major industrial accident or was responsible for a long-lasting cancer corridor, a record of much death and sickness around their factories, invariably covered up or, I think the expression is, glossed over, by . . . spinning doctors?"

"Spin doctors," I muttered. "The Conscious Circle— Are there those who are . . . conscious or—or powerful, esoterically powerful . . . who are opposed to—to the Conscious Circle?"

"Yes. It is possible to be conscious but to be sick—to be conscious does not mean to be good," Mendel said. "There are very few such people—only a handful. But there are only 23 conscious people in the circle—only 23 *good* conscious people in the whole world."

"Only 23!"

"Your mouth is hanging open, Ira," Paymenz said. "It is a grotesque effect."

"But—how can you know there're only 23?"

"We know," Mendel said dismissively. "As for the sick ones, the dark magicians, they may manipulate hundreds of others, using certain abilities that come to such people when they become partially conscious—telepathy, psychic control, and so forth. They have their own agenda, you see, but it is not that they are *opposed* to us particularly. They are indifferent to us as long as we do not get in their way. They wish to make themselves gods. They believe that each can rule his own universe, his own cosmos, and exploit it for his pleasure, if they become powerful enough."

Paymenz said sadly, "Some people become the apotheosis of selfishness and call it exalted."

Mendel nodded. "Now as to—" He broke off, looked at the ceiling, and frowned. He shivered and buttoned the top buttons of his shirt, though it was quite warm.

Melissa said suddenly, "I'm worried about my cats, Dad."

Kind of a non sequitur, I thought, but typical of Melissa. The remark was something that I loved her for, though I don't know why.

Nyerza looked at her with lifted eyebrows. "Cats?"

She scowled at him, knowing what he was thinking. "Yes. Cats. I know—the world is being eaten alive. All those people. And I'm worried about my cats. That's just how I am. I need to know they're okay."

"They have water and dry food, my dear," Paymenz said, patting her hand.

Brows knit, Mendel glanced again at the ceiling—then in the direction of the conference room where we'd met the demons.

Nyerza snorted softly, was saying, "Well, this is so American—to be concerned about cats at such a time."

I looked at Nyerza and thought, with a little flush of mean-spirited triumph: *Being "awakened" apparently doesn't necessarily make you always compassionate, always empathetic. It doesn't make you perfect. And it doesn't take away lust.*

Nyerza looked at me. I had the uncanny sense that he'd read my mind. I looked away.

"You're quite right," Mendel said, smiling gently at me. Mendel! Not Nyerza. "We are imperfect, even—even then."

Melissa looked at Mendel, then at me. "Ira didn't say anything . . . did he?"

Suddenly Mendel lifted his head and seemed to sniff the air. He looked at Nyerza, and both looked at the ceiling. Then at the hallway.

"The forbearance is at an end," Mendel said.

"Is it?" Paymenz said, going pale beneath his beard. "It was always surprising—"

"What are you *talking* about?" Melissa asked, her voice rising, breaking, the knuckles white on her clenched hands.

I reached out instinctively and took her hand; she let me do it. Her hand opened in mine like a blossom.

She looked at Nyerza, then at me. "Could we go somewhere and—and talk, Ira?"

Then the screams from above began. The room shook; a subterranean thunder rattled the pipes; plaster sprinkled, then rained down like flour from a sifter.

Nyerza ran to the police guards, shouting.

Drawing their weapons, the men hurried into the hallway, a ramp slanting gradually to stairs leading to the next floor.

Mendel had slipped away, off to the room he slept in—to hide?

Then a reptilian stench rolled into the room, a wind laden with a palpable reek that seemed to coat the inside of my nose and mouth with viscosity—like the putrid discharge you get on your fingers from handling a garter snake.

Nyerza was trying to herd us back from the hallway entrance when something rolled down toward us, down the ramp to our feet: a furry ball; the severed head of one of the guards. Then another came rolling down seconds later to bump with a wood-block clunk into the first. Someone screamed—I think it was me, not Melissa—and the demons we'd encountered in the conference room upstairs were there: the Gnasher and behind him the great sinuous bulk of the Tailpipe.

I remember thinking: *Just as things are beginning to make sense, chaos comes for me.*

I pulled Melissa back—she sagged on rubbery knees, making it hard to move her—and I wanted Mendel to be there, to explain, to make things rational again.

As if I'd summoned him, Mendel entered the room. At first he seemed the emblem of absurdity: He'd changed into a costume. Mendel carried a silvery broadsword. He'd taken off his coat; over his shirt he'd draped a tunic that was also a sort of banner, called a tabard, front and back: a red Christian cross on a white background.

"A crusader!"

the Gnasher hooted gleefully, gnashing its teeth loudly. The Tailpipe was too big for the hall but somehow oozed into the room like lava behind the Gnasher, who struck an elegant pose and swung his genitals like a zoot-suit chain.

"What a delight! And with a sword! I'm almost disappointed you can't slay me like Saint—who was it?—Saint Someone."

This last was addressed to Paymenz, who was murmuring something that might have been an incantation and might have been a prayer in what sounded like Hebrew.

"It was Saint George," Mendel said, and ran toward the Gnasher, shouting, "For Saint George! For Jesus, the King! For the King!"

"Oh, for Christ's sake,"

I heard the Gnasher mutter.

Then the sword whistled down, cleaving the demon to its groin, like some mighty blow in an Arthurian saga—but the wound sealed up behind the slash. The demon smiled sadly as it healed itself, almost disappointed. It gripped Mendel's wrist, crushing, making him fall to his knees with pain.

"Run, you imbeciles!" Mendel shouted, as the Gnasher with its free hand wrenched the sword's grip from Mendel and drew the sword casually from its own gut as from a scabbard.

Paymenz stalked toward the demons, incanting louder, raising his hand. The Gnasher laughed in Paymenz's face and ignored him, turned the sword on Mendel, gutting him like a chicken. Paymenz raised his voice and was almost in the Gnasher's reach as Melissa screamed, "No, Daddy!" and I strained to hold her back as she tried to run to him.

Nyerza strode up and struck Paymenz on the back of the neck, so that Paymenz buckled.

"You must take care of the girl and the Gold in the Urn, Israel!" Nyerza shouted to Paymenz as he dragged him back a few steps. Then Nyerza lifted Paymenz, threw him clear—even as the leviathan tail of the steaming, oozing black Tailpipe lifted and slammed at him. Nyerza dodged aside, was hit glancingly so that he was spun back away from the demons to fetch up against the wall, dazed but uninjured.

The Gnasher had slashed Mendel open, so that blood spread in a widening pool. Mendel was quivering, but his eyes were empty; he was dead or in shock. The Gnasher seemed to be probing for something in Mendel's insides . . . with his hands, with his sword, with his mouth, searching more and more frantically through Mendel's wet wreckage.

"Where is it? Where!"

Its fury made its voice resonate through my head.

"The spark! Where!"

After that it raged in the language we called Tartaran: the language of demons. But a baseline meaning was conveyed: rage, pent-up seeking, frustrated hunger. The Gnasher stepped back from the body and roared.

As if expressing the Gnasher's frustration by proxy, the Tailpipe raised its tail and smacked it down on Mendel's body, so that bone ends ripped into pink-white view and teeth rattled from a shattered jaw.

Melissa swayed; her mouth dropped open. She whimpered. I only felt like doing those things.

The Gnasher took a step toward us. Paymenz stepped in front of me and Melissa. Nyerza got to his feet.

Suddenly Mendel was there, intact, apparently alive, as we'd last seen him. But somehow I knew that it wasn't his body I was seeing. "Here is the spark you seek," he said, though his mouth didn't open.

The Gnasher turned to him and slashed with curving talons that went through Mendel, as if through a hologram. Mendel smiled distantly.

"You cannot harm me thus," said Mendel. "What you call my spark is a flame, and it burns in the realm of All Suns, where you cannot reach it."

Mendel turned to Nyerza and said, "Use the Gold as a shield."

Then Mendel was gone. It wasn't as if he blinked out, it was more like the passing of a memory.

The Gnasher bellowed,

"One spark gone, these remain, calling to their inheritor! Purchase ye my insurance, one payment only! Live forever within me and immediately cash in your premiums! We are a full-service organization!"

And it strode toward us.

"There has to be a way out!" I said, backpedaling, dragging Melissa with me.

Nyerza shook his head. "They will pursue: The only way out is through."

So saying, he took Melissa by the wrist and swung her in front of him.

And pushed her toward the demons.

I shouted something—I don't know what it was—and ran after her to pull her back as the Gnasher opened its great jaws to snap at her head, and then felt Paymenz and Nyerza gripping me, each taking an arm. Melissa put her hands in front of her face—

The Gnasher stepped toward her—

Then there was an effulgence. No, a scintillation, a sparkle from just in front of Melissa issuing from the area of her sternum. I saw, now, a sparkling, a slowly turning ball of sparkle, each spark big as my hand, the whole growing as it emerged, stabilizing at the size of a bushel; a grand, turning sparkle of gold and violet and electric-blue, the gold predominating, the whole giving off a keening sound so high-pitched you couldn't quite hear it and yet you felt it in your joints. Slowly turning, the orb of unfading sparks hung in the air between Melissa, who seemed in a trance, and the Gnasher . . .

Who reached for it . . .

And then recoiled, the demon whimpering so pathetically I wanted to say, There, there . . .

The wheeling ball of sparks moved toward the demons, seeming to draw Melissa like a sleepwalker behind it, and the Gnasher wailed in his own language and clawed its way up onto the steaming black bulk of the Tailpipe, as if taking comfort there, and then scrambled back away from Melissa. The great quivering, steaming, many-mouthed eelskin flank of the Tailpipe still barred our way, as we stumbled after her, but then the Tailpipe oozed itself into two parts, a kind of macroscopic mitosis, one part splitting off to the right, the other to the left, like the Red Sea in the Moses story. There was a clear path between the quivering ends, and we hurried between, through the oily stink of it, and up the ramp, past headless bodies, and to the stairs. I turned to see the Tailpipe flow seamlessly together behind us, and it commenced to follow, until the Gnasher shouted something in Tartaran, and it held back.

"This way," Nyerza said. "We go to the helicopter."

I looked at Melissa; the globe of incandescence had vanished, receded into her. She stared into space, listening, with tears in her eyes, as Paymenz whispered something to her.

"Okay," I said. "A helicopter. That's fine. I'll go for that. Sure. Let's do that."

———

Paymenz held Melissa in his arms, at the back of the chopper; I sat near the front, behind the pilot's seat. The pilot was a dour, stooped, gray-haired black man in a paramilitary uniform without markings: Mimbala, whom Nyerza said had once been an army chief of staff for some African country. Mimbala had started the chopper and left it running in some kind of idle, having gone to consult with a spindly white man from the FAA who was trying to provide a strategy for flying safely past the drifting Spiders, the darting Sharkadians. We could see them, instead of airplanes, speckling the sky here and there in the distance. Our chopper's blades were chuffing so slowly I could have hung on to them and swung around, like a child at play; and I had an impulse to do just that—to do something meaningless, mischievous, anything to deny the darkness pulling at our hearts like G-force tugging an astronaut who realizes his shuttle won't make it into orbit. Like the astronaut, I wanted to take to the sky.

Mostly to keep my mind busy, I began to question Nyerza. "The thing that came from her, that drove them back, that saved us—was it the Gold in the Urn that Mendel mentioned?"

"Yes. It needs a human being to be the Urn, the repository, for a time. We planted it in Melissa."

"Is that . . . is that what you were doing with her last night?" I asked, leaning toward him so Melissa wouldn't hear, my voice as soft as possible over the humming of the idling engine, the chuffing of the rotors.

He looked at me in frowning puzzlement. "No. That was . . . just a man and a woman. Spontaneous, as you say."

"Not a ritual?"

"No. It was quite natural." He looked out the window, signaled to the pilot. Mimbala raised a hand, palm outward, to say wait a moment. Nyerza turned back to me, sighing. "I will miss having Mendel physically near. The Urn . . . the Gold . . . this is what the demons call sparks, the being force of many lives, who're consolidated, in this case, to one purpose. They meditate together, and this keeps them together. They are like— In some cultures they are called bodhisattvas, the awakened, who return to help us. When we realized that the catastrophe was coming—though we did not know what form it would take—we consulted with these beings, these Ascended Masters, and asked for their help in its most powerful form: the Gold in the Urn. But our connection to it needed to be kept in one place and protected. A few years ago, Melissa was selected as the bearer, the Urn."

"She knew this?"

"She did not. I'm embarrassed to say it was done without her knowledge, as she slept. But this was done with the cooperation of her father. Harmlessly and painlessly."

"A few years ago . . ."

I remembered. Melissa had been depressed, gloomy, much more into the goth thing. Writing bleak songs like the one the demon had mocked her with. Then she'd changed—almost overnight. Becoming more centered, more confident, optimistic.

"The Gold . . . it possessed her?"

"Not at all. It only rode there, in her. But there has been some influence on her, I have no doubt. Its radiance would have been felt, though they try to keep themselves secreted deep within. The demon was trying to drive the Gold from her, perhaps, when it recited her song—a song from a time when she was ruled by, as you might say, quiet despair: that thing that, in some people, opens the door for the diabolic."

I thought I should be angry that Melissa had been used this way. But then, the Gold seemed to have helped her; and it saved us all today.

"The demons can't hurt her, at all, while the Gold is with her?"

"In time, they will make their own dark orb and hunt her down—destroy the Urn to destroy the Gold—using their own merged darkness to get to her, surely. Or they may use humans to attack her. But this, you see, will take time. How much, we only speculate. A month or six weeks perhaps, Mendel told me. . . . Ah, here comes Mimbala."

Mimbala returned to the chopper and threw switches, pulled levers; and it thrummed, and the rotors swished faster and faster, the world tilted, and we angled into the sky.

We are alone, Melissa and I, in the professor's chilly, dark apartment, alone with restive cats and dead lava lamps. Except Melissa is never alone, even when I've left her in another room. The Gold is with her, though unseen. It is silent, transparent; it is singing and scintillating: all of these.

I finished writing all the foregoing yesterday. Yes, it's amazing what people can get used to. We've been here for weeks, since the chopper pilot landed on the roof of the building.

"There's canned food and water stacked floor to ceiling in that back storeroom," Paymenz had shouted, over the throb of the chopper. "My divinations, you see, led me to stock up: *I*, at least, took them seriously! Now you may sing hosannas of praise to my foresight!" He grinned; he was trying to make light of his departure.

"Dad—stay with us!" Melissa shouted. "Or take us with you!"

The engine got louder. "Arrangements . . . They won't come here. . . . Must go with Nyerza . . . Events are shaped by . . . various convergences . . . luminous . . ." Luminous something. Repercussions, maybe? "We're going to try to locate the—" I couldn't make out the rest. They took off as he shouted, "Back in touch when possible. You are safe if you stay with her, Ira."

That's not good for my masculine vanity, but it's true: Melissa keeps me safe.

I don't go out, because I could be killed; Melissa doesn't go out because she doesn't want to see anyone killed. And the looters, the gangs, could take her; use her and kill her, as they have with too many others.

The Spiders departed the balcony some time ago. But

streamers of black smoke twist up randomly across the glassy vista of the city.

Depression comes sometimes, like a wolf prowling at the edge of a campfire's light. I throw what fuel I have on the fire.

The first few days we slept most of the time, she in her room, me on the living room couch, where I could keep an eye on the front door, pretend I was useful as her guardian. We slumbered away a weighty emotional exhaustion, absorbing, in riotous dreams and dozing depression, all that we'd seen. The demons, the flight through the city, the Gnasher, the flare of sex, the reshaping of paradigms, the brutal killing of Mendel and his triumph, the revelation of the Gold in the Urn . . . the Gold, the living wheel of burning spirit that possessed Melissa and yet didn't possess her; that seemed to hum in the background, unheard but felt by those feeling parts of us that are usually dormant.

———

What people can get used to . . . People managed a routine even at Dachau; they found ways to survive psychologically—harder than surviving physically.

In Cambodia, in the days of the Khmer Rouge, people adapted to being forced into an insane plan for an anti-intellectual agrarian utopia, a utopia based on mass murder and the destruction of ideas and common sense; masses of people, after seeing their loved ones butchered, forced from the cities onto farms, forced to work fourteen-hour days, seven days a week, 365 days a year; to give up all their old culture, their music, their traditions, every single one of their beliefs; to wear black pajamas and nothing else ever; to be slaves to a demented scheme of social engineering. They adapted; they survived.

Demons invade the world; people find ways to adapt, to get used to the horror.

Is it, really, any worse than the Killing Fields?

———

But often I felt a craving for the ordinariness that had reigned before the demons, for the very banality I had sometimes railed against. The mindless, childish ubiquity of mass media and consumerism; the welcome distraction of dealing with traffic and laundry and phone bills. What a relief real banality would be . . .

———

We passed the time as we might, making a pact, for the sake of sanity, to leave the TV and its battery in a closet, and listen to a radio news show only once a day. After two weeks Melissa asked me to listen alone, away from her. She spent the time meditating, every so often muttering in some language she shouldn't know; in reading, writing feverishly in a journal.

She encouraged me to paint, to draw, with whatever was handy. I felt tense, my art balled up inside; I was reluctant to let it out, to express it. But she gently insisted and came to muse over my drawings, my pen and inks made with all the wrong sorts of pens and inks.

Sometimes, as I drew, I seemed to see, in my mind's eye, a pentagram superimposed over a city I didn't recognize. I reproduced the city as a simplified map, street lines intertwined with hermetic symbols, and figures of myth.

———

One night, in the light of battery-operated lanterns, we sat around the living room, trying not to hear the distant sounds of shouting, combat, sirens, and, from far off, the *crump* of what might be a plane crashing. Some nights were worse than others; this was one of the bad nights.

She'd asked me to read to her, anything I wanted. I chose the Sufi poet Rumi—consciously or unconsciously. I glanced up at her from time to time as I read. She was curled sideways in an easy chair, with two cats nestled in her hollows; she wore a dark purple sari, no shoes. Her feet were drawn up onto the cushion, one hand toying with a silver ring on a toe, her eyes hidden by the drape of her hair. She made me ache.

"A lover gambles everything, the self,
the circle around the zero! He or she
cuts and throws it all away.
This is beyond any religion.
Lovers do not require from God any proof,
or any text, nor do they knock on a door
to make sure this is the right street.
They run and they run . . ."

I felt her looking at me then and glanced up at her, and our eyes met. Her gaze seemed open, as never before. I found myself putting the book aside and crossing the room to her, bending to kiss her. She lifted her head to return the kiss, and moved aside on the big chair so I could slide in beside her, the cats irritably jumping to the floor and slinking away. Then Melissa eased herself onto my lap, and I drew her into the circle of my arms. We kissed more deeply. My hands found their way to her thighs, and she let them explore upward from there. . . .

Suddenly I stopped, and looked down at my hand. It was as if there was a cold, bony grip on my wrist, holding it back, though nothing could be seen. Nothing except a blue-gold sparkling, a throbbing shimmer, that never quite declared it-self. Did I see it? It was as if, instead, I felt it and made some accommodation in the visual part of my brain.

She felt it, too, and went pale, looking up at me. "They . . ."

"They don't want me to. I'm not . . . while they're there, it has to be . . . someone like . . ." It hurt to say it: "Someone like Nyerza . . ." I took my hand away from her thigh; the invisible grip went from my wrist. It all seemed so . . . lawful. So in-evitable. We didn't question it.

She laid her head against my shoulder. "But the time will come."

"I don't know if I'll ever be . . ."

"You might, but that's not what I meant. They won't al-ways be with me. Not in the way they are now."

"If we live."

"Yes. If we live."

"But you'll belong to Nyerza."

After a moment, she said, "No, I don't think so. He's . . . a great man. But though he knows better, it's difficult for him to think of a woman as his equal. And even when I'm close to him I'm not close to him. And . . . there was a sense, when he was—was in me . . . that he was talking to them . . . like I was the phone booth. I didn't care for it. I should be honored, but . . ."

"Do they—do they speak to you? Inside?"

"No. Well, yes and no. They hide their light so I am not blinded. Sometimes I think I feel . . . sort of feel them saying something . . . but I hear no words."

"Saying?"

"I don't know how to put it into words."

We said no more that night, and soon she went to bed. I haven't tried, since. But sometimes she takes my hand, or I take hers, and we hold hands; sometimes she comes into the circle of my arms, and we stand quietly in the middle of the room.

In our area, the police are still operating, in a furtive kind of way. Mostly curtailing the gangs of looters, trying to suppress the parades, because there are always deaths at the parades or in their wake.

The parades wind through the streets, the paraders clashing garbage can lids, clanking bottles together, chanting, many of them naked and bright with fanciful body paints. How it began, no one seems quite sure. The parades skirt the areas where the demons are roaming, seem to flirt with them, to invite them. They seem to believe, according to a radio report I heard, that if they thus offer themselves up en masse, the participating individuals have a better chance of survival: Choose from us but choose not me.

I watched with binoculars, one dusk, as one of these spontaneous parades of the half mad wended, clashing and banging and chanting with an elliptical rhythm, into the square below the apartment building. I watched as a Dishrag fluttered down from the sky like a wet autumn leaf just broken from the tree, coming down, soon, to tumble across the ground, now like a tumbleweed but not tumbling at random. It was seeking and finding, as it closed on one of the paraders. The demon colloquially called a Dishrag is like fuzzy, blotchy gray-and-blue terry cloth crumpled up into a ball, about ten feet in diameter, capable of partially unfolding to entrap its victims.

The Rag bounced in pursuit of a short, fat man—perhaps picking the easy kill from the herd—as the parade parted for the hunt, the crowd gawping in awe as the demon's bounce became a pounce, knocking the man down, closing over him like a sea creature enfolding a fish. The victim's arms and feet protruded from opposite sides of the crumpled, furry ball. As it crushed him, squeezing the juice from him, something else was expressed from him, pressed out by unimaginable psychic pressures, a visible emission of his mental battery, a kind of electric-blue discharge of images, key psychological moments sketched on the air. It was something like the smoky shapes I'd seen coming from the victim of the Spiders—but this was like the movement of a light pen caught in slow time exposure: the brief, streaky-blue glow outline of the victim with his parents, his mother beating him with a coat hanger, a priest making him kneel before an altar and then before him, a girl surrendering to him, a college degree handed to him, a car accident where the girl dies. Then the light cartoons faded, as the man's screams became muted. The crowd was parading around the feasting demon, clashing and clanking and chanting rhythmically, some chant I couldn't make out, and now a Sharkadian was darting down from above.

I turned away, sickened and feeling suddenly claustrophobic. But something else had caught my attention from the corner of my eye.

I went back to the balcony railing and looked down to see a nondescript bus pull up, men with guns get out below, far below. Men with guns going into our building.

"Oh no," I said.

I think that's what I said. And I went back inside the building.

Shephard's people, maybe. The black magicians had sent mortals, unaffected by the power of the Gold, to take Melissa away.

I had no way to stop them, but maybe I could misdirect them.

———

I ran downstairs, got as far as the second-floor stairwell landing, before the soldiers burst into the stairwell and surrounded me. There was a gun shoved against the side of my head, one arm twisted behind me. "Let's see your pass," someone growled in my ear.

"I don't have one." I told them I was from Paymenz's apartment and then wished I'd bitten my tongue, thinking I shouldn't have told them that.

But it turned out to be the right thing to do. They let me go.

I went into the lobby and saw the front door was ringed by a semicircle of soldiers. None of the other buildings in the area was guarded. Our guardians seemed almost relaxed as they checked a nervous old woman's building pass. Maybe the soldiers were glad to be here, because the demons were afraid of this building—because the Gold was here. Word had gotten around that the demons wouldn't attack the building because they were afraid of Melissa.

Laboring back upstairs—the elevator was broken, of course— I realized the soldiers had been sent here, through Nyerza's government contacts, specifically to guard the building against Shephard's mortal associates. The bus I'd seen had brought relief soldiers for the next watch; they were protecting Melissa, not threatening her.

Then perhaps it was safe to go to the roof . . . to get *out*, after all these weeks, really outside . . .

Enjoying the exercise, I climbed to the roof. I wasn't alone up there.

I didn't see them at first, though I heard a tinkling piano from somewhere. There was a little building containing the elevator engine housing and the top landing for the stairs, and when I came out of it, they were on the other side, behind me. I strolled across the transplas-coated roof to the railing, reveling in the open air but scanning the sky for nearby Sharkadians or Spiders. I wasn't protected up here. I was too far from Melissa, from those who were called the Gold.

Then they raised the volume, and I turned at the sound of

someone playing an electric piano. It sounded like a perverse take on honky-tonk ragtime.

I walked around to the other side of the building, following the sound, and found two figures standing at an electric piano, the tall skinny one fingering a bass part, the stocky one in the hat tinkling away at the upper register. The electric piano was portable, on folding steel-tube legs, battery powered, and sounded fairly close to an acoustic piano. Up here, it sounded lost, plaintive. I took half a dozen steps toward them, before I realized that the guy playing the upper register, the guy wearing patchy jeans and work boots, and a shabby vest unbuttoned over a dirty white T-shirt . . . that his clothes had grown on him, were not real clothes, were part of his skin.

His? *Its* skin. The demon seemed to sense me, as I realized this, and though I very much did not want to see its face, the Bugsy snapped its whole body around and showed its face to me, and we both knew I couldn't look away.

A thing projected from its mouth that looked like a smoldering cigarette and gave off a greasy steam, only the projection wasn't a cigarette but an excrescence, part of its lip, a growth projecting three or four inches, camouflage complete with a yellow cigarette filter. I had no doubt there would be a brand name on it, too—and the "cigarette" never burned down. The Bugsy's face was ostensibly human, with a stub of a nose and flat blue eyes that were a tad too wide; a slack, froggish mouth; and jagged, uneven yellow teeth. Its proportions were not dwarfish—but its hands were, except for the curving talons on them. Its clothes grew from its skin like the shell of a turtle; and there were blotchy red and yellow running sores on the "cloth" of its vest, pants, and on one side of its neck. Bugsys grew different sorts of "clothes," but they all had those sores.

On its head was a hat, a real hat, taken from some human

victim probably; a bashed-up gray fedora that had mostly lost its shape.

A Bugsy, I thought. *There is a fucking Bugsy on the roof.*

It had a human companion—as they often did for a time. They kept human pets for a while—sometimes for a week or more, I'd heard—and then killed them. The human sidekicks were inexplicably oblivious of their fate until close to the end.

The Bugsy's voice was slurred like a drunk's, by turns guttural and squeaky. "There'sh my man, there'sh my man," the demon said. "Here he ish. Robert, you see this guy? Is he a bleshing or what?"

The skinny, ragged human sidckick, a man who might have been thirty, with hollow eyes so red I couldn't make out his natural eye color, tittered and rubbed his pointed noise with a grime-caked hand. His nails had grown long and begun to curl, as if in grotesque imitation of the Bugsy's talons. "You think he got any dope on him?"

"No, no I don't schmell any, Robert. I mean he's a bleshing for you, because I was jush gonna killya, for somepina do, and here he chiz. He's like a bleshing from uh-BUUUUUUUUUV! Gorblesh 'im!"

Robert laughed hysterically, glancing sidelong at the demon. *What* had it said about just going to kill?

Hoping to get them to turn their backs again, I said, "I was enjoying the music. Like to hear some more, if you've got any more in you."

"You wantsa shee what Robert's got in him huh ya?" the demon said, "cigarette" wagging with each syllable. The Bugsy hooked a talon under Robert's chin, so that blood spiraled down the skinny, grimy neck. There were lots of little scars, half-healed cuts on Robert where the Bugsy had toyed with him.

Robert giggled, still pinned by the talon the Bugsy was

absentmindedly digging in like a man vigorously picking his nose. Robert looked at me desperately, as if he wanted to say something.

It was useless, I knew, to tell the demon, No, I don't want to see you hurt him. I wondered how fast the Bugsys ran, how far they could jump.

Could I make it to the door of the building?

I tried to stay calm, forcing myself to breathe evenly. A little rain began to skirl down . . . to fall, to ease up, to fall again . . . A scrap of paper blew spiraling by . . .

I said, "I was hoping for music. I'd just about do anything for live music about now."

"Really! You do anyshing? Thasha what I wanta hear from more ya pepple—mansy, alla mansies don' wanna do this, don' wanna do that, boring tuh kill, boring to keep company wid-shem. You do someshin for me firsh"—the cigarette-shaped growth waggling—". . . and I'ma playin' you a bigshing . . . There'sh a girl downstairs, I'm a let you live, be the king, the king, the king of the shecrets, if you let my friend here in to talka her jusha little minute . . ."

"Just lemme talk to her," Robert said. "Just a little minute."

"Certainly . . . I'll bring her up here," I said. "Just a moment."

I backed toward the little building . . . the door to the stairs.

"No, thatsh not cool, mothuhfuckuh mansie—you lie to me, yuh fuckin' guy, yuh lyin'—now we goin' down the hall, you and Robert, ya goin first. Robert . . . he . . ."

And Robert kills her, I thought.

"Oh fuck it," I said, aloud. *Just run.*

I half turned to run for the door. The Bugsy let Robert go and crouched, preparing to spring. I'd never make it to the door. Then I remembered something I'd heard.

I turned back, dug in my pocket, and came up with a quarter with lint and crumbs stuck to it. I polished it with my thumb, saying, "Hey—I'll bet you anything you want I get heads, you get tails."

The Bugsy froze, then straightened, eyes glazing. They're said to have difficulty resisting an opportunity to gamble. They prefer cards, especially stud poker, but the coin toss seemed to be working. "Shrow it," the demon said.

I tossed the coin, caught it, flipped it, slapped it on my wrist. "Heads!" I announced.

"But ya didn't make a bet!" Robert blurted, blinking.

I realized that Robert reminded me of someone: my mom's boyfriend, Curtis. Long time ago.

I said, "I bet—I bet our lives, Robert's and mine—"

"Shrow it, fuckin' shrow it. I takeuh headsish time," the Bugsy hissed, staring at the quarter in my hand, drooling.

"Sure." I tossed the quarter up—toward a farther corner of the roof. The Bugsy ran for it.

I mouthed *Run!* at Robert. He only gaped at me, blinking stupidly, tears starting from his eyes.

I sprinted for the door to the stairs.

"No, don't, man!" Robert yelled hoarsely. "He . . ."

The Bugsy made a sound like a furious boar, and, as I ran, it shouted, "I won thatsh tosh!"

"Wait!" Robert yelled. He said nothing else after that—there was only the scream. It was such a piteous cry, I paused at the outbuilding, just around the corner from the door, to look back. Always a mistake, to look back at a demon.

"You don't wanna see whush I gotferya here?" the Bugsy said, "cigarette" bobbing as with one set of talons it held Robert facedown, the other claws digging deeply into Robert's back, demonic grip closing firmly over the writhing human's spine. One hand pushing, the other pulling—with a practiced motion, pulling Robert's spine from his body, the whole spine, as from an overcooked fish, though it was still attached to his skull. Until, there, the spine was yanked free, and the Bugsy waved the vertebrae spatteringly at me. "We cud be friendsh, give ya immortality, shecrets—all tha' shit, teach you do shit like thish, whatcha shay . . ." And as it spoke it strode toward me, waving the segmented dripping red wand of Robert's spine, holding my trapped attention.

I broke free and ran for the door, for the stairs, and vaulted over the railing, fell twelve feet—maybe more—to the next landing, a painful landing, hearing the unnaturally soft boot steps on the stairs above me as the demon came after me, seeing the red bony splintery thing flung past my head and down the stairwell.

I was down just ahead of the Bugsy, through a doorway, down the hall, running to Paymenz's apartment door. With terror-focused concentration putting the key *very exactly right into the lock*, no wasted motions as I inserted, turned the key, got the door open, removed the key, and ran in, slammed the door, shouting for Melissa, feeling like such a goddamn little boy, calling for the protection of his mother.

But when she came to the living room, put her hand on the door, I heard, almost immediately, the hasty retreat of the Bugsy padding away down the hall outside.

A little later we heard a rustling outside the window and saw a Sharkadian flying the Bugsy down from the roof in its arms, the two of them pausing to look toward us, about fifty feet past the balcony railing, hovering to stare before flapping awkwardly away.

———

The day after the Bugsy, with radical foolhardiness, I decided to visit some kids I'd been giving art lessons to. The soldiers wouldn't accompany me. I got there without running into the gangs. On the way I saw the things I described near the opening of this narrative. The Grindum, the man in the Volvo, and me on my way to teach an art lesson.

On the way home I had to dodge a van full of drunken, glue-sniffing kid fundies. Gangs of hysterical teens who think they're supposed to bring about the final judgment by punishing the enemies of God, which is whoever they happen on when they're out on the town. Half the time, happily, the demons get them. They nearly ran me down, but I cut through a burned-out Tofu Chef place and lost them in the alley.

Since then, some days of quiet. A Lull. I think it's a Monday afternoon. It's dull gray outside, like a Monday afternoon should be, anyway. The only noise is the occasional gunshot. The looters, I guess. Shot on sight, lately.

Quiet. But Melissa and I can both feel it: the imminence. Something is about to happen. Meanwhile, she's meditating in her room and I'm wondering if I'm—

Hold on, there's a pounding at the door. Someone pounding. Going to check it out.

Why don't we have a fucking gun here?! Going . . .

———

I'm back; I washed out my mouth but still taste vomit. My hands are shaking. Hard to write.

When I went to the living room, Melissa was opening the door—why, I don't know. Stupid to open the door, though the metal chain was across the gap.

Standing in the hall was a young guy in a Day-Glo orange VR-connect jumpsuit, the kind with all those little jacks on them and lots of peeling stickers from software companies slapped on between the jacks. The VR doesn't work very well, and when they use it they look like idiots, walking on their squirrelly little treadmills, and if they aren't real careful the goggles get disconnected or the wires pulled out of the suit. VR heads get into it anyway. This VR head was shaved, even his eyebrows; he'd have been rockstar-good-looking if not for that. He seemed clean, and, at first, he seemed sane: He didn't seem like a Bugsy slave. And he wasn't one.

"Do you need food?" Melissa asked. "We have a little to spare. Some canned stuff."

"I could use some," the guy said. "I live in the building here, you know, just a floor down." He stuck his hand in the space between door and frame as if to shake hands.

Melissa made as if to shake it. I pulled her back. He withdrew the hand, grinning, showing pearly white teeth. His manicure was perfect, too. "Look, we should stick together—the people in this building. I've got a good wireless Internet connection, the very best, if you wanta come and check it out. I do that Clan Collector website. That's mine, you know. My name's Dervin. Just Dervin." He looked at Melissa, then me. "You don't know the name?"

"No . . . The *what* website, did you say?" I asked.

He seemed genuinely surprised. "Clan Collector. You never heard of it? You're kidding! It's the third most popular site in the country. All seven clans of demons are totally represented . . . even some interviews!" He spoke fast, clasping his hands again and again to emphasize each statement. "We've got the best graphics showing them from different angles, rundowns on clan-specific styles of killing—the whole thing. Files on all the different worship cults, chat rooms, fan voting—right now the Gnashers are the most popular. There's a lot of Bugsy fanatics out there, though. Me, I think there's something majestic about the Tailpipe. And I think if we could learn the Tartaran terms for the clan types we could give them names that are, you know, more fitting, that honor the whole gestalt of that demon type. And I'm working on that."

Melissa and I looked at each other, then at the stranger. "Did you say fans? And . . . Bugsy fanatics?" She turned to push one of the cats, a fat tabby named Stimpy, away from the door. The cat wanted to get to what he thought would be outside, and he was pacing behind us, staring at the partly open door into the hall.

"Sure. The demons have a major fan base."

"A fan base?" she said. "But they're slaughtering us. In huge numbers."

"Well, yeah, but serial killers had a big fan following, and so did Hitler. Still does. I spoke to a Gnasher online—he said he was a Gnasher and I think he was, but that's, you know, controversial in fan circles—um, spoke to him in the chat room, right? And he said Hitler is actually—" He broke off. Chuckled. "You guys are staring at me like I'm nuts, but you're really the ones who're out of it. There was a Fox Channel special—they have that mobile Fox Channel transmitter, on that bus that uses that satellite info and dodges the demons. They have that show *The Clans* and it's just pure demonophile stuff."

"O-*kayyyy*," I said. "Whatever. We can let you have some canned goods, what you can carry. I know the building's been getting unevenly supplied—there was a raid on the Army convoy or something, and uh . . ."

"Ahh actually . . ." He was exchanging stares with the tabby cat. "I'd rather have one of your cats. One or two. You have, what, five?"

Melissa tilted her head as she gazed at him, trying to see if he was kidding. "You're joking, right?"

"Um—no. I can trade you all kinds of stuff for a couple of cats. Or as many as you want to give me."

"Food's that hard to get?" I asked. "I just offered—"

"No, it's for sacrifice. I've got an online relationship with that Gnasher—it's online and ongoing. It's safe, online. But to continue the contact, he requires sacrifices, and he'll accept animals."

"No," I said. "Not a chance. Good-bye. Move away from the door or I'll shout for the soldiers."

Then I saw that he was staring at Melissa's chest. I thought, at first, he was staring at her breasts, but his gaze was lower. And he was reaching behind him. *I've got an online relationship with that Gnasher. Online and ongoing.*

"Oh shit," I said. He put his shoulder against the door so we couldn't slam it, and he whipped the automatic pistol around to shove it through the opening. "Run, Melissa!" I yelled.

I jerked the wrist of his gun hand toward me with one hand, the other pulling his elbow, pulling him off balance. He instinctively pulled his arm back a little so the gun tilted up, and I pushed, hard—and Melissa helped me, ignoring my glare— and the gun muzzle went back as the gun went off pointing into Dervin's right eye socket, blowing his eye back into his skull, his brains out through the top of his head in a sudden, brief, thick-red fountain.

We threw his body off the balcony. I don't expect anyone will come and ask about it.

Then I had to run to the bathroom to vomit, as Melissa knelt by me, sobbing softly and stroking my hair.

I'm going to go brush my teeth again. At least my hands have stopped shaking.

———

In spring 1989, I came home from school to find our television taken apart, all over the living room floor, and my mom and her boyfriend, Curtis, crouched, tweaking amidst the parts.

"I know what you think," she said, grinning, so cranked

up it was an involuntary grin. I saw she'd lost a couple more teeth.

I snorted and tried to ignore them, skirting the wreckage of the TV, the tools they'd used to take it apart, trying to escape upstairs. Curtis was glaring at me, jaws working, grinding—like a Gnasher, it seems to me now. There was a buzzing in his deep-hollowed eyes, a vein throbbing on his forehead. (Yeah, the Bugsy's doomed pet, Robert, looked like Curtis, except Curtis was somewhat cleaner.)

"You got a problem, kid?"

"No." I was almost to the stairs. Then I stopped, staring. My boom box my aunt had given me. They'd taken it apart. They'd destroyed it. I stared at it, tears in my eyes. It was almost the only thing I owned. I loved music. And they . . .

"There was a—a bug in it. Curtis found a bug in it," Mom was babbling. "There was a whatdoyoucallit govermint govermind mind-control controller bug in it. Hon, we found it—where is it, I'll show you!"

She scrabbled in the parts and came up with a piece of the CD laser.

"That's for reading CDs," I said, barely audibly. "That's not—"

But Curtis heard me and snarled, "You're saying I'm full of shit?"

I shrugged, dazed, wiping my eyes. "You just . . ." I wasn't thinking about what I was saying anymore, which was a mistake. "You just do what crank cases do. You guys are tweaking and you take shit apart and you can't get it back together because you're on a tweaking thing. They all do that. It's a simple inevitability."

Curtis guffawed. "You hear that pretentious shit?" He put on his lame version of an English accent: "It's a 'simple inevitability'!" He stood up, locking his eyes on me.

101

My mother was feeling the plunge, the crash, slumping where she sat. Her voice was dead as she muttered, "Oh leave him alone; let's put this shit back together—"

"You know why he talks that way, the little fucking snot? He studies *art*, he reads Jane fucking Austen! How come? To keep himself separate from us, that's what, to make himself higher—oh, he's on a real higher fucking plane, your little prick—"

"I don't know why I'd want to keep separate," I said, wishing I could shut up and run. "Why I wouldn't want to be a crank burnout, I don't know."

"You little *fuck*! What'd you call me!"

After that, he was up and hitting me, and I was trying to shield myself with my school backpack and he was tearing it from me and swacking me with it, knocking me down, kicking me, cracking my ribs. Then I was scrambling away as my mom tried to pull him back, babbling something about I was just a kid and didn't understand and forgive him, Curtis, for he knows not what he does. And then he caught me and was dragging me back by the shirttail and I was tearing my shirt to get away from him and running through waves of pain to get to the back door and shouting incoherently. He threw a stereo tweeter at me—it went through the kitchen window—and then he was hitting Mom because she was holding him back and I turned to pull him off her and he hit me, knocked me flat, breaking my nose, and then I heard shouts from the front door.

Some cop had been passing at the corner and a neighbor flagged him down; she'd heard the shouts, seen the window shattering.

Curtis went to jail and did time for assault and possession of a controlled substance, and I went to a foster home, lucked into some pretty nice foster parents, and for two years I focused on doing art that had nothing to do with me or my life and never thinking about anything except what kept me out in front of the pursuer, the dogged pursuit of what it hurts to think about.

Later, 1999, I was out on my own, pretty young, and believing that pure art was the only way out of human suffering. Then I heard about my mom's suicide. Nothing. I felt nothing. I was out in front of feeling anything about it, way out in front and going at a good clip ahead of it.

And then one day I was given an assignment I didn't want—to do some art inspired by a newspaper article, any article. I tried to be inspired by a science article, but nothing came. The only article that seemed to transfer onto the canvas was a long piece about the slave children of Haiti. Was it December 1999? I think so. There were, I read, an estimated two hundred thousand children in Haiti sold into virtual slavery, into indentured servitude and worse, by their parents, sometimes for as little as ten dollars. More often than not the child was given a box in the yard to sleep in, was not allowed to meet the owners' eyes, not permitted to play with other children, not acknowledged at birthdays or Christmas. They were unpaid, underfed, barely clothed, oft-beaten servants. It was technically illegal, but the authorities in Haiti shrugged and said there was nothing they could do because it was "traditional." I began to draw photo-realistic images of the children—I began to see *particular* children who, I felt, were not imagined, who really existed, who were actually living in these conditions, often competing with dogs for scraps to eat; working despite having fractured bones, fractures received in beatings . . . dying . . . and replaced by others. And I couldn't sleep. I began to feel them out there, to feel their suffering like radiation in the air, like heat or a burning UV light. Then I heard about several thousand Albanians kept in prison by the Serbians even after we'd bombed them into submission in Kosovo: twelve-year-old boys crammed in with men, fifty to a room made for eight, forgotten by the diplomats. I could *feel them* there. I read about children in Africa forced to join roaming gangs who called themselves revolutionaries—forced, as initiation, to shoot their own sisters and brothers in the head. I felt their feelings as if they were my own, shared them in waves, transmitted through some unknowable medium. Children in the United States whose parents were crack addicts, speed freaks, brutal drunks; children who were taken away from abusive parents and, because there were not enough foster parents, were put in juvenile detention lockups and forgotten—though they'd committed no crime. I could hear the whimpers, the groans of the suffering in the world, and I heard something else—sardonic laughter behind it all. I saw the indifference of those who committed these crimes, and I saw the motivation behind that indifference: simple abject selfishness, pure appetite. And I saw, beneath that selfishness, that unfettered appetite, the faces of demons . . . of demons . . . of demons.

The nervous breakdown was swift in coming. But I was in the hospital for only three months. I quit the medication the day I quit the hospital. I simply learned to plug my ears, to not hear the groan of the world. To deaden myself. To go back to sleep.

I managed it most of the time, anyway. Most of us do. It's a skill you learn.

Then the sky thickened, and the clouds hung heavy, and gave birth to the Seven Clans . . .

7

$\mathcal{H}$ as it been three days or four? With all that's happened, and happened so fast, and the journey across the various time zones—I don't know.

A few days ago I woke to hear Melissa talking to someone. It wasn't the way she talked to the cats.

I sprang from bed, afraid there'd been a break-in, found her in the living room—on a cell phone I hadn't seen before. She was looking at a drawing I'd done . . . done and done and done over again.

"No, I think this is it. Come and see it. Now, seriously. Okay." She broke the connection, turned to see me staring at her.

"Where'd you get that phone?"

"Nyerza gave it to me. I just haven't needed it till now. They gave it to me for something specific. We're here about you, as much as anything else, you know. They felt you needed a haven, a familiar place to go to ground for—" she pointed at the drawing "—for this, I think. They're on their way here. I have to meditate. Wait out here, okay?"

"But . . ."

She wouldn't say anything else and didn't come out of her room till they arrived four hours later, in the same helicopter they'd left in.

Nyerza and Paymenz came into the living room, looking around with, I thought, relief. Cluttered and eccentric, but it was a home, even so. I wondered what conditions they'd been living in. Both men looked haggard; Paymenz wore the same clothes I'd last seen him in. He embraced Melissa, shook my hand, greeted the cats, as Nyerza stood at a small wooden table I used for my art, looked at one of my drawings.

"Have you had enough to eat?" Paymenz asked.

"Sure," I said. With the intermittent famines going on out there, it would've been childish to complain about the quality of the food. We were lucky to eat anything.

"There appears to be a corpse on the roof," Paymenz said. "The birds have been at him, so it's hard to tell, but he seems to have been . . . filleted."

"Yes. There was a Bugsy up there, but the Bugsy wouldn't come near Melissa. The guy on the roof was supposed to get at her, some way. He failed and—"

"And have there been other human attacks?" Nyerza asked, looking up from the table.

"One. Prompted by some guy's Internet contact with the demons, oddly enough."

"Not so odd," Paymenz said, sitting wearily on the arm of the easy chair. "They've been very playful that way." He smiled crookedly. "The Gnashers have developed a real affection for mass media. I expect them to sign with William Morris soon."

I was pretty sure he was kidding. About the William Morris part.

Nyerza looked at me, and I knew he wanted me to come to stand beside the table. "Yes?"

"This drawing, Ira. Do you, then, know what city this is?"

"I don't. I assume it's an imaginary one."

"No. We have been surveying American cities. This is certainly Detroit. This symbol, here—what does it mean? I have seen it somewhere, but that sort of arcanum is not my specialty."

"Astrological symbol of the planet Saturn. I don't know why it's there. It just felt right."

"We will go there, to that part of Detroit—and find out. You have been chosen as an interpreter. The Solar Soul—the Gold in the Urn—has been guiding you. It resides in Melissa, but sometimes speaks to you. Come—the roof—"

"Wait," Melissa said, with her head cocked, as if she were listening to something only she could hear. "I . . . think I should bring some broth."

Nyerza looked at her in surprise. "Broth? I can obtain government food supplies. We don't need—"

"Broth. I have some chicken soup in cans. I'll put it in a thermos."

Paymenz looked at Nyerza and shrugged.

———

A short, stomach-churningly turbulent trip by helicopter to a private airstrip in a Marin County eucalyptus grove, then a tense, smooth trip in a private jet to Detroit. I felt disoriented, shaken, as the trip wore itself away. Melissa simply slept. Paymenz would answer none of my questions. "Let's just see," was all he would say.

A drizzly evening in an armored limousine. The limo drove around abandoned cars on the freeway, around rubble on the street, to a deserted refinery on the edge of Detroit. A Grindum leapt from the trees beside the road, bounded toward us, each leap closer making my heart thud louder. The limo screeched to a halt as the Grindum blocked our way, a hundred feet off. As it stalked snufflingly toward us, Nyerza said, "Hit the accelerator—drive right at it!"

The driver—Mimbala, who'd piloted the chopper—shook his head doubtfully but obeyed. He floored the limo, and we roared at the Grindum—and it leapt straight into the air, just before we'd have struck it. I didn't see it come down from the first jump, but a few seconds later I saw the demon in the distance, bounding away from us.

I glimpsed the shadow of a Sharkadian ripple over the road's shoulder, as if it were pacing us some distance overhead; less than a quarter mile behind, a Spider drifted like Hell's own dandelion puff through the sky after us. But never coming too close.

Melissa and the Gold in the Urn again.

Paymenz had a flashlight on my drawing, was comparing it to a detailed map of the area. He pointed to a gravel road that led off to the side; there was a chained steel gate in a hurricane fence blocking the way. "There!"

We'd passed the turn; we had to stop and back up. Mimbala got out and broke the lock with a big iron mallet and chisel from the trunk of the car, and then drove us through.

"Touch nothing," Paymenz said, as we got out of the limo. We stood between empty-looking cinder-block buildings in the shadow of a rusting oil refinery. "This area is blighted—there was an industrial accident here. You remember—almost the same time as the one in Hercules. About twelve hundred people died in the toxic cloud. How much they've cleaned the surroundings since, I don't know."

We looked around the dark, nondescript buildings—and then we saw the faintly phosphorescent shape of a man step out from a doorway. It was Mendel. Wearing medieval armor, now, and the tabard, red cross on white—gesturing for us to come.

He turned and vanished into the closed door. We hurried to the door and found it double locked. Mimbala and his chisel again, a prolonged, painfully loud pounding with the mallet that echoed off the deserted buildings around us. I was sure the dissonant ringing would bring someone, or something. But no one came.

Then he had the door open, and we went in. There was a grudging, dim yellow light over a stairway that led underground.

Deep underground. Ten flights down, another door opened into a sort of antechamber within which was a stone structure: a mastaba of some reddish stone—but it had been built recently: a reproduction of a low, slope-sided, oblong structure used as an entrance to certain Egyptian tombs. There were Egyptian gods painted on the front in the hieroglyph style—on one side of the door, an image of Set. On the other—

"I don't recognize that one," I said.

"Aumaunet," said Melissa, "mistress of infinity."

"And there—" I pointed at other symbols "—hermetic symbols, pentagrams, symbols from the kabbalah—they don't belong with Egyptian images. They've mixed all the symbology up. . . ."

"It's not mixed up, exactly," Paymenz said. "They're symbols from various cultures but meaning the same thing. And what is symbolized in iconography is repeated, here, in text." He pointed to an inscription over the door. "I think that one is Sumerian . . . and here, I can read this one—in ancient Greek. It refers to a simple exchange: 'To the dark god, we give life; from the dark god, we receive life.' "

Nyerza seemed impatient with the mastaba. He gestured, and Mimbala, increasingly nervous, set about opening this last door, which was made of gnarled black wood.

A few strokes of the chisel, and the dark wooden door swung inward onto a short flight of stone steps, leading down to a brief concrete corridor and another door, of blue-painted metal, lit by an overhead bulb. This door was unlocked and opened onto a vast subterranean chamber—a room as big as a football field.

We stepped inside, trying to take it all in. The room was awash in the harsh glare of fluorescent strip lights on a ceiling so low Nyerza had to stoop. Under the lights were hundreds of portable hospital beds; on each one, a recumbent figure, a man or woman, to all appearances dead. They wore ordinary street clothes, their skin seemed grayish, and there were cobwebs on some of them. But they did not seem to be in a state of decay. From somewhere came the hum of powerful ventilation fans, the whisper of an artificial breeze.

"These people," Melissa said. "They're so . . . they seem so still. Are they dead?"

"I do not believe so," Nyerza said. "They are asleep and be-yond asleep—in a state of suspended animation of some sort. Almost the catatonia that mimics death . . ."

"A vast premature burial," Paymenz murmured. "Poe would be most distressed to be here."

Melissa gasped softly, grabbed my arm, and pointed. I saw Mendel, in the center of the room, head bowed in prayer. An apparition, he was there but not there. His form ever so slightly transparent.

"Oh thank God you've come," came a croak from someone else in the shadows to my right.

Shephard limped into view, shuffling painfully to within a dozen steps of us. I barely recognized him. His suit was in tat-ters; he wore a ragged beard streaked with what might have been old vomit and dried blood; his eyes flickered in deep sockets. He seemed bent; his clothes hung on him so loosely, a shrug might have dropped them to the floor.

"Stop there," Paymenz said, drawing a small automatic pistol from a side pocket.

Melissa looked at the gun and her father in surprise.

"I think it is all right," Nyerza said. "Or—all right for now. I do not believe he can hurt us."

"Nor would I," wheezed Shephard. "This place is supposed to be demonically protected. There are dozens of them, all seven of the clans, roundabout the building's exterior. Yet—yet you have entered unmolested. The Gold in the Urn must indeed be here with you . . . yes?" He looked at Melissa. I saw her squirm a little under his febrile gaze. "But yes, yes . . . inevitably yes."

"Why are you here now—and not entranced?" Paymenz asked, looking around for Mendel. The apparition was no longer visible.

Shephard licked his cracked lips. All his former insularity, his machinelike poise, was gone. He seemed a shell, sustained by will alone. "I . . ." He shook his head, unable to speak for a moment, coughing, covering his mouth with bony fingers.

"Sit down, Professor Shephard," Melissa said. "Rest yourself." Adding to herself: "Now I know who the broth is for. . . ."

She'd been carrying the thermos in a big leather purse, looped over her shoulder. She knelt beside Shephard and helped him to sit up, giving him a red-plastic thermos cup of broth. He drank it eagerly. She had to restrain him at times, so he didn't overdo it.

At last he pushed her hand away. "God bless you, my dear."

"God's name is defiled on your lips, Shephard," Nyerza rumbled.

"Yes," Shephard said, looking sleepy now. "Yes, perhaps. I

do not intend defilement. I ask forgiveness—and I have suffered, Dr. Nyerza, for the sake of my penance, yes, suffered before God these many weeks in this very room. I brought a little food and water with me, but it was not enough. And I was sick, for so long . . . so sick. . . . And the visions . . . the terrible visions . . . But you see, I was sure the Gold in the Urn would come, if only I could survive a day longer, an hour longer . . . a minute longer. . . . And so it proved. I thought I heard Mendel whispering to me. Dear Mendel, whom I hated—yes, hated!—at one time." He laughed sadly. "Oh how deep is my fatigue, deep and cold as the . . . long since I could sleep . . . How I have envied *their* sleep . . . and feared it, too . . ."

He seemed to droop but straightened a little as Paymenz moved to stand over him. "You will not sleep," Paymenz said, his voice hypnotically commanding, "but you will tell us what takes place here and your part in it."

"I was—was to be one of these," Shephard said, pointing at the hundreds in the vast room suspended in the sleep that mocked death. "I was to be in the final group. The ushers, we were called, preparing the way, enacting the final rituals. But then—then I saw what became of the world . . . and in the eyes of the demons I beheld a mirror. And in that mirror I saw my soul. And I crumbled, and it all fell apart for me. . . . I came here—to try to wake them and could not. I sensed that if I left—the Tartarans would destroy me, and suck my pitiful little spark away. May I have some water?"

Paymenz shook his head and opened his mouth to deny the water; but Melissa said, "Quiet, Daddy. And put that gun away."

She took a little plastic container of bottled water from her purse and helped Shephard drink a little of it. He wiped his lips and patted her hand. "Thank you. And those who accompany you . . . I thank them . . . I thank all who—"

"Speak!" Nyerza said. "Finish your story!"

Shephard hugged his knees, and in a cracked voice went on. "There are not so many demons as people think, but many reappearing, helter-skelter. There are a few thousand, sometimes bilocating. Even one can be terribly destructive, of course. They are . . . also these." He pointed at the sleepers. "They are possessing the demons."

"You mean—the demons are possessing them in some way?" I asked.

"No, Ira. They possess the demons. The demons in their own world are just . . . complex appetites, minimally self-aware creations—almost like artificial intelligences, but of a spiritual variety. Self-aware and yet—" he paused to swallow, to gather his strength "—and yet not self-aware. Living, to some extent sentient but not imbued with soul. They are the—the side effects of humanity at its worst—the psychic consequence of our cruelties, our selfishness, our brutality, echoing in the planes of metaphysical creation, finding its own level. Not Hell, not Sheol—that is just the sunless absence of God—but a world that parodies our world at its worst. There are many more than seven clans, of course. Only seven have come so far—but more will come, oh yes, when they're through: This I have seen. . . ."

Paymenz and Melissa looked questioningly at Nyerza.

"Yes," Nyerza said. "More will come unless these are stopped. Speak on, Shephard."

"If I must . . . The Tartarans are long lived but in a way more temporary than humanity—the root souls of human beings are eternal, you see. Early in the last century certain practitioners of ritual magic came into sufficient consciousness to create *real* magick. With this . . . with only this stupid little magickal tool . . . they sought to secure immortality for themselves—to remake the rules, to achieve not only immortality but a state of what they believed would be godhood. Each would, they hoped, become the ruler of some personal cosmic realm. As of old, this called for human sacrifice—but vast numbers of sacrifices were needed. Thousands, thousands, thousands of deaths—and there were two methods: Many could be killed, *all* together . . . or many could die over time as the result of a deliberate act and by a kind of slow poisoning. You see?"

"Not—well, not entirely," I said.

He gestured as if waving a fly away from his face. "A mass human sacrifice that in some cases came about in minutes—as in Bhopal, as in Hercules, as here, in this half-forgotten little suburb of Detroit. Or, in other cases—other ceremonies—the sacrifices came about over a generation or two. Slow, roasting cancerous death in the cancer corridors of Louisiana, in other places in this country, in other countries . . . In rooms like this one, men and women chanted and carried out their ceremonies as those around them died. Sometimes the entire rite took place in one night; sometimes the ceremonies were repeated at the solstices. . . . When environmental regulations in some countries tightened, they resorted more and more to industrial 'accidents.'. . ." He chuckled, a miserable sound. "That Certain One, with whom such deals are struck—*he* told them how to carry this out. Eventually it became obvious that industrial pollution caused cancer, emphysema, and so forth. Yet the industries denied and denied and covered up. For many decades they did so—they did not care. Some were simply blinded by greed and indifference—yet that fed the demonic, too, of course. Others worked actively for their dark brotherhood . . . and set up the sacrifices quite deliberately, oh my yes. It was all for the greater good—that some human beings, at least, would become 'like gods'. . . so they told themselves. So I told myself. The sacrifices were acceptable losses. Like Roosevelt's sacrifice of Pearl Harbor, to galvanize the country into a war—like Hiroshima to end the war. Acceptable losses of life for something great . . ."

"And you believed this—about its being acceptable?" Melissa asked gently.

Shephard nodded mechanically. "I did. I was the great rationalizer, always. Until forced into . . . a kind of involuntary *vigil* here, in this great ugly sensory deprivation tank of a room, and inevitably I could not help but see myself as I was . . . see my colleagues in conspiracy as they are. . . ."

"The actual mechanics of all this?" Nyerza prompted. "Anything more?"

"Yes . . . a little water . . . yes the—the industrial areas, those 'industrial parks' and factories involved in the sacrifices, were not—were not laid out at random, oh no, my good friends, no."

Nyerza seemed to grind his teeth at the term of endearment coming from this man, but he kept his silence, as Shephard, after sipping water, went on.

"Each ISZ as we called it—"

"An acronym for what exactly?" Paymenz asked sharply.

"ISZ? Oh yes, of course—Industrial Sacrifice Zone. The primary ISZs are where the sleepers are found now, all underground. Here you'll find those who did the deed at Hercules, other places, as well as Detroit. Each ISZ was laid out in the shape of a particular rune—seven runes in all, you see. Even—even the shapes of the oil refineries, certain other mills . . . those at the ISZs were adapted from their necessary shape, in the science of refining, so that against the horizon they etched runes in the seven names."

Nyerza and Paymenz exchanged startled glances. I thought I saw a flicker of admiration in Paymenz's eyes as he looked at Shephard. Paymenz murmured, "The scale of the undertaking—astounding, almost majestic."

Nyerza threw Paymenz a pantherish look of warning.

"But," I said, waving a hand at the tranced figures on the multitude of gurneys. "But the trance, the sleep. They—"

"It was supposed to be temporary. It was supposed to be over weeks ago. Occupying the demons, they were to take many souls, many sparks from the pleroma—to consume them for the second half of the undertaking, the transfiguration into gods. But . . . it never came about. That Certain One Who Cannot Be Named spoke just once when we ventured to inquire. It said— We have argued what it said . . . but it was something like, A promise to men is in the words men use; such words have no single meaning. Words mean what I say they mean—" He broke off and began to sway to and fro, cackling to himself. "Yes, we ventured to inquire! Heeeee-uh-heee—we ventured— we ventured to—"

"Stop it!" Nyerza growled, hunkering near him, so that Shephard slunk back, scrambling clumsily away on the concrete floor.

"Don't hurt me! I've been through enough! Or just . . . oh, simply cut my throat. But don't hector me . . . I am a house of cards inside! I'm going to need therapy and—and medication!"

"Stop whining and answer! How may we waken these sleepers? How may we end the demonic attack?"

Shephard clutched himself and tittered sourly. "You have just said it: You end the demonic attack by waking the sleepers! They are the extrapolation of all mankind. Men sleep even when they think they are awake—the true self sleeps—and because it sleeps we are ruled by the egoic, by vanity . . . by the *demonic*. Unchecked, unchanneled, it rages where it will! Sometimes in quiet cunning, friends, dear friends—sometimes in overt brutality! Even those—those of us who managed some higher consciousness—it's in all the wrong parts of us! We're all . . . we're like—like the Elephant Man—all overgrown in the wrong places, inside. . . ."

"How can they be awakened, Professor?" Melissa asked more gently.

"I don't know! If I knew, I'd have done it! I came here with drugs, various drugs, to awaken them, and I administered them. Nothing worked. I used those drugs to keep myself awake, for weeks at a time, for fear I might become like them. You see before you the result—I am a wreckage. But these— these sleepers cannot be awakened by any ordinary medical means—not by ice water—not by blasting symphonies in their ears!"

"And if you kill them—you render the demons permanent, or so I suspect," Paymenz murmured.

"Yes. They are what they are. As the sleepers sleep, each has a corresponding demon who rages in the outer world. And how the demons look, what they do, is partly sustained by what path the sleepers chose, by their acts—but also by the sleep of the rest of humanity! If the human race—even some great portion—saw itself as it was, there would be a—a ripple effect that would be some help." As he went on he slowly slumped into a fetal position, lying on his side, muttering, the words more and more difficult to hear. "But the *shock* required to wake those who sleep this sleep . . . well, it's too late to be self-generated by the sleeper. Such a shock comes only from— from a kind of grace coming from something greater than all of us, from the solar level, the next higher plane. But how, how to—to focus that, to— I don't know . . . I thought perhaps . . . I don't know." He shook his body, as he might have once shaken only his head, and fell silent. And then he went limp.

We looked at him, at one another, back at Shephard. I asked, "Is he dead? Asleep?"

Melissa touched his neck. After a moment she shook her head. "Neither. Unconscious." She stood and looked at the sleeping multitude. "Or in a trance of some kind. Perhaps he has become like one of these others."

"No," Nyerza said. "Not yet."

DEMONS

"Mendel was here," I said. "He must intend something. You who are . . . you in the circle. Didn't you know about all this?"

Nyerza gazed at the sleepers and mused, "We knew almost nothing of all this . . . because they had suffused the world in distractions and darkened the world with media, with wave after wave of their dark suggestions. We knew they were hiding something—but we guessed at nothing so vast." He added, "Then again, some guessed. And they were not listened to."

"Yes," Paymenz said. "Mendel suggested something of the sort. So I've heard. We knew the Brotherhood of That Certain One were using some aspects of industrial civilization for evil, but the obvious evil blinded us to the subtle, the Great Plan. We thought it was all for the sake of chaos, to keep humanity off balance, easy to prey on. But that was only half of it . . . and even now the waves of darkness hide the truth—even from the ascended masters."

"No longer,"

said Mendel. His voice resonated with that unnatural, psychic vibrancy the Gnashers sometimes had. But where the Gnashers' tones had radiated impulses to self-doubt, to raw fear, Mendel's voice gave hope and subtle energy.

We saw him again, standing amid the sleeping multitude.

"We now see what needs be done. Only one more was needed—myself—to add to the noospheric energy, to dispel the darkness. Follow the woman, one sleeper to the next. Be guided by her."

With that he was gone. And Melissa drew her breath in sharply. She touched her solar plexus, and shivered.

We followed her. From one sleeping figure to the next.

They were all adults, of every possible age, of every type, of every race—though there were perhaps more middle-aged white males than any other type.

As Melissa came to the first sleeper, the Gold in the Urn emerged from her, resplendent.

She quivered, her knees buckling, as it came fulminating, sparkling, and shining; a birth pang that left her shaking, gazing with parted lips, with eyes reflecting the shimmer.

"This—this golden thing," I murmured to Paymenz, "could it awaken me? Could she use it to—to make me . . . enlightened?"

"No, enlightenment, and the states of consciousness *beyond* enlightenment—the recognition of true essence in oneself, the creation of real being—these things must be earned. They must be paid for by personal effort, by conscious suffering. What will happen here is only a return to ordinary consciousness—and I suspect the Gold will show them one thing more."

She turned to Mimbala, and in a voice that wasn't quite hers, said, "Go there—to the box on the wall. Shut off the false light."

He looked at Nyerza, who nodded. Mimbala trotted to the power box and threw the switch. We were dropped into a vast well of darkness that was immediately abated in a hemisphere of light around us—the light of the Gold.

Then she put out her right hand, palm upward, and the shimmering orb floated to suspend the core of itself six inches over her palm, so that its energies all but hid her hand from view and lit up her body . . . and lit her face and eyes from beneath, blue and gold.

She moved her arm to the nearest of the sleepers, a young

man, and lowered her hand so that the energies swept over the sleeper's head, and almost instantly, he awoke.

He awoke with a wrenching cry of authentic agony.

We heard that sound repeated hundreds of times, as we passed from one recumbent figure to the next.

The awakened seemed inconsolable, though some drifted into groups, here and there, and clutched one another for comfort, weeping. Others crept under their gurneys and hugged themselves, crying, quivering with horror, eyes wide, staring around yet looking somehow inward.

Seeing themselves, through the power of the Gold in the Urn, as they really were.

There were many cries of agony.

———

We found out later . . .

. . . that a seven-year-old Hispanic boy and his young mother were making their way on foot to a government emergency food distribution center, when a flying Sharkadian, carrying a Bugsy, spotted them crossing a street.

I don't know if the Bugsy was "my" Bugsy, but it came to them the way it had left us. The Sharkadian lowered the Bugsy on one side of the terrified mother and son, then flapped to obstruct their escape down the rubble-filled street.

The young mother whispered to her son: "Run, when I give the signal."

The Bugsy told her that she should tell him, instead, to run right to the Sharkadian. It'd be over faster that way. Unless the Bugsy itself decided to take the boy as his "li'l pal." The Bugsy said it hadn't had a "li'l pal" quite that little before. But perhaps the lady would like to dance first. "The two of us," said the Bugsy—"a polka, perhaps."

"If I dance, if I do whatever you want, you let my son go?"

"Depends," said the Bugsy, "what you mean by let him go."

Then the Sharkadian, impatient, leapt forward, clapped its talons on the mother's shoulders, opened its jaws to snap her head away, as the child screamed.

"That's when the one who had me was pulled away," the mother said later. "Like something had him by the tail and was pulling him. I don't know why he couldn't pull me with him— it was like he had no strength in him then."

The Bugsy gave a whimpering cry and tried to crawl under a car, but it did no good. The same thing that was happening to the Sharkadian happened to the Bugsy. The demons began to fall away into themselves.

We heard the description again and again, and always more or less the same: The demon was like something receding into the distance at great speed—as if you'd dropped the demon off the roof of the Empire State Building and watched it fall, shrinking as it went. Only, it was falling into itself some-how, into the center point of where it had been. It vanished into the distance—without moving an inch.

The boy and his mother clutched each other and watched as the two demons shrank into nothingness and were gone. Mother and child fell to their knees and thanked God and went safely home.

The story was told again and again in thousands of places across the world.

And each vanished demon corresponded to a human being, a conspirator of the Brotherhood of That Certain One, awak-ened by my own darling Melissa and the Gold in the Urn. When the demon's corresponding human woke, the demon was hurled back into its own plane, back to where it was and wasn't; and that which made it possible for them to inhabit our world returned to its originator, and woke the invoker to an agony of self-knowledge.

———

As Melissa finished waking the sleepers at the first ISZ, Nyerza switched the overhead lights back on, and she turned to see Mimbala pointing a gun at Shephard's head.

Shephard was on his hands and knees, weeping, crawling toward her, across the room.

"Dr. Nyerza!" Melissa shouted.

Mimbala cocked the gun.

"Mimbala will not pull that trigger!" Melissa bellowed.

Nyerza looked at her. She'd raised her voice to a volume I'd never have thought possible. "You will let that man be!"

She strode toward them, and as if in retreat from her anger, the Gold in the Urn vanished within her, for a time.

Mimbala fired the gun.

Most of Shephard's left ear disappeared. There was a red smear down his neck, and he clutched his head and rocked in pain.

Mimbala's old hands were shaking. He steadied his right hand with his left—

Melissa came to stand a few yards away. Mimbala hesitated, looking at her and then at Nyerza, but kept the gun extended, aimed at the cowering Shephard.

Melissa spoke in a gentler tone. "Nyerza? Please. Leave him be."

"Let them kill me," Shephard said hoarsely.

"No," Melissa said. "Nyerza?"

"He's one of them—and soon," Nyerza added, "he will be a sleeper, like those you've awakened. He is lying to us about his intentions—perhaps misleading us completely about everything."

"No," she said. "I don't think so."

She looked at me, and I sighed and walked over to stand beside her.

"So you can be conscious, Nyerza—and without compassion?" I asked.

"I can kill if necessary," said Nyerza. "I believe that if we let this man live, he will become like these others—when we cannot reach him. And another demon will walk the Earth. How many will it kill? To save those people—kill him now."

I turned to Melissa. "Unless—can you wake him now?"

"No . . . it doesn't—doesn't feel like it." She looked sharply at Nyerza. "Here's the irony: Some part of *you*, Nyerza, has gone to sleep. Maybe it's the burden you've carried the last few weeks. No one could bear it. Don't feel bad, but see this impulse to kill Shephard for what it is."

Nyerza opened his mouth, as if to speak--then seemed to gaze into space for a moment, or into himself.

Paymenz was watching the others, who muttered and groaned and cursed in the room. "I think we'd better make up our minds and leave. Nyerza, she is guided. Trust her."

Mimbala looked at Nyerza questioningly. Nyerza closed his long fingers over Mimbala's wrist and shook his head.

"Let him be," Nyerza said reluctantly. "She is right."

Melissa strode up to them.

"Shephard will come with us," she said.

"This?" Paymenz said, pointing at Shephard. "He is one of them! How many have died because—"

"Daddy—be silent!"

Paymenz fell silent out of sheer astonishment.

She went on, more quietly and even more authoritatively, "He comes with us. He will lead us to the others."

———

Shephard required a wheelchair. Nyerza's government contacts provided military helicopters and transport jets normally used only for the brass, and an Army nurse for Shephard.

We traveled, with snowballing exhaustion, from one primary ISZ to another, Shephard guiding us. Six more—there were three more Industrial Sacrifice Zones in the United States—one in Chicago, one in Louisiana, one in New Jersey; then we skipped to three overseas, flying across the Atlantic. We hopped the globe, traveling to primary ISZs in Africa, India, and Malaysia.

Behind us, those forcibly awakened slowly emerged from the vast underground rooms: some retreated into madness; some went into a long depression and then a sort of amnesia; a fair number committed suicide; some found their way to synagogues, Buddhist temples, churches, mosques, cathedrals, even sweat lodges, to ask intercession and forgiveness. One man crawled forty-three miles on his hands and knees till he was grinding bone ends on concrete, as some sort of inarticulate act of expiation; many simply let their health tumble apart, in alcohol and drugs. And died. They all had this in common: a fear of sleep; a determined sleeplessness.

We crossed the Pacific to the last ISZ—in the Los Angeles area.

———

They were waiting for us . . .

. . . in California. We saw them twenty minutes after we trudged wearily down the ramp. Melissa coming down the ramp out the back of the squat plane first, and then the men hiding behind the woman: Nyerza, Paymenz, Mimbala, myself, Shephard and his nurse, four buddhist Monks, a Sikh teacher, two Catholic priests, and an Islamic Sufi we'd picked up in India. We emerged, blinking in the sunlight, from the military transport plane we'd appropriated, with the blessing of the Air Force, in Hawaii. The plane had landed on a broad road that led to the chemicals factory twenty minutes north of the San Fernando Valley. The site of an "accident."

We looked up at the ISZ: The factory stood against the yellowish late afternoon sky in a shape that was largely vertical but with pipes and catwalks crossing horizontally, diagonally: the now-obvious silhouette of a giant rune.

But our small group wasn't alone: three trucks of National Guardsmen arrived almost at the same moment, looking pale and frightened, sent to help us by a Presidential administration encouraged by Melissa's successes. They climbed dutifully from their trucks, checked the clips on their rifles, gazed pensively around them.

As we approached the side road that led to the underground chamber of sleepers, I felt a constriction, a chill, seeing long lines of dark figures issuing from the grove of dead oak trees to cither side of the road; the leafless, twisted, blackened trees themselves looking like freehand runes in some fanciful, forgotten script signifying only decay and death.

But those who paraded from the woods to block our way were human—most of them. There were, however, three Bugsys, looking almost identical, in the forefront. Milling around the Bugsys were some four hundred men and women, many of them naked but for sandals and garish body paint: painted in ribald imagery, geometric designs, or pentagrams; crude pictoglyphs of Spiders and Tailpipes. Others wore papier-mâché heads resembling Gnashers, Grindums, and Sharkadians; hand-sewn costumes mimicking the demons' shapes.

These were people, I thought, who had been terrified into making their own desperate accommodation with the new demonic reality.

Some carried hunting rifles, pistols, axes, baseball bats, and steel pipes.

The National Guardsmen looked almost glad to see them. These people, at least, could be shot dead, and they would stay dead.

D E M O N S

A Bugsy stepped forward, with his hand on one man's shoulder, guiding the man toward us like a parent gently urging a child to step forward and recite a poem.

The lanky potbellied man, with a ragged gray-streaked red beard, was almost naked, painted mostly blue, with bands of bright red around his limbs; his genitals Day-Glo orange; on his head was a hand-sewn cloth hood that was a sort of pathetic muppet of a Sharkadian. In one hand the man held a staff made from an old television antenna, with bits of mummified human parts dangling from its remaining crossbars: mummified fingers, a string of ears, a whole hand, a head—the head mostly just skull, now.

There was a teasing familiarity about the face of the man in the Sharkadian hood, despite the paint and the beard and the gauntness. Hadn't he been an important candidate for governor before the invasion?

I put an arm instinctively around Melissa's shoulders; we heard a snorting, a flapping, and glanced up to see Sharkadians wheeling a few hundred feet overhead, to see Spiders drifting in from three directions.

Some of the soldiers whimpered, seeing the demons gather.

"More are coming," said the man in the Sharkadian hood, stepping forward; the Bugsys holding back. The man adopted a low, portentous voice. "Your destruction of the new world will end here."

"We destroy nothing," Paymenz said. "We only awaken."

"And what becomes of those you damage with your waking?" the man demanded. "They go mad; they kill themselves."

"Some do—awakening such people brings to them a particular remorse, one that's hard to bear. They have more to be remorseful about."

"You are murdering them with your black magic," the man said, perplexing us all.

126

"Black magic?" I blurted.

"The angels whom your magic has blighted, darkened, have been winnowing the human race, removing those whose souls were not pure enough to ascend at the great dance to come."

I had to laugh—maybe from a weariness-bred hysteria. "Angels! Is that what they've told you? Winnowing? *Purifying?* You see them torture and mangle people and you still believe they have some kind of good intentions?"

"We see the distortion your dark magic has brought about!"

I looked at the rest of the parading mob. I saw there were at least fifty who were dressed more or less normally; and among those painted faces were many expressions besides hostility: dismay, confusion, confoundment, uncertainty. It gave me hope.

"Yes, Ira," Nyerza said, voicing my thoughts. "Doubt can be heartening—some of them do doubt. Doubt is the gate that opens to truth."

"Shith on themth, fugemall," said the Bugsy. It gestured to three men near him who raised their rifles. "Killum bathuds!"

Nyerza opened his mouth to speak, but an echoing crackle of automatic fire erupted from the guardsmen.

And the three mob riflemen fell dead.

The crowd fell back—retreating but not dispersing—an electric uncertainty holding us all in place.

I tried to pull Melissa to cover, but she gently pushed my hands away and fell to her knees, facing the mob, her lips moving in prayer. The holy men with us followed suit; each of them praying in the posture of his tradition.

There was a single gunshot from the mob, which whistled over our heads—a rifle shot from a shaking, skinny young man, naked and gaping. His tentative gunfire was returned by the guardsmen—returned conclusively. He spun around with the impact of a dozen bullets. The crowd cried out and drew back farther, away from the fallen man; most of them throwing themselves down for cover or hunkering behind trees. A few dropped their guns and raised their hands.

Others took up shooting positions behind the trees.

The demons in the sky veered closer. The Bugsys raised their fists.

The guardsmen took aim; the gunmen in the mob took aim.

Then the sky grew dark.

There were no clouds. But in fearful silence, the sky darkened of itself. I looked at the sun—there was no eclipse. All the sky, instead, was eclipsed—not blackened but darkened so that a deep twilight reigned.

Then the Gold in the Urn emerged from Melissa.

The Gold shimmered and sparked in the air in front of her as she continued to pray. The orb seemed to grow—to become thirty, forty feet across. And as it grew, details became evident. I seemed to make out a swirl of faces within the light—men and women of all races, ancient races and modern, Asian and European and African and Latin. Was that Mendel? It seemed so.

Everyone gazed at the Gold. It was the greatest source of light, with the sky blotted; even the Bugsys seemed frozen with a kind of profound misgiving as they stared into the swirling radiance of sheer conscious being.

Melissa's voice came from somewhere—from the Gold as much as from Melissa—and it seemed to carry that more-than-human resonance that vibrated in the heart and the head as well as the ears:

"There are those held captive here only by their fear and their uncertainty: To those I say, pray for self-knowledge, pray to see yourself as you are, pray to see your connectedness to the Higher and to see the false for what it is. Pray to see

your rootedness in the nature-mind, in a self that is no individual but that delights in your individuality; pray to see your essence; pray to see your sleep; pray for awakening. Pray for the murderers and the murdered. Pray for That Certain One; pray for demons and the demon ridden; pray for your enemies; pray again for yourself. If you know that you know nothing, your prayers to know will be answered. Pray to see yourself as you really are."

There was an immediate response from many in the mob, a cry of despair paradoxically mingled with sudden hope. I saw almost half of them go to their knees. Praying, praying to see themselves as they really were, the bad with the good. 1 saw their anguish, their relief. I heard them shouting many things but all the same. I heard Shephard crying out, sobbing. I saw the Bugsys jumping up and down with fury. I saw Gnashers coming through the crowd from the rear, rending as they came . . . then freezing in place, to make ready for what came next.

Then I saw the incubus. That's what I call it, anyway.

It didn't come all at once but seemed to come in questing fingers of iridescent black ooze that streamed across the dirt between the dead trees, streaming from a gathering of demons behind the mob. The demons froze in place like statues as the ooze nosed its way from them in rivulets and shiny-black glutinous branchings to merge into a great pool before us—before the Gold in the Urn.

Like a sentient pool of petroleum, the black syrup purposefully churned and took shape: many shapes, seven shapes.

Seven black imps stood before us. I stared at them, expecting to see shapes that corresponded to the seven clans. But they were all the same shape, a silhouette of a human being, an androgynous human being, both male and female, each about two feet tall. Each was filmed with an iridescent sheen that was almost exactly like the brackish colors gasoline makes on a puddle of water.

The imps rushed toward one another, and then bounded into a manic, circular dance, as we stared in disgusted wonder. The circle grew smaller, and they began to clamber, to cluster, to crawl stickily onto one another, like a sickening mockery of acrobats who make a tower of human bodies. They stood one atop the other, clutched together, and formed a shape synthesized from the sum of their small bodies, an almost Escherian formation of the big out of the small: a seven-foot-high incubus made of oily, iridescent, faceless imps, tightly clasped one against another. Its own face was a crude suggestion of eyes, nose, and mouth, a contemptuously unfinished sketch. The imps that constituted its body seemed to squirm up and down, outlines visible within the androgynous shape of the incubus.

It turned its eyeless face toward us, and we felt its gaze on us like a swarm of lice.

One of the holy men screamed and threw himself flat. With a hoarse cry, Mimbala tried to rush at the thing. Nyerza pulled him back, but not before Mimbala fired a pistol at it. We could see the vitreous surface ripple with the impact, but the bullet was drawn into it and swallowed.

But still Melissa knelt, praying, serene. Still the Gold in the Urn burned and turned in the air, unperturbed. The holy men prayed; Paymenz prayed; Nyerza prayed; and I . . . I'm ashamed to record that I only stared at the scene in paralyzed fear.

The incubus reflected a little of the light of the Gold in the Urn. It took a step toward the Gold and put out its hands, and the Gold reacted with a spasm that was a kind of retreat or revulsion. Melissa only twitched; her face showed a sickened grimace and then became serene again.

The demons howled in glee.

The incubus made to advance once more.

Then Shephard was up, staggering from his wheelchair, past the orb of light, directly into the path of the incubus. He shouted wordless defiance and flung himself at it, fists raised— and vanished shrieking into it as wholly as the bullet had.

A useless sacrifice, I thought, choking with a grief that Shephard perhaps didn't merit—but then, for me, Shephard was all wretches who wanted redemption, and my grief for him was very personal.

Melissa stood and spoke. She was smiling, her voice calm and clear:

"He's there still—our lost friend Professor Shephard! All of you, here! Pray for this man who betrayed us all—pray for him!"

The incubus seemed to hesitate at the edge of the circle of light—and took a step back. The light expanded to encompass the space the incubus had occupied.

The demons raged and stamped forward in desperation at this, but the light of the Gold, expanding warningly, held them at bay.

And we prayed for Shephard, who had vanished within the incubus of the seven imps.

That was the incubus's undoing: a prayer for another, for an enemy, predicated on prayer for self-knowledge.

So it seemed inexorably right when we saw Shephard's face emerging from the incubus— gone!—and then reappearing for a moment, one of the half-seen faces in the Gold in the Urn, weeping with joy.

And as Shephard appeared, the incubus began to fall apart— first into its component imps, then into a pool of black that seeped into the cracks of the earth, and vanished from sight.

The demons roared in frustrated fury but fell back before us as we followed the Gold in the Urn and Melissa, marching forward through the gate into the final Industrial Sacrifice Zone, down underground, where more than a thousand slept in their own fluorescent-lit purgatory.

Those among the mob who had heard Melissa, who had prayed for self-knowledge, followed us joyfully through the gate into the underground place. And out again after it was over—back to what remained of their lives.

The demons lit into their remaining followers, rending in fury—but many escaped as the awakenings began and the demons ran in terrified confusion and began to fall away into themselves, falling into nowhere. Vanishing from the Earth.

Getting smaller with distance as they went nowhere at all.

———

Almost a year since I wrote the above.

The Gold in the Urn passed from Melissa that day, months ago, as soon as she emerged from the final ISZ. She collapsed—but only from exhaustion.

She opened her eyes once as I wheeled her on a gurney to the plane. She murmured, "All sparks are struck . . . from . . ." Her eyes closed.

She was asleep—the good sleep—before she finished saying it. I said the rest for her: "From the same forge."

She slept for two days. When she woke, the Gold was gone, but she was changed. She awoke . . . *awake*.

Melissa is two months pregnant. I'm hoping for a boy. She's hoping for a girl. We argue about the name. Right now I'm in our bedroom, working at a little wooden TV tray table. I'm looking forward to us moving out of here soon and into our own place, something larger. Just now she's teaching a seminar at the Hall of Remembering; I'm supposed to meet her for dinner. Chinese food.

We're living with her father, who's had not only his electricity returned, and water, but has had an unspeakably large government grant quietly bestowed on him. "Perhaps"— Paymenz chuckled—"the grant will go the way of this administration, if this rhetoric continues."

He said this the night we watched with real amazement, on the evening news, the government giving its official opinion that the demons had not existed as a physical reality, that it had all been some kind of hallucinogenic gas attack by a cult of industrialists who had had an obscure world-domination plan.

There is, somehow, no existing footage of the demons— nothing on video or digital. Nothing. It has all gone black. We have our own explanations for that; the officials have theirs. It doesn't matter.

All the deaths, the spokesmen said, were carried out by human beings, some of them in costume, possibly some robotically augmented. Those who remember otherwise, said the spokesmen, remember hallucinations formed by suggestion, spawned by faked video and mass hypnosis. The previous President was allegedly killed by a hallucinogen-addled assassin.

The world tries to forget, as of course it must. A World's Fair is planned, an Olympics. There is much reconstruction. But there are enough of us who remember—millions who are sure of what they remember—and who know that the spiritual world is the material world; that the material world is the spiritual world; that the universe is just a conception in a mind that dreams what it must, that calls for us to return to its deepest places, through awakening to who we really are.

Me, I'm doing a little writing and some graphics for *Memorial* magazine, which Paymenz funds and which I oversee. Melissa is just Melissa—most of the time. She only rarely chooses to show her true self to me. Her higher self is hard for me to look at—there are no sunglasses for that light. But she opens the shutters a little when she teaches the hundreds who come to her, to hear her speak at the unprepossessing little edifice they have built for her, the Hall of Remembering, in an oak grove on a former cattle ranch near Martinez.

And a sadly smiling, mustachioed little man named Yanan has come from Turkey to live near us. He was sent by Nyerza, he said, to be my special instructor, to prepare me for the time—maybe soon, maybe years from now—when I will enter the Conscious Circle.

Every so often, I take a step closer to that place where I see myself as I really am; where I see *who* I really am; where I forgive the unforgivable. Every step toward that place is joyful—but every step hurts.

BOOK TWO

UNDERCURRENT

"I believe that Demons take advantage of the night to mislead the unwary—although, you know, I don't believe in them."

—EDGAR ALLAN POE

Nine Years Having Passed . . .

1

San Francisco

Let us speak plainly. Let us not be cute about it. Stephen Isquerat only dreamed what happened in the little room at the
top of the pyramid of the West Wind building. There is such a
building, but there is no such room, not precisely. It exists only
in the dream and, perhaps, in the place where dreams refract
reality.

You woke in bed remembering it, he said to himself, all that
working day. *It was just a dream,* and again, *just a dream. So let go
of it.*

But the memory of the dream had dug into his mind like a
tick. The squirming faces, the mushroom trays.

———

Stephen was still thinking about it at five that afternoon as he sat in a squeaking chair in Dale Winderson's office in the West Wind building in downtown San Francisco, waiting for an audience with Dale himself, West Wind's CEO.

"An audience with the pope!" his supervisor, Quellman, had said, laughing off his envy. Envy because it was young Steve Isquerat who had been summoned to see Dale himself in person, privately. It had to be an opportunity; the CEO didn't fire anyone in person.

Stephen wished he could change seats. The deathly dry breath of the air conditioner snuffled and whirred at the back of his neck; he could feel it lifting the little hairs there. But Winderson's receptionist glanced at him sharply from time to time across her track-lit domain, the dust-blue expanse of synthetic carpet; he might seem eccentric if he abruptly changed seats. She was young and flare coifed and sullen, behind that vast U-shaped desk situated under the enormous WW logo, a small thorn of a woman compressed between the huge symbol and the huge desk.

There were no windows. Outside, he knew, it was a crisp late-autumn day, pleasantly misty. In here, seasons didn't exist.

He shifted in the seat, and it squeaked reproachfully. The seats squeaked whenever you sat down or moved in them at all. They were made of a West Wind product, Inimicalene, a polymer that had always made Stephen recoil when he touched it. A variant of it was used as a kind of cellophane, and having to open things wrapped in the squeaky, repellent substance always made him react as if a cold drink had hit an exposed tooth nerve.

He squirmed again under the air conditioner's chill breath on the back of his neck . . . and twitched at the squeak of the chair.

As a supervisor of new product development, he'd suggested they might replace Inimicalene with a variant that was less uncomfortable to the touch. Everyone at the meeting, he remembered, had stared at him.

Uncomfortable? What did he mean?

No one admitted the stuff was loathsome, but he saw them all shudder when they touched it.

And there was something in that experience, he reflected, that he couldn't grasp, something connected to the dream—a feeling of revulsion that could not be articulated.

The dream played itself again in his memory, even as he tried not to think about it, even as he tried to ready himself for his meeting with Winderson.

Don't think about climbing those concrete steps to the little room. Following the sleepy-eyed old woman, climbing up from what should have been the top floor of the narrow, pyramid-shaped skyscraper. Spiraling like a nautilus, those steps, up and up.

Don't think about the old spinster's face . . . though it wasn't at all a sinister face. But when she turned to him—rosy-cheeked, bright eyes of some dark color you couldn't quite identify; bluish hair in a bell shape, like that of any number of old ladies; her teeth so perfect and white, much too perfect for a woman her age—it affected him like touching Inimicalene.

"Almost there," the spinster had said brightly, eyes dancing with delight. "Never quite but almost! Goes on forever. Who was that old Greek gent, said you couldn't go anywhere because any distance could be divided again and again, smaller and smaller, so it went on forever? Yet here we are, here we are!"

In the dream . . .

In the dream they had stood on the topmost landing of the entire building; and she had opened a shabby plastic-amalgam door to the topmost room, a room no bigger than a broom closet, itself shaped like a pyramid. Then she stood aside and gestured for him to enter. Her manner was that of a kindly nurse in a maternity ward, ushering him into the presence of one of life's sacred joys.

He had stepped through and seen that the only furniture in the room was an old, flaking wooden kitchen table—a table he almost recognized, perhaps from his father's tiny kitchen— and on it, a wooden tray filled with dirt. In the dirt were human faces—unfamiliar yet almost known to him—seven of them, staring straight up as if the faces were the caps of big mushrooms. Each one—though only a face, its temples and jawline flush with the black soil—was alive, was squirming, fidgeting within itself. The eyes rolling; the mouths opening, gasping, murmuring without words, a little drool escaping the corners of their open, mumbling lips: five men and two women.

As he had stepped closer, seven pairs of eyes had swiveled to fix on him, and the babyish fear in their expressions turned to idiotic joy.

"Now if you'll just feed them," came the old woman's chirpy voice in the dream, "everyone's future will be happy . . . happily . . . joyfully . . . to"—her words fragmenting as the dream broke up—"completionate . . . fantastible, joynicating . . . razzle suckle . . . Steve . . . Stevie."

"Mr. Isquerat?"

He nearly leapt from his seat. "Yes?"

"Mr. Winderson will see you now."

———

"Coffee, Stephen?"

Here was Mr. Dale Winderson, the billionaire, offering to pour him, a junior executive, a cup of coffee. But it wouldn't do to be obsequious, to insist on pouring his own coffee.

"Sure. Thank you, sir."

"You can call me Dale, Stephen. Your *father* called me Brat-boy." He chuckled. Winderson was a tall, good-looking man with thick black hair, wearing a silk San Francisco Giants jacket, jeans, and cowboy boots. He had permanent smile lines etched around his eyes and mouth.

"Bratboy, sir? Not really."

"Oh yes, really! I didn't mind."

The office was enormous—it was a good eighty feet to the ceiling with the square footage of about a two-story house. The sparseness of its furnishings reflected an elegant mini-malism that only emphasized the volume. There were a sofa, Winderson's broad, Chinese-lacquer desk, two chairs—leather, not Inimicalene—and a few paintings. The window wall re-vealed the stalagmite caviness of downtown San Francisco: a few copters darting like mutated dragonflies, the new monorail slithering over the Bay Bridge.

Winderson stood in front of the tinted window, pouring coffee at a mahogany serving table on casters. Despite the tint-ing and the gray sky there was a certain glare, and only when Winderson brought Stephen his coffee—in a black mug with the WW logo emblazoned in gold on the side—did he realize that Winderson had hair plugs of some kind and that the ex-pression on his face, with its cheerful lines, was more or less printed there. His expressions were garments, like his casual clothing.

Trying not to stare, Stephen sipped a little coffee and pre-tended to admire the view.

"Your father was a great guy," Winderson was saying, as he sat on the edge of his desk, stretching his legs out.

Stephen sat in the black leather chair across from the desk; the big office seemed to whisper of opportunity, of privilege.

"Old Barry . . ." Winderson shook his head as if at some cherished memory. "Your dad took me under his wing when I came to Stanford. He was my roommate, a year older—but it was more than an obligation. He *liked* helping people find their way. And he'd go the distance for a pal."

Stephen felt grief pierce his giddiness for a moment. His father, a grade school teacher, had indeed been a good man. He'd had his problems—a tendency toward moody withdrawal, and he'd almost destroyed his marriage with an affair—but he'd loved his son, and made sure Stephen felt it. He had died two years before of cancer, after a cruelly protracted battle. *The insurance companies crapped out on me, son. The HMO dropped me, of course, long ago. So I spent everything on treatments. I shouldn't have. I should've known it was too late. What that means is I've got nothing to leave you—except a tired old favor. A man owes me a favor. You've heard of Dale Winderson . . . what I did for him—well, he owes me. We were roommates, and he can get you in at the top of his company. I don't really know what they do there, exactly—chemicals or refining or something. But if you don't like it, you can always move on. You'll be one of the people you wanted to be. . . . I mean, you know—you can use your MBA.*

What had he meant, "one of the people you wanted to be"? Why had he put it like that?

Stephen had dabbled in online day trading, stocks of all kinds, since he'd turned eighteen. He'd lost as much as he'd made at it, but it had always been small investments, and hence small losses—and the excitement had whetted his appetite.

He didn't want to be like his father, teaching kids who didn't care. He wanted to be one of the people who mattered in the world.

"Your dad," Dale was saying, "well, he was really there for me. I owe him. I mean it was more than just shepherd-

ing me through school. Did he, um, tell you what it was that
he, ah . . . ?"

"No, sir. Dale."

"Well. All that matters is, what he did for me got you the job.
I won't pretend that your grades did it, though they were re-
spectable. And now it's going to get you another opportunity. . . ."

He paused, sipped coffee, looking at Stephen over the top
of his mug. Waiting.

Waiting for what? Stephen wasn't sure. He cleared his throat
and took a stab at it.

"Dale—I'm here at WW because I want to be. I mean—I
want to be part of the—"

"Team, right? You want to grow with the company. Son,
you've already been hired. You don't have to give me that tired
old speech. I just wonder . . . do you know what the world is
really like? And what our place in it really is? Of course you
don't. Almost no one does. You're an alert kid—and you caught
our interest with that Dirvane 17 business you brought up."

So that's it. Stephen maintained what he hoped was an interested, impartial expression. But inside he writhed. He was
going to be fired after all. Maybe Winderson thought he had to
fire him personally, for his father's sake.

Researching new products, Stephen had learned that
Dirvane 17, a pesticide soon to be marketed by West Wind, had
been called seriously carcinogenic and neurologically toxic by
independent researchers. Remarkably small amounts of it would
cause convulsions in children and liver damage in adults. There
were also indications of neurological complications. And it persisted in the environment. But it killed the Glassy-Winged
Sharpshooter, the bug that threatened California's wine industry, more rapidly and definitely than any other pesticide.

"You pointed out the downside of Dirvane 17."

"Yes, sir—I was only concerned that—" He broke off as Winderson raised his hand.

"I know, son—you were concerned about the company. That we'd face lawsuits. That it'd generate a big backlash—bad publicity—that in the long run it'd cost us more in settlements than we'd make in profits."

Stephen exhaled through his nose, in relief. "Exactly . . . Dale."

"Very sharp. I've asked that the stuff be reviewed. Maybe we can cover our asses with some sort of warning label and special handling instructions—more of that kind of thing than usual, I mean—before we market the stuff."

Winderson went to stand in front of the window, his back to Stephen, striking a pose with one hand in his Giants jacket, the other holding the mug in front of him. "Look at that big ol' world out there. Steve, you ever ask yourself which way is up or down?"

"Um—well success is up, and to get there . . ."

"Don't need that speech either, Steve. No, I mean—morally. Is there a moral up and down?"

"Well—sure."

"Sure there is—yet it's all relative. Personally, I think of the moral good as being the greatest good for the most people. Now this world of ours—did you ever consider that *up*—the literal *up*, toward the sky—isn't up? You'd know if you were an astronaut. Those guys know. See, it's all relative to where you stand. It's *up* if you're on the ground. But in space there is no up. I mean—why don't you fall off the Earth? Looking toward the South Pole, why, that's down, right? So why don't you fall toward the South Pole and then out into space? Gravity. But that's all that prevents you going one way or another. Get out into the Solar System, the galaxy, there's no up or down. We orient ourselves according to what works, son."

What's the point of all this? Stephen wondered. But he said, "Um—sure, I can see that."

"So . . . gravity . . . where's *our* center of gravity, so to speak? Yours and mine? Where's our *moral* center of gravity? Like I said, it's whatever's the most good for the most people. I have my own notions of what that is. Have to operate by my own notions—they're all I've got."

He turned to face Stephen but didn't look at him; he put his coffee mug down very carefully on his glass-topped desk beside the computer terminal and the speaker phone, frowning with concentration, as if putting the mug down was a matter of life or death. "Stephen, you remember the so-called Demon Hallucinations about nine years ago?"

"The Demon Hallucinations?"

"Yes. What's your notion of what happened?"

Stephen hesitated. "Um—I really don't have one. I was doing graduate work, helping create a business in Thailand—a computer-manufacturing base." He chuckled, trying to sound like an experienced fellow businessman. "We did all of the work and got none of the profits. I wasn't much more than an intern then, and it wasn't much more than a sweatshop, as it turned out. I couldn't wait to leave. It was an island just off the Thai mainland, very isolated. They could avoid the international labor laws there. But I was stuck there for a while. I wasn't in the States when any of the—the demon hysteria went down. I saw some of it on TV, but it all looked like a hoax to me, special effects, that, uh—"

"Yes, no doubt," Winderson interrupted with a dismissive wave. "So you thought it was a hoax, and later—hallucinations, you said?"

"Right—they said there was a terrorist attack, with hallucinogens—all these people went nuts and wrecked the—"

"Yes, all right," Winderson broke in again, briskly this time. He gazed blankly down at Stephen. His eternal smile had seamlessly melted into a grimace of strain.

I said the wrong thing, Stephen thought. *But how?*

Winderson gave a soft grunt that sounded like cynical amusement. "Well, some of our people were accused of being involved in spreading the poison gas, or whatever, that caused the hallucinations. I wanted to know where you stood on it. There are lawsuits pending. Groundless, I assure you. It was pulled off by terrorists, who put rye-mold-based hallucinogens in the water around the world. Of course, a great many people still believe . . ." He shrugged as if waiting for Stephen to finish the thought for him.

"Uh, yeah, a lot of people seem to think it really happened, in some literal way—but there's no TV footage of actual demons. At the time I saw some clips—but they were all sort of blurry. . . . After a while, they stopped showing them. I've always wondered what happened to that footage."

"Do you know how much footage there was out there? Too much to find and erase. Yet all the people who claimed to have home video footage of the demons, or to have taped news reports about them, came up with erased tapes. Digital stuff was blotted out, too. So—they were lying."

"But how could there be footage of hallucinations in the first place?"

"There wasn't—there was some footage of people hallucinating, rioting, killing one another, some of them in bizarre costumes. Many of them with extraordinary strength—a side effect of the drug."

"Costumes. I saw some of that—people parading around in homemade demon costumes, their bodies all painted up. . . ."

"Right. It was mass hysteria, fueled by the attack. Some people succumbed, and some didn't. The footage was confiscated, taken for the government investigation. Anyway, the terrorist cell was wiped out so that's that."

"Well . . ." Stephen stood, assuming the interview had come to an end.

"Not so fast, son! That's not the only reason you're here! I was just wondering what you thought about all that. No, there's something more we have to discuss. You have a special opportunity ahead of you."

Stephen sat down again, a little too heavily, his mouth dry. At last, here it was.

"They've asked for you, Stephen."

"Who has?"

"That's not what you need to know. You should ask *why* they've asked for you—that's far more important."

Is it? Stephen wondered. Some survival instinct stirred in him.

"Yes," Winderson went on, perhaps reading the doubtful expression on Stephen's face. "Yes . . . *Why you?* is the question. It's because you're a kind of tabula rasa, it seems. You have special qualities. . . ." He seemed to be thinking aloud. "And I can only envy you . . . but—" He shrugged, then turned to the speaker phone, and hit a button. "Latilla?"

As he straightened up, an older woman in a gray-blue suit bustled into the room through a side door.

The woman from Stephen's dream.

"I've got to make some phone calls. Take Stephen to see his opportunity, Latilla," Winderson said. "I'll be along."

———

At the back of the penthouse office, a door opened onto a stairwell: a dusty stairwell that spiraled upward.

Heart hammering, Stephen found himself following Latilla exactly as he'd followed her in his dream, though she had been dressed differently then. She didn't say anything as they ascended, just hummed tunelessly to herself as they came to a narrow landing, a door.

Stephen felt himself close to hyperventilating as she put her hand on the knob. The faces in the tray.

She looked at him quizzically. "Are you all right, Mr. Isquerat?"

She pronounced his name almost like *Issk-rat*. Making him think of *muskrat*. He wanted to correct her, tell her it should be closer to *Iss-carrot*.

No. There was something else it was more important to say: *Don't take me into that room!*

"Yes—yes, I . . . but perhaps, really, I'm . . ." He wanted to say he wasn't right for this. But he wasn't supposed to know what was there.

She gave her head a little shake of puzzled impatience, then turned the knob and stepped into the room, holding the door open for him.

Inside was another short hallway to a small office just big enough to hold its five workstations.

Stephen looked around. *Just an office.* He shivered.

He was dizzy with relief. The dream had been just a dream. He blew out his breath, relaxing a little.

The cubicles weren't cubicles, really—though partitioned with the usual white soundboard, they were oddly shaped, each one a triangle, with the point outward, the computer operator sitting at a desk with his back to the center of the room, where Stephen and Latilla stood. It was a windowless room; vaguely New Age Muzak oozed from hidden speakers. A sixth man joined them, his smile somehow the same quality as the music. He was a pale man with a high forehead and fishy lips, wearing a white lab coat. He carried a digital clipboard.

"This is H. D.—Harrison Deane," Latilla said, squeezing Deane's shoulder hard enough to make the man wince.

H. D. blinked at Stephen. "This is . . . ?"

"Yes, this is *him*," Latilla said.

"Really! And he'll be starting here with me soon?"

"First there's a plan for, ah, some kind of fieldwork. Just the way Dale likes to do things."

"Fieldwork?" H. D. looked at her in confusion. Then something seemed to dawn on him. "Oh, yes, of course . . ."

"I'm a little at sea, here," Stephen said, trying to laugh it off. It was as if they were two people who knew about a surprise party and were trying to talk about it without clueing him in.

"H. D. is George Deane's son," Latilla said, as if that explained things. "George started psychonomics."

"Psychonomics . . ." Stephen couldn't quite bring himself to admit he didn't know what it was.

Latilla smiled. "The use of psychic power in business, which in turn increases your psychic influence over the world. *If* you've developed your ability with psychonomics."

Stephen wasn't sure he'd heard her rightly. Had she said "psychic"?

"So this room is for . . . psychonomics training?" Stephen asked.

More urgently, he wanted to ask *Where's the men's room?* He needed to pee badly. But somehow it didn't feel like the right moment.

"Ye-es," said H. D., noncommittally. "Have a look at Al in station number three. I think he's got some kind of groove going here today."

They went to stand behind a gangly, round-shouldered man with thinning brown hair, stooped before a flat-screen monitor. He was staring intently at the screen. There was *no* keyboard.

The screen itself was divided into two columns of numbers, scrolling jerkily down. "On the left," H. D. said, "you see numbers generated, as you might suppose, by a random-number generator. On the right side, Al is trying to induce in the stream of random numbers consistent patterns—increases, especially. When he succeeds, the computer chimes."

As if eager to demonstrate, the computer chimed, and numbers flickered in bright green on the right side of the screen.

"It rewards me," Al said. His voice seemed distant, as if he spoke in his sleep. "The computer rewards me. I can feel it."

"How does that happen?" Stephen asked, shifting from one foot to the other. He tried not to squirm, though he increasingly had to pee. "The reward part?"

But H. D. went briskly on, "So you see, he's changing the pattern by the power of his mind alone. Something like this might be used to influence the stock market, for example, one way or another." He droned on, and Stephen glanced around for a men's room door.

"Are you quite all right?" Latilla asked.

"Yes, well, actually I was sort of wondering if I could just pop into the men's room."

"Right out that door and to the right. You can't miss it," H. D. said, pointing. He turned his attention back to his clipboard.

Stephen hurried through the door, found himself in an unfamiliar hallway. He followed it around two bends, then located the men's room. The New Age Muzak sang in soothing redundancies as he relieved himself in the urinal. He set off again to find the computer room, opened the door he thought led back into it, and realized he was lost.

Instead of the psychonomics computer room, he found himself in an antechamber, facing a glass door. On the other side were two women in nurse's uniforms, bustling around a dim figure on a bed.

Some other aspect of psychonomics, he supposed. He could ask them the way back to the room with the five computers.

He went diffidently through the glass door into a room that smelled of hospital disinfectant overlaid by the perfumes of an enormous bouquet of flowers on the broad windowsill. A bone-thin older man in a hospital gown, his back to the door, lay on his side in a wide, comfortable-looking hospital bed. Top of the line, Stephen supposed. The room was all white, pastel, and chrome: a hospital suite transplanted whole into the upper floors of an office building. There was a television, switched off, on the wall over the sink; a bathroom, a metal table with bed pans, catheters, coils of tubing. Stephen went a little closer to the old man on the bed.

"I don't think you were given a pass to this suite," came Latilla's voice, low and brittle, as she came in the door behind him, making him jump.

"I was looking for the, uh . . ."

He found he was staring at the man on the bed. He recognized him from his research into the company: George Deane, the cofounder of West Wind. The onetime company president was staring into nothingness with a look of frightened despair, his lips moving soundlessly. His stick-thin arms were drawn up mantislike in front of him, his fingers tapping, quivering in front of his mouth like questing antennae.

"That's Mr. Deane—H. D.'s father—isn't it?" Stephen asked.

Winderson came in then, behind Latilla, and stopped, eyebrows raised, looking at Stephen.

Latilla turned to look at Winderson. It was remarkable how unafraid of him she seemed.

Winderson pursed his lips. "You find your own way in here, Stephen?"

"Took a wrong turn coming back from the bathroom."

"Did you? You recognize him, I see. Well—you're here now. You may as well have the full tour. And maybe it's good. Maybe there's a reason for it . . . maybe they . . ."

Winderson glanced at Latilla. She shrugged.

"We just finished bathing him," said the Filipino nurse, hurrying past them. "Don't be long. He needs to rest."

The other nurse, a black woman with pensive eyes, glanced at Stephen as she followed her colleague out of the room. He had the feeling she wanted to say something to him.

Latilla walked around to the other side of the bed. Deane didn't seem to react to the people around him. He scarcely blinked; now and then he squeezed his eyes shut convulsively and snapped them open again. There was an IV in his arm, closed off at the moment. His bedclothes consisted of a single crisp sheet, tautly tucked in, covering him from just below his waist.

"They've had to feed him intravenously most of the time," Latilla said. "Poor man. How are you, Mr. Deane?" She didn't seem to expect an answer as she reached over and tugged his pillow a little more squarely under the side of his head. He didn't so much as glance at her. "Resting comfortably today? Mr. Winderson is here to see you."

Deane groaned, then. And went on as before.

"Winderson is here, George!" the CEO announced· cheerily, bending near Deane's ear. Deane only groaned and turned away.

Winderson straightened up, looked at Stephen a moment before remarking musingly, "You must be surprised to find a room like this up here."

"A little—but I suppose you wanted to look after him personally."

"Exactly. We can afford it, so why not."

"A stroke?" Stephen asked softly.

Winderson shook his head and patted the recumbent old man on his bony, shivering shoulder. "No. Not exactly. More like . . . *sabotage*. Psychological sabotage. We have enemies, Stephen. Perhaps it's just as well you meet a fallen warrior now and see what the stakes are. What we're up against. You'll learn more about all that in time. Just know that George here was a real pioneer in psychonomics."

Winderson reached out to give George Deane's hand a squeeze. "We'll let you rest, George."

Deane jerked his hand away from Winderson's touch with a groan. Winderson grunted angrily and turned away. "You can go, Latilla. Don't put any calls through to me."

"Well, I'm sure I don't know why you even carry a palmtalker, you use it so little," she muttered. Then she left the way they'd come in.

Stephen watched her go. Was this really the woman he'd seen in his nightmare? A woman he'd never seen in life before today?

No. Not possible. It must have seemed like it because the nightmare was still on his mind. He must have misremembered what the woman in the dream looked like . . .

Winderson chuckled. "She's been with me a long time. I let her get away with murder. This way, Stephen. Since you're here, I might as well show you the rest."

They went through a side door into what appeared to be some kind of trophy room. There was another window wall, with a view over the misty, gray city. Beyond the skyline, San Francisco Bay looked like a pool of mercury. The room's other three walls were crowded with shelves of civic awards, plaques,

and framed photos of George Deane shaking hands with famous people: politicians, movie stars, Presidents. There was a
leather sofa with a few Edwardian chairs facing it. "We bring
George in here from time to time," Winderson said, settling on
the sofa. "Have a seat."

Stephen sat across from him, changing his position several
times, trying to look sufficiently relaxed yet sufficiently atten-
tive. "This room is, um, encouraging to him? Psychologically?"

"Smart boy. Yes, it's a sort of gallery of his triumphs—to re-
store his confidence, his belief in himself. We don't know exactly
what happened to him, really, because he's never said a word
since it happened. But the MRIs—all the tests indicate it wasn't
a stroke. And we've seen others in variations of this condition."
He paused, watching as a streamer of cloud skated past the
window.

"God, I miss smoking. Love to have a smoke now." He put
his arm across the back of the sofa and gestured. "Sit over here,
boy. It makes me feel more comfortable if I don't have to raise
my voice."

Stephen sank into the yielding cushion at the other end of
the sofa.

"Stephen, you've just had a little glimpse into psychonomics. Let me fill you in on a bit of history. It began for George
in the early nineteen-seventies. He was interested in self-
improvement, therapies of all kinds—Esalen, Gestalt, Janov,
what have you. He was particularly impressed with the man
who called himself Werner Erhard. George was involved in est
and Forum—all the time husbanding his investments in oil
and chemicals research. Therapy was an avocation, but he was
looking for ways to fuse it with his industrial vocation.

"Then he became involved with a Professor Shephard in
something called pragmatic postmodernism—it involved the

biology of economics, a kind of sociobiology of capitalism. He and Shephard developed the notion that business was a spiritual power—spiritual and telepathic being related—and they dubbed it psychonomics."

"Like those Christian businesses that try to use spiritual ideas in their workplaces?"

"Not . . . as such, no. It was more like the *power* of the spirit and how businesses could enhance that power. That is, it assumed that there was a kind of invisible world of— of cause and effect that could be influenced by our state of mind."

"Psychically?" Stephen was for the first time more intrigued than nervous.

"Well—yes. For lack of a better word. Some of it was expressed in psychic energy that flowed through a physical work structure—how a business, or a refinery, for example, was laid out."

"Sort of like feng shui?"

"It did, in fact, employ some of those principles. And more. They went beyond that to what they called Psychic Pumping Stations. Certain individuals, in communication with certain, ah, you might say, spiritual influences . . . influences that could be spread psychically through a corporation. People in a corporation could be yoked together psychically to become of one mind, more or less. The result would be loyal, hardworking employees who would contribute their individual energy to the collective energy of the corporation."

"But that would still be only a—a psychological effect, wouldn't it?"

Winderson smiled wearily. "Only on the surface. I assure you, there's also a psychic influence in business. Stephen, do you remember, a few weeks ago, being asked to take a test for us? You tried to guess what images completed a pattern. You also had to draw pictures inspired by numbers."

"Oh, yes. I thought it was some kind of psychological exam. I was hoping they picked me at random—spot-checking, so to speak, for unbalanced people."

"It wasn't a psychological test, Stephen. And it wasn't random. It was a psychic test. You're not a psychic as such, but you do have a certain special potential, and that's one of the reasons that you're here. When your father asked me to give you a job, I had you tested along with some other people, and was gratified to discover just how remarkably strong your aptitude was."

"We weren't told it was a psychic test."

"Again, it doesn't test whether or not you're a psychic. It tests to see if you have a certain psychic *potential* that can be . . . encouraged. Some have more than others. You have lots of it. And I want you to use that ability to take up where George Deane left off.

"I want you to be the new director—and primary test subject—for the next step in the George Deane Foundation. You will become the point man, the living vector, for the new psychonomics."

Ash Valley, California

The sorceress had arrived just at dusk in this little Northern California town. She had confirmed that there would be no more spraying that day, yet she wore a respirator and goggles, walking from the van to the outbuilding in the park at the center of town. She was walking to the room where *it* was waiting . . . if waiting was a word you could use. The Spirit Prince didn't exist entirely within the mortal time flow, after all. . . . And would it really be there? They couldn't enter our world completely until the working was done. At best it would be projecting its image—and perhaps some of its power—into the human world.

She crossed the sidewalk to the rectangular cinder-block building marked PUBLIC REST ROOMS. Her pumps skidded just a little on the brown pine needles coating the cement. The town was quiet. There wasn't anyone in the park, at least no one she could see. She supposed most of the townspeople were at dinner, eating in the living room and watching television, like they were supposed to.

The tall old trees creaked in the breeze. There was a dead robin, seething with ants, lying just beside the closed metal door. She found that her hand was trembling as she brought the padlock key out of her purse.

Shaking with anticipation, she told herself. *Not fear.* She should not be afraid of them: They were, ultimately, her servants.

That morning she had risen and faced west. With the sun at her back, she had spoken the words, the sacred Names of Power, over and over, with her own mind and her whole being focused on the act of magical declamation. And she had visualized the rune in the heart of Saturn, had seen herself, in her mind's eye, grow as big as the Earth, big as the Sun, big as the Solar System, big as the galaxy, a cosmos-spanning sorceress. And she'd truly believed in the vision.

On the conduit of her belief, power had flowed into her. She summoned that power now, from the center of her being, as she unlocked the padlock.

Everything was symbolic when you were dealing with the astral realms, the sorceress reflected. Simply leaving your vehicle to enter a building had its mythological significance: Imagine an ancient priestess leaving a chariot, entering a pyramid. Unlocking the padlock was symbolic always. It symbolized

another milestone in the attainment of her own freedom, symbolized all the risks of Pandora's box, symbolized unlocking the
shackles put on her by the tyrant who had tried to keep humanity as pets in the Garden of Eden.

When True Will brought about the convergence of worlds, she
thought, *the astral and the material, a tension arose, and synchro-
nicity was bent to the service of symbolism.*

She replaced the key in her purse. It was time to go inside,
to face the Spirit Prince.

Remember, she told herself, *when any two meet, one is always
the servant.*

She glanced over her shoulder. The men in the van, in their
military drab, would see to it that she was not interrupted.

Removing her gas mask and goggles, letting them dangle
around her neck like grotesque necklaces, she entered the
dank, noisome building and thought about how the secrets to
the keys of power were found in the darkest, foulest swamps of
the sorceress's inner world, the place within her that corresponded to this reeking box.

She paused, just inside.

The windowless rectangular room was shadowy on one
side, where an overhead light was burnt out, harshly lit on the
other side. The fly-specked light was enclosed in a metal cage.
It burned relentlessly. But suppose it went out?

You are in charge, she told herself. *You are beyond fear.* And she
spoke the names in her mind.

The walls separating the men's and women's rest rooms
had been torn down by her associates at her request. Even that
was symbolic! The subsuming of male and female into one! But
the toilets remained, still reeking of old urine and faintly of
feces. The urinals were still there, on the men's side, and the
graffiti on the walls over the urinals.

The room was only apparently empty. She knew *it* was there.

She closed the door behind her and walked to the lit part of the room, her heels clacking on the tile floor, echoing from the concrete walls. She told herself she chose that part of the room only because it would be easier to see the design. She drew the vial from her purse, uncorked it, found the little paint-brush, and dipped it into the red fluid, which was only partly blood. She painted the symbol around herself on the floor, chanting as she did so, feeling those particular energies rising up inside her.

Doubts flickered, and were gone.

She was queen here.

She spoke the names again.

"Well? You said something, maybe?"

The voice was by turns fruity and reptilian, mocking a human ethnicity.

"You're asserting dominance over me, I believe, dear lady?"

It laughed—or made a sound like a musical saw in the hands of a lunatic, a sound that she took to be laughter.

It was a male voice, more or less, but there seemed to be more than one voice, and certainly more than one timbre; and she knew that the princes, despite the implication of gender in that human term for them, were neither male nor female. Some of them, when they showed themselves on this plane, possessed humanlike genitalia—but these were affectations, decorations, and sometimes weapons.

She looked around and saw *its* head thrusting out of the wall, as if through a porthole that didn't exist, between the polished metal mirror and the old stainless steel paper towel dispenser. Issuing from the wall itself, quite seamlessly, it almost looked like another kind of bathroom fixture.

It was the head of what some people, during the invasion, had called a Gnasher.

Mostly jaws, that head, with rather pretty blue human eyes set along the top of the flattish skull—set in a way human eyes would never be: like the eyes of a manta ray. The flexible, shark-toothed mouth wrapped most of the way around the head, which was now tilted back a bit on its dragon-skin neck, to grin at her.

"Come over here and give us a wet one!"

it said.

"I remain centered in my power," she said, both ritually and declaratively, "and you at my periphery. So be it."

"Oh, don't be so stuffy!"

The head turned in place, as if in a socket, upside down, then right side up again.

For a vertiginous moment she felt that it was she who was extending from a wall, standing on the wall in defiance of gravity, and the demon—as ordinary mortals called them—was sticking its head up out of the ground, like an animal emerging from a burrow. She felt as if she might fall into those gaping, mocking jaws . . .

She growled at herself in quiet fury. It was exerting some kind of influence, some sort of psychic disorientation on her; and she was falling for it like a tyro. *Idiot! Wake up and take your throne! You are its queen or its victim. Choose to be its queen!*

She found her orientation again and muttered names of control.

"Yes indeedy,"

the Gnasher said jovially, effortlessly reading her mind.

"You do deserve to be a queen—and you must have all a queen's trappings. Hence and therefore . . ."

Suddenly, behind her, there was a metallic squealing, the grating crunch of dislodged concrete. She only half turned before something thrust under her from behind. She fell back onto a toilet.

The toilet, she realized, had pulled itself from the wall, extending on pipes and scraping across the floor, leaving bits of porcelain behind. It had scraped through the magic diagram; but it didn't matter. The diagram, she knew, was really just a device that forced her mind into the proper state to control the entities summoned.

The toilet induced her to sit, like a magic chair in a Disney cartoon, and the demon threw its voice, so its laughter was now reverberating from the bowl of the toilet and up through her hips. She squelched an urge to leap up, screaming, slapping at her rump—an infantile mental picture formed of the toilet and its hinged seat having grown teeth, snapping at her. Instead she forced herself to lean regally back, as if all this was her own will.

"Any seat is a throne for the queen of sorcerers, even in mockery, even in irony," the sorceress said. "Why not give me a plunger for a scepter? But it won't diminish my power, which increases in every light, even in the garish light of ridicule."

"Well said!"

the demon crowed with an utter lack of sincerity, its voice still coming from underneath her. The Spirit Prince began to move easily up within the concrete wall, as if it were liquid, making it ripple faintly. As it went, its body began to emerge from the wall projecting horizontally—first shoulders, then upper breast. It began to declaim the demonic glossolalia that some adepts in the Undercurrent imagined to be of great significance but which she felt was just an oblique method of seeding disorientation.

"Undertake to appreciate the undertaker, for the identity in question is held to be contingent, and not a matter of necessity, i.e., of the meaning of the terms used to report observations of the two kinds in question. Let us then celebrate Jeremy Bentham, British philosopher, mouthpiece for the quantitative comparison of the amounts of pleasure and pain that will occur as the consequences of alternative courses of action. Had I been there!"

It threw out a number of phrases in Tartaran she could not handily translate as it emerged to its waist, wading through the wall, up toward the ceiling. Its soliloquy returned to English.

"Oh! Had I but been there when Bentham enumerated the Dimensions of Pain and Pleasure. Do y'know, he laid 'em out according to intensity, duration, certainty, propinquity, purity, fecundity, and extent! And how much more directly he can study the dimensions of pain, in particular, and the

*pleasure in others quite beyond his reach, now that he be-
longs to the Lower Princes!"*

The sorceress snorted. She knew that "the Lower Princes"
was a term used to describe the "devils" employed by "Satan"
in "Hell" to feed on those who had insisted on remaining outside what the Conscious Circle called "God's Sphere of Light."
Every so often the Spirit Princes tested the leaders of the Undercurrent, to see if such mythology frightened them.

She stood and said, "Cease the projection of your voice."

"How's this, girlfriend?"

it asked. Its voice was coming from the air, about ten feet to the
left of its head.

"That will do. Now let us proceed to our Great Work. The
preliminary steps are completed."

The demon had reached the ceiling now, and was upside
down like a repulsive chandelier. Its arms were not quite free—
the hands were still sunk into the material of the ceiling.

"The preliminary steps are completed, she says . . ."

It was just possible, she knew, that given the chance—once
her head, say, came within reach of its talons—the Gnasher
would kill her, and kill her gleefully, even if it did disrupt the
Spirit Princes' agenda. It was more than just impulsiveness—
the Princes had no sense of human values and did not always
place planning ahead of murderous delight.

Its drool fell from spike-glittering jaws, to sizzle on the
floor.

"How nonchalant she is! 'The preliminary steps are completed!' Oh, really? I think not!"

Its voice continued to project across the room, and she realized it was attempting to divide her attention, to make her giddy. She decided to act as if it didn't bother her. Though it did.

"And, you know,"

it went on,

"I really do think 'not.' I think: Not! Not *is what I specialize in thinking. And I am here to tell you that you rubbery-bag THINGS do NOT!"*

It snapped the word NOT at her with its cymbal-clashing jaws, its upper body lashing at her like a cobra, so that she staggered back and fell onto the toilet again, banging her tailbone painfully. It laughed like the mad musical saw and drew casually back, continued speaking, now and then darting its head forward with the louder words, just to see her twitch.

"You temporary bag-fluid THINGS do NOT have the necessary item. Cease all prevarication! You have it NOT! Nor do you truly have control of the retriever of the necessary item! Such as I cannot go into the place where the necessary item is—it would be like a human swallowing its own brain! But one of you pink primate THINGS can go there. In the sequence you experience, YEW"

—its accent had suddenly become Texan—

"do NOT have the necessary I-TEMMMMM!"

"Hear me now, O Prince!" she said, standing. "You are a prince, truly—but I am a goddess as well as a queen. I am She Whom You Will Obey! Stand your ground outside the circle! Your queen and goddess commands you!"

"Oh, sure. Whatever,"

it said, its accent becoming Southern Californian. It waggled its head in an impossible mockery of human affectation. Since it was hanging upside down from the ceiling, it looked like a spastic bat.

"You're all, 'stay out of my space, yo,' and I'm all, 'don't GO there, girl.' "

"Cease this banter," she commanded. "It does not confuse me. And harken now: The necessary item is soon to be in place. We've only just located the retriever."

"Now hear this, SKIN THING,"

the demon snarled, mocking her tone.

"What you think of as the schedule within what you call the 'flow of time'—the choreography of probability, my little queen—will have to be subjectively accelerated. Am I speaking two-dimensionally enough?"

"I am a three-dimensional creature," she said, trying to refute its intimidation.

"There you err. Only in trivial aspects are you three-dimensional."

It said something rapid, almost gibbering, in Tartaran and some form of ancient Latin she couldn't translate, then went on in English.

"Now I tell you this: The Retriever must be exposed to your worldly workings; his hands must become dirty or we cannot guide him. He must walk through the fields and smell the death and not repent."

"This we understand."

"Listen your maj-hystery—O, Queen of Grit and Sour Smells—LISTEN! It must be what you call 'sooner'! Your enemies are seeking the Retriever, too! Too, too solid, this flesh—only your flesh, my dear, is really like a balloon filled with red, diluted mud and just a spark of life, and how easy it is to pop a balloon!"

It waded once more across the ceiling, down the wall, into the floor, this time turning right side up, coming at her through the floor. Sunk into the floor up to its waist, its hands hidden in the tile as if it were a bog.

It giggled delightedly.

"My darling dear, my queen, go little Queenie, oh!"

It jerked its arm up and its taloned hand came free of the floor as it lashed out at her.

She stood her ground, exerting her magical Will to maintain the integrity of the circle's bubble of protection—so that the demon's raking talons stopped at the boundary of the circle.

Then it laughed, its laughter a demented song.

And it reached through what she'd supposed to be her infallible wall of protection, its arm extending, stretching like soft plastic . . .

And it tickled her under the chin with its claws. Then it pinched her right nipple.

She hardly dared breathe. It could have touched her whenever it wanted, she realized. *It could kill her whenever it chose.*

Its jaws widened, as if the back of its head were unzipping to open them all the way around. Three hundred sixty degrees of jaws, so that they should have fallen apart, upper separating from lower, head from neck. But instead, the complete circle of upper jaws oscillated like a coin spinning on a table just before it falls flat. And then the jaws snapped shut, the demon chirping,

"Hee!"

Other heads emerged from the ceiling, the wall, the floor. There, a head popped up from the tile—it looked like a man's head with the features scrambled, set free to move about, so that they wandered about the front of the skull: The eyes crawling like snails, the lips humping along like caterpillars, the nose sliding to dance around what appeared to be a cigarette made of flesh. Then the features found their organization, wandered into place, and became the Prince people had called a Bugsy.

"Be minth, Valentinth,"

it said.

"I've got somethingth for yewww, about ten feeth under the floor here."

A Grindum, roaring so that the walls shook, was shouldering its way from the wall. The raggedy feelers of a Dishrag waved and beckoned from the ceiling. A Sharkadian was moving across the floor toward her like—

Like a shark.

And she was backing toward the door.

"Your advice is understood, O Prince," she said, managing to keep her voice from quavering much, hardly able to hear it herself over the pounding of her pulse. "I will accelerate the program. And now—I banish you back to—to your—"

The Sharkadian leapt up from the floor like a killer whale leaping from the sea, and came at her—

And grabbed her as she turned to run. It gripped her shoulders from behind.

"You . . . you will release me. . . . Now . . ."

There came a metallic singsong cackling, and then she felt herself propelled, like a drunk from a bar, out the door . . .

To fall on her face on the sidewalk, skinning her nose and palms. She heard the door slam behind her.

Panting with fear, face and hands burning, she got to her feet and almost fell again, swaying on rubbery knees. The men in the van stared at her, but didn't come out to help. The treacherous cowards.

She steadied herself and turned to look. The rest room building's door was closed—and the lock was locked.

She hurried to the van. She got in and gasped, "Turn on the filter."

The air cleanser hummed. She sat quietly in her seat as the van hastily backed up, then barreled down the road. The others looked at her but chose not to ask why she'd been ejected that way. They were afraid of her, perhaps—or afraid to know.

Her hands gripped her knees; her knuckles were white.

It couldn't be, she thought, *that we never had control of them. That couldn't be. I must've done something wrong, incanted something badly. My Will must have failed. They couldn't have been toying with me all along.*

I am queen of the sorceresses. I am a goddess, Becoming. I am no one's plaything!

When they got to the highway, the sorceress spoke aloud. "Anybody got anything to drink?" she rasped. "I mean, something strong?"

2

Portland, Oregon

There were twenty-three people sitting in a circle around the large, cluttered, musty old room. They sat on straight-backed chairs or, straight-backed themselves, on floor cushions. A conference table had been moved out in order to make room for the group. The window shades were drawn, and a small electric chandelier overhead had been dimmed to the brightness of a few candles.

The room was just a little too warm, and Ira was wishing he'd taken off his sweater before the sitting. He didn't want to distract the others by taking it off now. It was a raw November evening outside, and most of them had overdressed. Ira sat in a light sheen of sweat, directing his attention to his inner world, to his sensations, to his feelings, to his heart and the heart within his heart, and to a certain place in the very center of himself. He watched detachedly as his train of free associations slipped endlessly by. He was distantly amused by many of them.

There was something else, something indescribable . . . something that flowed out of the present, from the silence that lay within the innermost circle of his watchful detachment.

Everyone was completely silent; it had been some time since Yanan, the leader of the meditation, had spoken. Ira could feel him there, but he couldn't read him. Yanan was an enigma.

But no—they weren't completely silent. Though they didn't speak, it was just before dinnertime, and their stomachs gurgled and mewed, absurdly loud in the quiet. Sometimes it sounded like an orchestral section, tuning up. Santos, from Brazil, cleared his throat; an Egyptian woman sitting nearby shifted in her chair, grimacing with discomfort. They'd all been sitting on the hard seats for an hour and a half.

A man to Ira's left sniffed, probably trying not to sneeze; someone's stomach made a soft *eeep* sound. Ira had to smile.

Ira usually chose to do his sitting with his eyes open. He found himself looking at Paymenz. Beardless now but bearlike in his enormous brown sweater, Paymenz sat across from Ira, eyes closed, deep in meditation. He wasn't yet used to Paymenz without a beard—his face looked too round, too pale, too tired without it. The erstwhile professor was going through changes, despite his age. He'd discarded as "energy-wasting and distorting" his old interest in ritual magic and divination. Paymenz instead had chosen the purity of the struggle for higher consciousness.

Ira himself had taken the same path—but sometimes, as now, he felt it was more a fishhook than a path. He felt, at times, impaled by the methods of this esoteric school; at such moments he felt himself squirming in the struggle to suffer all things consciously—like a shrike's victim squirming on a thorn.

He was young in this school, he knew, despite having a certain gift for it. And he knew that he was still a slave to his lower impulses—like his resentment over Melissa's absence, her going abroad with their son, Marcus. He knew the boy missed him, he could feel it, even now. Why couldn't she have left Marcus? Her mission would take her to an obscure monastery in Turkmenistan, and the boy might succumb to some exotic Middle Eastern bacterium there; or he could be kidnapped by militants, taken hostage. Nine years old, wandering through the wastelands not far from the Afghanistan border.

But not alone. There were guides, protecting them. And of course, Nyerza was there.

He was ashamed at the naked surge of jealousy that rose up in him. Nyerza—who'd gathered her in his arms that night, as they'd hidden beneath the city . . . Nyerza in charge of his wife—and his son. If she'd had to insist on taking Marcus to that hard land, couldn't she have told Ira why?

It would've been better if Melissa had lied. But instead she had said, with her typical disarming openness, "I don't know why. But he has to go with me."

She didn't even know why she'd taken him there.

Ira was yanked back to the work at hand when Yanan spoke, bringing them to the end of the group meditation.

"And now we return our attention to the normal flow of events, to the social world, and the world of time." His accent soft, faintly Middle Eastern. He was a small, compact man with a boyish brown face, though he was at least sixty. His curly black hair showed only the faintest peppering of gray. His wide flexible mouth was always on the verge of a smile—perpetually implying one, even when he didn't smile.

Ira sighed inwardly, annoyed with himself for letting his mind wander. But there wasn't any point in beating himself up about his lack of discipline. Anyone in his position would find it hard to stay cool and detached. He should have insisted on going with Melissa himself.

He'd *tried* to—but Yanan and Paymenz had made it sound as if it were a test of his faith and humility to stay here. If he hadn't seen the demons nine years ago, if he hadn't felt what he'd felt then, seen what he'd seen, he'd wonder if he was in a damn cult now. Perhaps, after nine years, it had deteriorated to just that.

Yanan stood and stretched, and that was the signal for the others to do so. Ira stood, grimacing as sensation came back into his legs but grateful to be able to move.

Yanan was there, gazing up at him. "Many kinks in the arms and legs today, eh?"

"My damn back hurts as soon as I stand up."

"And why is that, do we know? Hm? Eh? It is you who put the hurts in with your tension. You sit today like a crocodile biting down. Crunch, all of your muscles. Big tension. Who's in charge, you or the muscles, eh? Hm?"

"The muscles. My aunt Edna. Anybody but me."

"You have an Aunt Edna? Is she with us?"

"No, that was a joke, I don't have an Aunt Edna."

"Ah! A joke! Too bad it's not funny, eh? Hm?"

"Yeah." Ira laughed softly. "Too bad." The others were shuffling out of the room, carrying chairs, fetching the coffee table, saying nothing. "Okay, I'll work on relaxing."

"You're worried about the Urn, the wife, the baby. You feel trapped in all this. Sometimes you like to be in it; sometimes you wish you had never started. Yes, eh?"

"Yes, eh."

"Now you're making fun of me?"

"Yes, eh."

Yanan laughed and punched at Ira's midriff. "Come on, let

us have some coffee. No, first I make my evening prayers. Then we have some coffee. Eh? Hm?"

THE JOURNAL OF STEPHEN ISQUERAT

It only happened twice. The first time was when I was thirteen, the second time I was fifteen. I guess I'd convinced myself—sort of—that it hadn't been real, that it was some kind of dream. And I kind of suppressed it. But when I took the psychonomics test, I remembered it, and it felt like the memory of something real.

Then I talked to Mr. Winderson, and met Latilla and got the tour of the psychonomics training room where those people sat at the desks. (None of them ever looked up! It was weird.) And after visiting that place and stumbling onto Mr. Deane, I remembered again. So I guess I'll write it down in my journal. Maybe I can copy and paste it later for some psychonomics project.

It was winter, that first time, and we were snowed in. That was when Dad worked at that school in the Idaho panhandle. Nice kids, but the parents got really uptight when he mentioned evolution. Dad stuck it out there for two years.

The second year the snow was so high it buried the back of our one-story house and drifted halfway up the picture window; it was heavy enough it made the glass creak. We were way out in the boonies, away from anybody. I only saw my friends at school. It was Christmas vacation, and the power went out and we heated with wood, used lanterns for light. The County people kept saying they were going to plow our road, but somehow it never happened. Dad made arrangements for groceries to be brought out by a neighbor who had a snowmobile. Without power there was no TV, no Internet, no computer at all. I read, and we tried to enjoy the snow, but days passed and the claustrophobia, the cabin fever, got worse and worse.

It was snowing, sleeting really, early one night, and Dad wouldn't let me go outside. But it had been just too long like this. I was sitting by the fireplace, staring into the flames. Dad was up in the loft reading something. I just sat there and stared, and the fire sort of sucked in all my attention. It was like I was escaping into it. It was like the whole world was blue and red and orange flames. Then suddenly one of the logs—I don't know if it was because of pitch or trapped water—burst in half, and I jerked back.

But my body *didn't* jerk back. It was whatever rides around in my body—my spirit or mind or both, I don't know. It wasn't much more than a *moving point of view* really. It was moving back away from my body . . . so I saw my body sitting by the fire, leaning back on outstretched hands, staring blankly. I was floating upward, away from that body.

I remember thinking, *Is that what I look like? It's not like seeing yourself in a mirror. I look goofier than I thought.*

I wasn't scared at all. It was like I floated away from fear when I floated away from my body. Then I saw some wood, dust, and spiders, and I knew I was going through the ceiling. I saw my dad, his back to me. I tried to call out to him, but I couldn't speak.

Then I was falling, but falling *up*—that's how it felt, like I was free-falling but upward, really rocketing up over the cabin. Up was down, down was up, and I was falling up. I watched the roof of the cabin receding below me and the melted outline of the snowy fir trees. A white owl perched near the top of a pine. The owl seemed to see me as I passed. Then I fell upward into a hole in the sky. It was like it wasn't sky anymore—it was another world. I

saw men and women rising like threads of smoke around
me, each of them changing: They were a baby, a child,
they were adult, they were old, they were babies again . . .
flickering through that whole sequence and babbling to
themselves. I seemed to see a sky filled with stars that
were actually *words* of some kind, written in some language I couldn't understand. The stars seemed to be talking to me, all of them at once.

I remember thinking: *I'm dying. But what about Dad?*

That thought seemed to trigger a change, and I burst
out from the other world, back into the sky over the cabin.
It wasn't like I came from up or down or sideways, it was
like I *exploded into being* there, like fireworks expanding
from a small missile of chemicals to a big, flaring, burning, shining shape in the sky, all at once.

Then I was just a point of view again, and I was drifting down through the roof and down to the fireplace.

There was a nasty clicking feeling—definitely not
pleasant, it was like getting a hammer in the elbow—and
then I was back in my body, lying on my side, feeling sick
to my stomach. Shaking and crying.

My dad heard me and came downstairs to see what
was wrong and I tried to talk about it and couldn't. So finally I told him I'd fallen asleep and had a nightmare, and
after a while I almost believed that's what had happened.

The second time was almost a year later. I was at a
school in L.A., and I was depressed that day to start with.
I had PE first period, we were doing softball; and I missed
an easy catch—I just choked up—and then I struck out at
bat, and the other guys jeered at me big-time. Screwing
up in sports was standard for me. I was feeling pretty
down on myself. Then a girl I was interested in, Trisha,
who was editor of the school literary magazine, walked up
to me with a look on her face like she was going to eat
something tasty.

She said she'd gotten my note in her editorial cubby asking her if she wanted to go to the spring dance, and she said, "The answer is, please don't embarrass me again by asking. Some people heard about you asking me and they gave me a lot of crap. Capish?"

I don't know why I thought she'd be sensitive, editing the school literary mag. It was a lot of dreck anyway.

So I was even more down on myself after that encounter with Trisha, and then a big lunk of a kid named Greg Monnard spotted me after school. He was a kid with died-white Eminem hair, a thick, naturally brawny body, big feet that turned outward, and his pants hanging low off his ass. He walked up to me, with no expression at all on his face, and just knocked me down, *bang!*, with a right to the side of my head. I went down, I rolled onto my side. Then Greg sat on me, and whenever I tried to get up, he bent over and backhanded me or ground his heel into my knee. As he sat on me he lit a cigarette. "Sit still, till I'm done with my cigarette. I don't want to sit on the grass. I think there's dog shit on it." So he used me as his bench while he smoked his cigarette, just smiling a little bit, as if at all the irony in the whole world, while a crowd gathered to watch.

That's when it happened again. I just couldn't *stay* there. I had to, but I couldn't. So the part of me that can leave my body backed out and was hovering over Greg and the crowd and my body down there. Suddenly all the pain and misery was gone. I flew upward and I didn't want to come back to my body at all. I went through that hole in the sky and was back in the place where smoky spirits, changing from baby to child to adult to old, were floating upward, transforming as they went. The stars were talking runes again. And then I seemed to fly right into one of those stars, or through it like it was a door.

I passed through a world of living lightning bolts and then into a place where there was nothing but a constantly changing landscape, as if the land shifted like the sea does in a storm, and there were wailing, miserable spirits trapped there. Above them all was a being who was as big as a mountain, towering over everything. He had a beautiful face, and he had twisted horns, and he had wings that were broken and bleeding. His lower half was hidden because he was stuck in ice up to his waist—the ice was the only thing that didn't shift and change in that world.

He turned his head to look at me, and *I felt his looking* like an ant would feel the beam from a magnifying glass. I felt myself shriveling up under that gaze, and I knew I was going to be trapped there, too, if I stayed. So I thought about my dad, and my body, and how I wanted to grow up to be a rich and powerful man, who people wouldn't beat up on, and then I was back in my body, twisting out from under Greg Monnard.

I felt sick and disoriented, but different, and even stronger in some way. I guess it was that I wasn't afraid of Greg anymore. He seemed so *small* after what I'd seen.

So after I squirmed out from under him, I grabbed the cigarette out of Greg's mouth—he was pretty surprised!—and shoved it down his shirt. He backed away, yelling and slapping at himself, and then I kicked him hard in the pit of the stomach. He fell on his ass, gasping, and smoke was coming out of his shirt. I reached down, tugged it so the cigarette came out, and flicked it away. Somehow, taking the cigarette out of his shirt so it wouldn't hurt him anymore gave me some kind of style or grace, like I had some character he didn't have.

"I tried to let you be the big man," I said, "but you went too far. And you are just so *small.*"

Some of the people watching applauded, and Greg didn't bother me anymore after that.

But for the next couple of days I was afraid to sleep, afraid of my dreams, of feeling like the real world wasn't real enough. I decided that what I'd seen was some weird mental aberration, like a seizure, a hallucination like the things epileptics see. It worked in my favor this once, because in my disassociated state I'd lost my fear of Greg. But I decided I had to never let it happen again, because if I did let it happen, I was going to end up being put away somewhere. I'd get lost in my own head, and they'd put me in an asylum.

I saw ten minutes or so of a show about Out-of-Body Experiences—OBEs, they call them— on the Discovery Channel, a year or so later. I turned it off pretty quickly. *No,* I told myself, *bullshit. Not real.*

So I talked myself again into believing it hadn't been real.

But now, somehow, I know it was real. It was a real OBE. And maybe I have a kind of talent for it that Winderson wants to use somehow. So maybe it was a good thing.

I hope I can deal with it. Just seems to me that a person could go insane after a few experiences like that.

"I don't think we've met, have we, Mr. Isquerat?" the woman with the red-blond hair asked, riding up the elevator with him.

A little more blond than red, that long wavy hair. Stephen thought of a pinup girl from the middle of the last century, painted on some bomber: an almost perfect face, dimpled chin, something glittering in her crystalline blue eyes. She wore a red leather coat opened in the front to show off voluptuous curves tautly wrapped in a cream-colored blouse, a pantsuit, and red pumps to match her coat. Her nails were the color of her suit. He didn't usually note so many details, but this woman made Stephen stare. She was perhaps a little short, a little too plump, but she carried herself with the supreme confidence of an over-paid cover girl.

"You *are* Mr. Isquerat?"

"Hm? Oh, I'm sorry, I didn't answer you." He felt his face burning. He'd been staring instead of listening. "I mean, in my mind I answered yes."

"I'm not usually a mind reader. Only every third Wednesday."

He chuckled dutifully, trying to identify her perfume. Gardenias? Yes, but very understated gardenias. The elevator reached the eleventh floor of the West Wind building and he followed her out. "I'm *Stephen* Isquerat. . . ."

"I'm the boss's niece. Better be nice to me!" Her face was deadpan, except her eyes laughed.

"There was never any chance I wouldn't be. I'm . . ." *No, don't say "I'm only human."* "Anyway—if you're Mr. Winderson's niece, then you're Jonquil? He mentioned you to me once."

"Well, he better had. He's under strict instructions to mention me to every up-and-coming guy he brings in around here."

"I don't know how up-and-coming I am. . . ."

"I hear he's got great plans for you. You're going to revive psychonomics, I think?"

"Maybe—soon as I figure out what it is."

She chuckled. "You and me both."

But somehow he thought she was just playing along, that she knew *exactly* what it was all about. It gave him an uneasy feeling, but he quickly forgot it, looking into her eyes. What was that song his dad had liked? *"Crystal Blue Persuasion"?* "Well . . . uh . . ." He looked around in confusion. Eleventh floor.

She pursed her lips to keep the smile out this time. "Wrong floor?"

"No, no I just . . ." He sighed. "Yes, okay. Wrong floor."

"I'll take that as flattery. See you later . . . two floors up, I think."

"Sure. Later . . ."

But he didn't see her till it was almost time for him to go to Ash Valley.

———

Ira was sipping coffee flavored with roses. Seated across from him, at the small table of the Turkish-style café, Yanan watched and almost smiled. Paymenz, sitting on his right, glowered into his own undrunk coffee, chewing fitfully on a gooey wedge of baklava. There was canned Turkish music playing, but Ira was only vaguely aware of it.

"You like the rose coffee?" Yanan asked. "You got such a look on your face, maybe you don't like it."

"I do though," Ira said. "It interests me. It's like . . . the taste of the coffee is interrupted by something anomalous—like planting a coffee bush in a rose garden—normal expectations are stretched, opened up. A certain delightful tension in the two flavors. And the smells are oddly harmonious."

Paymenz looked at him dourly. "All this from a sip of coffee? What, you're Proust now?"

"Well, I . . ."

Yanan laughed. "Look at Paymenz! He's in a bad mood! Why do you identify with your bad mood, Paymenz, eh?"

"You know my inner state so well? Just because I'm not kicking up my heels?"

Yanan only smiled. Paymenz shrugged and glanced at Ira, both of them thinking along the same lines: Yanan might well be able to see into Paymenz's inner state, even if the professor put up a good front.

Paymenz *was* in one of his dark moods; typically, he'd swing abruptly from ebullient to dark. It was an inborn tendency: He knew it, and everyone else knew it.

After a moment, Yanan said, "It's possible, Professor, you are not truly identified with your depressed mind. But I think you are. Like Ira, you worry about Melissa and the boy. Nyerza is with them—they will be all right. But perhaps it's more selfish than that, hm?"

Paymenz nodded, smiling sourly. "Yes indeed. It's also a feeling that the important part of my life is over. I did too much damage to my soul before the invasion. And now . . . I have lost hope for myself. I'm too tired to find what I once had. I don't even know what to do professionally anymore. I'm angry that all that was revealed to the world those nine years ago is . . . lost. So even that effort seems wasted. I know—it's self-pity. Or sounds like it."

"My friend, you are traveling through a desert called the terrible truth of old age. It is long before the oasis. But the oasis will come. And . . . in the meantime—eh?"

Paymenz nodded. "I know. In the meantime."

Ira sipped his coffee and glanced at his watch. He had an art lesson to give in forty-five minutes. He reached for his baklava, but then withdrew his hand; he didn't want to get honey on his fingers. He had his portfolio with him, leaning against the wall, and there was artwork he was supposed to show Yanan. "You really think—" He broke off as the Turkish music came to a sudden stop. Suddenly the little café was jarringly quiet.

They were the only ones in the place besides the proprietor—a bald, swarthy, stocky man with a white handlebar mustache, who was flagrantly breaking state law by smoking a cigarette as he moved about the little kitchen. The cessation of music made Ira lower his voice. "Do you really think that people can have forgotten, Professor?"

Paymenz snorted contemptuously. "Humanity wants to sleep. They want to believe it was a terrorist attack and a few lunatics in costumes, some explosives. Computer-animation on television. Hallucinogens in the air and water. They want to believe that the terrorist cell the government identified is real, that one of those men killed the President. They want to believe that what they themselves saw wasn't real. Or anyway they want to tell their children that. It is a conspiracy to pretend. There are no photographs, no film of the demons anymore . . . nothing to contradict the easy explanation."

"I've heard a hundred theories about what happened to all the visual records," Ira said, "but nothing convincing. I mean, some of it *was* confiscated—but they say even that went blank. And the government's reconfigured the refineries, destroyed the Zone rooms—but they pretend that nothing supernatural happened. A collective, willful amnesia. Even the videotapes have gone amnesiac."

"Maybe," Yanan said, "God Himself wiped it clean. Perhaps, maybe, eh? So that we may have faith and believe in the invisible world without evidence."

"My opinion . . ." Paymenz looked at Yanan, asking if he should give it. Yanan was teacher to both of them.

Yanan nodded.

Paymenz went on. "My opinion is that Yanan is partly right—God *permitted* the erasure. But it was That Certain One who did it. Or spirits at his command. They know that nonbelief is their ally. If people have evidence of the dark side of the supernatural world, then they know that there must also be another side. Demons imply angels! And God does not want human beings to expect angels to come to their aid. God wants *humanity* to help humanity."

Yanan nodded. "God works through men. The good works of God are the good works of men; the good works of men are the good works of God."

"But I don't understand how people can disbelieve what they saw with their own eyes," Ira persisted. "Well, of course— not everyone does. I've got a friend who's an old hand at taking psychedelic drugs. He says he knows when he's hallucinating. And he knows he wasn't hallucinating then. He says he knows what he saw, and I sure as hell know what *I* saw. But there was a TV special about the invasion, and *everyone* they spoke to said it was a hallucination augmented by hysteria, mass hypnosis, elaborate costumes, or something . . . people psychologically adapting to mass murder. The show claimed people couldn't deal with the thought of so much mindless carnage, so they had to imagine demons instead of people." He snorted. "But given history— Who was it said 'History is a list of crimes'? Humanity slides into its worst behavior at the slightest excuse—" He broke off. Yanan was staring at him. "I've been pontificating again."

"Yes, but also—your faith is weak." Yanan leaned toward him. "Still, eh? Yes? It's good to ask—how can people fall so easily the victim of this nonbelief, denying what they saw with their own eyes? Exactly, yes. There is a reason people are so willing to forget—so I believe. There is another *influence* at work, my friend."

Ira looked at him, shivering a little at the thought. "You mean that the same force that erased the pictures erases people's minds? Or just blurs their memories?"

"Ah. Minds are connected to souls—and souls resist this erasing. But the influence is there. It tries. And many weak souls give in. It is as Paymenz says: People want to sleep, eh?

But not everyone." He leaned back in his chair and slapped the table. "But you, Ira! What help are you? These others at the group sitting today, they are like our children. You and Paymenz and I—we are to take care of them. They think it is a Sufi meditation. It is that, eh? But we, you and I, we know the greater meaning—we know what honey is made, when it works." He picked up a bit of baklava, rolled it between thumb and forefinger, put it to his lips, and tasted it. "Honey! Another kind of honey. The food that feeds the Gold in the Urn. But what do you do? Let yourself go to sleep in your dreams of worry. All dreams of worry! When I need you to be the—the *sustainer* for the energy, for the transformation, the making of the honey I am cultivating there. Paymenz, he did his part. But you! You are the self-pity man! Hm? Yes?"

Ira cleared his throat. "Yes."

"Good. Try again some more next time. Now, you said you have pictures for me?"

Ira hesitated. He wanted to ask about Melissa, but most likely if Yanan knew anything else to reassure him, he'd have told him. He nodded and opened the portfolio. "You asked me to do that . . . the certain meditation you taught me. To draw afterward what came to me. Nothing much. Just this."

He handed Yanan a large pen-and-ink drawing, colored in lightly with felt-tip pens. It looked at first like an abstract image: a shiny roundness pressed off center into an iridescent web of lines with just the faintest suggestion of a face, bent and ghostly, in the round shape. Paymenz looked at it and shook his head. Yanan stared.

"It's not much of anything—" Ira began.

Yanan raised a hand for silence and sat back, closed his eyes. He seemed to settle into himself. His lips moved. There was a faint murmur now and then—words in Greek, Ira thought—though Yanan wasn't Greek.

Ira exchanged glances with Paymenz. Yanan was in contact with others in the Conscious Circle.

A moment more, and he opened his eyes, shuddering. "It is the Black Pearl," he muttered wearily. "The Undercurrent has all of us in its grip—and there is one who can turn the current another way and give us a chance to swim free."

"Who?" Ira asked, thinking it would be Melissa.

"His name is Stephen . . . something like Iskiera, I think. Or something close to this. If we can create a strong enough circle, the Urn will find a way to touch him. But it is probably already too late for Stephen. And therefore too late for all of us."

THE JOURNAL OF STEPHEN ISQUERAT

Am writing this on my laptop, while I wait for my breakfast. I'm in a chain restaurant, didn't even notice the name, halfway to Bald Peak, my first new West Wind assignment. Got the keys to my company rental from Jonquil Winderson just this morning. Our hands brushed as she gave it to me. I kid myself her hand sort of lingered. But no way. She had peach-colored nails today and a peach-colored dress. Very tight, that dress. She should have pity on guys like me who don't get laid.

People in the booth behind me are talking about the Demon Hallucinations as if it'd all been real, and I wish they'd keep their crank ideas to themselves. I've got a raise, on my way to a promotion, I should feel good, but I've got some kind of butterflies.

Is it second thoughts, or is it just nervousness I'm feeling? Just a kind of stage fright because I'm about to do some serious work in front of the bosses, and they're like critics ready to judge how well I dance to their tune? But

there it is again, that feeling of doubt or cynicism or something. I'm confused, I guess.

Ever since I watched Dad die, knowing if he'd had
better insurance, more money, he'd probably have beaten
the cancer, I've just wanted to make money and be one of
the people who're taken care of when he gets sick. One
of the people who gets listened to. They don't listen to
schoolteachers like Dad. No one does anymore. They stick
the kid in front of an Internet tutor half the day and they
play games that're supposed to be educational. There's no
room in that world for guys like my dad.

I don't know why I'm obsessing about it. It's not like
my options are "Be Like My Dad" or "Be Mister MBA." I
could do lots of other things. The world is crazy—people
hallucinated demons and pretended to *be* demons. In a
world like that, if a man stays rational, stays alert, he can
clean up. When everybody else is flipped out, he's watching for the *opportunity*.

So now I see my opportunity. I kiss up to Winderson
by playing his psychonomics game for a while. If I have
the ability to leave my body and do some business spying
for him, what the hell. I get that over with, then I get
some field experience, I'm groomed to be a VP and then—
who knows?—director of marketing. So I've got to put all
these weird doubts behind me.

I remember having that dream about the old lady and
then seeing her. I see Mr. Deane on that bed, that senile
anger trapped in him, even though he seems frozen somehow, I start to get nervous. I think it's my dad's voice in
my head, like the transactional therapy people would say.
"Son, you've got to do something that's useful for the
world, for everyone—not just yourself. That's what feels
right in the soul." And that dad in me is trying to get me
to back off West Wind.

Except that doesn't make sense, because he set me up

with West Wind in the first place. But, somehow, I figure that he did that out of disappointment. That he was hoping I'd see what it was like and want to do something else.

Just shows how he didn't know me. He never understood the high I got doing online trading. But I've got to wonder, with all the money at West Wind's disposal, if they can't help George Deane, if they can't heal him—how much does money really help? Maybe, when something wants to get you, it just gets you. No matter what.

I'm still adjusting to the idea that my OBEs were real, that I can use them in a practical way.

Something else occurred to me. If those experiences were real, then there *is a soul* that can leave the body. What if that means there's life after death! Otherwise, why have a soul that can live without the body? So if there's life after death, then maybe my dad isn't really dead. His soul is out there somewhere. Maybe I can see him again. And my mom. Maybe, all kinds of things. It makes me feel like I could melt into this chair. Why'd I write that, about melting into the chair? It doesn't make sense.

Another thing. If there's life after death, then maybe some other parts of religion are true.

Okay, here she comes with my eggs and ham. Don't know if I can eat much. Queasy.

I've got to shake off this nervous bullshit and focus on the job.

Turkmenistan: between Uzbekistan, Iran, and Afghanistan

Melissa closed her eyes against the insistent cloud of dust, and she blew at the inside of her veil, trying to keep the fine brown desert powder from caking there.

She sat in the front passenger seat of the Jeep parked on

the dirt road, next to the old pickup truck. She checked on Marcus, hugged to her side, to make sure the blanket was still cocooned snugly around him. She wished that Nyerza would return from the little stucco building off to one side or that they might go in with him. She could just make out the truck, parked beside the Jeep, whenever the clouds parted enough to admit some moonlight. The two Turkmen escorts in the wind-scoured Ford pickup were trustworthy enough, but the dark and the dust and the wind all seemed part of some malignant entity bent on demoralizing her. She knew it wasn't—she knew enough about discorporate malignant entities, and herself, to know what was a real diabolic influence and what arose from her own worried imagination.

The dust subsided, and she felt Marcus stir under her arm. "Mom?" His voice came sleepily.

"Shhh . . . go back to sleep."

"Can we get out of this Jeep, Mom?"

"Not for a while. Soon."

The boy coughed under the blanket. Maybe they *should* go inside, regardless of the warnings their guides had given them. Nyerza was in the little building where the gravel road forked, just a hundred fifty feet away. But their guides had warned them about the Tekke tribesmen who sometimes took shelter in these old Soviet outposts. Some were known to take outsiders, and sell them to the outlawed Islamic militants, who then held them for ransom. In the post–Soviet era, the Turkmenistan government, though independent of Russia, was still semisocialist, based on the iron-handed Soviet model but more concerned with their oil and gas pipelines than policing the Tekke. And some had reverted to their nineteenth-century brigandage.

The cold wind rolled across the plains like a breaker, gusting imperiously out of Russia, slapping them with dust from the Kara Kum desert. She glanced toward their guides' truck. One corner of the truck's dark side window pulsed red with a cigarette's ember as one of the Turkmen sucked at the harsh Russian tobacco. What were these guides good for if they didn't even know the way to the Fallen Shrine? She coughed, and had just decided to take Marcus inside, when firelight sketched the edge of the building's opening door, and she saw Nyerza stooping to step through. He turned back and waved to someone inside. She glimpsed a stocky bearded man wearing a *telpek*, the shaggy brimless hat of the desert Turkmen. Nyerza made a farewell gesture she'd seen Muslims give—he could seem utterly Muslim when he chose—and strode out toward the Jeep, fighting the wind, picking his way over the rough ground, an absurdly elongated, wavering figure in the streamers of dust flickering in the dawn light.

She found herself thinking of someone else entirely as she watched Nyerza approach: Ira, back home in a more familiar world, giving his art lessons, studying with Yanan, drawing, worrying. She felt a surge of warmth when she remembered the struggle in him—she'd felt it so palpably, when he'd agreed to let her come without him, to bring Marcus, to go with Nyerza. Knowing his jealousy of Nyerza but letting her go.

She asked herself for the hundredth time why she'd come. She asked something within her, but her connection to the Urn had gone silent some time ago. They were preoccupied or chose to be unresponsive. They gave no answer. Perhaps they'd withdrawn from her entirely.

Perhaps she was unworthy.

Drawing his robes closer around him, the tall African ducked down behind the windshield, settled back in his seat. He bent and spoke behind a cupped hand into her ear, to be heard over the wind. "They gave me a map. Perhaps it's good.

The wind will ease as the daylight comes. We'll go to the foot of Mount Rize before we rest."

She would have liked to put up their tents somewhere sheltered. She was grittily tired; her eyes ached; she was hungry. But Nyerza had said they were to move as quickly as they could.

He glanced at her, seemed to cast about for a subject to take her mind off her fatigue. He bent near again. "Do you know how many of them are in that building?"

"Couldn't be room for more than twenty at the most."

"I counted sixty-three, mostly men, a couple of crones, one young wife, a handful of children."

"Sixty-three! In that little building!"

"Not only that but two horses! The less valuable horses are out back, in improvised shelters. It's crowded, but more protection than a yurt. They travel in extended families—and no one is to be left without shelter. But that is how I left you! I'm sorry to leave you out here. Those oafs in the truck should have traded places with you while we waited."

"It's all right. I think Marcus has gone to sleep anyway."

As he put the Jeep in gear, the window of the truck rolled down, shedding dust, and a bearded face peered out through a wreath of smoke. Nyerza gave a thumbs-up and said something in Russian. The Turkmen spoke a combination of Turkish, Russian, and Azeri; they understood Russian well enough. They nodded, and the truck roared to life. The Jeep led the way, jouncing along the rutted gravel road.

The road cut straight across the plain for eight miles more, then advanced windingly up the spine of a ridge. The great sea of dust parted before them like the Red Sea before Moses, settling as the wind dropped. Now and then, following the road— or did the road follow them?—there were standing stones.

They might once have been sculpted, but windblown sand had removed any traces of man, except for their stubborn, precariously balanced uprightness.

The two vehicles bounced up the ridge's spine toward the foothills of Mount Rize. In the distance, where the first sunlight shifted indigo plains to reaches of lifeless blue and outcroppings of stony dun, there were points of unsteady flickering. "What is that—city lights?" she asked.

"No—you see how it wavers? It's flame. Those are the new natural gas fields—they're doing some burn-off. When the gas reserves were discovered, the Russians were sorry they'd let Turkmenistan go. And there are new oil wells, too, south of here."

"Oil! When will it be enough? We have hydrogen cars now, and electric cars."

"Those are only prevalent in America and Europe, somewhat in Japan. Most of the world still burns gasoline and slowly melts the ice caps. Is there any bottled water left?"

"Yes, I think Marcus has it. How far to the shrine?"

"About a hundred and fifty miles, but some of it we will have to go on horseback."

She reached under the blanket for the plastic water bottle Marcus held in his arms as he slept and felt a dreadful clamminess on the boy's wrist, a throbbing heat from his forehead. "Oh, no. Marcus? Are you all right? How do you feel? Marcus!"

The boy didn't reply.

"Marcus?" He remained limp, unresponsive. With trembling hands she fumbled the Mediscan kit from the satchel on the floor, found the general indications scanner, and pressed it to his temple. "Stop the Jeep—I can't read this with all the bouncing!"

Nyerza signaled the truck, and the two vehicles lurched to a stop in a plume of dust. She pressed the scanner to the boy's sweat-beaded forehead, and squinted at its miniature, green-glowing screen.

"What is it?" Nyerza asked.

She let out a long, ragged breath. "I can't wake Marcus. His blood pressure is mortally low. And he has a temperature of a hundred and five."

3

Bald Peak, Northern California

Stephen was poised on the edge of paradise, or so it seemed to him.

He stood on a cliff's edge, on the grassy grounds of the old Bald Peak Observatory, gazing down over Ash Valley. He stood there in the gentle breeze, his hands in the pockets of a heavy black overcoat, ducking his head so that the thin, drizzling rain didn't slant past his plastic-coated hat brim.

Three parallel slanting shafts of light transfixed the great green and golden bowl of Ash Valley, sunlight breaking through gaps in the uneasy roof of blue-gray clouds. The beams of light shifted like spotlights over the rolling, piney hills, the winding olive-dun river, clusters of tree-hugged houses, and stubbly cornfields cupped by the Northern California highlands. At the northern end of the valley, the ground dipped to the silvery snail tracks of rice field canals.

"It's an experiment," said a feminine voice just behind him. He turned and saw a short, slightly plump woman in a rust-colored windbreaker, the hood up. Stephen found he was startled by her lively golden-brown eyes, the lustrous brown hair trapped by the hood, churning in curls and framing her face. She smiled, dimpling cheeks red from the wind. He thought about Winderson's niece, Jonquil, so different from this woman, but it was a bracing difference.

"Which experiment is that?" Stephen asked. He didn't yet want to ask her name; he wanted to remain suspended in the delicious uncertainty of the moment there on the edge of a rain-softened abyss.

"The rice fields. I thought you were looking at them with a kind of what-the-devil-are-those look. That's wetlands there, at the north end of the valley. It's stocked with wetlands birds who eat insects and grubs but not rice. The birds are supposed to take care of the rice, while the rice fields provide wetlands for them. And wetlands, of course, protect the rest of the valley from flooding. But since West Wind has bought most of the valley, I'm not sure what they'll do with that land."

He could tell she was trying to keep regret from her voice.

"You live down there?" he asked.

"Me? No! I live at the observatory now—of course, it's not used as an observatory much anymore. I work for West Wind, like you. I'm Glyneth Solomon. You *are* Stephen Isquerat, aren't you?"

"Thank you for pronouncing my name right. It's refreshing. I hear Isk-rat a lot. I haven't checked in yet. West Wind already knows I'm here?"

"Seems so. They sent me out to ask if you needed to know how to get into the building. I guess—" her smile flashed and hid itself again "—they couldn't figure out why you'd be standing out here looking at the valley."

He turned and looked back at Ash Valley. "I just thought it was . . . beautiful. Even in the rain. Even more in the rain, maybe. I don't know. My mood today—" He broke off, wondering why he was telling her this.

He looked at her but couldn't read her expression. It might have been sympathy and it might have been puzzlement. She said, "Did they tell you I was to be your new assistant?"

He shook his head. "No, but . . . that's great. I mean, they said I was to have an assistant. Good to meet you." He cleared his throat. "Well, I'm just getting soaked out here. Can you take me to the coffee?"

"I sure can. I know right where it is. Then we'll locate Dickinham—he'll want to show you around."

Portland, Oregon

Ira had a cat in his lap and a laptop on the worktable in front of him. He was waiting for Melissa to call.

He was searching online for the name Iskeriat or Isqueriat and all the variations he could come up with, working in the cone of light from a gooseneck lamp, now and then elbowing art supplies out of the way. And he was waiting for Melissa to call.

Why did she have to take Marcus? he asked himself for the hundredth time. The boy should be in school. He should be here, where he could be safe and live a normal child's life. He should be here *playing*, for God's sake. He thought about Marcus playing with Paymenz's cats. Getting down on the floor, on his hands and knees, butting heads with a cat, laughing when it flopped on its back, a sign it wanted to play. "How'm I supposed to play that without any claws like you got?" the boy had asked. "You give me some claws, then I'll play that . . ."

"Very wise, Marcus," Paymenz had said. Right then, Marcus was showing off a tumbling move he'd learned, somersaulting into the side of Paymenz's overloaded desk, jarring it so that papers showered down on him. "It's rainin' paper!"

"Hey, Marcus," Ira had said, "you could've knocked off his expensive laptop." He had tried to scowl disapproval at the boy, but it was hard. Marcus's eyes were his mother's; the boy's smile was at once a paragon of innocence and sly humor.

A week later Marcus had gotten into some trouble in school. A parent-teacher conference was called. Marcus had apparently been singing a song he'd heard on the video channel. " 'I'm a sex god from the thirteenth hell, love in my touch but sulfur in my smell—oh, yeah, oh darlin' yeah.' " Singing it, moreover, while dancing around a little girl, Ira was told.

At the school, Marcus's pleasant, pretty Vietnamese-American teacher, Nhe, told him earnestly that the boy was guilty of sexual harassment.

"What's that?" Marcus had asked.

Ira shrugged. "They claim you were getting all sexy with the girl or something inappropriate like that."

"What girl?"

"Diane," Nhe said.

"When?"

"When you were dancing and singing that song about sex gods." Ira sighed—trying not to laugh.

"I only sang it once. I just like the sound of it. I didn't notice Diane. Is she that red-haired girl?" No, he was told; she was the girl with long black hair. "Well," Marcus said, "if I notice her, I won't sing it around her anymore. But if I don't notice her, I might sing it on accident."

"*By* accident," Ira had said automatically.

Ira told them he would see to it that the boy sang no more inappropriate songs at school.

They said fine, but Marcus would have to do some detention.

Marcus had taken it in stride, Ira thought tenderly, never sulking about the extra school time, though he had no enthusiasm for hanging around school unnecessarily. He had only smiled and said, "Okay."

In the car with Ira, on the way home, the boy had said, "I wasn't sexing at anybody."

"I know you weren't."

"But they thought I was. They were protecting her." More to himself, than to Ira.

Ira looked at the boy in admiration. He understood completely.

Marcus asked, "What is a sex god anyway?"

"Hell if I know, son."

They'd both laughed at that, the laughter between them like two colors in a painting, Ira thought, blending into one shade, making a single statement of affinity.

Now that laughing, forgiving boy was traveling with his mother through a desolate wasteland.

Ira had been trying not to think about it. Again and again doing the inner exercises Yanan had taught him, to stay centered, present, nonidentified. They worked for a while, but then he noticed the digital wall clock. She was supposed to have called through the satellite uplink. Both she and Nyerza had the equipment with them. He had checked with the international cell phone company. No problems there.

When he accidentally brushed his markers off the table, and they clattered on the floor, he didn't bend to pick them up. The sleek black cat stirred in his lap and looked into his face.

"Settle down, Daumal," Ira told the cat.

He couldn't find a meaningful match for his online search. He noticed the clock again and typed in a new search subject. TURKMENISTAN AND HUMAN RIGHTS. He selected a website from the list found by the search engine. He skimmed and scrolled down the page.

U.S. Department of Foreign Services Security and Human Rights Report: Turkmenistan

The government's human rights record remains extremely poor. The government continues to commit serious human rights abuses, and Turkmen authorities severely restrict political and civil liberties. A number of political prisoners have died in custody under suspicious circumstances. Security forces continue to beat and otherwise mistreat suspects and prisoners, and prison conditions remain poor and unsafe. Both the police and the KNB operate with relative impunity and abuse the rights of individuals, as well as enforce the government's policy of repressing political opposition. Arbitrary arrest and detention, prolonged pretrial detention, unfair trials, and interference with citizens' privacy remain problems.

The government completely controls the media, censoring all newspapers and rarely permitting independent criticism of government policy or officials.

Ira stopped when he came to one comment in particular. He reread it:

The government imposes restrictions on nonregistered religious groups. The law allows the government to tighten control of religious groups. It is required that all religious organizations include at least 500 Turkmen citizens as members in a given locality in order to be registered legally. This has prevented all but Sunni Muslims and

Russian Orthodox Christians from legally establishing themselves.

Ira found himself squeezing the cat against his belly so hard that it clawed at him to get away. He let Daumal jump to the floor and tried to marshal his thoughts.

Melissa and Nyerza were going to the Fallen Shrine. Surely what remained of the ancient school at the Fallen Shrine would be regarded as a nonapproved religious group—though they were not actually religious at all, in the usual sense. But a government wouldn't distinguish between a metaphysical science and a religion.

He leaned over the laptop, scrolled farther down the page.

The government imposes some restrictions on freedom to travel abroad. Domestic violence against women is a problem, and women experience societal discrimination. The government generally gives favored treatment to men over women and to ethnic Turkmen over minorities.

In January, the Organization for Security and Cooperation in Europe (OSCE) opened an office in Ashgabat. In September, Georgei Garayev, a political prisoner and Russian citizen, was found hanged in his cell in the maximum security prison in Turkmenbashy. The government has rejected requests from the Russian government and international human rights organizations for an investigation into the suspicious nature of Garayev's death (see Sections 1.c. and 1.e.). The 1992 constitution makes torture or other cruel, inhuman, or degrading treatment illegal. However, there have been widespread credible reports that security officials frequently beat criminal suspects and prisoners and often use force to obtain confessions.

There have been credible reports that political prisoners are singled out for cruel treatment. Security forces also use denial of medical treatment and food, verbal intimidation, and unsanitary conditions to coerce confessions. Jehovah's Witnesses reportedly were beaten while in police custody in September (see Section 2.c.). Prisons are unsanitary, overcrowded, and unsafe. Food is poor, and infectious diseases are rampant. Facilities for prisoner rehabilitation and recreation are extremely limited. Some prisoners have died due to overcrowding, untreated illnesses, and lack of adequate protection from the severe summer heat. Women political prisoners are routinely prevented from seeing their children, who are often placed in state custody.

"Oh, shit," Ira said.

Bald Mountain Observatory, Northern California

It was chilly in the echoing, curved area of the telescope room, as Harold Dickinham gave Stephen and Glyneth the tour. "There's the telescope, still operational. Mr. Winderson comes and uses it once in a while. But most of us regard this room as wasted space. We could use a lot more lab room, and we're hoping Mr. Winderson will turn it over to us eventually."

Dickinham was a broad-shouldered, balding man with newly transplanted hair cropping out. Below squinting, almost colorless blue eyes, his nose showed broken red veins like those of an alcoholic, but which Stephen also associated with people who worked a great deal around pesticides. You saw them on the faces of exterminators. He associated cancer with that condition also—but more often than not cancer could be cured, nowadays. If you had the insurance coverage.

Looking around the big, shadowy, windowless dome, Stephen reflected that a converted observatory seemed an odd base of operations for a chemicals company carrying out a field experiment.

West Wind ostensibly fit the usual corporate paradigm. Like most corporations, they used temps whenever possible so as not to have to pay into retirement funds or insurance plans. They downsized personnel whenever they felt it would help their stocks; they arranged the usual tax loopholes; they maintained the usual corps of lobbyists and campaign-financed politicos; they pushed to be "self-regulating" so they could pollute without constraint.

But every so often, something peculiar cropped up at West Wind, like that one-patient hospice high in the pyramid building—and like psychonomics. And now this: a refitted observatory. Above Stephen, aimed at the closed hatch, the telescope looked like a giant insect, stymied as it sought to spring into the sky. Stephen wondered briefly what miniature stars and galaxies it could see in the paint-flaking, rusty metal hatches.

They left the observatory, going into a long curving room that followed the arc of the observatory's base. It had been retrofitted for use as a chemicals- and animal-testing lab, with long tables of beakers and sealed containers, each sporting its warning label, and cages and microscopes and PC monitors.

Dickinham rattled on proudly. "We've pulled all the old computers out of the digital-scan room and donated them to UC Davis. We use the site for agents-testing now, though we do have other plans for this section."

Stephen swallowed, looking neither to the right nor the left as he walked through the room—seeing only peripherally the cages of rabbits, rats, and chickens. Some of them were dead, some weren't.

What is this weakness I have for animals? he asked himself angrily. *It's stupid.*

It wasn't as if he were a vegetarian. But he didn't—couldn't—think about chicken or beef as coming from living things, things that walked around and breathed and suffered as they were slaughtered, before he ate them. His uncle had laughed in his face when he'd taken him on a hunting trip as a boy, and he'd burst into tears, watching the deer writhing from a bullet wound.

"Why don't you finish 'im for me, Stevie boy? Here—just put the muzzle right behind his ear. Come on, shoot 'im—your dad'd be ashamed if you don't do it."

That'd made the boyish Stephen take the rifle, shove the muzzle against the back of the deer's head, and pull the trigger. But he'd gotten sick when he'd blown its eyes out the front of its skull. And his uncle had laughed again.

Now, he felt Glyneth watching him, and he was relieved when they left the testing room and passed into other labs that were mostly storage—some of it refrigerated—for sundry volatile chemicals. There were complex devices for safely decanting them; and in room-sized glass boxes men in antitoxin suits, complete with helmets, worked with beakers of a rather pretty blue fluid.

Without thinking, Stephen commented, "Those suits—it's as if they're handling nerve gas. Is the stuff really that dangerous?"

Stephen regretted his outburst when Dickinham glanced sharply at him. "No. It isn't. It's just . . . before it's combined with other chemicals, it's pretty toxic. By the time it gets into the field, it's not bad at all. You know—diluted and muted. And we overcompensate here, for the safety of our employees."

"Sure, of course. I forgot. My specialty was always general business and marketing. I'm a little weak on the science side."

Dickinham grunted and led the way into a one-story rectangular building attached to the dome, into the smell of hot food and coffee. "Well now, Steve . . . Glyneth . . . what would you say to some lunch?" He gestured with humorous grandeur at a steaming buffet table laid out at one end of the little cafeteria.

Glyneth responded instantly, not quite deadpan, "What would I say? I'd say 'Lunch, I'm ready for you, so I hope you're ready for me.' "

Dickinham smiled apologetically at Stephen. "Those little jokes are a staple of Glyneth's."

"Makes the workday go faster, I'm sure," Stephen said, wincing inwardly at the forced sound of the remark.

"Is that our young Mr. Isquerat?" came Winderson's voice.

Stephen turned and jumped when he found Dale Winderson standing between him and the buffet table, beaming, thrusting out his hand. Winderson seemed eerily backlit by a wall light, his face half hidden in its glare.

"Well, Stephen, you going to shake my hand or just leave it there for a bird to build a nest on?"

"Sorry!" Stephen crossed to him and stuck out his own hand—which went right through Winderson's. He stared, then experimentally ran his hand through Winderson's middle. "A hologram!" The light behind Winderson's head was actually a little mobile projector that hovered like a flying penlight in midair.

Winderson laughed. "A damn good hologram, though! Most of 'em fall for it, and you did, too!" In the background, Dickinham was chuckling politely as the boss went on. "I've had projectors and surveillance put in most of the important West Wind research centers. I like to maintain an on-site presence of one kind or another." Winderson turned to Glyneth. "Who's the charmin' young miz?" Though he was in a transmission booth back at West Wind headquarters, his hologram mimicked his every movement.

"Ms. Glyneth Solomon," Dickinham said.

"Mr. Winderson," Glyneth said, pretending to curtsey, smiling just the right amount.

"A curtsey! I like that. Dickinham, why don't you curtsey? Call me Dale, Glyneth. I was just touring the facilities and thought I'd see if I could pull a fast one on young Stephen here. But you guys look hungry. You'll find West Wind does well by its employees in these outlying research centers. It's all catered in hot."

"It's damn good, too," Dickinham said redundantly.

"Well, I'm out of here. Just remember, Harry, Stephen's important to us. But see to it that he does plenty of bottom-floor work to get his feet wet, so to speak . . . all right?"

"Yes, sir, that was the memo. I'm on it."

"All righty." The hologram wiggled its fingers good-bye at them. "Check you later!" And he blinked out . . . gone.

Stephen shook his head, laughing softly. "Am I a chump or what?"

Glyneth said, "Or what. You hungry?"

They heaped their sectioned trays with boeuf bourguignon, surprisingly fresh vegetables, rice, and apple crisp, then sat at tables near the long strip of windows looking out over the valley. Out there, a rainbow shimmered in and out of view through leaden gossamers teased from the clouds. Inside, cutlery clicked, and for a while no one looked up from their food except to make an occasional casual remark.

Other workers came to the buffet and sat at tables in twos and threes, men and women in white coats and hairnets, with rueful smiles or an air of quiet brooding. Some of them had reddish noses with broken veins.

A white-haired man with long sideburns, purplish lips, and doughy features slapped his tray down across from Stephen. Dickinham introduced him with a notable lack of enthusiasm. "This is Fritz Crocker, our head of D17 research."

Crocker grinned at them. Some of his teeth were a little too white, a little too straight, in contrast to the others, artificial perfection side by side with natural snaggles. "How're you likin' that French beef dish, there, Steve?"

What accent was that? Maybe Florida? Stephen nodded approvingly over his meal. "Much better than I expect from a buffet."

"You can't taste the Dirvane 17, of course," Crocker said casually, "but it's there—you know, residual, from the feed the beef got. We wouldn't test anything on the public we weren't willing to digest our own selves, right, Steve?"

Stephen, chewing a mouthful of beef, glanced at Crocker and then at his plate. Reluctantly, he swallowed the stuff, almost choking.

Crocker exploded with laughter.

And Dale Winderson blinked back into the room, appearing seated in a chair at Crocker's elbow, saying, "Don't mind this chowderhead, Stephen."

Crocker jumped, almost as startled as Stephen at Winderson's magical arrival.

"Crocker's having his little joke," Winderson continued. "Of course we don't eat Dirvane-contaminated food ourselves."

"I suppose we run enough risk of exposure to organic compounds, just working in the business," Glyneth remarked, as if she weren't talking to a hologram.

"Hm? Yes, exactly." The hologram of Winderson appeared to squint at Glyneth, as if to see her better, but it was looking a bit to the left of her.

"I was just havin' some fun with the new guy," Crocker said. "Food's safe, Stevie, don't worry about it. Pullin' your leg."

"Practical jokes seem to be popular around here," Stephen said, trying to find the right smile and tone to convey what a good sport he was. "Maybe I should think up one or two of my own."

"You do that," Winderson's hologram said with a wink. Then he seemed to look intently into nowhere—at something in the room where he actually was. "Jonquil! It's all right, my dear. No great need for privacy here. Come into the projector field and say hello. You remember Stephen . . . and Dickinham. There, in that screen."

Suddenly half a woman was there—the right half, split down the middle. A holographic projection of part of Jonquil. "Hi, Stephen. Hi, you guys!" she said, all the words said with half a mouth.

"You're only half there, Jonquil," Stephen said, his heart thudding. "I know the feeling. Great to see even half of you again."

She chuckled and stepped farther into the field, the rest of her appearing. She looked as if she'd been poured into what might have been, on some other woman, a simple coatdress. Silver-gray and blue, conservatively cut, but on her the garment had the impact of lingerie—quite possibly it was a little too small for her. "Is that better? Am I all there yet?"

"As much as you'll ever be!" Winderson said, the joke coming rather distractedly. He seemed to be staring at something else again that was out of hologram range.

Stephen tried to think of something to say, to keep her there. She was such a relief, after this bleak place, these mostly unrelatable people. Her blue eyes glimmered, even in a hologram. Her pearly smile seemed to beckon him, and she tossed her head a little as if the long wavy blond hair had gotten in her eyes, though it hadn't. "I came to tell my uncle he's expected for a business dinner with the second most powerful Japanese businessman in the world, and here he is trading jokes with you guys. That's so typical. I don't see how he makes any money, I really don't."

"The other corp heads just take pity on me, honey dear,"

Winderson said. It seemed to Stephen that Winderson's hand went behind her, as if to cup her shapely ass; and she stiffened, her smile strained. But that couldn't be right—she was his niece. "Okay, muh dear, tell 'em I'm rushing down there right now. I don't want to keep Mr. Koto waiting a second longer than I have to."

"Like he'll believe that. But I'll tell 'im." She turned to look approximately toward Stephen. "Good to see you."

He wanted to think of something that would convey his eagerness to see her again without upsetting the social apple cart. But all that would come was, "Me, too." He winced, thinking, *That was lame,* but then she was gone.

And Winderson put on his serious face. "Joking around is fine—even important sometimes—but never forget that our purpose here is serious. You are the vanguard of West Wind, all of you. We're counting on a revolution in pest control and in marketing. That's your cue, Fritz."

"Yes, sir, you bet—"

But Winderson blinked out again.

Stephen stared at the empty chair. "How does he project himself—his image—into a chair so . . . I mean, a standing image in the middle of the floor I can figure but sitting . . ."

"We have the best communications technology available," Dickinham said proudly. "Projects him right where he wants to be—and how he wants to be."

"I see." Stephen remembered his discussion with Winderson about the so-called demonic invaders, and found himself wondering if this kind of holographic technology could have been used along with other devices—robotics?—to create the *illusion* of a demonic invasion. For a moment he wished he were back on that white-sand island, with its patchy communications, even its badly ventilated factory and its blissful ignorance of the whole hysterical, apocalyptic mess.

There was a moment of awkward silence in the cafeteria, broken by the murmurs from other tables, arcane discussions about chemical compounds, talk of stock options, and the distinctly annoying sound of Crocker chewing. Stephen found that he was uncomfortable—even afraid. He had no idea why. It wasn't Winderson's unseen presence, really. It was some other unseen presence.

He looked around. It seemed to him for a moment as if everyone were chewing in unison. Dickinham and Crocker both had their mouths open, chewing green vegetables with march-like regularity.

Stephen looked away. Sipping cranberry juice, he glanced at Glyneth—and found she was looking at him. It wasn't as if she were staring at him. It was as if, somehow, she were looking for something in his face. Watching and waiting.

A gust of wind rattled the window—like a distant, frustrated roar.

To relieve his unease, Stephen asked Dickinham, "Do you have a specific agenda for me here? Frankly, Dale was kind of vague about it." He wondered how much they knew about psychonomics. Winderson had told him firmly that he wasn't to discuss it with anyone.

Crocker put a lot of jeering into one syllable: "Dale?"

Stephen shrugged. "He asked me to call him Dale. Although it's true I didn't have the nerve to call him that to his face just now. Mr. Winderson, then."

Crocker grunted and seemed about to say something else, then glanced at the chair beside him and thought better of it. Winderson might be listening.

Odd, Stephen reflected, knowing that Winderson could be watching them electronically, eavesdropping on them like a trickster god from mythology brooding over his minions.

Dickinham seemed to be pondering Stephen's question.

Then he put down his fork, made a tent out of his fingers, and said, "Okay, it's like this. They've got you slated to do some kind of special work—some kind of experiment. They're preparing for all that in some way—and meanwhile we're supposed to get you ready by giving you experience in the field. Stuff you wouldn't ordinarily do. West Wind fieldwork."

Crocker snorted. "Like a silver-spoon kid who has to do a little work on the assembly line before he gets to inherit."

Dickinham shook his head. "No, there's some other reason. I don't know what it is, though."

Stephen thought it might be good if he didn't seem entirely out of the loop. "As far as I can work it out, from what you're telling me and what . . . Mr. Winderson . . . has said, it's probably about getting me ready to market Dirvane 17 and other West Wind products, and to get ideas for doing that I need to get out into the field, see the stuff doing its work firsthand. Like when we did that Petrochemicals Changing Lives campaign. Some of our copywriters went out to the oil rigs and got a sense of the way the oil comes right out of the ground. Then, in the commercial, we traced it all the way to the production of plastics used in a kid's toy. From the guy programming the rig robotics to the kid playing with the plastic truck."

Dickinham blinked at him. "Yeah. It could be. You know. Something like that."

Portland, Oregon

"You could do it if you wanted to, Yanan," Ira was saying. They stood in the chilly entryway of the old, rented Odd Fellows' lodge hall where they'd held their meeting that evening: a little room of excessively lacquered wooden floors, mildewed walls, and a rack of rain-musty coats. "They were supposed to call me today—and they didn't call at the fallback time. Both she and Nyerza have palm communicators. There should be a good satellite fix now. *But they didn't call.*"

Yanan nodded. His dark eyes were full of understanding, but they were also unyielding. "Yes, I see. There could be many reasons, eh? You are too soon panicking. I cannot call them any better than you can."

Ira's heart was pounding. It was a terrible thing to have to confront Yanan in this way. Yanan was a father figure to him, really. And he'd never known his own father.

"You *can* talk to Nyerza. You're part of the circle. You can . . . you know . . ."

Yanan looked at him blankly. "No. I don't know, hm?"

"The Conscious Circle. Like the other day in the café . . ."

"And what happened the other day in the café?"

"You . . ." Ira lowered his voice. "You contacted the Circle, telepathically or presciently."

"Did I say to you I did such a thing?"

"Not exactly, but you closed your eyes, you went into a sort of trance, and you came out of it with information."

"It was only a reverie. Perhaps—perhaps someone had told me something earlier in the day and I remembered it then, eh?"

Ira turned away, grabbed his coat, jerking it off the hook. He began to put it on, but in his angry confusion he couldn't find the sleeve. He knew he shouldn't make a decision in anger and fear, but the feelings had taken him, and he couldn't stop now. He didn't really want to stop.

"You are too lost in your anger, taken by it, you cannot even put on your coat, Ira." Yanan helped him into the sleeve, showing not the least exasperation. There was no sense of tension about him to match Ira's.

Ira turned toward him. "So you don't trust me enough to speak plainly." *Or perhaps,* Ira thought, *he's taken a vow never to speak of such things outright—some adepts did.* "But you *know* you could help me find them."

Yanan sighed gently and gazed into the middle distance. "Something . . . prevents me."

"Some impulse prevents you? Meaning you don't want to. Fine. But I'm going—I have some money put aside. I'm going to fly to Ashgabat."

Yanan smiled. "You will find it difficult to find a direct flight to such a place from America. Perhaps in Turkey."

"I'll do what I have to," Ira said flatly, again turning away.

Yanan laid a gently restraining hand on his arm. "No—I cannot allow this. You stay here and work with me. Have faith, hm?"

Ira struggled within himself. He felt he was about to be caught up in some powerful internal momentum; he was poised on the edge of a long, dark path into a trackless wasteland . . .

. . . And plunged down that path, making up his mind not to look back. He said, with finality, "I've lost touch with my wife and child. I'm going to find them."

He turned and stalked out the door, hurrying to leave before Yanan could use the force of his personality, if that was the word, to stop him.

"Ira—wait now! This is not a good time for this!" Yanan called from the door, as Ira plunged into the cold, brittle, windless night.

Ira hurried to his little hydrogen-cell scooter, straddled and started it, then U-turned into the street. He felt some satisfaction—and shame at the satisfaction—hearing Yanan shouting after him to stop.

He decided to go right to the airport. *Long-term parking,* he thought, *very long-term*. He would call the professor about feeding the cats. He could buy clothes and supplies in Turkey.

It wasn't till he was boarding a plane for New York that he remembered Yanan's words: *Something . . . prevents me.*

And he realized that he had probably mistaken Yanan's meaning.

4

Turkmenistan

Melissa was the first on that cold, windy morning to see the Turkmen state security agents. The trucks quivered in the screen of the digital binoculars.

There was a caravan of four vehicles crossing the sere basin below, about a quarter mile off and coming right for them: one covered Jeep and three twentieth-century SUVs, painted olive, with the insignia of Turkmenistan state on the sides.

She didn't say *Oh, shit.* But she thought it.

She and Nyerza were pulled up on the edge of a bluff, overlooking the basin.

A crumbling road, not much more than a wide trail, snaked down the side of the bluff into the basin. Across the lowlands rose the foothills of the mountain where the Fallen Shrine was supposed to be. "What do you see?" Nyerza asked her, removing his dusty goggles, as she lowered the digital binoculars. The cold, sleety wind scoured at them.

"Four vehicles—with government insignia. From what I read, a state security roving team."

Their guides had pulled the tired old truck up behind them—and she knew, without even turning around, what it meant when they gunned their rackety engine. The truck's suspension creaked in protest as they turned it around.

Nyerza tried to shout after them, but his voice betrayed his resignation. Their guides were running, abandoning them to the tender mercies of Turkmenistan state security.

She and Nyerza couldn't follow. The nearest help, if any, was at the shrine. And she had to get Marcus to medical help at any cost.

Nyerza sat down with a shrug. "They weren't much use anyway." He took the binoculars and had a look for himself. "You're probably right—state security agents in the field . . . far afield indeed. Perhaps you should try the satellite phone again."

"I just tried it. It's no good. There's some kind of interference—or else it's broken. I don't know . . . Ira must be worried." She turned to look into the nest they'd made of blankets in the back, where Marcus was curled up; she lifted the scrap of canvas that sheltered him from the wet wind. The boy was shaking, pale, sweating. His lips were cracked; his eyes open slightly, seeing nothing, at least nothing in this world. She poured water from a plastic jug onto a cloth and draped it over his head. She tried to get him to drink, but he pushed the jug away. Her stomach twisted, and she wanted to scream at Nyerza, *Get us to help!* But she knew he was doing everything he could. "How far to the shrine?"

"Only thirty miles. But the security men are in the way. We're clearly in their view. I don't see a way around them—unless they're not interested in us. However, I suspect they are."

She shivered as another spatter of sleet whipped over the Jeep. Long since the Jeep's canvas roof had been blown off.

"And," Nyerza added, "I think we're nearly out of fuel."

She centered herself, stepped back mentally from her inner agitation. "We shouldn't assume they are after us. We've done nothing. We're not on any kind of mission that should worry them."

"You're speaking as if state security is rational in a country like this, or even efficient. But as you say, we cannot know. Let us go on as if we were not worried about them."

"Who knows—maybe they can help Marcus."

Nyerza said nothing to that.

They descended the sickening, twisting track to the basin, where a road graded with sharply broken rock angled through a stony scrubland. The state security men were waiting for them at the place where the road bottomed onto the basin, their vehicles lined up to block the way. Nyerza braked the Jeep but kept the motor idling. Four men in cammies and furry, ear-flapped brimless hats, all carrying assault weapons, approached their Jeep.

Melissa was thinking, *Why am I here at all? I had a vision of the Fallen Shrine. Nyerza said, "Then, we must go there. Yanan feels it, too. He is sending us. And the boy . . . especially the boy."*

Why had they brought Marcus? It had felt so right back in the States, but now . . .

We're lost . . . we're lost. It was all hallucination and now we're lost.

Nyerza glanced at her. "Do not lose faith. Do you not remember the Gold and orb, and what became of Shephard, and how the demons fell away into themselves?"

She was about to answer, *I thought I remembered—but did it all happen, really?*

Aloud she murmured, "I was sure of myself, when I was in touch with the Gold . . . but everything's gone dark. It's like a radio silence—like with the satellite phone. Only it's inside me . . . and I don't know what's real anymore, what was real then—what to believe."

"I know," he said softly, as the soldiers surrounded their Jeep. "Perhaps the darkness is diabolic—or perhaps it is just the rhythm of the spirit. It comes and goes according to its own drumbeat."

She thought: *It's like the Cloud of Unknowing, perhaps, or the Dark Night of the Soul that the Christian mystics spoke of: It withdraws so that we can grow, like a parent who steps back from the infant to encourage his first independent steps.*

Or perhaps, whispered another voice, as the men came to point their guns into the Jeep, *perhaps it's simply darkness. Everything, after all, ends in darkness.*

A short, stocky man with gold on his uniform's shoulder seemed to be in charge. He had a bushy mustache, his eyes shut away in aviator sunglasses. He spoke to the others in one of Turkmenistan's dialects, and two of them came close enough that Melissa could smell their sweat and clinging cigarette smoke as they leaned to glare into the Jeep. Seeing no weapons, they stepped back, gesturing all-clear to their commander. They stood by, seeming bemused by the sight of a small western woman sitting beside the jet-black giant who was too tall for his vehicle's windshield.

The commander approached, looking fairly affable. Nyerza gave him a broad smile and spoke to him in Turkish. She had heard their cover story often enough to know what some of the words meant: They were anthropologists, here to study the

Fallen Shrine. Nyerza spoke the jargon of anthropology fluently and could sound quite convincing.

The security commander smiled skeptically. He spoke briefly, pointing at the sky, then across the desert.

Nyerza laughed dismissively and shook his head, making a brief explanation, his veneer unruffled. He turned to her to explain, choosing his words carefully in case any of these men spoke English. "Like a lot of countries, they buy time on corporate surveillance satellites. They were using them to track those Tekke men who gave us directions. You remember? They were apparently outlaws of some sort, nomadic bandits. They've been attacking supply trucks going to the gas fields. Supposedly they're being paid by environmental terrorists from overseas. Rather an improbable connection, but anyway, the government sent these fellows out here because they saw us speaking with the bandits—they think we have some kind of deal with the bandits. He doesn't know what our connection might be, but I think he supposes we're the contacts with the overseas environmental group."

"But there isn't any connection! We have nothing to do with any of that!"

"Right. He's jumping to conclusions. But that is their method."

She thought: *That is their method.* Meaning they come down like a hammer on anyone who might be even remotely dangerous to the state. A choking cloud of fear provided an effective deterrent.

"Well, tell him that we've got to get help for Marcus—he could be dying!"

The Turkmen commander spoke again, his head cocked to one side, looking at them speculatively.

Nyerza responded wearily, shaking his head and pointing at the boy. He spoke a soft aside, nodding to Melissa. She heard the name Greenpeace. "The tribesmen have apparently been getting weapons from someone. He wonders if we're the ones providing them. He mentions Greenpeace—though they have never given weapons to anyone, they are entirely nonviolent."

Melissa felt a sickening rage rise up in her. While these fools blocked her way, her son was dying!

"We're *anthropologists!*" she said sharply to the commander, amazed to hear such self-righteous outrage in her own voice as she repeated the lie.

"Leave off, please, Melissa—"

The mustachioed man spoke again. The soldiers strode up and gestured with their weapons, reaching to jerk open the Jeep doors.

Melissa understood. They were to be taken into custody. They might take Marcus away from her.

The commander spoke briskly. Nyerza swallowed, and said to her in a tone measured and careful, designed to be all reassurance: "They want to take us to Paskhir for questioning."

"Oh, no, they can't! It's too far! We need help for Marcus now!"

Then another, very different sort of stranger drove up, in a rollicky, three-wheeled electric jitney, its roof a slanting solar-power collector. He was a big, thick-bodied man with a drooping white mustache, long white hair, a hooked nose, big furious brown eyes, a dusty turban, and yellow-and-black robes that flapped in the wind. Shouting in Turkish mixed with Russian, then in English, he leapt from the jitney. "Keep these foreigners away!" He stalked up to the car, waving his arms as if warning of an avalanche. "Keep them away! Take them with you! I don't want anthropologists here! They are nosy! They want all our sacred secrets! They sniff around for treasure! We have no treasure, we have no artifacts except wretched old ruins, but still they come!"

"We have a sick child—" Melissa said.

"I cannot take care of children! We have no hospital! We don't like anthropologists!"

The commander, whose name, it emerged, was Akesh, spoke to the angry old man in his own dialect. As they shouted back and forth, Nyerza bent to whisper to Melissa. "He's asking how this old Sufi dervish knows we're anthropologists. The old gentleman says he knows full well who we are: 'notorious' anthropologists, famous ones of the worst sort, always coming around bothering him. He shouts at the commander to take us away."

Akesh was shouting back now, not liking to be ordered about. He turned stiffly to Nyerza and Melissa and spoke with disgusted finality. Nyerza translated: " 'I have ordered him to take you into his monastery . . . this fallen-in old place here across the plain. He will find that we do not take easily to commands from old fools in stinking robes.' Something like that . . . Says he will have some men stay with us to keep an eye on things while he and the others go on to find the bandits. The commander isn't so sure what is going on, but—" Nyerza smiled "—he vows to get to the bottom of it."

The old man shouted in outrage at this news, swearing in several languages. But, less than a minute later, driving the jitney, he led the Jeep and one of the SUVs back to the Fallen Shrine at the base of a sheer sandstone cliff.

———

Melissa's first impression of the shrine was meager—most of her attention was focused on Marcus—but she had a sense of a multitiered edifice carved from the yellow sandstone of the mountainside itself, much of it indeed tumbled down, other parts shored up by wooden beams, with a smaller building of stucco and cinder blocks attached to it, obviously of recent construction. Smoke wisped from a chimney made of cement and tile; long shadows hid the sand-blurred features of a three-armed angel—or demon?—carved from a single boulder, forty feet high.

Then they hurried inside. Nyerza laid the shivering boy on a pallet in a warm room lit only by a lantern and the flames of a stone fireplace that was burning natural gas. The three state security men waited in an outer room where the walls and floor were covered in Persian-style carpets. They were served tea by a silent old woman. They joked with one another, laughing, happy to be given this cushy assignment in a comfortable room.

The hawk-faced old man with the drooping mustache closed the door of the inner room, muffling the raucous voices of the security men, and knelt beside the boy.

Confused, Melissa watched the old man wonderingly. His expression was completely different now. His face conveyed only gentle concern as he touched Marcus's head, felt his pulse. "The boy is quite sick," he said in English. "Some form of cholera, perhaps. He must've drunk something he shouldn't have. But perhaps we can heal him. I have some medicines coming."

He flashed a broken smile at them, and turned to a younger man in contemporary khakis and wire-rim glasses, who had bustled into the room carrying what appeared to be a mason jar. The jar was filled with black liquid in which floated lumps of unidentifiable muck. The word "ball" was written on the side of the jar in calligraphed relief lettering.

Marcus lay, turning his head this way and that in feverish unease, his eyes shut.

The old man sat beside the boy and held the jar in his hands; he winked at Melissa, and closed his eyes. He held the jar up, and his hands trembled as if something were passing from him, through his hands, and into the jar. The dark material in the jar seemed to dance. The old man just sat there . . . sat there for a long minute, and another, holding the jar.

There was a burst of cynical laughter from the state security men in the next room, as someone tossed off a witticism in Turkic. The sudden sound seemed to push Melissa to the edge of some inner furnace she hadn't known was there. She felt she would fall in, incinerate in her terror for Marcus, her sense of abandonment by the forces that had guided her life till now. Nyerza patted her shoulder. The thin, dark man in khakis and wire-rims remained standing by the door, watching quietly.

But I am here at the place we have journeyed so far to be at, she told herself. *We are safe for now. There is help for Marcus here. Perhaps.*

Or perhaps the old man was just another charlatan. There were so many.

Then he opened his eyes and gestured for Melissa to come and prop the boy up. She knelt awkwardly beside her son and lifted his limp head and shoulders. Marcus moaned and opened his eyes a crack. The old man held the open jar to the boy's mouth, tipped in a spoonful or two—and the boy recoiled, coughing, shaking his head, making a face.

"No—it's—*no!*"

"You will drink it, boy, yes," the old man said gently. "You drank something that was bad for you; now drink something good, even if it tastes bad. That is often the way of it."

"No! Mama, it's going to make me throw up."

"What is this stuff, please?" Melissa asked.

The old man shrugged. "Herbs. Some good quality, infused. A long story."

"This is more response than we've had from Marcus for some time," Nyerza pointed out. "After a few sips."

She nodded slowly. "Marcus? Please? We don't have time to get to a hospital."

Marcus tried to squirm away from the jar, covering his mouth. "No!"

"Okay," said the mustachioed old man. He gestured to the younger man—his assistant, Melissa supposed—and spoke a few words in his own tongue. The assistant smiled and brought from the fireplace an old-fashioned bellows. Marcus's eyes widened as the old man went on. "Okay, boy—your name is Marcus, yes?—we put the medicine here, in this pumping thing, and—" he made two duck-quacking sounds close together "—it goes up your behind. We don't need your cooperation for such. Now, Hiram, bring the butter. We will use it to get the instrument in. Turn the boy over."

He said all this with a straight face, but Melissa hoped desperately that he was bluffing.

Whether he was bluffing or not, it worked. Marcus shook his head, popped his mouth open wide. Keeping his poker face, the old man put the jar to the boy's lips, and Marcus drank. He gagged, choked, but swallowed half the dark brew. "That is enough, I think," said the old man. "Hold the boy up against you in your arms. Pray for him. He will sleep."

Marcus shuddered deeply, and closed his eyes. He began to relax against her.

The dervish winked again at Melissa and gestured to his assistant. The two of them bustled out, taking the jar with them.

Melissa looked at Nyerza in puzzlement.

Nyerza chuckled. "So the old fellow fooled you, too, out on the road?"

She nodded. "I guess he did."

He whispered, "He knew if he seemed to want us here, the government's thugs would take us away. But if he demanded that they take us away, they would bring us here. He's used to dealing with them. He is the man we have come here to see."

Ash Valley, California

Stephen was standing at the edge of a muddy pool, watching Death as it floated, slowly turning, on the stained surface of the water. There were two dead mallards, a male and a female, floating on their sides, their eyes milky, tucked nose to tail with each other, turning in an eddy as if deliberately doing a grotesque imitation of a yin-yang symbol. Flies clung to them like swamped sailors on a life raft. But looking closer, he realized that most of the flies were dead, too.

The clouds shifted, and the light with them, so the wetlands pool mirrored the thin cloud cover, looking like the interior of an abalone shell. And in the reflection the two dead birds seemed to float in the sky like some forgotten ancient symbol of cosmic decay.

Stephen shook himself. *Get a grip, Stevie boy—focus!* He turned to look for Dickinham and Glyneth.

They were about fifty feet away, hunkered down at the pool's edge with the sampling equipment, both of them wearing rubber gloves that protected them up to their elbows, preventing contact with the contaminated water.

Glyneth glanced up at him as he walked over, her expression sadly amused. "It seems the stuff works," she said dryly, turning to look at the water where two red-winged blackbirds, three dragonflies, and a stiff frog floated, half tangled together in an association they would never have tolerated in life. The animals weren't long dead—only since the rain had flushed the fields above the floodplain that morning—and there was just a slight odor of rot plus another scent, perhaps from the faintly iridescent, oily slick that clung around them.

"Yes, it works, a treat!" Dickinham said without irony, clearly pleased as he used the grabber to place a dead dragonfly into a test tube. He put the tube into a red-plastic case, like a fishing tackle box, that he'd set on a low boulder by the rushes.

"Is there something I can do?" Stephen asked dutifully.

"Today, just observe," Dickinham said. "The job has to be done with the right toxics protocol, or you can accumulate the Dirvane on yourself, make yourself . . . queasy. Tomorrow you can help us with the osterizing scanner."

"Osterizing scanner?"

"It cuts things up, purees 'em like a blender—animals, plants—and tells you what their chemical components are."

"Ah. Crocker said you'd be checking to see if the stuff breaks down prematurely," Stephen said.

"Right."

Looking at the dead animals, Stephen added, "Looks to me like it doesn't break down soon at all. It's definitely sticking around and doing its job."

"Not sure, though, if it's staying at the levels of concentration we want to see."

"What sort of pest are we aiming at here?" Glyneth asked, straightening up from her sample collector. "Mosquitoes or Mothra?"

"Oh, a broad spectrum," Dickinham said absently, using a touch pen to write something on a digital clipboard. "Kinda like one of those heavy-duty broad-spectrum antibiotics but for agricultural pests and not bacteria. Of course, I've always thought of unnecessary bugs and animals as just, you know, the bigger disease organisms of agriculture. Well, come on. Let's head up into town, get some lunch."

Unnecessary bugs and animals? Stephen thought. One of the first things he'd learned in college was that they were almost all necessary, in some way, to the food chain, the biosphere. But he'd since learned to be skeptical of making such assumptions at West Wind. Its scientists delighted in pointing to the resilience of nature. Sometimes, though, he worried about it. Very quietly.

Dickinham picked up his red-plastic case and headed away from the water, trudging up the muddy trail between the terraces of rice fields above the wetlands. Stephen started to follow, then held back, distracted by a rattling among the rushes and swampy reeds. With an inexplicable feeling of gladness, he turned to peer at the rushes, watching them shake as something tried to thrash its way free. "Something, anyway," he murmured. He didn't say the rest aloud: *Something, anyway, had survived here.*

Then the reeds across the muddy channel began to dance—and a dog, a mud-spattered retriever, splashed blindly out of the rushes, coming from the island of mud on the farther side. There was something desperate in the way it thrashed toward them, its head making unnatural, spastic movements, jaws now and then snapping at the air. The frantic animal made it to the open water but seemed to bog down anyway, though a large retriever like this should have been able to swim comfortably. There was red foam, he saw, trailing from its muzzle, and its eyes had the milky glaze he'd seen on the ducks.

"Jeezus," Stephen whispered, taking a step back. "Is it rabid?"

Glyneth shook her head, pointing at the dead birds. "Were they all rabid? No."

As he and Glyneth watched, the dog whimpered and coughed, paddled in a circle, clearly confused, more and more weakly with each motion of its legs—and then it shuddered, ceasing to swim . . . and sank.

Instinctively, Stephen started toward the water, as if to wade in after the distressed dog—but, quickly peeling off a tainted rubber glove, Glyneth caught up with him and gripped his elbow. "Uh-uh, no—don't go in that water."

He hesitated, watching the water bubbling where the retriever had sunk, as the dog drowned.

"What was it doing out here?" he wondered aloud. "We're quite a way from any houses."

"Dirvane 17 attacks the central nervous system. I guess it got a dose somewhere, got confused, wandered out here," Glyneth muttered, her voice hoarse.

The dog suddenly bobbed to the surface of the murk, on its side—rigid, its jaws open, head twisted to one side—and began to slowly drift in circles, looking as if it were already locked in rigor mortis, though it could only just have died. It turned in the syrup-slow eddy, beside the dead mallards and the dead frog and the dead dragonflies.

Stephen tore his sickened gaze away, and trudged with Glyneth up the muddy path. He didn't allow himself to run.

———

"You're not hungry?" Dickinham asked, with surprise, as they pulled up to the drive-up order window of Burger Urge.

"No, still, um, full from breakfast," Stephen said.

"I mean, if you're worried about the local produce, these fast-food people ship everything in."

"No, I just . . ."

"Can I help you?" the talking plastic burger on the ordering sign asked them.

"Yes," Dickinham replied briskly. "An Urgent Burger, a double strawberry shake, fries, and—Glyneth?"

"Just some coffee."

They got Dickinham's food and drove the rented Hydrogen Hummer over to the little park that occupied the center of town.

There they sat in the hydrogen-fuel-cell-powered Humvee, Dickinham and Stephen in front, Glyneth in back. Dickinham ate and made vague small talk about West Wind. The car filled with the smell of salty carbohydrates and meat.

Stephen looked around, able to see most of downtown Ash Valley from their vantage point. There wasn't much: small shops in a square around the little half-block park, with its tall fir trees, rusty swing set, and child-tramped dirt. There were two basketball hoops, bent from people jumping up to dunk and dangle; the concrete court was humped and cracked by tree roots.

The shops were touristy, for people on their way to Mount Shasta, and there were some fast-food places—Wendy's and Burger Urge and a Soylicious and a Japanaquick. Surprisingly few people showed themselves on the streets; a small boy wobbled vaguely down the center line on his bicycle, his eyes equally vague. A single car passed through—moving quickly, for a small town—and, as Stephen watched, tensing, the electric sedan almost hit the boy, but it veered crookedly around him.

The boy on the bicycle didn't react.

A concrete-block rest-room building stood in the park, and someone had done an elaborate spray-paint graffito of a demon, one of the seven clans, on the back wall in Day-Glo red and green: a Gnasher, if Stephen remembered the mythology rightly. Someone else had tried to blot it out with a red Christian cross, like a religious version of a cancel sign over it.

"What the hell is that?" Dickinham growled rhetorically.

"Um," Stephen began, "I suppose it's left over from—"

But Dickinham wasn't listening; he'd meant something else. "What *are* those idiots doing here," he muttered, getting out of the car. He paused, then turned to them long enough to snap, "You wait here, you two, please—I gotta have a word with . . ." He let it trail off and slammed the door loud enough to make Stephen jump.

Glyneth and Stephen exchanged puzzled glances, then watched as Dickinham strode across a corner of the park to a large solar-enhanced white van, its rear toward them. It was parked in an alley beside a hardware store. "So that's what he was talking about," Stephen murmured, as Dickinham banged on the back doors of the van. They were opened by two men, who glared out at him. "Some kind of company car."

"I don't think that's a company car, exactly," Glyneth said.

The two scowling white men wore nondescript green jumpsuits and shiny black shoes; they had identical buzz cuts. A third man—red-faced, long-haired, bearded, shabbily dressed, looking drunk—tried to push his way out of the van. The two men pushed him farther back in. There was something odd about the drunk man's eyes.

"You see that license plate?" Glyneth asked casually. "That sequence—G-two-four-four—that's typical of certain kinds of government vehicles. Pentagon research."

Stephen looked at her. "How do you know that?"

She shrugged. "I did some checking once, about military research programs, for a paper I was writing. The information cropped up on the Internet. I almost went in to government research chemistry instead of private."

She said it, then looked quickly away, and Stephen thought, *She's lying.*

But that lie had been seamlessly delivered. Why was he so sure of it?

He heard a slam, and glanced out the window to see that the back doors of the van were closed now, the van moving away down the alley, and Dickinham was returning. He opened the passenger-side door and reached past Stephen to the glove

compartment. "Just need my cell phone a second . . . here it is."
He hit a speed-dialed number and put the phone to his ear.
"Crocker? Why are the boys in green here already? Well, it's
broad daylight, for one thing, and they're taking subjects for—"
He paused, seemed to feel Stephen listening. Shot a cold look at
him, then closed the car door and walked away, talking on the
cell phone, gesturing vigorously.

"Something confidential," Glyneth murmured. "We speak
no evil if we hear no evil, I guess. We learn not to see it. I wonder if we can *feel* it."

Stephen looked at her. "What do you mean?"

"Just thinking out loud. Anyway, there was a rumor going
around the observatory . . ." She looked at him blankly. "The rumor is that Dirvane 17 wasn't really developed as a pesticide."

"What, then?"

"I'm not sure. The people who were hinting about it were
pretty mysterious themselves. But, you know, lots of pesticides
are chemically related to nerve gas. Some of them were basically
nerve gas *first*: Diazinon, for example, which people've used
since the last century, is an organophosphate—one of the neu-
rotoxins developed during World War II. I thought maybe . . ."

Stephen stared at her, then turned to peer around at the interior of the Hummer.

She raised her eyebrows. "What are you looking for?"

"Cameras, maybe one of those flying cams . . . they make
them so small now." He turned back to her, a little sheepish. "I
thought you had to be pulling my leg, and Winderson was going to appear again, projected into the car—'You bought that
one too, huh, Stephen?' Or maybe he'd just be watching."

She stared, then shrugged and turned to watch Dickinham,
who was returning. "I wasn't kidding, but I was just speculating. I mean—people talk. I don't worry about it. This job is all
about going with the flow."

"Go with the flow? But—people would be dying in the streets if Dirvane 17 were nerve gas. They—they've sprayed the stuff all around the town."

"I don't think it's nerve gas *exactly*. They also experiment with— Actually, we shouldn't be talking about this." She changed the subject. "So, how do you like your new office?"

"What office would that be?" Stephen asked, as Dickinham got back in, looking grim.

"Oh, that's right," Glyneth said blithely. Her manner changed around Dickinham. She smirked at Stephen, "You haven't seen your executive suite yet."

"No need to be sarcastic, young lady," said Dickinham, buckling his seat belt. "It's just a cubby in the building attached to the observatory, Steve. Just temporary, but this whole operation out here is temporary."

"So what was up with the van?" Stephen asked.

Dickinham waved dismissively. "Just . . . one of our teams, jumping the gun."

"It looked like there was someone—the guy with long hair—trying to get out?"

Dickinham started the vehicle but didn't put it into gear. "Him? Oh, he's one of the local yokels, ran into the D17 seepage pond. We're going to detox him just to be on the safe side. Wouldn't want anyone . . . you know. He was drunk, is all—not really trying to get away. Listen—hand me my fries, will you? And, uh, when we get back, speaking of detoxing, we all ought to go through the regimen—special shower, the whole trip."

"Special shower?" Glyneth said, straight-faced. "That sounds kinky."

Dickinham snorted and shook his head. "One in every crowd."

"Have we been exposed to anything dangerous?" Stephen asked, trying to sound as if he weren't really worried about it.

"No, no . . . It's in the nature of a drill. Part of the experience you're supposed to be getting . . . all part of the program . . . We—" He broke off.

A group of people marched toward them through the park. They were led by a man in a long black coat and muddy boots, who was gesticulating wildly: a man with a bubble instead of a head.

As they got closer, Stephen saw that the bubble was a transparent helmet, like the toy space-suit helmets little kids sometimes wore. But this wasn't a toy. He'd seen other models before, in highly polluted areas. There was a filtration unit located just below the chin; toxins were separated from air, excessive water vapor was vented, keeping the inside of the helmet from misting over. There was a voice-amplification device of some kind so you could hear the wearer clearly.

"Is that one of those new helmet cell phones?" Glyneth asked.

Stephen knew what she meant. People who wanted cell phone privacy sometimes wore helmets. Heads-up displays showed e-mail and the like.

"No," Stephen said. "I'm pretty sure that's an air-filtration helmet."

The man also wore rubber gloves. The five people trailing along with him—two old women, an elderly Hispanic man, a young teenage couple—wore gloves and other, more-compact filtration masks.

The man in the helmet seemed to notice the hydro Hummer, and he changed course, making a beeline for it. "It's that lunatic, Reverend Anthony," Dickinham muttered.

"If he's a lunatic, perhaps we should beat a strategic retreat," Glyneth suggested.

"No. I want to know what the son of a bitch is up to."

Stephen glanced at the frowning Dickinham. Why should he care what some street crazy was doing?

Reverend Anthony stopped, about five feet away from the car, his back to the part of the cloudy sky that hid the sun. The brightness leaking through the clouds transformed his bubble helmet into a halo as he glowered through the glass at them. He had thinning red hair, a wide, flexible mouth, weariness-smudged blue eyes—a big-boned face that had once been pudgy, Stephen supposed, now looked gaunt. When he spoke, he exposed gapped teeth, and he pointed with a rubber-gloved hand.

"You are here to witness for *your* Lord, are you? Well I am here to witness, as well, friends! I witness for the Good Lord and Him only! Who will you testify for, West Windies?" There was a Southern twang to his voice—maybe Louisianan.

Dickinham snorted, and powered his window halfway down. "Mr. Perry Anthony—I was about to say reverend but then I remembered . . ."

The street preacher became very still.

"That you've been—what do you call it?—defrocked, right?" Dickinham went on mockingly. "Got your church taken away. What happened? Get too friendly with the church's children? Maybe somebody's wife?"

"They called me a *heretic*, friend," Reverend Anthony said softly, but his voice was tense and electronically amplified. "Because I said that the demons were not the coming of the End Times . . . because I said they were the works of men. Because I said they *were* men, men who were joined with demons!" His voice got louder with each phrase. "Because I said that the Cursed Spirit was clever enough to work through men, and that men were evil enough to do his work, with so little encouragement! And later, when churchfolk changed their story, when they took the government's money to convince us it was all a hallucination—why, sir, I *denounced* them!

"For a deceit the demons were—but they were also real, raging through this world! I will witness the truth! Many are the false prophets—few there are who speak with the spirit! I told my superiors that they slept—they slept and they sinned in their sleep, friends!" He underscored every phrase with a jab of his fist in the air. "They said I was mad to demand a wakening every morning, that I was mad to shout Wake up! Wake up! through the streets. The day for making the choice is always here, and *EVERY DAY IS JUDGMENT DAY!*"

Dickinham was laughing now, shaking his head, and then there was a loud thump on the hood of the car. A seagull—they were only ten miles inland—had fallen from the sky. The bird was flapping frantically in death throes, on the hood, its broken wings a sorrowful asymmetry, its cracked beak oozing blood.

"Oh, God," Glyneth breathed.

Anthony's followers drew back, gasping, murmuring, as Anthony pointed at the dying bird.

"I witness for the Good Lord! *Behold!* The poisoners serve their dark master and they sicken the world—like the sickness of sin in their souls, they spread poison over the world, and the Good Lord's blessed creation withers and dies!"

Stephen saw an odd movement from the corner of his eye—a squirrel on a tree trunk in the park. It was hanging on to the trunk by its front claws, the rest of its body was twitching, spasming. It managed to get a grip with its hind paws, went a few feet farther up, stopped, shaking its head violently—then fell, dying convulsively in the grass at the base of the tree.

"Dickinham," Stephen whispered, "do me a favor: Roll up that window."

"*BEHOLD!*" the erstwhile Reverend Anthony shouted, turning up his helmet amplifier, so his voice boomed and echoed like the voice of God. " 'BY THEIR FRUITS YOU SHALL KNOW THEM!' They sicken the Earth! Behold!"

Dickinham grinned at the preacher—a strained, skullish grin—gave him the finger, put the vehicle in gear, and drove hurriedly away.

———

It wasn't until that evening, alone at his laptop in his Bald Peak cubby, that Stephen began to ask himself in earnest why Glyneth had talked so frankly about the Dirvane 17 rumors. She was his assistant—wasn't she afraid of getting fired, for being loose lipped about such things? Might she have been planted to test his loyalty? Did they suspect he was some kind of bleeding heart?

The questions came seething up in his mind as he skimmed through the material she'd sent him, a file beamed from her palmer . . .

In 1931, the Rockefeller Institute for Medical Investigations injected human subjects with cancerous cells. The Institute's Dr. Cornelius Rhoads later set up the U.S. Army Biological Warfare facilities. Later still, working for the Atomic Energy Commission, he initiated radiation exposure experiments both on soldiers and civilian hospital patients—the subjects had little or no understanding of what they were being subjected to.

In the 1932 Tuskegee Syphilis Study, 200 black men diagnosed with syphilis were not told of the diagnosis and were denied treatment. They were used as lab subjects in a study of the progress of the disease. They all died from syphilis. They could have been successfully treated.

In 1946, patients in Veterans' Affairs hospitals were

utilized for medical experiments. Scientists were ordered to say "investigations" or "observations" instead of "experiments" when discussing the study.

In 1947, the U.S. Atomic Energy Commission issued the highly secret Document 07075001, which blandly noted that the agency would begin injecting doses of radioactive substances into uninformed human guinea pigs. . . . Also that year the CIA began studying LSD as a possible weapon. Human subjects were subjected to the powerful drug either without their knowledge or without a clear understanding of the risks—risks known to the administrators of the experiment.

In 1950, the Department of Defense began to detonate nuclear bombs—and to monitor people living downwind for resultant illnesses and radiation-induced mortality. It is assumed the DoD knew there would be a measurable increase of such consequences in the American citizens downwind of the blasts.

In 1950, the U.S. Navy deliberately discharged a cloud of bacteria from ships so that it would drift over San Francisco. The city was monitored by devices, which could be safely checked later, to see how far the infection spread. A significant number of San Franciscans fell sick with apparent pneumonia.

In 1951, the DOD started its own open-air tests of disease-producing bacteria and viruses. The tests continued through 1969. Subsequent investigators believe that people in the areas around the open-air testing were exposed—no one knows for sure how many sickened and died as a result of the tests.

In a 1953 test of chemical warfare capability, the U.S. military sprayed clouds of zinc cadmium sulfide onto various cities including Winnipeg, St. Louis, Minneapolis, Fort Wayne, the Monocacy River Valley in Maryland, and

Leesburg, Virginia. The long-term health consequences of the tests are not definitely known.

Also in 1953, the military and CIA undertook airborne micro-agent distribution experiments, exposing thousands of people in New York and San Francisco to the airborne germs *Serratia marcescens* and *Bacillus glogigii.*

In 1953, American intelligence services launched Project MK ULTRA, designed to test drugs and biological agents specific for mind control and psychological operations. Human beings were sometimes used as guinea pigs in the project without their knowledge. There is at least one well-documented case of a subject committing suicide as a result of the project. The evidence suggests there were other casualties.

In 1956, the U.S. military released mosquitoes infected with yellow fever in Savannah, Georgia, and Avon Park, Florida. Army agents pretended to be government health officials in subsequent tests for effects on unwitting victims . . .

In 1965, intelligence services commenced Project MK SEARCH, attempting to control human behavior through mind-altering drugs . . .

In 1966, the CIA initiated Project MK OFTEN, a program that tested the toxicological consequences of certain drugs on humans—and on animals, the experimenters making no great distinction . . .

In 1966, the U.S. Army spread *Bacillus subtilis variant niger* through large parts of the New York City subway system. Army scientists dropped lightbulbs filled with the bacteria onto ventilation grates, exposing about a million civilians. Lightbulbs were used presumably as camouflage— if noticed, they would be ignored, unlike lab flasks . . .

According to *Military Review*, November 1970, the United States had two years earlier intensified its development of so-called "ethnic weapons," designed to selectively target and eliminate ethnic groups that were susceptible due to genetic differences. . . . In 1977, senators were told in hearings that 239 major metropolitan areas and smaller towns had been deliberately exposed to biological warfare agents since the program began in 1949.

It went on and on, through the 1990s and the first decade of the twenty-first century. . . . Stephen shook his head and put his finger on the button to delete the file.

"Stephen?"

He turned—and there was Winderson. Stephen shifted his chair so he'd block Winderson's view of the screen with his body. Which might have been a mistake: Winderson glanced toward the screen, as if wondering what Stephen was covering up.

This is ridiculous, Stephen thought. But he didn't unblock the screen.

"Just checking in. Didn't mean to startle you, Stevie boy."

Stephen could see a file box through Winderson's torso. As he watched, interference rippled the hologram.

"You didn't startle me. Glad to see you. I just hope you don't get sick from that flickering, boss," Stephen added, making a nervous joke.

"Hm? Oh, is my image messy? *Ha!* Well, my boy, how'd your first day in the field go?"

"Um . . . fascinating."

"Dirvane 17 is pretty effective, isn't it?"

"You could say that, yes."

"Do I detect a certain ambiguity in your response? You know, we're really hoping you can start coming up with some ideas for marketing the product. Right after a little foray into psychonomics, I mean."

"Marketing? Oh—of course. I'm already, um, thinking about it."

"No misgivings? I mean, I recall your initial concern that it might generate bad publicity for us."

"Well—it is a bit problematic. I take it that some of it blew over the town itself today. That shouldn't be a big problem—but there were people wearing gas masks."

"Right, well, they're the sort of kooks who love dramatizing. We sprayed near the town, the wind blew a little there but— At any rate, you have to always look at the big picture, Stephen. Our society is soaked in so-called toxins. Some of them *are* toxic—but there are naturally occurring cyanides in almonds, and arsenic is naturally present in oranges. The body eliminates them, as a matter of course."

Stephen knew that thesis. Common sense suggested the counterargument: The trace toxins naturally found in produce occurred at almost undetectable levels, and the human body was better able to filter out some toxins than others.

Wanting to be a team player, though, he replied, "And of course pesticides can be made to break down, after they first take effect. Some of them."

"Certainly. Exactly. And what we try initially doesn't have to be the final concentration—we may dilute it hundreds of times. Perhaps. And if at first we make a mess here and there—down the line everyone will benefit. It's like dams. You may cover up some pretty valleys, but you provide millions of people with energy."

Stephen nodded. He wondered why Winderson was taking the time to rationalize D17 to him. He was pretty sure the chairman wouldn't bother with most employees. It was kind of flattering, really, as if Winderson thought him especially important.

He knew, in some part of himself, that he was swallowing all this because it comforted him. A conceptual tranquilizer.

But this was his job—he needed to survive in it.

As if sensing his line of thought, Winderson's projection went on, "It's a tough world—competition is fierce. From people and from nature. Nature is always chewing away at us with millions of insect mandibles. Pesticides are among our only defenses."

"Sure, I know that," Stephen said, feeling a little better.

He'd been more disturbed than he'd realized by what he'd seen today.

And by Reverend Anthony. Crazy, that man—but very *convinced*.

"Just giving you food for thought—maybe you can use it in marketing somewhere. I remember when I was a boy those old Raid commercials on TV. 'Kills bugs dead!' Now that was style! But you know, a corporation, my boy, isn't about its product. It doesn't matter what we make. We've diversified—and we'll diversify further. But what really matters is the—the *organism* of the corporation. And whether or not we're in harmony with that organism."

"Organism?" Stephen realized he shouldn't seem surprised.
"Yes, of course—if you're incorporated, you've got a, what? A whole that's more than the sum of the parts. Organization—and organism . . . I mean, they're close . . ."

Okay, he thought, *now I'm babbling.*

"Oh, it's more than that, Stephen, m'boy," Winderson went on, putting his holographic hands in his holographic pockets. "Harken back to the late nineteenth century. The Supreme Court made a decision. It was, in this case, in favor of a railroad to the effect that corporations were to be regarded as having the rights and privileges of individuals. They were considered to be as real as human beings, legally. They were, of course, more powerful than individual human beings. And that was the turning point: We began to think of corporations differently. First they became extended families, and then they became *entities*. They've taken on a life of their own in a more literal way than you realize, Stephen. A corporation is a living thing in the astral realm . . . but you'll learn more about that in psychonomics."

"I'm . . . looking forward to it." Stephen couldn't think of anything better to say. What did you say to *"a corporation is a living thing in the astral realm"*?

Winderson nodded gravely several times, then looked at something Stephen couldn't see. "Anyway, just wanted to check in. We may have another assignment for you later tonight. You may see me again. Gotta go. Call coming in from—good grief, from Turkmenistan. Can you imagine? Always something."

And he blinked out.

Was he really gone? Stephen wondered. Winderson could see Stephen, somehow, when he chose to. He might still be watching. Stephen turned and, as quickly as he could without looking like he was hiding something, he deleted Glyneth's cranky e-mail. He switched off the computer and thought, *I'll get a cup of coffee.*

But he didn't move. He didn't get up. He just sat there staring at the dead screen, gnawing a knuckle. Thinking.

Why *had* Glyneth sent that file to him? What was up with her?

Suddenly he felt claustrophobic, trapped in this little cubicle. He got up and went down the empty overlit hallway to the cafeteria in search of coffee.

He smelled gardenias, before he saw Jonquil. He turned, and saw her sitting at the far end of the cafeteria, with her back to him, looking out a window—though nothing much could be seen in the darkness outside.

People who looked out into unbroken darkness were actually looking into their own minds, he supposed.

She was wearing a dove-gray suit. A short jacket hung over the back of her chair. The harsh cafeteria light flashed on her white silk blouse. He knew it was Jonquil from the red-gold spill of her hair across her shoulders.

He started toward her, then stopped, not wanting to startle her. "Hey," he called, softly.

She looked over her shoulder. Even from where he stood, he could see tear streaks. "Hi." She turned away, wiped her eyes. "Come and have some of this hot chocolate."

He crossed to stand beside her. "I was sort of looking for coffee. You okay?"

She swallowed, then looked into her plastic cup. "I'm . . ." She shrugged. "Yeah, sure."

" 'Sure,' she says. I'm not so sure, though. Can I help, Jonquil? I mean, I barely know you, but—"

"It's really very sweet of you to ask. I'm not so good at hiding things, but I can't really talk about it yet." She sipped at the hot chocolate and made a face. "Grew a skin on it. Gross."

"I'm kind of surprised to see you out here at Bald Peak. I didn't think it was your . . . I don't know, I thought you worked in the throne room of the castle, so to speak. We're mostly peasants out here." He looked at her and chuckled. "You *are* here, aren't you? I just had a visit from Winderson—only he wasn't really here."

"His idea of keeping people on their toes. You're not seriously asking if I'm here?"

She turned to look up at him, and he almost fell into her deep blue eyes. He could feel the warmth of her body.

"No, you're definitely here."

"I don't want to be. I want to be in my stupid little cell of a room drinking some cognac." She stood up and put on her jacket.

"You're staying here, at the observatory?"

"It's just too far to a decent motel."

"There's something in Ash Valley, I think."

She looked at him as if wondering if he were serious. "Oh, I wouldn't stay *there*." She shrugged. "So—you coming or not?"

"Um—where?"

"To drink cognac, of course. You wanted to do something for me. You can have a drink with me. That'd help."

She didn't wait for his answer. She swept past him toward the door, swinging her purse. He followed, feeling dreamlike.

Don't kid yourself, Stephen, he told himself. *You're not that lucky.*

A hundred uncertain steps later he was standing with her as she unlocked the door to a little dorm-type room. There was just space inside for a queen-sized bed, a dresser, an open closet—with a garment bag hanging inside and a suitcase—a desk with a closed laptop, a gooseneck lamp that provided the only light. Beside the laptop was a bottle of authentic cognac and two snifters. He didn't think about there being two snifters till a long time later.

Just now his mind was full of the sight of her taking off her jacket, tossing it over the desk chair. "Close the door. We haven't got enough of the good stuff for Dickinham and those other clucks," she said.

He closed the door. Not wanting to seem to assume too much by sitting on the bed, he stood awkwardly in the middle of the little room. He crossed his arms—then, feeling that he looked vaguely hostile, he put his hands in his pockets.

She uncorked the cognac, poured them each half a snifter, and looked at him in feigned dismay. "For heaven's sake, sit down! You're making this little room seem even smaller, standing there like that."

Heart pounding, he sat on the edge of her bed and accepted the snifter. She sat down next to him, setting the cognac bottle within reach, and leaned against the wall. She raised the glass to him, said "Chin-chin," and drank deeply. "Hoo, boy. Stephen, I'm telling you, this is the good stuff. Dale's private stock. Organic French grapes."

Organic? he thought. *Winderson prefers organic?*

It was, anyway, a delicious cognac, but it had a kick; already his head was swimming. "Whoa. Strong stuff."

"What's the point of weak stuff?"

Looking for conversation, remembering the ask-women-about-themselves rule, he noticed an old, leather-bound book sticking out of a side pocket of her open suitcase. "You take books with you when you travel? I do, too. Is it fiction or . . . ?"

"That book? No. Not fiction. What do you read when you travel?"

He had the distinct impression she was changing the subject. "Me? I like old novels. Stuff that seems kind of gritty. Like old twentieth-century detective novels. Dashiell Hammett. And C. S. Forester's Horatio Hornblower stories. Historical fiction."

"Sounds like escape into the real world—or the world people think of as real. Escape from what?"

"Oh, when I was a kid . . . well, it's tied in with the psychonomics stuff." This might be a good time to find out more about the psychonomics division. She might be more forthcoming, now, after a few drinks.

But he really didn't want to think about it. He wanted to savor being here in this little room, drinking with a girl who made him weak in the knees when he looked at her.

She kicked off her shoes. Small white feet, petite white

toes. Red-painted toenails. "You like the nail polish? Almost fire-engine red. I was inspired by a Monroe movie."

"Yeah. Vivid."

She took another drink. "Almost the color that's coming into your cheeks."

She seemed to get more brash with each sip.

He laughed lightly; he hoped it was convincingly. "Am I blushing? Or is it the drink? Or do we care?" He was trying for lighthearted banter. He tried to remember the Noël Coward he'd read in college.

She took another sip, and then pulled the two pillows out from under the white bedspread, plumped them behind her against the wall. She leaned back with a sigh—and stretched out her legs across his lap. His erection was instantaneous.

"We're forgetting toasts," Stephen said, trying to find some conversation that wasn't just a reaction to hers. "What should we toast? West Wind?"

"Not today. How about—to life. Make that *long* life."

"Sure. To life! *Long* life!"

They drank. They refilled their snifters and drank some more. He felt warm and very much in the moment. There was nothing beyond this little room, nothing beyond himself and Jonquil.

He realized he'd let his left hand fall onto her knee. Her skin was smooth, warm. But he was sure his palm was sweaty. He wondered if she could feel his relentless, almost painful erection through the fabric of his pants.

Another toast, he thought. *Be suave.* "In fact," he said, "the devil with long life—let's make it a toast to *eternal* life. Why not?"

She looked at him oddly. Her smile was crooked as she said, "Yes, why not." And she drank deeply from her snifter.

She bent her right leg—his hand was on her left—and the motion pushed her skirt up, showing a great deal more thigh and a triangle of white panty.

A little surprised, he took his hand from her leg. She said, "Why don't you put your glass in your left hand?"

He laughed a bit drunkenly. "Why—does the cognac taste better that way?"

She cocked her head and closed one eye. "Umm, I think it will, yeah."

The room was beginning to whirl, just a little.

He took the snifter in his left hand and drank. "Weird. It does seem better."

"You just pay closer attention to the taste that way." She re-filled his glass; he drank half of it almost immediately when she added: "But I wanted you to put your drink in your left hand so you could put your right hand on my leg. You can reach farther up my leg with your right hand, see . . . Do close your mouth—you're gaping at me like a fish."

"I am?" He laughed nervously, smiled shyly, and returned his right hand to her leg, let it slowly slide up her thigh. The skin of her thigh seemed fractionally more moist. His palm cupped her flesh, and the tips of his fingers seemed to drink in the sheer, vibrant life of her.

"That light on the desk," she said, "is bothering my eyes. Could you just turn it so that it's facing the wall? It's adjustable."

He got up, and instantly found he was more drunk than he'd thought. The room rocked around him. He focused on the lamp and walked across to it as steadily as he could. "This boat seems to be hitting some rough water," he muttered. She laughed at that. He turned the shade so the light faced the wall, making the room candlelight dim.

He found his way back to the bed and saw she'd put her

glass on the floor and unbuttoned her blouse. "This damn brassiere is killing me. I can't breathe in it. Would you mind?"

He put his glass beside hers, then fumbled with the bra hook, in front between the cups, and at last managed to undo it without pinching her. "Good man," she said huskily, tilting her face up to his. He bent to kiss her.

It was a long kiss, and her lips seemed to melt into his. Then she put her hands on the back of his head, and drew his face down to her full breasts and moaned. "I'm sad tonight," she whispered, pressing his face into her cleavage. He smelled her skin—her perfume, her musk. "Make me feel better. . . . Make me feel better, Stephen."

Somehow she squirmed out of her skirt and underwear without taking his face from the lusciously soft world of her skin as he tongued the tautness, the electricity of her nipples. Somehow she fairly clawed his clothes away, and he almost dove into the center of her, and only the sweet distancing of the liquor prevented him from ejaculating too soon. He forgot himself in her, and that was the key that opened chambers within secret chambers, within others. They made love for at least an hour, and he slid into the dark waters of sleep without a ripple.

———

Stephen heard a woman's voice. It wasn't Jonquil's.

"They're ready for you now, Mr. Issk-rat."

Stephen sat abruptly up in bed—and regretted it. A hangover backhanded him in return for the suddenness of the motion. "Ow . . . shit." His mouth was paper dry; the skin of his face in his hands seemed disgustingly oily. He wasn't an experienced drinker.

He looked around the room. Jonquil was gone.

The closet was open; her bag was gone. Her clothes were no

longer hanging there. The laptop was gone. There was a note written on the desktop in lipstick.

Early meeting. See you soon. J.

He looked at his watch. Seven A.M. Take some aspirin before facing sunlight.

He pulled on his pants, his head throbbing. He was desperate for a drink of water. Was she used to drinking that much? She must be.

Dressing sloppily in dirty clothes, he wondered what last night had meant. He'd made love to Jonquil, and it'd been something powerful, at least to him. Had it mattered as much to her? Was she as used to that kind of intimacy as she was to drinking?

"They're ready for you now, Mr. Issk-rat."

Had someone spoken to him? He was sure he'd heard someone . . . he thought it might have been Latilla's voice. Maybe something left over from a dream. He wished Latilla would stay way, far, completely clear of his dreams.

But maybe someone had been there; maybe they'd said something at the door. Did they know he'd spent the night with Jonquil?

He went to the door, opened it, peered up and down the hall. "Hello?" He heard male laughter from the little coffee nook at the end of the stretch of dorm rooms. Crocker. If he went for coffee, he'd run into Crocker. He definitely didn't want to talk to Crocker now, one of those guys whose every word mocked you, but they never quite crossed the line enough that you could call him on it.

He walked ploddingly to the cafeteria, in search of water. Maybe someone would have some aspirin.

Jonquil. She'd filled his senses last night. All five of them. He was beginning to feel the emotional ache through the hangover ache. Waking up alone like that had been jarring. The note seemed impersonal.

How did she feel about him? They'd known each other so briefly, but making love to her had sure as hell broken the ice.

There was too much light in the cafeteria. He'd cheerfully pay a hundred dollars for any pair of sunglasses.

———

Almost fourteen hours later, in the first march of the night, Stephen put on his overcoat and hat and went down the hall, looking for the nearest exit. He'd spent the day, and part of the night, outlining marketing ideas for D17. He couldn't get over the notion that it was just busywork, that it wasn't even part of what Winderson wanted from him. That made it unsatisfying work.

Moreover, Jonquil hadn't called him, hadn't shown up. She never had explained why she'd come to Bald Peak in the first place. Had she come there to see him?

He found the exit, went through into breezy nighttime gloom.

He took a deep breath, found himself wondering if you could taste darkness when you breathed in the night air—an odd thought that made no real sense.

He crossed the field between the old observatory and the place where he'd stood looking out over the valley when he'd arrived here. The grass wiped the wetness from a recent rainfall onto his trousers, till they began to cling and scrape his calves.

He thought about calling her, but something about her terse note suggested she preferred to get in touch with him. So why didn't she? Had he been lousy in bed? Hadn't seemed like it at the time. She'd seemed to be riding a roller coaster of multiple orgasms.

But maybe it was a one-time thing for her. She'd been

depressed about something. He'd been someone handy to help her forget about it, whatever it was. But that didn't mean he was serious-relationship material.

Face it, he told himself. *You're not particularly good-looking,* and *you're low on the corporate totem pole. You don't even have stock options. You were comfort food for a night.*

He kicked angrily at a tall weed. She was a capable woman executive, paid a helluva lot more than he was; she wasn't going to be impressed with him anytime soon. And if he made a serious play for the boss's niece and it went sour—so would his career.

Maybe when he saw her, she'd act as if nothing had happened. How should he react to that?

He approached the edge of the cliff. But this time he looked up at the stars and the moon. The wind had torn the cloud cover and was drawing the curtains for a celestial display. Raggedly framed by black clouds, the stars glittered blue-white. He tried to remember what constellations he was seeing, but they all seemed new to him. The moon was low, its cold light making the broken clouds starkly black in their hearts.

At last, almost reluctantly, he looked down at Ash Valley.

Lights shone in clusters and stippled the lines of streets, marking residential blocks. Some parts of town seemed darker than they should have at this hour, he'd have thought. But over there, to the north of the town, there was a bustle of spotlit activity. He could just hear the rumble of earthmovers, and he could see they were making a road. Working through the night to gouge a new, ramrod-straight artery extending from the town—and another, coming at a slant to meet the first one, so that they converged to make a point. Pointing right at him. And on the farther side of the town, directly opposite the first work site, more spotlights, catching blue smoke from diesel engines. Yet another road.

Why were they working so hard in the middle of a winter night, some of the time in the rain, to make these roads?

"They're ready for you now, Mr. Issk-rat."

He turned, almost jumping, feeling as if he'd been caught at something he shouldn't be doing.

"I didn't mean to startle you," Latilla said. The elderly woman, with her bell-like hair, her lizardlike hooded eyes, was gazing at him unblinkingly—or so it seemed to Stephen. She wore a woolen overcoat and rubber galoshes. She came nearer, stood so close he could smell coffee on her breath. Suddenly she smiled, tilting her head to one side inquisitively. "I guess I just get all *jumping-bean-enthusiastic* about Mr. Winderson's projects. It's so exciting, don't you think?"

"Um—jeez, Latilla—I didn't even know you were out here, I mean, at the observatory. Mr. Winderson sent you all the way up here? Oh—then he must be here, too, huh?"

"No, not in person. He may project in later. They're ready for you in the observatory."

"Ready for me?"

She nodded, adding only, "You betcha life they are!" And didn't seem inclined to explain. But after a moment, as if a badly timed afterthought, she winked at him.

My policy, he thought wryly, *is to pretend I know what I'm doing. Best to stick with it.*

He nodded and smiled, made a lead-the-way gesture. She turned and they walked back to the main observatory building.

They went through the propped-open exit door, into light and stale warmth, down a curving corridor to the telescope room. Here, Latilla took his hat and coat and gestured toward the telescope.

The big room was even dimmer, duskier than during the day; the only illumination in the echoing, chilly observatory came from up under the telescope: a cone of light from somewhere on the telescope, shining yellow as a cat's eye over what looked like an operating table, but without the IV stands and monitors he somehow expected to see. Someone stepped out of the shadows into the cone of light next to the operating table, on the metal landing—a man in a white lab coat, half-frame glasses, pale, high forehead.

Stephen looked around hopefully for Glyneth, not sure why he was looking for her, why he wanted her to be here. But there wasn't anyone in the room except Latilla and the vaguely familiar man who stood above him.

Stephen found himself frozen in the middle of the room, gazing up at the man on the landing of the telescope gantry.

"Stephen Isquerat, I think, isn't it?" the man said, his voice hollow and metallic in the observatory space. He beamed a patently false smile of cheery welcome.

"I think you've met Professor Deane," said Latilla, pausing to gesture at the man. "Harrison Deane? We call him H. D."

"Oh, yes! We met, once before, in passing."

"I understand you met my father, George Deane," H. D. called down to him.

Stephen nodded. "Sort of." Stephen smiled, climbing the metal steps to the landing, and asked lightly, "So, H. D, okay if I ask, uh—what are we doing here, exactly?"

"You weren't briefed?" H. D. seemed genuinely surprised. "Oh, but Dale did say the timetable had been moved up. Something about the men in green. Yes—tonight is your first experiment for the George Deane Foundation. Your first direct experience . . . with psychonomics."

He stepped back so Stephen could see the operating table. That's when Stephen realized, for the first time, that the cone of light wasn't coming from anything attached to the telescope—it was coming out of the eyepiece of the telescope itself. The glow was somehow filtered down through the instrument, from the night sky, outside.

There was a disturbance in the air and a blurring of the details beyond—then Winderson appeared, smiling at Stephen. It was an encouraging smile, a hopeful smile, a don't-disappoint-me-you're-like-a-son-to-me smile.

Stephen nodded. "I guess we'd better . . . get to it. Whatever it is."

But he didn't move.

"Righty-oh, as Felix the cat liked to say," Latilla said, taking Stephen's arm firmly. "We'd best get to it. Right this way."

Feeling numb, Stephen moved obediently to the table in the cone of cold light.

Ash Valley

Late afternoon. The air heavy, the air hurting the back of the throat.

Bonnie Halpern was sitting on the stoop of her little house in Ash Valley, and she wasn't thinking at all about the dead baby girl in her crib.

It should have been surprising and horrifying that she didn't care about her little girl being dead in the house. But she was way beyond feeling surprised.

Horace hadn't come home that morning. She was trying to think what that meant. She had a vague sort of feeling that it should mean something. She was trying to think about the baby, too. Something hurt in her, and it had to do with the baby, somewhere, but there was no connection between the place that hurt and her mind. She knew it was there, but she couldn't feel it herself. It was like she was all cut up into jigsaw puzzle parts, and the parts weren't quite fitting together anymore. They were barely connected at all.

She was wearing her nightgown, with nothing under it, and her slippers. Nothing else. Normally she'd never come out to the front steps dressed that way. But it didn't matter today.

The phone was ringing back in the house. Bonnie knew who it was: her boss, Larry, asking why wasn't she at work waitressing at his place over near Shasta. He'd been calling all day. She'd heard his voice leaving messages on the answering machine, a little more irate with each call.

She could answer the phone and say, Hi, Larry, little Rosalie's dead. Dead at nine and a half months old. Yesterday I loved her, but today I don't seem to care that she died during the night for no reason. My husband's missing. I don't care about that either. If you were here I'd probably hurt you.

Too much trouble to go to the phone and say all that.

She got up and looked around, her eyes burning. She squeezed them shut and rubbed the lids, then looked again, trying to see the street. Some of it she could see, and some of it she couldn't. It was like a big color photograph, and someone had cut random pieces out of the photo. The street looked cut up, fragmentary—and she felt like the street looked.

Bonnie could see the little pine-lined side street she lived on that led down to the town square, with its park in the middle, where the fir trees had stood. They cut them down yesterday. But the houses across the street were snipped away, too; there was a strobing gray nothing where the houses were supposed to be. Part of the street in front of her was there, and part of it wasn't.

Something was calling to her. It was too low-pitched to hear, but she could feel it in her joints.

The call shivered into her, like the chill that comes before a fever, and it filled her loins and the emptiness at the center of her with a hot, delightful presence. She felt complete, now, and was grateful for the feeling. It told her what it wanted, and she complied without a second of hesitation. Anything to keep it inside her. She felt so much better now.

She got up and went into the house, went to the crib and picked up Rosalie's dead body by a pudgy, still-soft arm. Soft—but cold now. She went back to the front stoop, holding the dead child by her small wrist. She dangled like a handbag. One of her blue-green eyes was open, the other closed, like a broken baby doll.

Bonnie walked down the two steps to the sidewalk, and down the street. She saw Mrs. Schneider watching from her living room picture window. Old white-haired Mrs. Schneider: She had one of those paper breathing masks on and she lifted her hand to the mask and she shook her head, staring at Bonnie and the baby. She closed the drapes.

Bonnie followed the call's vibration, walking down the middle of the street. It was coming from the center of town. Maybe from the park. As she walked toward its source, the call got stronger and stronger.

Now she saw the others, walking that way—men and women. Two were naked, most were dressed as they ordinarily dressed; a few others dragged bodies along behind them. One man was dragging the body of his ten-year-old son. She knew them both, though she couldn't remember their names now. A woman was dragging her husband's body after her. It looked like the front of his skull had been smashed in.

The crowd got bigger and bigger as people came from the houses and joined the procession. It was a silent parade, no one saying anything, just marching along, all of them looking kind of contented, some even crying with happiness.

There were others, too, in uniforms she'd never seen before: men in gas masks. They didn't join the procession. They just watched.

The procession continued toward the center of town. No one walked too fast or too slow.

Someone screamed, "No, no, no, sweetheart, no, no, no!" from the little condominium complex on the corner. Then the screaming stopped.

They kept on another block and came to the square at the center of town, Bonnie swinging Rosalie's little body in time to the cadence of the procession. Rosalie's diapers were hanging half off her body now. Her skin was turning blue.

They paraded onto the street that ran next to the park rest room. Two other processions came from other directions. Across the way, there were houses, burning.

There were already some people there in the street. Most of them were dead. The marchers were laying more bodies down, smiling, some of them patting the dead affectionately. Then, she saw Mr. Harrison—wasn't that his name? The man who owned the hardware store.

Mr. Harrison from the hardware store, handily equipped with a new ball-peen hammer, walked up to the stout middle-aged Mexican lady who watched the kids of the farmworkers, during the season, and he smashed her head in with the hammer. Methodically, *chunk chunk chunk,* smiling vacantly.

When she was dead, he dragged her to the pile. A voice boomed from a white van, parked on a side street. It was an amplified voice calling out a name in a language Bonnie didn't know. But she knew somehow it was the name of the person who'd called her here.

The vibration that had called them was audible now. It was a rhythmic thrumming that made them all dip and straighten again, a slow, spontaneous group dance, in a circle around the mound of bodies. Bonnie danced slowly, swinging the dead baby at her side in counterpoint.

Above the mound, Bonnie could see a face. It seemed to

make itself out of the smoke from the burning houses. It grew more defined as she watched. It had an enormous toothy mouth, and its eyes . . .

But then she heard someone hoarsely calling her name. She looked down and saw her husband, Horace, lying on his stomach, on the edge of the mound of the dead. Only, he wasn't dead. He was wearing his mechanic's overalls but had lost his shoes. He was trying to crawl out of the mound, and she could see that he was fighting the voice, the vibration, the call.

Bonnie walked over to him, swinging the baby. She dropped the baby on the ground in front of him. He crawled toward it, his mouth working like a puppet's. The puppeteer was a mute.

Horace reached a hand out to the baby, and at the same time Bonnie knelt. She reached out her hands to his neck and began to strangle him. He was too weak to resist. "This is for you," she said to the face forming itself over the mound of the dead. "Please give me that feeling again. . . . This is for you . . . this is for you. . . ."

Bonnie kept squeezing her husband's neck for several minutes after he was dead. Then she looked up to see Mr. Harrison standing over her with the ball-peen hammer.

"This is for you," Mr. Harrison said. He wasn't talking to Bonnie.

He brought the hammer down hard on her forehead, and she fell into a hole that passed through the entire world—and the hole, she saw, was a mouth, and the mouth swallowed her.

She heard something thinking. It was not thinking in her own language, but she understood it anyway.

The spark, the spark, the spark, oh, if only it would remain with me.

Then there was a flash of black light. After that, Bonnie was as dead as anyone ever is.

5

On approach to Ashgabat, Turkmenistan

Dawn, and Aeroflot 233, shivering in its metal bones and reeking of jet fuel, was en route from Athens to Aleysk, Russia, with one stop in Turkmenistan. Ira hadn't been able to sleep on the flight. The jet was a relic of the twentieth century, and whenever they hit any turbulence he could hear bolts rattling in their sockets.

The pilot made an announcement in Russian. The scarf-wrapped old woman in the print dress sitting beside him translated. "He say we are on approach to Ashgabat." She seemed like a babushka, but she'd informed him that she was a retired college professor. She watched serenely as he took out his palm viewer, set it on the tray table, and once again unzipped his home video files of Marcus.

"Is lovely child," she murmured. "Very good heart, you can see. Is true?"

"Yes, yes indeed," he said, his own heart wrenching as he watched Marcus, a diminutive figure lost on the small screen, Marcus, just a month ago, trying to ride a skateboard. Too young for a skateboard, his mom had said, but Marcus admired Ira's cousin Varnie, who was a skateboard champion; who made balletlike ollies look easy; who carried off "variel flips to 5-0 grinds, heel flips to 360-shove-its in the half pipes," all this with aplomb and only the occasional cracked femur. Varnie had given him a skateboard, and Marcus was showing off for his dad, trying to learn how to turn corners and do the most simple skateboard jump—an ollie. Marcus japed at the camera, then skateboarded toward it, wobbly but determined, singing the lyrics to a popular song as he came, making fun of his own feeble attempts to shred, his voice full of pleasurable self-deprecation:

> *"Ever'body rides, everybody jacks*
> *Ever'body paysa jumpin' tax*
> *You gotter pay a toll to shred my site*
> *Look uppa me getter dizzy widda height—*
> *I'm all wheels . . . all wheels . . ."*

Then he fell on his rump, laughing, Ira's handheld camera shakily dipping to keep him in frame. Marcus cracked, "I needa mediscan—but not if the girls are around . . . ow damn."

Did Melissa take a portable medical scanner with her? Yes, Ira was sure she had. He'd made sure, and he'd charged its battery, too.

As she watched Marcus on the little screen, the babushka professor laughed. Eyes stinging with tears, Ira nodded, smiling, and fast-forwarded to another scene: Marcus playing with

Kenny, the little Chinese kid who lived down the street with his grandparents. The kid was eleven but was as small as Marcus, and he didn't seem much more mature. The two boys were playing a holographic game, in which they darted in among projected images and tagged treasures from the capering 3-D figures of elves and pretty witches. But one of the figures, a troll, looked a little too demonic . . . and the boy burst into tears. The boy's parents had been killed by a Sharkadian, Ira knew. Marcus switched off the hologame and, with an amazing lack of pretense, put an arm around the sob-wracked boy. Comforting this child who was two years older than him, he said, "I know what you mean, Kenny. I do."

As his Russian companion leaned into the aisle to argue with the attendants—demanding coffee and apparently being told they were too close to landing—Ira went to another file, artwork he'd made on a portable digital-art pad.

He stared at the image, shook his head, baffled. He'd been trying to sketch Marcus from memory. He'd done it before, without difficulty, but this time his sketches of Marcus's face seemed blurred, mixed with some other face, seemed too grown-up, and . . . different.

A male flight attendant signaled him to put away his palm viewer and put up his tray table. They were about to land in Turkmenistan.

The airport near Ashgabat

Customs.

He was drooping with fatigue in a Tower of Babel, voices in Greek, Turkish, Russian, Farsi, and some local dialect. He stood in a long line in a room with flaking pale-green walls and fluorescent lights on the low ceiling. He looked at his watch. Only eight minutes had passed since the last time he'd looked. He'd been sure at least half an hour had passed.

The line finally moved a step or two. He pushed his overnight bag ahead with his foot, took the step, and prepared to wait some more.

He checked his palmer for the third time since arriving. No messages from Melissa. He felt a gripping tension in his shoulders and stretched, then pushed his overnight bag ahead with his foot. He got out his passport again, thinking: *As if having it ready makes the line go faster.* He grimaced at his photo.

Someone took the passport from Ira's hand. He snatched at it, but one of the strangers—there were two of them—slapped his hand away.

Ira had an impression of unfamiliar uniforms, of jet-black eyes, solemn, almost bored expressions, and glossy black mustaches. But his eyes were drawn to the Uzis they cradled.

The shorter one pocketed Ira's passport. When he started to protest, they flashed cryptic identity cards at him, gripped him firmly by the elbows, and dragged him out of the room.

Everyone in line was careful not to show too much interest as Turkmenistan state security took Ira away.

They hustled him into gray daylight, sleeting wind, and a street braying with car horns, and then quickly into a military-green Jeep. The shorter of the two men drove; the larger man sat in the back with Ira.

They drove down a service road and out into the stony desert flecked with shrubs, and past the mazy pipes and gray towers of a refinery. There was a new chain-link fence around it, topped with razor wire. They didn't enter the refinery grounds, but Ira found himself staring, as they passed, at a sign next to the gate, its text repeated in Turkish, Cyrillic, and, at bottom, in English:

A WEST WIND INTL REFINERY

IN COOPERATION WITH THE REPUBLIC OF TURKMENISTAN

They left the refinery behind, continuing for three, maybe four miles through more of the bleak landscape. The Jeep reached the warehouses and junkyards on the outskirts of Ashgabat, which gave way to a warren of old, perhaps ancient, buildings of stone and clay and tile, tenements relying on one another to stand straight.

"If we could swing by the American embassy," Ira said, "I think all this can be straightened out, whatever the misunderstanding is." They ignored him. "Could you at least tell me—"

The big man beside Ira took his Uzi in his left hand and backhandedly smacked its muzzle against Ira's lips—not hard but sharply. It stung, and Ira got the message.

They passed a mosque, and down a side street Ira saw the distinctive cross of the Russian Orthodox church. He felt an urge to shout out the window for help, and shook his head at the foolishness of the impulse.

Next came a zone of more spacious streets, of high glassy buildings, skybridges, squat state edifices of beveled concrete. Here solo copters buzzed by overhead, natural-gas scooters crowded the street, and now and then a limo drove by. Cops in elaborate uniforms waved them through checkpoints.

Within thirty minutes of leaving the airport, they pulled up in front of a tall building of tinted glass and pitted concrete. They hustled him around the corner and through a back door, past two checkpoints, and down four flights to a sparsely lit level of what appeared to be detention cells. Down to whimpers and hoarse, despairing laughter.

They pushed him into a nearly barren, cold little room with brown-stained cement walls, a hole in the floor, and a cot. He tried once more to demand to speak to an ambassador, a lawyer, a supervisor. One of them, before locking him in alone, said, "Soon begin interrogation, sit quiet."

He never saw those two again. The ones who came later wore no uniforms.

Turkmenistan, the Fallen Shrine

"Mom—come on, wake up! You gotta see this three-eyed guy out here! He might embarrass you but he's pretty cool. Mom, you have to check it out."

Melissa sat up, blinking around at the little room where she'd been sleeping beside Marcus on a pallet. She hadn't been able to see it much when they'd gone to sleep—but there wasn't much to see: a lamp in one corner and no decorations, daylight coming brightly through the open door. She shook her head at Marcus, starting to laugh at his excitement. Then she remembered all they'd been through, and the laughter died on her lips. "Marcus! Sit down. You're sick, and we've got to have you looked at before you go running around. You couldn't be recovered already; you'd need food and—"

"I'm *fine*! Shaikh Araha told me I could do what I wanted now."

"Shaikh who?" But then she remembered who it was. "Oh."

"The old guy with the long white mustache! Shaikh Araha, Mom. He already checked me, he said I was good, I was okay. I ate some curds and honey and stuff. Come on, I want to show you the statue and the caves!"

She hastily dressed in jeans, sneakers, and a T-shirt, and let him lead her out into the pale winter sunlight. The air was crisp; she could smell coffee somewhere. "Where's Nyerza?" she asked as they went.

"He's up in one of the caves, praying," Marcus said

distractedly. "I'm gonna find him. Look at the idol in daytime—check it out. Is that thing cool or what?" Marcus gazed up at it, amused and awestruck, just standing there staring—then he ran to a crevice at one side of the idol and began climbing toward a shadowy overhang.

She had an impulse to forbid him to climb. He must still be weak and sick—mustn't he?—and she didn't want to let him out of her sight for a while. But she couldn't quite say it.

Just let him go. . . . He'll be all right. . . . We'll watch over him. . . .

"You be careful, Marcus," was all she was able to say as she gazed up at the statue.

Its sandstone cracked, blotched white by bird droppings, the idol—almost Egyptian in style but not quite—stood half-emerged from the beetling sandstone cliffs. It was as if it had been hidden away in the stuff of the Earth and then had tried to force its way out, freezing partway. Shielding her eyes against the morning sun, Melissa understood immediately what Marcus had meant by something embarrassing her. Just two yards above eye level, the idol was clasping an enormous erect phallus with its lower right hand—lower right because it had three arms, two on the right side, one on the left. The upper right hand was touching its forehead, with surprising delicacy, just to one side of its third eye. Its left hand was touching a shape made enigmatic by time and decay, close above its navel. Perhaps, she thought, it was a lotus, or a sunflower. Or what was left of a carving of the sun.

"It once had nine points on its corona, that sun," Araha said, strolling up beside her. He scratched a shaggy white eyebrow, gazing up at the idol. "We've been meaning to clean him off. This bloody awful bird mess. To clean him not out of any sense of worship, you understand, but out of respect for the monks who carved him."

"Monks? I'd have thought . . . I mean, I don't know much

about the history of the place. I thought it was an old pagan temple of some kind taken over by, I don't know, some Christian sect. But you'd have thought they'd tear down this—this fellow."

"So our friend Yanan did not tell you? Yanan was my student, you know, once. The monks who were here for several centuries were the ones who carved this idol about six hundred years ago. They knew it would be mistaken for a far more ancient pagan god. They wanted this confusion. They wished it to be mistaken for something other than what it was. Various archaeologists have assumed it to be Baal or perhaps a variant of Vishnu from some lost Hindu sect. But this one has no name at all. The idol is a *legominism*, only: a message from the past—a teaching in a code of visual symbols."

"The three minds of man," she said, looking at the statue, the three places on it controlled by the figure's three hands.

"Yes. The heart mind, the mental mind, the carnal mind— this last not only sexual but also—what would you say?—all bodily nature. Instinct and so on. His hands, you see, stand ready to guide the mind, to open the soul to the energy of creation, and to control the instincts, the sex center, redirect its power. You see, if you look at the hand, he is not caressing. He is protecting, sheltering that part of himself. He keeps the energy but does not release it in the carnal way."

She nodded. The hand, she saw now, was in front of the carved phallus, but not quite touching it. She stepped back and gazed up and down the idol. She nodded. "His arms are symmetrical, with relation to each other, to symbolize these things in balance. And his third eye is the biggest, open widest—for a consciousness that is, so to speak, open wide."

"You are right." He nodded solemnly. "So—is that you speaking of this figure's meaning, young lady, or . . . ?"

She looked at him, puzzled—and then she understood. "Or

them? They have not . . . spoken through me for a long time. I'm not sure they're still there."

He nodded gravely. "Perhaps not as before but 'Lift the stone and find me; split the wood and there I am. . . .' "

"I've been trying to place your accent—if you don't mind my asking. Your English is very good, and you seem to have a bit of a British accent. But it doesn't seem to be your native language."

He made an eloquent gesture of acknowledgment and self-deprecation. "I was educated at Eton and Oxford, but I am in fact Iranian. I lived in England, and after graduation I traveled a bit—then went back to Iran. After the Shah fell, I fled to . . . shall we say, a certain monastery in Egypt. And they sent me here. I have been here for perhaps eighteen years, a sort of caretaker and . . . like a telephone operator for this place. It is a powerful place."

"After the Shah . . ." She looked at him more closely. This man was far older than he looked. Then she remembered what he'd done for Marcus. "Oh! I am so sorry—I'm still a bit sleepy, overwhelmed. I haven't thanked you! You saved my son's life!"

"I could do not less. And I'm not certain he would have died. I suspect that he was attacked, you know. They bend the laws of probability, sometimes, the servants of That Certain One. They may have directed the tainted water to him."

Her breath caught in her throat. "You think they . . . really? They're targeting him?" She looked up the cliff side and couldn't see Marcus. If there were malign influences against him, could they make him miss his footing up there?

"Perhaps. I understand they have a *tepaphon*."

She blinked at him, waiting for an explanation. Wondering more, each second, where Marcus was.

"I see you don't know—but of course you don't. The FOGC Lodge—one of the precursors of those who brought the demons about—have an instrument. It was used by the Teutonic lodges to destroy enemies at a distance. They use it to transmit what they call 'odic' force—we call it something else, of course. Or they can draw away one's odic energies, inducing sickness and death from afar. It was made out of lenses and copper coils and copper plates. An image of the victim is placed in it, electricity is then passed through it, and one uses psychic force in guiding it. It can be used for projecting souls to other realms for various purposes. A truly arcane device. I understand that some modern devices can be adapted to become *tepaphons.* . . ."

She was only half listening now, staring past the worn, enigmatic face of the idol at the cave entrance just above the head and right shoulder. "Marcus!"

"Where is the boy?" Araha asked, a note of concern creeping into his voice.

"He climbed up there, looking for Nyerza, I think."

"In there? But it is too soon. I have not prepared you for what will happen to him. . . ." He laid a hand on her shoulder, a touch of sympathy—and it frightened her.

She pulled away from him. "What are you talking about? What will happen to him? Why were we summoned here?"

"Mother! Is that you?"

Marcus's voice—it was his voice, wasn't it?—coming from above.

She looked up, flooded with relief, to see him climbing down the crevice from the cave mouth. Nyerza emerged from the cave, peered down at her, then came down by a path that zigzagged over the cliff face. There was something like grief in the slump of his shoulders. Was she imagining that?

Marcus climbed down from the crevice. "How full of energy I feel. It's remarkable."

Melissa stared at him. "Marcus?" There was a look on his face she didn't recognize, one that didn't seem to belong there.

There was an unfamiliar depth in it, a new detachment. And—he had never called her *Mother* before. Only *Mom* or *Mama*.

He gazed up at her, in a kind of fond fascination. "My mother . . ."

Suddenly she felt the chill in the breeze, heard sand ticking against the stone. "Are you okay?" She took him in her arms, and he let her embrace him, but he seemed tentative, almost embarrassed.

Araha shook his head dolefully. "Nyerza should not have acted so soon. . . ."

"He did nothing—not directly," Marcus said softly, turning to look up the cliff. "His prayer was of a general nature, but it seemed to fill the cave with the light that cannot be seen with the carnal eyes. And then . . . I was here, fully here. The cave itself . . ." And then he said something in another language. It sounded Danish or . . .

Araha nodded grimly. "There are many ancient, powerful influences there."

Melissa felt fury welling out of her confusion. "What are you talking about?"

Marcus stepped back from his mother and took her hands in his, looking up at her with a sad compassion. He spoke gently. "Mother, what has happened is, my root soul has emerged into my mind. It was necessary for my protection and so that I could be of help in the coming battle. It's why we came here—so this could happen. We met before this life, Mother. I died and was incarnated as this boy—but that identity was lost, buried. Now, I am no longer a child—at least, not mentally. I am who I was when I died the last time. Last time, you see, my name was Mendel. If you like, Mother, you can continue to call me Marcus." The boy glanced up at Araha, sighed, and continued. "This is hard for me to adapt to as well. I wonder—do you have any brandy? I could drink a double."

Nyerza joined them; he looked at her and then at the ground.

"I'm sorry," he said.

A basement cell in Ashgabat

Ira was shivering and naked in a corner of the room, trying to decide what time of day or night it was. He was squatting on the balls of his feet, hugging himself. He was wet, though he'd tried to wipe away some of the cold water they'd dumped on him, and he was so cold it hurt. Two burly, mustached men had come in at three in the morning and stripped him, then—without a word, except a few casual remarks to each other in their own language—had dumped a bucket of cold, filthy water over his head. And then they'd taken away his clothes and his bed, and left, locking the door again.

Ira was the only feature of the room except for the waste hole in the floor and the relentlessly burning bulb in the ceiling. He was grateful for the bulb—he could feel just a faint heat from it on his head.

It was about five or six in the morning, he guessed.

He had wiped away as much of the water as he could with his hand, flicking it away to try to conserve warmth. He found the heat drained out of him faster when he leaned against the wall or lay on the floor, but he badly wanted to lie down. He *ached* to lie down. But he was afraid he'd die of hypothermia if he did.

A man who called himself Akesh had come at about two-thirty and, with the help of a veiled, dark-eyed translator, a woman who spoke middling-good English, had asked him some questions in a reasonable tone. It was strange, the man's words recycled through the woman—his sharp-edged questions in her soft female voice.

Where was his wife?

Doing anthropological work in Turkmenistan, he answered.

Why was his wife sending him messages via satellite from the distant parts of Turkmenistan?

Everyone communicated over long distances that way now, if they were out in the field.

Was he an environmentalist?

Not very actively. Mostly I'm an artist.

Was he aware that there were criminal conspiracies against the oil and natural gas refineries and processing plants in Turkmenistan? Conspiracies carried out by so-called environmentalists?

No . . . he didn't know that.

Why are you here?

To find my wife—I lost touch with her. I'm concerned about her and my child . . .

You are lying. You know where she is. Now, time for the true answers. We intercepted the transmission from a dangerous part of the desert, where we have had problems with these terrorists, who are calling themselves environmentalists, and with foreigners making deals with certain tribes of nomadic outlaws. We traced it and found the woman in question. This so-called anthropologist wife of yours. She is being watched.

Is she all right? *Please!* Are she and the boy all right?

Akesh had ignored the question. He merely lit a Russian cigarette—a stubby little thing—and went on.

I found out only yesterday evening that her claims to have a degree in anthropology are false. She is not known to be an anthropologist. So she is lying, and so is the man with her, and then so are you. And when we traced that transmission to you, we became interested in you, we did some research, and we were very interested to find that you had booked a flight here.

And now here we all are together. Now, you will tell us the truth. Let us start at the beginning. Why are you here?

I told you . . .

When it became apparent that Ira would not change his story, Akesh smiled, showing smoke-yellowed teeth, and nodded. Then he winked at Ira and went into the hall—ignoring Ira's requests to speak to the U.S. embassy or a lawyer. In the corridor, he issued orders to the guards. A little while later they came and stripped Ira naked, took away the bed, and brought in the bucket.

Crouching in the corner, rocking on the balls of his feet, aching, teeth chattering, he knew it was going to get worse. He was a little surprised he wasn't more frightened. He felt a deep, resonant remorse. He'd blundered ahead; he hadn't made a conscious choice. He'd run down the forest trail of his life on a moonless night without a torch, and he'd fallen into a ravine. And his son would be deprived of a father, his wife of a husband.

They were going to hurt him, he knew. It didn't matter that there wasn't even a reason for it. There wasn't even the reason of war, or because they thought he was a spy. It would be utterly meaningless, really. It would be inflicted mindlessly. But then, that was, he reflected, what many people experienced anyway every day. Ira knew it was so—he still felt it, sometimes, as he had of old. What was it his mother had said? The lightning seen from space . . . marking, in her view, the mindless discharge of human brutality.

Then the door opened, and three men and the translator came in. The men were Akesh and two others he hadn't seen before: a bald man with a pitted face and sallow skin and a stocky man who looked as if he would have been a harem eunuch. Both wore boots and paramilitary garb without insignia.

Akesh had a steaming mug of coffee in his hand. The smell was the worst torment so far—a hot drink would have been rapture.

The two men with Akesh had electric batons in their hands. Akesh sipped his coffee and nodded. Ira guessed what was coming; he closed his eyes and tried to cover his head.

They beat him with the electric batons about the shoulders, arms, knees, genitals, and back. The batons sent electric jolts into him at each thudding contact, and the shocks somehow delayed the feeling of the actual impact but imparted something nastier—a sensation that made him think of a crocodile jerking its prey back and forth. The electricity crashing into him felt like jaws clamping into his flesh, shaking it. Then the pain of the impact came through like earthquake aftershocks and seemed to stretch feelers to the other places of impact, so there was a network of pain; and the shocks seemed to make the network pulse with its own weird internal blue light. . . .

Ira glanced up at them from under a sheltering hand, trying to make eye contact; perhaps if he let them know he was a human being, they would ease up a little. He looked into their faces, but they did not look into his. They simply went about their work. The stocky man beat him methodically, like someone beating dust from a rug. He probably would have preferred another assignment. The bald man was smiling, his eyes growing brighter with each smack of the batons: He was enjoying this. It excited him.

Ira was lying on his side, choking with vomit, and he knew he was soiling himself; he knew his skin had split in several places, and the blood was at least warming.

"Are you ready to tell us?"

His torturers stood back for a moment and, as if through a pulsing membrane, Ira saw the translator's brown-black eyes above her veil; he saw pity there, genuine pity, and he could see she wished she could do something for him. She seemed to be silently urging him to cooperate. He felt a profound connection to her, then; he felt for a moment that he was her and she was him—that he was everyone, even the men beating him, in other incarnations. And then he felt he was outside himself and he followed the feeling, the sense of objectivity, trying to use some of the techniques he'd learned to become detached, to move above the pain and despair, the fury at his helplessness and their mindlessness, the frustration and humiliation that hurt almost as much as their blows, and then . . .

Then they hit him again.

Ira remembered an expression from his boyhood. Mom's "Boyfriend Thing" had used it. *You'll find your ass in a world of pain*

And here it was—the world of pain. Mountains and valleys, seas and winds of pain. Some pains dull, some sharp, some spiking brightly colored, others like an ashen plain.

He wanted to make something up, to make these men happy, to make it end, but he couldn't talk; his mouth was quivering in some kind of rigor like lockjaw. It just wouldn't work, and he felt himself slipping away.

Don't let go, he told himself. *You'll die.* But death would make it end, at least. *Marcus needs you. Melissa . . .*

He struggled to hold on, to speak, and he struggled within himself. Looking up at the men standing over him, he saw that they were there, and then again they weren't there. They were simply human appetites and responses, a kind of robot but entirely biological. And as time slowed for him, the batons coming at him in slow motion, the men shimmered, and for a moment he saw their true selves hidden by the masks of demons: The men hitting him were Grindums, scaled down to human size, with grasshopper legs, insectile heads, twists of horns, jaws that spun on their heads like drill bits, and Akesh had become a Bugsy. . . . But . . .

But the demons had hollow eyes, and inside their empty

eye sockets there was another face entirely, looking frightened and trapped: a child trapped inside the demons.

And then the vision vanished. They were just men again—and the batons struck and bit and ripped at him. The frightening part was that he wasn't able to feel the batons as much now. The numbness was terrifying, too. They could be ripping him apart and he wouldn't know it.

Then he saw someone else: a man from his own country, he thought, judging by the man's face and clothing. He was a tall, middle-aged man with shiny black hair; he wore a silk San Francisco Giants jacket and jeans tucked into cowboy boots. Maybe he was from the embassy. Maybe the man was here to help. He gestured, and Ira's inquisitors stepped back.

As Ira lay there panting, the pain sweeping over him again in mounting waves, he glimpsed something small and metal-glass shiny hovering in the air near the ceiling—a silvery bullet-shaped flying projector with a glass tip. Was it something hallucinatory, a vision like the demons he'd just seen?

But no—this was real technology; he'd seen it before. And Ira realized that the figure was slightly transparent. The man was a life-sized hologram, projected by the hovering device so that Akesh could see this man, talk to him. Talk to the hologram. The actual man might be anywhere in the world.

Ira felt himself close to slipping away again . . . afraid that if he went he'd never come back. Marcus needed him. Melissa needed him.

Akesh spoke to the translator, said something like, "Mister Wondasham?" and then asked a question in the hybrid language of Turkmenistan. The translator whispered something to the little flying machine as if talking to a hovering insect. The machine transmitted the question to the man, somewhere far away.

"Yes," the hologram responded, the voice coming rather tinnily from the little floating projector. "He is known to us.

JOHN SHIRLEY

Until recently he was protected by proximity to certain people. If we'd gone after him and the girl, the others, the Circle—they would've been able to trace the attack back to us; they'd have moved against us. But now he's blundered into our hands, away from those who shielded him. You did well to tell me. No, don't translate all that. Just tell Akesh that I know who this man is and that, ah—" The image flickered with interference, then sharpened again. The hologram went on. "And tell him that this man is not one of the environmental terrorists. But he's something even more dangerous to West Wind—to his government's partners. He must be made to tell us where the Gold in the Urn has gone. You fools have lost her—so where is she going next? What are they doing at the shrine with the old Shaikh? Ask him—but first, let him lie there and think. Give him a blanket and some soup so he doesn't die on us. Then give him another . . . treatment. If he doesn't respond, after one or two more treatments, make all record of his coming here disappear. And then I'd take it kindly if you'd kill him, if he isn't already dead by then."

Akesh asked one more question—his gestures made clear it was a question. The translator whispered it so softly Ira couldn't hear it over the booming, the off-key singing in his head. Pain had its own sound, today.

The hologram's only answer to the question was yes.

Then the hologram vanished, and the little bullet-shaped projector flew away.

Ira thought: *Isn't that a funny way to put it:* "I'd take it kindly if you'd . . . if you'd . . ."

But he began to slip away again.

There was just time for one more thought: The man had said they had lost track of the Gold in the Urn. They had lost track of the woman. So she at least was safe from them. Oh, thank God. Melissa was . . .

277

The sheer misery of being conscious was too much. He stopped fighting. It was delicious to slip into unconsciousness. Nothingness never felt better.

Elsewhere in Turkmenistan: The desert

Shaikh Araha sat in the front passenger's seat of the Jeep, beside Nyerza; Melissa rode in the back, beside the boy who called himself Marcus, who sometimes spoke like a dead man she'd known as Mendel.

Now, as she glanced at him, as the Jeep bounced over the rutted road in the predawn grayness, he seemed like an ordinary boy. A grave expression on his face, but boys sometimes were grave, weren't they?

The word *grave* made her want to sob. Wasn't that where her boy was, really? Wasn't he dead?

He was here but not here. She shivered and pulled the blanket more tightly around her.

The sky was clear, but it was cold. The stars seemed points of ice overhead melting where the dawn was coming in the east.

"I'm glad you're coming with us Shaikh Araha," said Marcus. Then he muttered something else in Dutch—a language Marcus could not speak.

"I am not glad of it," the old dervish said. "I had more to do at the shrine. But when I drugged the sentries, had my people tie up the men they left to watch you, it was—what is the expression?—casting the die, don't you know. Now I am a fugitive. I just hope that Hiram and the others get away. They should be all right with my Tekke friends."

Melissa leaned forward to speak to Nyerza. Her tone was cold, as it had been with all of them since she'd learned what they'd done to Marcus. "The message from Yanan—did he say when exactly Ira got to Ashgabat? Where he was going?"

Nyerza spoke without taking his eyes off the road, just turning his head a little so she could hear him over the clunking and rumbling of the Jeep. "No. We presume he was attempting to go to the Fallen Shrine. He seems to have landed, but he never came through customs, according to the dervish Yanan sent to meet him."

"What? What does that mean? How could he have landed and not—" She broke off, shaking her head in disbelief. "Oh, hell."

"We don't know," Nyerza said. "He might be fine."

After a while, the Shaikh said, "He is not 'fine.' I have a friend who works in the government. Sometimes he can arrange to have people deported or transferred to another facility. If we were to get in and out with the right papers . . ." He sighed. "I don't know. Maybe. It will be a great risk for him to do this. But . . . I don't know." He shook his head just once and the gesture had so much resignation in it.

Melissa had fought weeping, ever since the revelations of the previous morning. But now she let it come. The chill desert wind sucked away her tears before they reached her cheeks.

THE JOURNAL OF STEPHEN ISQUERAT

Writing this early evening, in my cubicle. Still recovering.

Psychonomics. They call it psychonomics.

I was lying on my back on the bed in the observatory, and I was looking up through the telescope eyepiece, some kind of little mirror really, and I was seeing an orb in there. I heard Harrison Deane say (I remember his exact words), "That's the planet Saturn you're seeing. It's seeing you quite as much as you're seeing it."

He asked if I felt anything strange, like a pulsing in my skin. I said yes. He said that an electromagnetic field was taking hold of me. It was quite harmless, he said, but it would put me into a kind of trance, and then my spirit was going to be projected into another place. I asked if it was going to Saturn. He said it would be just passing through there. My spirit was going into another universe, of sorts.

He said I would find myself passing through "certain unusual scenes." He said, "You can't be harmed there—you'll just be passing through in a way that protects you."

Then he said I'd find myself in an office. An ordinary business office, and all I had to do was speak to the man I found there. "Speak with your mind only but as clearly as you can. That will be your first real use of psychonomics." He said I had to memorize these words: *Yes to the West Wind buyout offer.* He made me repeat them.

It was as if all I could see was that ringed orb, filling up my whole sight, getting closer and closer. I managed to repeat, "Yes to the West Wind buyout offer."

"Good," I heard him say. Then I couldn't hear anyone say anything for a while, because there was a sort of white-noise staticky rushing sound that was getting louder and louder.

Then I felt a *snapping* feeling, like something broke in me except it didn't hurt, and suddenly I was standing there, *standing next to Deane* and staring down at my own body, which was still lying on the gurney-type table, staring up into the telescope lens.

Standing outside my own body, I could see that my mouth was slightly open, and a little drool was dripping onto my chin. I tried to reach out and touch my arm, but the white noise got so loud I was swept away by it, and

> then I was falling toward a glowing sea of energy that changed color from one second to the next. I crashed through it, and it was like turning inside out and outside in but without any pain. I could see Saturn again, hanging there in space above me, it seemed.
>
> But then the planet was below me and I was falling toward it.

Stephen stopped typing. He couldn't think of a way to describe what had happened next. Was that it—or was it that he couldn't bring himself to write about it? He leaned back in the desk chair in his cubicle and reached for his Styrofoam cup of coffee. He sipped, then put it down. The stuff didn't taste good cold.

He looked at his laptop. Maybe it was unwise to write this stuff down at all.

It had been a way to get the images out of his head. Project it into his computer file. He had to think about it. It wouldn't leave him alone. It demanded attention. And it demanded a decision.

He leaned back and closed his eyes. *Think about something else. Think about Jonquil.*

But his mind's eye was filled with the planet below him. Saturn. Or so it appeared. Torn from his body, projected through space, up had become down. He had rushed down into the planet's atmosphere: an endless storm of multicolored smoke. He passed through layers of shimmering liquid metal, one inside the next. Then he found himself traveling over a gleaming, seething landscape, no longer feeling he was going down—it felt like straight-ahead movement.

All this time, Stephen's mind was in a receptive, observational state—it was as if he were racing ahead of his emotional reactions, ahead of his disorientation at being torn from his body, his world, as if he were being pursued by his human feelings and he just managed to keep them from catching up.

If they did catch him, he would, of course, go quite mad.

There was something ahead written in living fire in the sky: a kind of glyph, or rune, big as a mountain, and he could feel that the rune was somehow alive and intelligent. It was watching him fly toward it. Stephen was just a soul, a spirit, but it could see him.

It was shaped like a cross with a wicked hook at the bottom; there were crosshatch elaborations that seemed to shift through a series of meanings.

As Stephen hurtled toward it, he almost understood its meaning.

It was a symbol that was also a place; it was a creature that was also a door; it was exactly on the cusp between good and evil. It was physical, but it was purely mental. It thrived on contradiction.

He flew into its center, and *through* it, like going through a door . . . a door to another world.

Then Stephen found himself in that world, no longer winging along but standing on solid ground. He was on a crag that reached up out of a sea of iridescent mist. The sky was crowded with symbols. There was no sun, no visible light source. Everything seemed to add its own faint glow to the collective illumination.

He looked at the ground. Nothing here was really solid; but the *probability* of the ground being solid under his feet was sufficient, was just enough, that it remained solid.

He looked down again and realized he couldn't see his feet. He looked at his hands, but they weren't there. He could feel them, but he couldn't see them. He had no eyes to look around with, but somehow he looked around. He was a node of perception—yet he was walking along the top of a mountain peak. It was shaped like a rough stone ax blade, this peak, and he walked along the edge of the blade to its highest point.

There were other mountain peaks in the distance, rising out of the pensive sea of mist.

Stephen found some comfort in this plane's almost earthly orientation. At least, the ground was under him; there was a sky above. A strange sky, to be sure. It was indigo around the horizon, becoming gunmetal blue overhead; a sky nervous with flocks of spinning runes, almost like spinning airplane propellers as long as he only glanced at them. But if he looked at them closely, each took on a particular runic shape, became a three-dimensional figure of quivering blue-black ink hanging in the sky. In his peripheral vision they became spinning propellers again. There were hundreds of them, floating in the abyss below the rim of the peak, hovering over the iridescent mist. There were hundreds more in the sky, thousands, some distant, some near. But when he looked at the distant ones, they suddenly seemed near.

He knelt on the stone, on his unseen knees, and looked over the edge into the churning sealike mist, which seemed to shift between violet, purple, beetle-green, second by second. When he looked into it, it seemed to react, as if it sensed the pressure of his attention.

The sea of mist developed faces, the mocking faces of infants that became old faces, then rotted in fast-forward to become oozing skulls, with tongues waggling in their eye sockets. These blew up suddenly into showers of something like flower petals— that might have been sparks of feeling, feelings of regret.

The mist churned faster, and a wave of the iridescent fog surged in slow motion into a spout that spun, shaped itself into familiar forms.

The spout of mist shaped into Jonquil. Jonquil nude. She reached for him. Then it fell back, like a waterspout falling into a sea, disintegrating. Another spout surged up: his father, trying to say something to him, shaking his head—

"Dad?" Stephen murmured.

Then his father disintegrated into the sea of mist, and the spout surged up again, spinning to a new shape like wood on a lathe, becoming something not quite man-shaped, something hideous—a demonic creature whose fang-rimmed mouth grew out of all proportion to its head, its maw becoming cartoonishly gigantic, gaping to swallow him.

Stephen jerked back from the edge of the abyss. *Don't look down there again.*

He muttered aloud, "What the fuck am I supposed to do here?"

Then he heard a voice—Harrison Deane's voice—echoing in the telescope room, as if that room were all around him as much as this place was.

"Guidance is . . . not quite connecting . . . Increase the . . ."

"Where are you?" Stephen called out. "What am I supposed to do?"

For a moment he could feel the table under his back, the cool air of the telescope room. In the next moment there was only the mountaintop in the sea of mist.

He touched the stony ground with his unseen hands—it was no particular temperature. Its color was black, seamed with white veins, but the craggy facets of its surface altered again, constantly recrystallizing, the veins rethreading. Somehow he knew that this mountain was composed of the stuff of mind: It was the production of mentation, like everything here. The stones, the mountains, were crystallizations of ideas held in common, somewhere. Some society's assumptions, formed into rough, irregular blocks of inwardly shifting stone.

Stephen wrenched his mind away from that. *Think too much about what this place is, and you'll get lost in your mind and never get out. Follow the thread of your purpose.*

He walked down the slope of the peak, and at the farther edge found what might be a crude path, carved—or *assumed*—into the cliff side. He descended the path, careful not to look into the abyss to his left. He was still well above the sea of mist.

As he descended, he felt a kind of sickening flip-flop in his middle and felt himself to be upside down; looking down the cliff path was looking *up*. Now he was ascending, though the path continued the same way. Above, on the mountaintop—what should have been the *bottom* of the mountain—he saw a wretch, a frightened, insubstantial ghost, terrifyingly familiar. Stephen wanted to reach out to that person to comfort him.

"Reach for him," H. D.'s voice came again.

Stephen reached out to the miserable ghost at the bottom—the top—of the mountain until he had leaned too far out and was falling. Falling up or down—he couldn't tell which. He was rushing toward the open arms of that wailing, ghostly figure, and into it, through it, just like he'd gone through the rune creature at the heart of Saturn.

He passed into dark interstellar space, black space occupied only with constructions of black-light traceries, photo-negative outlines, forming themselves into vast structures that were like castles, castles built on castles built on castles, each multifaceted fortress whirling like an asteroid through the void. In each was a tangled maze where demons—what else could they be?—ran and crawled and jumped endlessly after one another, endlessly preying on one another.

The seven clans, he thought. Some marched in endlessly ugly parades with banners that looked like waving arms holding stretched flaps of human skin, each banner embossed with a living human face, its eyes darting around in terror . . . a sort of nightmarish Valhalla, squirming with Tailpipes and Bugsys and Gnashers and Spiders. And the castles they bounded about in were creatures themselves: some other kind of demon . . . something more powerful, masterful.

Stephen felt himself rocketing toward one of these whirling, photo-negative castles, and felt the swarming creatures turn to face him, howling in anticipation.

He felt real fear catching up with him then. But he heard H. D.'s voice . . .

"The way has been prepared. You have only to say to yourself, 'West Wind's needs, West Wind's goals . . .' "

Stephen said it, in his mind, and as aloud as a soul can speak: "West Wind's needs, West Wind's goals . . ."

Then he was flashing past the tumbling castle and toward a star, a living star, that whispered, *"Here, come hither, hence from there, hie you here . . ."*

And he fell through the gateway of the star.

He found himself rushing down at the sea of multicolored energy again, crashing into the energy sea's surface, going down into it, *and coming out* of its surface—down becoming up again.

He was launched straight into an ordinary elevator shaft.

It was an ordinary human construction. He could see cables and, stenciled on the wall of the shaft: SAFETYPROMISE ELEVATORS, INC.

Stephen slowed to a gentle upward drift till he came to elevator doors. He passed through them as if they were gossamer and came to a halt in the hallway of an ordinary earthly office building.

———

Stephen shook his head. He couldn't write that stuff down. He started typing again.

I passed through a series of strange worlds I can't really describe, including a sort of space filled with floating, spinning castles swarming with demons. It was as if H. D. was guiding me. I found my way to a star that was a kind of entrance back to our world. Then I was in our world, on Earth, but I was there astrally. OBE-like. Disembodied. Whatever you want to call it.

But I was really there. I could feel the carpet under my feet. It felt good: Anything to be away from the other place. Though I hadn't realized it, I'd been on the verge of dissolving into terror in that place, and now I was somewhere more or less familiar. It was the hallway of an ordinary office building.

There were people walking past me, going about their business. Ordinary people, but I had the sense that *they were just riding their bodies around—and the bodies, not the souls, decided where they would go.* Not one of them looked at me. I was invisible.

There was a guy from Pakistan or India, pushing a cart full of racked computer disks; there was a woman whose bald head was painted different colors—I recognized it as a style some people sported in cities like New York. I'd seen a commentator making fun of it on TV. I heard people talking, in a fuzzy kind of way; some of them had New York accents.

I felt a sort of inner tugging that told me where to go. I walked through a door without opening it. I walked right *through* the wood, then down a hall, through another door, then I found myself coming up behind a man who was standing at a floor-to-ceiling window, his hands in his pockets, gazing out at the Manhattan skyline. There was a scaffolding on the top of the Chrysler building—it was still being restored, I remembered, because people suffering from the demon hallucinations had destroyed it somehow. The man looking at it wore a white shirt, a tie, tailored trousers. He was blond, but partly bald, I think. I never did see much of his face. He was frowning as if at some thought. It was as if he was trying to remember something.

I came to a stop. Whatever had directed me here was waiting. There was something I had to do. What was it?

I couldn't remember.

Out of the corner of my eye I seemed almost to see those hideous faces in the iridescent mist—faces created by my own fear, I knew, but hideous anyway. I focused my attention on this office, this view of the city in the early morning.

What was I supposed to do?

Then I remembered. I tried to speak but found I couldn't make a sound. I could sort of feel my mouth, but I couldn't make a noise with it. Then I remembered just to think it, clearly: *Yes to West Wind buyout offer.*

I thought those words over and over, staring hard at the man, and he seemed to lift his head and nod as if in answer to an idea.

Yes to West Wind buyout offer.

And then I heard H. D.'s voice. He said something like: *"Just relax. Feel the table under you . . . those warm pulses going into you. Go with the feeling they bring to you . . . ride them back to the sound of my voice."*

There was a rushing as I passed back through the shining sea, past a mountain, through a storm, through a living white noise, and suddenly I was back on the gurney, staring up at a small, bright light. It moved—it was some kind of doctor's examination light.

H. D. was leaning over me, shining the light into my eyes. He was frowning. I was back in the observatory. I blinked and turned my head (the light was beginning to hurt) and he straightened up, nodding with satisfaction. Looking up at him was like looking up a cliff to the top of a mountain. Peering down from somewhere above his head was a frightened ghost.

I found myself sobbing and clawing to get off the table. They undid the straps and gave me something hot to drink in an Inimicalene cup. I think it had a tranquilizer in it, because the peculiar old lady and Harrison Deane had to help me to my bed.

I slept for a while, and when I woke up, I felt I had to write this down, to remember, to be sure it wasn't a dream. Or to be sure it was

But it wasn't a dream. Even more than the mushroom faces in that tray of dirt in the pyramid: not a dream.

I want out of this. I'm going to tell them today. *I want out!*

Maybe I'll just leave. I'll send them an e-mail later or something. Jonquil obviously doesn't intend to get back in touch with me. So there's no reason to stay.

I should just leave.

6

Ira didn't want to open his eyes.

Eyes shut, he stayed in the dream. If he opened his eyes, he'd be back on that soiled, icy stone floor.

But here, in the nothing place, he was floating on a multi-colored sea, a sea that was the border between two worlds; and here he was safe, floating on liquid energy. He could feel Yanan and Melissa and . . .

No, Marcus was strangely absent. Marcus was there, but then he wasn't.

There was a wedge of cold stone forcing its way into this world. He could see it in the roiling, misty sky: a giant stone ax, primitive as the men who first wielded it, men who lived within his torturers. Angling down at him, a giant ax to smash him.

It was a feeling, really, the feeling of the stone floor under him as he began to wake. *Leave me dead! Don't kill me, just leave me dead.*

But the stone ax of the waking world slammed down into him, though he tried to hold on to the other place by squeezing his eyes shut.

He could hear their footsteps; he could hear their voices. He knew what they were going to do.

"Ira?"

Now he was hallucinating Melissa's voice, her touch on his face. Then a great multiple crackle of pain flashed through him as someone picked him up.

He opened his eyes—more in a convulsive reaction to the pain than for any other reason—and looked up between swollen eyelids at a great blur of a face. The face came in and out of focus. There: an old man with drooping white mustaches.

"Who the fuck are you?" Ira said, before lapsing again into semiconsciousness. Gone was the sense of the ecstatic otherworldly place; only a foggy limbo remained, echoing with voices, familiar and unfamiliar. They were the voices of people around him, yet they were infinitely far from him, too.

"We must hurry," the man carrying him said, this time speaking in English.

Ira felt another, agonizing, many-forked lightning strike pass through him as he was laid onto some sort of stretcher. He arched his back with the crackling pain.

A hand patted his shoulder, stroked his cheek; a blanket was draped over him. The pain subsided to merge into a swinging nausea as the stretcher was carried somewhere, someplace slightly warmer. The echoing footsteps around him suggested a corridor. He heard a muted scream from some other cell. Or maybe it was his own cell; maybe it was himself screaming back there still. Maybe these demons had come to carry his soul away, to wrap it in cerements and carry it into their world. It made a change, anyway.

"Quickly," someone said. "My friend in this place cannot help in person, so if the papers he gave us are questioned, we are lost. Your veil, adjust your veil."

Then he heard a voice that made him want to shout with rage: Nyerza's voice. "We're almost there."

So they weren't demons, except in the way that any human could be a demon: They were humans who'd betrayed him. And Ira shouted: "Damn you, fuck you, you hypocritical bastard. You stole my wife and child!" Forcing the words out as loudly as he could, though every syllable hurt coming through his swollen face. But he seethed and burned with rage. Nyerza was in league with his interrogators!

"Quiet!" Nyerza's voice said urgently above Ira's head. "You'll give us away!"

"Fuck you, fuck you! You're working with them, you son of a—"

"It's all right," came the other man's voice from near Ira's feet. He sounded as if he had his back to Ira—carrying the stretcher from the front. "Let him rave. He would, as a prisoner being transferred to a madhouse."

All this in the gray mist, the limbo place—he still didn't want to open his eyes. He couldn't bear to see.

He heard them talking to a sentry. An explanation was whispered in English to someone. There would be a delay of perhaps half an hour before they could be allowed to leave, because the sergeant with the authority to let them go was off somewhere eating.

But in time they would transfer him to a mental hospital. Who knew what cruelties they would inflict there? Brain-wrecking drugs perhaps.

His rage made him forget his earlier, dazed passivity. Ira

struggled to get free of the blanket, to roll off the stretcher—shouting without words—and then he felt a hand take his and gently squeeze. He knew that hand, that small soft hand.

It couldn't be her, really, could it? He might have looked to see if it was her. But if he did . . . he knew what he'd see: only the translator. And Nyerza, his betrayer.

Enemies.

Strangers.

Traitors.

Better to keep his eyes shut, hold this stranger's hand, and pretend it was Melissa.

San Francisco Airport

Exiting the 797, Stephen was dazedly surprised to find a limousine driver waiting for him, holding a sign with his name on it. "You waiting for me?" Stephen asked him. "I'm Stephen Isquerat."

"Yes, sir," said the young Asian-American driver. "West Wind sent the limo for your convenience, with their compliments."

Stephen shrugged. "Lead on, then."

He'd told West Wind he was quitting, and yet they were sending limos for him. Maybe they were hoping to get him to change his mind.

Let them try. He wasn't going back there. The dead animals floating in that pond, the nightmares they'd sent him into, in another world—and in his own. He wasn't going back. But there was no reason he shouldn't take advantage of a free ride. Maybe it was Winderson's way of saying no hard feelings.

Stephen didn't really care. He was just trying to get from point A to point B without breaking down; and that meant he had to believe in the world as it was supposed to be.

It wasn't easy, because of the way people kept turning into

ghosts all around him. Or spirits. They were spirits, all these people: spirits in designer sneakers and loafers, spirits in sports coats and raincoats, spirits with luggage swinging in their hands, spirits speaking on cell phones, spirits watching television shows in the gate area as he came out. That feeling he'd had, drifting unseen through that New York office building, had never completely left him. These people were in ordinary human bodies, to be sure, but it was as if they were *riding* the bodies instead of *being* the bodies—carried within them, trapped in forms that were making all the decisions about where to go and forced to ride along willy-nilly.

This point of view was sickening. It made everything seem ephemeral, dreamlike, insubstantial. Only once did he see a man who looked solid, unghostly: a middle-aged Oriental, perhaps a Tibetan. The tote bag he carried looked like Tibetan craftsmanship. The man seemed to sense him, then turned and stared at him. Did he nod just slightly? Then he moved away, moved more purposefully in some indefinable way than the people in the crowd around him, though each no doubt had a destination. It was as if this Tibetan were more *here* than the others.

And then he was lost in the crowd.

Walking beside the limo driver, Stephen felt as if everything might melt away at any moment, and the only thing that kept the whole world in place was a *thought*. A Big Thought that was thought by something unknown. But if whatever was thinking that Big Thought stopped thinking it, then all this would go away, melt into a sea of chaos, a sea of energy.

They went down a moving-stairs device used for transporting spirits from one deck of temporary material to another: a crowd streaming down an escalator.

It was with relief that he made it out into the morning,

overcast but shiny from a recent rain. Here he could breathe cool air and feel a breeze on his cheeks and hands as he waited for the driver to fetch the car. The chill felt real.

"The white zone is for loading and unloading only."

A silvery stretch limo pulled up, its electric engine eerily silent. The young Asian driver got out, came around, and opened the door for him. "Here you go, sir," the driver said, smiling; the smile was locked away in his mouth, and he didn't communicate with his eyes at all.

Stephen got in the back, a little reluctantly. He hadn't asked for this. It felt close in here, smelling of leather and cigar smoke and—gardenias? He hit the switch to roll the window down, let the cool air shock his cheeks. "You're not cold, sir?" the driver asked, as they pulled away from the curb, jockeying with the taxis and shuttles.

"No. I need the fresh air this morning." Stephen found himself staring out the left side window at ruins. There'd been a restaurant there once, hadn't there, when he was a teenager? One of those circular restaurants on the edge of the airport. The shattered walls, marked off with yellow tape, looked muddy; the ground around them was covered with weeds grown through an ice field of broken window glass. And on one of the remaining walls were what looked like big, deep claw marks. "They tearing something down over there?" Stephen asked, to keep his mind busy.

"Yes, sir, they're finally clearing that away. Supposed to begin rebuilding it next month," the driver said. "That's what I heard. It's been there for nine years. The demons, the crazed people, they did so much damage at the airport, it's taken a long time to get it all fixed up. It only just got back up to full capacity like a year ago."

A tram full of passengers went by—a box of ghosts on

wheels, it seemed to him. He shuddered, thinking of the sea of energy, the mountain that stood on its own peak, the face.

Oh God, where did I go?

He wanted to sob. He seemed to see that terrible, frightened, hollow-eyed face staring at him again. Those disconnected pin-wheels, like propellers and not like propellers, hanging in the sky. That face—a raggy, threadbare version of his own soul.

A sob escaped him. When the driver looked at him in the rearview mirror, Stephen tried to turn it into a cough.

He noticed a rack of miniature bottles and glasses, under the window that separated him from the chauffeur. "Little bit of a croup. You think it's okay if I have a drink from this bar here? I mean it's sort of early, but it eases this, uh, cough."

"It's there for your convenience, sir."

Stephen opened a miniature whiskey, then another and made himself a double in a small brandy glass. He drank half of it down quickly, grateful for the familiarity, the mundanity of it soothing. Some of the lingering ghostliness retreated.

He began to think about the prospect of getting another job. He could find something. A lot of people had died nine years ago. There weren't really enough qualified people around. Most likely it would be much more entrance-level than what he'd had at West Wind. Or maybe he could pull a little invest-ment money together, get back into online trading. Most of the lines were back up.

Dickinham had stared at him and said only, "Uh-huh," when he'd caught Stephen heading out, carrying his grip, and Stephen had told him he was quitting.

Psychonomics? Had the process really projected him out of his body? It had been some kind of hypnotic experience, he told himself. A vision in a trance. A training tool of some kind, enhanced by his own morbid imagination.

Or it had been real. After all, the experiences he'd had as a boy now seemed to have been real.

But it didn't matter. Either way, he wasn't going back there.

They drove onto the freeway, but they were scarcely a mile toward the city before the limo took an exit onto a side street he didn't know. "Shortcut to another freeway?" Stephen asked.

The driver shook his head. "No, the hospital is right here. It's the new one by the airport."

"The hospital?"

They pulled into a parking lot and drove to the emergency room doors of a very modern hospital, a big building with sweeping curves of tinted glass, balconies tufted here and there with deck gardens. The breaking sunlight purpled on its rain-wet surfaces, reminding Stephen of the wings of a fly.

Winderson was there, standing under the Emergency sign, wearing an unbuttoned trench coat. Behind Winderson stood a big black man with wavy, greased-back black hair, sunglasses, and a black suit and tie. He wore a headset, and his hands were folded in front of him. *A bodyguard,* Stephen thought. Tongan, maybe.

But maybe not a bodyguard—maybe it was just a guy hanging out here, and Winderson wasn't really here, not physically. Maybe this was a hologram.

Then the CEO opened the door of the limo himself and bent down to speak softly to Stephen, who hurriedly put the whiskey glass away.

"She's up on the sixth floor, Stephen. It's faster to go in this way. They know me by now."

"Who's up on the sixth floor?"

"Jonquil! She was admitted just a day ago. Didn't anyone tell you?"

Ashgabat

The sergeant had taken thirty-five minutes. They waited with Ira in a sweat-reeking little holding room near the doors to the outer world, and Melissa wanted to scream from tension, sure that at any minute those who had incarcerated Ira would notice he was gone. She prayed they, too, were at their meal.

Araha had induced a kind of quiet in Ira somehow. Ira had slipped into semiconsciousness and now lay rocking slightly from side to side on the stretcher, lips moving soundlessly.

Then a uniformed guard with a pocked face and a slack mouth gestured to them from the doorway. They followed him to the checkpoint booth.

There were two sentries at the booth beside the exit doors of the state security building. They only glanced at Melissa in her veil and the head-to-toe garb of a devout Muslim woman; but they stared at Ira, then for long, muttering moments at Nyerza—there weren't many blacks in Turkmenistan state security and even fewer so tall they had to stoop to pass through the doorway.

Melissa and the others had agreed on a story ahead of time, and Melissa knew what Araha was telling the sentries, with much ironic gesticulation: that Nyerza was a security consultant from Nigeria, where this American on the stretcher had worked with the environmental terrorists. They'd had a Turkmen soldier helping carry the stretcher but the fool had disappeared, was loafing somewhere, so this dignitary volunteered to carry one end. Can you imagine? There will be a report on the slacker—one Amu.

The sentries chuckled—they all knew at least one Amu. Their sergeant took a second look at the papers.

We have a chance, Melissa thought. The papers of transferral were, after all, legitimate, having been obtained by Araha's contact in the government—legitimate, except that the name of the authorizing officer was fabricated. And it wasn't uncommon to transfer prisoners to a mental hospital, for holding until they were needed again.

Melissa's heart thudded and the fear was magnified when she found herself wondering if she were committing a sin against humanity—risking herself, members of the Conscious Circle, who were all too rare and all too important—just to rescue her husband. It was selfish. And if they were caught, Marcus would be left alone with strangers in this foreign land.

But then, Marcus was not Marcus. She forced that thought down, because with everything else, it was just too much to bear.

When would they be done looking at the papers?

Then the sergeant shrugged and said something in his own language. He pressed a button. The door buzzed, declaring itself momentarily unlocked. Nyerza pushed through, trying not to hurry, he and Araha toting the stretcher.

Their contacts—two tall, turbaned men in long coats— were waiting with the truck outside, Marcus with them. They were Turkic Sufi dervishes who sometimes worked with Araha. Brave men but both had been unwilling to enter the building, so Nyerza had been forced to be a stretcher bearer.

Marcus looked up at Melissa as she got into the back of the truck. Before the Fallen Shrine, he would have rushed to her arms, seeing his mother back, safe from danger. But now he only smiled encouragingly.

Their contacts gave them truck keys and good wishes, and hurried off down a side street.

———

It was only a short drive to the Iranian border, but here they stopped. There were four guards at the checkpoint in a glass-walled booth by the gate across the highway, playing a game with odd-looking dice. Two of them grumpily got up from their game and made Melissa, Nyerza, and Araha get out of the truck and stand in the chill drizzle as they peered in the back at Marcus and Ira, who mumbled in his delirium. Once again most of the guards stared at Nyerza; but a fat lieutenant in a turban and uniform, tugging at his pointed beard, gave his attention mostly to Melissa. His eyes were so small in the heavy folds of his face she could barely see them.

"You look back boldly," he said in English. She dropped her eyes, and he snorted. "She is American or British," he said flatly to Araha. "You will all be arrested, if you please."

"How could it 'please' us?" Araha asked mildly. "I have something around my neck to show you. Perhaps it will change your point of view . . . perhaps it will touch your heart." He said something else in Turkic.

Melissa despaired. She knew that around his neck, on a thong, he wore a silver nine-pointed geometrical symbol with a cross superimposed over it and on either side of the cross the crescent moon and star of Islam. Just an esoteric medallion, representing his syncretistic sect. Did he really think this man would respond? Or did Araha suppose this man was a dervish, a member of his order?

Not this man, she thought. He emanated lust and greed and self-satisfaction.

Araha drew out the medallion and a leather bag, also on the thong. He opened the bag and produced a roll of bills. She saw one of the colorful new American twenty-dollar bills—red, white, and blue with a green border.

Araha whispered something in what sounded like Turkish; perhaps, *How much do you want?*

The man snorted, and laughed, and said something that must've meant, *All of it, of course!*

Araha looked convincingly exasperated, made a few noises of protest, and nodded in reluctant agreement. As if suddenly realizing this stranger with the drooping white mustaches was an old friend, the fat lieutenant moved to embrace Araha. When he got close, he took the money with a practiced swipe of his hand, like a raccoon fishing. His girth hid the exchange from the other guards. The money vanished into his uniform. The lieutenant gestured to a corporal, who threw a switch, causing the gate to creak open.

Almost high with relief, Melissa climbed into the back of the truck to sit with Ira and Marcus. They trundled through the gate, and into Iran.

Later, when they had arrived at the little airstrip where the plane was waiting, Melissa asked Araha how much money he'd surrendered—hoping she could reimburse him somehow.

He laughed. "Not so much. Twenty on top, the rest all ones. He didn't look closely. Most of my money is in my boot. I always keep dollars ready for this day."

South San Francisco

The bodyguard, standing behind Stephen, breathed loudly through his mouth as if he suffered from asthma. The sound dominated the elevator as they rode up to Jonquil's room. Winderson was scowling at the spotless floor of the elevator, his hands thrust into the pockets of his trench coat. "They call it cancer, a tumor. I call it an attack, myself. I mean—it's cancer, but . . ."

"An attack?" Stephen asked, overwhelmed, his voice hoarse. "You mean—like a relapse? She was sick before?"

"Hm? No, she wasn't. It was an attack like— I'll explain later. Here's the floor. I'm making arrangements to have a room set up for her at headquarters, like George's private hospice, with her own doctors. But this was all very sudden, so for now . . ."

Stephen followed Winderson down a hall. How many West Wind people were tucked away in secret little hospice rooms—and why?

The room Jonquil was in, however, was the best in the hospital: large and sunny, gushing with get-well flowers and untouched baskets of fruit clasped by transparent Inimicalene. It was almost a suite, overlooking the freeway and San Francisco Bay beyond. There was an entertainment center near the foot of Jonquil's hospital bed, the wide-screen TV turned on but muted, a sardonic daytime talk show host waving his arms wildly at an audience of clapping people with painted faces.

The bodyguard waited at the door, watching the hall, as Stephen and Winderson approached Jonquil's bed.

She gazed out the window at an enormous cargo ship on the bay, the freighter's decks stacked with interlocked metal bins, easing toward Oakland. "That ship," she said, her voice weak, "it's like a skyscraper lying on its side, floating along. . . . It's so big. I never thought about how big those ships are before. It's funny the things you notice when you . . . when you're sick." She pressed a button, raising the head of her bed so she was almost sitting up. She was wearing a satiny blue low-cut nightgown; her skin was very pale, the orbs of her cleavage like twin moons. Her blue eyes had lost some of their luster; there was a smudge around them; her lips showed the faintest blue tinge of cyanosis.

She turned a stalwart smile to Stephen and her uncle. Her

long hair, looking redder than usual in this light, was spread across the luxuriant silk pillow, as if arranged by a photographer.

"Hi," Stephen began, not sure quite what was expected of him. "You . . . well, I guess it's stupid to say you look good, since of course you don't feel good. This all happened so fast. Just a day or two ago . . . well, you seemed fine."

"She was," Winderson said bitterly, slowly pacing the length of the room. "She was fine." He took a few steps, picking up magazines from a coffee table at the sofa, putting them down, picking up a knickknack, not really looking at it as he spoke. "Our enemies have attacked her, you see. That's the only way something so serious could happen so suddenly to someone in such good health."

"We don't know that, Uncle Dale," Jonquil said in a small voice. "The doctor said sometimes it happens this way."

So this is it, Stephen thought.

This is why she was crying; this is why he hadn't heard from her. She'd gone almost immediately into the hospital.

"You keep saying 'attacked,' " Stephen said. "You mean— like poisoned?"

"In a way," Winderson muttered. Then he looked at Stephen sharply. "Psychically poisoned. I think she was psychically attacked. You see, we're not the only ones with psychonomics. There are others who use it—competitors. Evil, sick, unscrupulous people. Oh, you're not in any danger. People like you, with natural abilities, you're protected. It's like you have a psychic immune system. But Jonquil here . . ." He shook his head.

Stephen felt dizzy. *This talk of being attacked, of enemies—it has to be bullshit. It sounds like bullshit.*

But what if it's not. Then I might . . .

In a way, Jonquil completed the thought. "If it's true . . . what Uncle Dale says—" her eyes glimmering with unshed tears as she looked at him "—you could help me. But, Uncle Dale says that you're leaving? Quitting? I mean—it isn't because of me, is it? Because I didn't get back in touch after we . . ."

"No!" Stephen swallowed. He badly wanted another drink. "It's just . . . maybe I do have the ability to . . . under certain conditions, to, uh . . . well, to do what I did. But that doesn't mean it's something I *want* to do. I mean, to use a corny example, if I had a talent for being a sumo wrestler, I wouldn't necessarily want to spend my life bashing sweaty people on a mat. I might be good at this, but I don't think I'm cut out for it."

"Stephen," Winderson said, looking at him with a kind of amazed disbelief, "don't you get it? You *succeeded!* You were a great success! No one else has done so well! The man you were sent to influence did just what he was supposed to do—within minutes! Totally reversing his earlier position! It can't be a coincidence."

Stephen looked from Winderson to Jonquil. "You know about all this?"

She nodded slowly, looking a little puzzled. "Ye-es. Some of it. Enough. It's like advertising—or salesmanship. But psychic. Psychic influence on economics." She winced and pressed a button for a nurse. "I need some morphine."

"My boy," Winderson went on in a hushed voice, his hand on Stephen's shoulder, "you succeeded—and that meant so much to us. We've been searching for someone with the gift, the ability to succeed at this, for a long, long while. The last one—well, now that you've succeeded at this—there's something so much more important we need you to do. Something that will change the world, and save Jonquil's life."

A young male nurse with a crew cut came in. "Can I help you, miss?" he asked.

"I need a little more medication—the pain."

"Sure, I'll—I'll get that. I mean, I'll get the doctor. He can . . . do that."

He hurried out, glancing at the bodyguard. There was something odd about the nurse. Stephen shook his head.

Then Jonquil took his hand, and the touch sent a shock of lurid electricity into him right down to his groin. "Stephen—I don't know if I'm being attacked, but I know there's something you can do to help me."

"I—I'd like to. Of course. But I don't see what I can do."

"You can go there, to the invisible world . . . find the right place in the spiritual ecology."

"Spiritual ecology?"

"A sort of technical term," Winderson interrupted hastily, glancing at her. "From psychonomics."

Jonquil licked her lips and went on. "I need your help—in that world. There's a thing called the Black Pearl. . . ."

"The Black Pearl . . . ?"

"I know it sounds weird . . . but this thing—this object—is a kind of mirror that can show me how to get well. And to get to it you have to go there. You have the gift that'll take you there. We haven't got anyone else talented enough. You are our retriever."

"But, that world, real or not—it's all a mental place. You can't bring an object *back*. Objects there don't exist in the same way, from what I can tell."

Winderson nodded. "That's true, but this thing won't be an object here. Not in the usual way. Nevertheless, you can make it *appear* here."

Stephen stared out the window. There was the freighter, still coasting slowly by. It was made of metal, and it was real. There was San Francisco Bay. It was cold, and you could drown in it. It was all *real*. "I . . . don't know if I can keep my sanity if I go there again."

She squeezed his hand and drew him closer; her lips parting as she looked directly up into his eyes. She looked at him that way for a moment, panting almost imperceptibly. Then, heavy lidded, she said, "You're *strong*, stronger than you know. I can feel it. I felt it from the moment we met." She looked away, embarrassed.

"There are some things uncles aren't meant to hear," Winderson said. "Maybe I should . . ."

"No, it's okay," Jonquil said. "The doctor will be here in a second anyway. I have to rest. I don't know how long I have, Stephen."

Stephen remembered the journey through the telescope, through the multicolored sea. He shivered, feeling again the terror of falling toward a living maze crawling with demons like a wound with maggots.

But Jonquil was dying, and there was a way, they said, to save her. This was his chance to be a hero, like Horatio Hornblower. To sail into unknown realms and bring back the prize. He was, after all, in love with her.

Wasn't he?

He wondered where Glyneth was. He found himself wishing he could ask her about all this.

"We need your decision now, Stephen," Winderson said gently but firmly.

Jonquil squeezed his hand, drawing his gaze back to her. She looked at him, lips compressed in a way that betrayed her hope, though she managed not to seem like she was imploring him. "Will you help me, Stephen?"

No pressure, he thought and almost laughed aloud. But when he looked in her eyes, he couldn't look away. Finally he said, "I'll do what I can."

"We'll need to take my chopper back to Bald Peak immediately," Winderson said, looking at his watch.

As if to seal a pact, Jonquil pulled Stephen close and kissed him. Then she whispered, "When I'm well . . . I want you. The two of us, again . . ."

"I—I'll be there. Just whistle."

He straightened up, and she lay back, as if the conversation had exhausted her, and closed her eyes.

In a daze, Stephen followed Winderson out into the corridor, the bodyguard trailing behind. They went down the hall, up a series of stairways, to a helipad on the roof of the hospital. A small gold-and-black West Wind chopper was waiting, a pilot already seated in the cockpit.

Winderson climbed in first. The bodyguard took Stephen's arm to help him, as if he were a frail old lady, and then climbed in to sit behind him. Stephen wondered: *Is this guy a bodyguard at all? Maybe he's more than that*

The pilot was a bald white man with dark glasses and a pencil-thin mustache. Winderson never said a word; the pilot seemed to know their destination. The chopper lifted seconds after the door slammed shut, and they tilted sickeningly into the sky, leaning toward Ash Valley and the observatory.

Stephen felt close to retching from the juddering of the chopper as, fighting turbulence, they curved through the air to head north. But at least most of the sense of unrealness had gone, his feeling that everyone was a ghost. Somehow Winderson had grounded him, got him involved with real life once more. He didn't understand the Black Pearl thing—it must be some kind of metaphysical object that would help Jonquil cure herself, some mind-body connection he could help her make. But the main thing was, he was back in the swing—and he had a chance to help a woman he desired to the depths of himself.

After they left the San Francisco peninsula behind, the helicopter's passage steadied, and so did Stephen's stomach. He tried not to think too much, keeping his mind occupied by looking at the roads snaking through the agricultural checker-board far below. But despite himself, he found himself musing: *Is what I'm doing really what my father wanted for me when he set this job up?*

He remembered his father reading poetry to him on Halloween, when he was a boy: "Quoth the Raven, 'Nevermore' . . ."

His father would be with him nevermore. Dad had been so dulled by pain and then drugs at the end, they hadn't talked much. And just after this, Stephen had gone off on a business trip, on money he'd earned from online trading, and his father had died. There had been no last words for Stephen.

But sometimes he thought he *felt* his dad trying to say something to him.

Suddenly he remembered the Reverend Anthony. The swirling death in the water at Ash Valley. The gull on the hood of the Hummer. People in gas masks. And what Glyneth had said about a possible military connection. It nagged at him. Maybe it was time to clear the air.

He was, after all, *in* with Winderson now—he would be saving Winderson's niece's life. Which meant he was empowered to ask awkward questions. He thought, *Ask about it—get it off your chest.*

He took a breath and plunged in. "Dale . . . I saw some stuff in Ash Valley that made me wonder. Dickinham said . . . well, I had the impression he was talking to military people about the D17 test . . ."

Winderson frowned, and then shrugged. "Yes, Stephen—the military. Well, the military wants to use the stuff to protect military personnel in places where there's a heavy mosquito presence, risk of encephalitis, tsetse flies—that sort of thing."

"But in town . . . I mean, people had to wear gas masks. And all the dead animals. I'm just worried about the publicity angle—if it gets out of hand. D17 seems so powerful. It just seemed like . . . overkill."

"Ah. Yes, it could be, Steve, that we . . . miscalculated. To be sure, the stuff was sprayed near the town, it was picked up by a wind, blown over the town. . . . There are always factors that are difficult to predict. But you see, my boy, in the long run we're trying to increase food production, find ways to fight insects that have grown resistant to pesticides. There are more than six billion people on this planet. You can't sneeze without hurting someone somewhere.

"You've got to see the big picture, Stephen. And from the top of the corporate ladder, I assure you, you will understand!" He smiled warmly.

Stephen felt some of the weight lifted from his shoulders. It was true: He had just panicked; he'd forgotten the big picture.

The chopper shuddered onward. At last Winderson said, "Almost there," and Stephen saw the observatory swinging into view ahead and below.

He glanced at Ash Valley . . . and did a double take. Staring.

The new roads that West Wind had been building were more clearly marked out now, though they were still just straight-edged gouges in the land. They extended raylike from the out-skirts of the town, sharply angling in convergent lines that made five points, symmetrical all around the town: a giant pentagram carved in the land, with the town at its center. And the trees had been cut down in the park, pulled right out of the ground. In their place was a symbol, in the very center of town, marked out with the same roadlike gougings, visible only from the air.

Stephen had seen that symbol before—in the heart of his astral vision. The rune that was a creature—it had been shaped like that.

Exactly like that.

Rostov, Russia

Melissa sat by Ira's comfortable hotel bed in Rostov. It was still dark out, but on the verge of dawn. She saw the transferral papers that had gotten Ira out of prison, folded in a side pocket of Nyerza's grip—they really must destroy them. She said a quick prayer, asking that Araha's friend in the government, a Sufi-in-secret, didn't pay for those documents with his life.

Nyerza had made some calls to associates from the Circle, who had arranged to have a private cargo plane waiting for them just over the border in Iran. They'd flown from there to the Caspian Sea and northwest to Rostov. Melissa had wanted to find a hospital in Iran, but Araha had warned that there were too many corrupt Irani officials who might, for a price, arrange for their extradition back to Turkmenistan, since by now they were being sought. She'd worried all through the journey that Ira might at any moment die of internal injuries. But, heavily sedated, he'd slept through the truck and jet rides, all the way to Rostov.

Nyerza hadn't seemed worried. He'd accomplished his mission. After all, she thought bitterly, Mendel was back. That was why they'd come to Turkmenistan: to annihilate her son's personality with the reawakening of a previous incarnation.

The hospital had been crowded and squalid. X-rays revealed no life-threatening physical trauma or serious internal bleeding in Ira—only a cracked collarbone, a minor concussion, a chipped kneecap, dozens of deep bruises, some broken teeth—and it was decided to take Ira to somewhere he could be more comfortable. Someplace quiet.

Now the only sounds were Ira's raspy breathing, the hissing of a samovar, the sound of men talking with Marcus over their teacups in the next room. None of them had slept much, but the old dervish and Nyerza were already up, talking. And Marcus.

Marcus.

Mendel.

A boy's voice, a strange man's words. She could scarcely bear to be around him.

They lied to me, she thought furiously. *They knew what would happen to Marcus.* They needed Mendel's consciousness back fully, and they'd sacrificed her child. They could claim, if they wanted, that Marcus had always been Mendel—that he'd only forgotten it. They could claim that being Marcus had been a kind of amnesia—an amnesia that had simply ended.

But something had died that day in the cave.

She brushed some hair from Ira's eyes; he stirred in his medicated sleep and groaned. Every movement hurt him, even in sleep: He was one great mass of bruises. They'd managed to get some broth down him, and the doctor had given him a vitamin shot. But he couldn't eat solid food. There was too much facial swelling, too many cracked teeth.

"My poor, foolish husband," she murmured. "Why didn't you stay home?"

She heard Marcus speaking, in tones measured, thoughtful, and grave, in the next room. All the innocence had been cauterized from his voice.

She was lucky to have Ira alive. He'd endured only a single day of torture; in many countries, prisoners were tortured over and over again, forced to endure unspeakable cruelties. Strange to think that this wreckage of a man beside her had gotten off *lightly.*

How would he digest the experience? she wondered. He was sensitive—no man was more sensitive—but he was tough in a lot of ways, too. His wounded childhood, the confrontation with the demons, the man he'd had to kill that day, the monster on the roof—all this had toughened him. And he had the advantage of Yanan's teaching; he might have been able to keep some part of himself safe, something to build on. But still . . . look at him!

The world had been induced to mostly forget the demons, to blur the memory, to distort the truth. What else, she wondered, had been suppressed through the psychic influence of That Certain One throughout the history of humanity? Perhaps some of the demons had invaded before, in one guise or another, and perhaps humanity had been made to forget that time, too.

A sickness was pervasive in the world—the sickness of humanity's vanity, its selfishness, its lusts, and its brutalities— and it was worse than ever.

It could be, she thought, a resonant pang of despair forcing tears from her eyes, *that we are losing the battle. That we have lost.*

As she had lost her son.

The radiator under the window began to hiss, drawing her gaze, as if whispering to her, *Look over here.*

She looked out the half-curtained window, at the hard-edged buildings, the contrasting cathedral set among them. The dawn light, shining behind the dome and Byzantine cross, made the Orthodox cathedral seem as if it were cut out of black paper. She watched as the light increased, to grant the cathedral dimension with a patina of rose and gold. The high-rise buildings around it began to seem like mere place holders, incomplete architectural notions; but the church looked permanent, like a fully realized idea.

She felt a glimmer of hope—until Marcus walked in. "Mel—Mother, how is he?"

"Sleeping."

"Good. Good." The boy stood awkwardly in the door, looking at her. Looking at her like an adult who wants to help but doesn't quite know how. Not like a child who needed a hug. And yet what would have helped her would've been the child who needed the hug.

"Best let him sleep," Melissa said hoarsely. "I'll watch over him."

"Certainly. Good. Yes." Marcus cleared his throat, then went back into the kitchen.

She bent over her husband, her face close to his breast, and wept, her head in her hands.

After a moment, the sound of Ira's breathing changed, and she felt his hand on her head, stroking her hair, comforting her.

Ash Valley

Glyneth felt another twinge and a particular wet warmth and said, "I have to make a stop."

"We're there," Dickinham responded, as he pulled the hydro Hummer up at a muddy construction site. It was late afternoon, the sky lowering, streamers of mist blurring the edges of the brown, wooden construction trailer at the end of the new gravel drive, where two new roads from the town of Ash Valley converged in a point. For the moment, there was no work being done. The site was vacant. There was an office trailer, along with a couple of inert, mud-spattered earthmovers, a large van, and a chemical toilet outhouse.

"I'll just run into that bathroom," Glyneth said.

Dickinham glanced at her, as if hesitating to give permission, which she thought strange, and then nodded. She climbed down from the Humvee, slogged through the mud. She glanced toward Ash Valley. There was smoke rising over there. It looked like a major fire, maybe two. Funny, she didn't hear sirens. But then, they'd closed off the roads to Ash Valley.

She went into the bright blue-plastic outhouse, with its

astringent smell of chemicals, its fruity rot of feces. She locked the door, opened her purse, and found a tampon.

Normally her period was comforting to her. Though it was the end of her cycle, it meant she could still have children. She wanted that, someday. But today she had the uneasy feeling that it was like a little death inside her.

It's just that death seems to've overrun this valley, she thought, as she finished and tugged up her jeans. They'd had to drive around two dead deer and a half-dozen dead dogs on the way here.

She stepped out into the cleaner air, then stopped and looked out at the wet fields. Even here, if she opened herself to it, she could feel the connection to the Earth, to the biosphere, that had brought her into environmental politics—and then, through Professor Paymenz, service to the Circle. A sense of something indefinably precious, and fragile at the same time as being mighty. Her responsibility to protect. So when they'd asked her to take on a false surname, a fake work history, and penetrate West Wind as Stephen's assistant, she'd said yes, though it meant lying down with dogs.

Why had Dickinham asked her to come out to this mud-hole anyway? Glyneth wondered. She was Stephen's assistant, not Dickinham's.

Slinging her purse strap over her shoulder, Glyneth trudged to the brown trailer and stopped near the door, to look at the van with the military plates parked at the other end. Wasn't that the van they'd seen in town? She found herself listening to the low, almost whispering voices coming from the trailer. Stealthy voices.

She moved to crouch under a small screened open window.

"She sent him a file with background on MK ULTRA, a dozen other projects," Dickinham was saying. "We just started intercepting her palmer transits, and no one got around to evaluating them till this morning."

A murmur from the other man—she couldn't make out what he was saying.

"I think she knows about the mind-control aspect, and I got a projection from Winderson just before I came out here. Told him about it. He says to assume it's our enemies. Assume she knows. That she's an initiate of some kind . . . one of *them*."

Another murmur.

Dickinham answering, "No, most of them are protected from that kind of detection, especially if they're associated with the Conscious Circle."

Listening, she shivered with a succession of chills that felt like the beginning of a flu. So now she understood why they'd brought her out here.

They *knew*—and they were going to kill her. Feed her to That Certain One.

She backed away from the window, and, as quietly as she could move in the sucking mud, she returned to the Humvee. No keys. Dickinham had taken them with him.

She popped the hood and found a confusing array of wires. She located the starter battery and tore it out, glancing at the trailer. No movement there. But any moment . . .

Her mouth felt dry, tasted metallic. She could feel her heart stuttering.

So this is what real fear is like, Glyneth thought, tasting it, seeing it objectively but not letting herself identify with it too strongly. Trying to stay calm, as conscious as possible.

She closed the hood—*too loud*—and hurried, crouching, to the van. It was unlocked but keyless. Trying to get its engine cover open, she cut her fingers, cursed under her breath in frustration. Finally it popped—and she couldn't find its battery. It was some kind of hybrid engine, and the battery was a huge affair underneath it somewhere.

She pulled at every wire she could find, ripping some out

with her teeth. Closing the engine cover, she saw a rather elaborate gas mask lying on one of the van's seats. She grabbed it, slung it around her neck so it hung down her back and, carrying the Hummer's battery, she started to run to the road. But the mud sucked at her feet, caking heavily on her shoes, as if purposely trying to slow her down. She was able only to trudge sweatily along till she got to the road.

Feet crunching too loudly in the gravel, Glyneth ran down the road, feeling like she was wearing ankle weights with the mud caked on her shoes. About fifty yards along, she tossed the car battery into a gurgling culvert. She noticed the sun setting, and wished it would go down faster, because she knew she made a good target on this road, with the flat stubbly fields to either side and a quarter mile of open ground to the nearest stand of trees. She needed darkness to hide her.

She heard angry shouting behind her. They'd noticed her absence; they'd discovered her sabotage. They would be running after her.

She heard a bee buzz past her head, followed by a cracking sound, and realized it hadn't been a bee at all.

She felt as if the middle of her back was exposed, cold—it was the place she was expecting the next bullet to hit. Another dark culvert opening yawned to her right, echoing with rushing water. She heard another bee, and a handful of gravel leapt up, stinging her calf. Someone was gaining on her, getting the range.

She looked around for cover—there was only the culvert. Oh, God, for a flashlight. Wait—she had a little one on her keychain.

Glyneth sprinted to the culvert and jumped down into the ditch, grunting with the impact as she splashed into the water, falling on her hands and knees. "Shit!" It was cold, a very sudden coldness. She straightened up, fumbled in her purse.

Where was it? At any moment they might come to the edge of the ditch and fire down at her.

She found the keychain and turned on the little penlight. If only she had the car that went with the keychain.

She hesitated. The culvert ran toward the town. She was afraid of the town now, but she could hear the rattling of their running footsteps on the gravel road above her. Would they follow her in here? Maybe they wouldn't have to. They might be able to call people at the other end.

She plunged into the musty, echoing tunnel, immediately running into spiderwebs, having to run, crouching, into wet, rushing darkness broken only by the thin ray of bobbing light shining from her hand.

Rostov, Russia

The old dervish hadn't picked Rostov, nor their hotel, at random. There was a certain priest who worked at the Orthodox cathedral just across the way. But this small chapel grotto, though connected through an underground passage with the cathedral, wasn't a part of it. The Conscious Circle did not want to interfere with the specific consecrations of the cathedral; the Orthodox church had its own spiritual-vibratory identity. Though the bent old priest belonged to the Conscious Circle, he would have regarded its Work as heresy were it conducted in the cathedral proper.

It was a paradox Melissa had never quite mastered.

She and Nyerza helped Ira onto a cot in one corner of the mostly bare, clammy stone room and covered him with blankets. It was an ancient chamber, she thought, straightening to look around. Its damp walls were carved out of bedrock; the figures painted into the floor were very like Araha's pendant.

The old, bent, gray-bearded priest, Father Spenskaya, wearing a dark cassock and hooded cap, regarded Marcus gravely and then Ira with pale eyes. His gaunt, lined face seemed itself etched in stone in the dim light of the candelabra standing in a wall niche, until he turned suddenly to speak to Shaikh Araha in Russian, in a voice that sounded like a squeaky winch.

Araha responded in the same language, then turned to Melissa. "He wants to know why we have brought a sick man. Says we have no time for healing anyone tonight."

Marcus stepped out of the shadows then, and spoke in halting Russian—but the somewhat surprised old priest evidently understood, nodding acquiescence. Melissa looked questioningly at Araha.

"He said that he wanted his father here. That Ira must remain. He cannot concentrate, when his father is so much in distress, unless he can see that he's at least safe with us."

She glanced at Marcus who went to help the old priest light incense in little bronze bowls laid at the nine points of the figure on the floor. Around the figure were low wooden stools, much worn with use. Enough for Melissa, Marcus, Nyerza, Araha, Father Spenskaya, and four others.

Araha knelt beside Ira. The shaikh's hands were clasped around an old pottery cup, brimming with water. He murmured over the cup—as he had for Marcus—and Melissa saw the water seem to stir. Then Ira, wincing, sat up and drank.

He'd had many such treatments from Araha since coming out of the prison. By degrees, he seemed to be coming back to them, healing and growing a little stronger.

The priest straightened, turning to look at Melissa. He spoke in uncertain English, gesturing toward her. "Is the—the Urn, *da*?"

Nyerza spoke for the first time in hours. "Yes, but the Gold is not with her. She grew angry, quite justly angry, and their

connection was already tenuous. But together . . . we may perhaps find a path to them. . . ."

The priest shook his head; he'd understood little. Araha
translated. The priest nodded. He went to a painted wooden
figure of Saint Anthony tucked away in a wall niche and knelt
in front of it on the naked stone; he began to pray in Russian.
He was entering into hesychasm, the prayer of the heart: a
prayer that was more an inner state than it was words.

Melissa hunkered beside Ira, feeling his head. It was
clammy cold in here; he really shouldn't be here.

"I'm okay," he whispered raspily, looking at her through
still-puffy eyes. He smiled crookedly.

"You'll live, sure, if that's what you mean," she said, just
loud enough for him to hear. "But they don't just torture a
man's body."

"It wasn't a long . . . interrogation. It was horrible. But people have worse. I don't want to sound—"

"Pious? Falsely humble? You're right on the verge. But
sound any way you want. Soon we'll find you a therapist, to
help you work through it."

"I've had my rage already. I can feel the depression. The—"
he licked his lips and groped for words "—the sense that people are all just . . . things, robots. Mindless, only pretending to
be . . . to care. But the men who tortured me probably love their
children. . . ."

"Perhaps. I doubt it, but maybe. Listen—you're strong,
you've been through a lot. You've looked the seven clans in the
eyes. You killed a man to defend me, and I remember how you
mourned for him and prayed for his soul. I don't underestimate
you, darling. But you mustn't underestimate what you've been
through."

He chuckled, showing broken teeth. "Every time I move it
still hurts. Don't worry—it's a reminder." He turned his head to

look as Marcus, Araha, and Nyerza settled on the little stools at the points of the sacred figure on the floor.

She remembered holding her husband in her arms that morning, when he'd awakened more or less cogent. He had silently eaten porridge, drunk a little tea—and then he'd begun to weep into his teacup. She held him as he sobbed against her for an hour, and then he'd gone to sleep. And when Ira had awakened, Marcus had bent near him, kissed him on the forehead, patted his cheek. Even now, Ira turned on the cot to look intently at his son.

Did Ira know? Did Ira understand what had happened to the boy? Had he heard her discussing it with the others, in his semiconsciousness?

Another man came in then, making her shiver at his sudden appearance. It was Araha's old assistant, Hiram. He nodded to them, smiling faintly, and went immediately to sit on one of the low stools.

Then another man came in, and both Ira and Melissa gasped in surprise.

"Yanan!"

Wearing a long overcoat, Yanan came and stood by Ira, smiling softly down at him. "I come right from the airport. I have not been to this room for some years, but it does not change. So—I am glad you are safe and with those you love, Ira, hm?"

"Yes, he is," Melissa said, giving Yanan a brittle look. She took Yanan aside, lowering her voice so Marcus and Ira wouldn't hear. "With his wife—and his 'son.' Did you know what they were going to do, Yanan?"

"I . . . only knew that they said he would be able to help. That he would be awakened through remembering who he had been, before."

"He hasn't only remembered it," she whispered, "he's become it. He lost who he was."

"Many died, nine years ago, in our circle, eh? And afterward, weakened, others died. There weren't enough without Mendel—we sensed he was close, in the boy. Araha was told he could be reawakened, if he was brought to a place where the influences were strong enough, you see. But as to how it feels for you . . . I feel that you suffer. And I had not thought it would be so."

"You wouldn't have changed anything, none of you, if you'd known how I'd feel."

Yanan led her back to Ira's side.

Ira was trying to sit up. "I . . . found something in myself . . . these last days . . . that could help. . . ."

Yanan smiled. "You are ready to help us now, Ira?"

Melissa shook her head firmly, pressing Ira back on the cot. "Marcus just wanted him here. We can't—I mean—Ira can't help. You don't know what's happened to Ira, Yanan. What he's been through."

"Yes, I do know," Yanan said tenderly. "I very much do. It happened to me before, hm?" He smiled with an ancient sadness. "We must all pay our bills, eh? Come, Ira." He extended his hand to Ira, to help him stand.

Melissa snapped, *"No!"*

Yanan stood there, looking down at Ira, hand extended. Ira swallowed, then smiled wearily, and took Yanan's hand. He grimaced as he allowed his mentor to pull him to his feet.

Melissa was close to walking out. What had they done to her family? First Marcus—now Ira.

Her father had taught her to trust them. Maybe her father was wrong.

Ira wore only pajamas and a robe and slippers, but he hobbled across the room, leaning on Yanan, and sat down on a stool. "I'm okay, Melissa," he said. "It'll take all of us—Marcus, too—to call him . . ."

"You understand who we call, eh?" Yanan said, looking at Ira.

Ira nodded. "Someone who's gone beyond—who can talk to their Retriever . . . Marcus . . ." He looked at the boy. He shrugged. "Marcus told me."

The old priest got slowly to his feet—she could almost hear his joints creaking. The priest turned to look at her, his eyes like pale blue fire. He waited.

She took a deep breath, and let the anger slide away to some dark place inside her. She crossed to her small wooden stool and sat down; it was so low she had to squat as much as sit.

The priest came and sat opposite her. They all joined hands— and it began. They set out to summon the ninth participant in their Circle—a dead man.

Beneath Ash Valley

Glyneth could hardly feel her feet now in the cold water. How far had she gone? Her back was aching from hunching over; her socks had gotten bunched in her shoes. Now and then something slimy and furry wriggled past her ankles, making her hiss with revulsion, but she kept on, afraid of something worse. Following the coursing of the stream.

She stopped and listened. Sounds came to her, down the culvert, distorted with reverberation. Ringing sounds, cracks, splashes—losing definition. She took a deep breath and went on, followed her weakening penlight beam around a curve— and cracked her head on a pipe.

Gasping with pain, she fell floundering back to sit dizzily in the water, on slime-coated concrete. After a few moments the throbbing subsided, and she gingerly felt the goose egg on her forehead—it was tender. "Ow. Fucking *hell*," she muttered. Then a moment of panic. The flashlight! Where was it? There was a dim glow in the water, like a phosphorescent fish. She snatched at the flashlight with cold-clumsy fingers, pulled it from the water. It blinked, twice, three times—and she whimpered. But it didn't go out.

Then she froze, fell silent, listening. There was a heavy splashing coming up behind her in the darkness. Or was it up ahead?

She stood carefully, mindful that there was a pipe above her and, not knowing what else to do, moved on. Slowly, the sounds receded. The fading penlight beam wavered over the dirty water; she caught the lights of yellow-pink eyes, small wet snouts regarding her more than once from small drainage channels oozing water. She swore softly at them, and the rats turned and swam away, naked tails rippling like agitated earthworms.

She began to feel sick from cold and realized that her core heat was draining away in the slow, cold push of the water. She started to shiver uncontrollably.

Another fifty steps, and she thought she could make out a light in the distance. She switched off the little flashlight and found there was still just enough illumination to allow her to make her way down the sibilating tunnel.

The culvert opened up a bit, so she could straighten, and she discovered that the light was coming from above: a rain-water grate and a manhole up there, side by side. The light was mostly coming through the grate. It looked like street light. She heard a car go whirring by.

She crossed to a metal ladder and climbed the rungs that were sunk deep into the damp concrete wall, thinking, *This is it! I'm getting out of this stinking hole!*

She reached the underside of the manhole and pushed. It didn't budge, not even slightly. She tried again. It was utterly unyielding. She guessed that it must have been one of those manholes sealed in place by asphalt.

The sewer grate was bolted down—she could see the bolts. "Like to get hold of the genius who worked on that street," she muttered through grinding teeth, descending the rungs, back into the damp darkness. "What is the fucking point of a manhole if . . . if . . ." She broke off, stopped on the ladder, peering downward.

There was something big, moving through the water, about a yard under her feet.

She squinted down in the dim light—her own shadow was obscuring whatever it was. She flattened against the ladder so the light fell on the thing.

It was a man, moving low through the water like an alligator, coming out of the tunnel that led toward Ash Valley—opposite the way Glyneth had come. He was dressed in a soggy sweatshirt and jeans, one shoe on, the other foot bare, and he was *pulling* himself through the water with his hands clawing at the bottom, and making excited babyish sounds as he went—cooing and sputtering and bubbling. The skin on the back of his neck looked bluish to her; she guessed he must be close to dying of the cold.

But he glided vigorously through the water to the branch she'd just come out of—there he hesitated, lifting his head to stare down the culvert.

Another man joined him, coming from the same direction. No, this was a woman. She was walking bent, crouched so low that her face was almost touching the water. She wore a torn dress, her wet hair plastered on her head, down her back, and dangling to trail in the dirty water.

The woman looked up, but not right at Glyneth; she seemed to be drawn to stare at the light overhead. Her eyes were milky, filmed over.

She returned her baleful attention to the opening of the

culvert, cooing to herself, giggling now and then as she waited with the man, the two of them staring into the dark tunnel, teeth bared.

Glyneth's arms ached. She shivered, and it was hard to keep her teeth from clacking together. But she was afraid of making any sound at all.

Another man came, a chunky guy in a white shirt and no pants. His shirt clung to him; she could see his naked ass, as pink as the tails of the rats. He was pulling himself along in the water like the first; he seemed to be keening like a lost cat.

He crouched alongside the other two, each making their own odd little noise, staring down the culvert the way she'd come.

And then a flashlight beam quivered from the opening. Someone said something. Maybe, "Who's that?" Glyneth wasn't sure.

The one she thought of as the alligator man seemed to dart forward, propelled up and out of the water. Someone yelled. There was a bang and a metallic echo; she smelled gun smoke, heard giggling. Then the other two moved into the culvert.

Now, Glyneth thought as a frightened yell and the sounds of thrashing came from the tunnel. She climbed down to the water and went into the tunnel the three had come out of.

Just as she entered, she realized the water was changing color around her knees, darkening, as if it were rusting, brown, red. Blood.

She heard a man scream like a small child.

She paused long enough to glance over her shoulder, only to see Dickinham, in the tunnel opposite, his face contorted with some terrible realization. He reached out to her imploringly, then the tunnel strobed as he fired the pistol again, into the ceiling. One of them had his wrist gripped in blue-white hands.

The two men and the woman bore him down. With inhumanly fast movements of their jaws, they tore red gobbets from his neck and shoulders, clawing bloody gel from one of his eye sockets, cooing and keening and giggling.

A ripple of sick disorientation went through Glyneth, something beyond terror, and she almost vomited. But that would make too much noise.

She turned away, looking inside for control of herself.

Fear, horror—it's all just internal weather, she reminded herself, *the weather of the mind. Let it blow—but don't let it blow you away.*

She began to splash determinedly through the darkness . . . then stopped, thinking: *How many more of them are there, waiting up ahead?*

There was a smell she recognized in the air, too: D17.

She remembered the gas mask and pulled it over her face, set it for high cleanse, and forced herself to go on—though it was even harder to see now. She brought out the little penlight's pathetic illumination once more. It felt good to move; it warmed her a little. A dozen steps onward, and then her foot struck an obstruction—a painful one. She bit back a curse and felt under the water. Found a piece of broken pipe, three inches in diameter, maybe a foot and a half long. Instinctively, she picked it up.

She went on, praying under her breath, then felt a sickening contact on her knee—she froze, afraid one of the madmen was about to bear her down as they had Dickinham. Something solid yet mushy, with bones inside it. Swallowing bile, she pointed the fading penlight beam down and saw the corpse of a Mexican man floating, caught against her leg. He was faceup, eyes glazed, lips dead white. A rat poised on its hind legs on the corpse's collarbone, like a dog begging, peering up at her. She could see a ragged gash where it had chewed away the flesh of the dead man's jawline, exposing bone.

She knew this time she was going to vomit. She got the gas mask off just in time as she splashed frantically away from the corpse, pausing to empty her guts into the water. She found herself laughing bitterly as she forced the gas mask back over her face. Breathing the smell of her own vomit. Hearing the sound of her own harsh breathing in there. At least the mask protected her face from wet, toothy little animals.

Keep going, keep going. Get out!

Another forty yards, and the penlight finally gave out. She shook it, fiddled with its switch. "Fuck!"

She shoved it in a pocket and continued on, feeling her way, thirty, forty, fifty steps, and saw another cylinder of wan light up ahead.

Glyneth hurried to the light, almost falling in her haste. She stopped abruptly in the opening to the shaft for the manhole. Up above was an open sewer grating. A way out!

But there were two people between her and the grating— both of them on the ladder.

There was a blond boy of about thirteen, wearing only his underwear, pale and skinny, whining, weeping, trying to get up the ladder, to get out; blood streamed down his back, his legs. One of the sopping, giggling madmen clung to the rungs below him, his right arm twisted through a rung, his hand clamped to the struggling boy's ankle. He was a slender, muscular man, perhaps half black, without a shirt, a handmade tattoo on his shoulder: *999*. His loose trousers were crowded with pocket zippers. He wore slimy tennis shoes. In his left hand he gripped a clawlike gardening implement, which he'd dug deeply into the boy's right calf. The wounds where it dug in ripped deeper and deeper as the weeping boy struggled.

Glyneth made up her mind. She had to get out that way—and she had to help the boy.

Fighting to keep control of herself, Glyneth hefted the pipe and came at the man from behind, grabbing a rung with her left hand, setting her foot on the lowest to hoist herself up, then bringing the pipe down hard on the back of his head.

He turned a milky-eyed gaze at her, startled, as blood gushed from his split scalp. He let go of the blood-slick gardening claw and grabbed her firmly by the throat, squeezing. She hit him twice more in the same spot. His eyes seemed to clear for a moment—he gaped at her in confusion, as if trying to remember how he'd come to this—and then he fell onto her, knocking her off the ladder.

Glyneth yelled as she fell back in the water, the weight of the man pressing her under, his blood curtaining the light away, closing the surface of the water with tightening skeins of red.

She torqued her body hard to one side, dumping him off, and struggled to her feet, swaying, looking for the boy.

Who was turning his own milky eyes to her—just as he leapt, snarling, laughing, at her.

Her scream was cut short as he bore her back into the water, onto the man's body. The boy gripped her throat, pressing his thumbs into her windpipe. She swung the pipe at his head, quivered with revulsion as it connected, hard, crunching into the boy's skull.

Sobbing, she rolled him off her, left him to float facedown in the water. Bubbles seethed up around his head. She let him drown. It was a kindness.

She climbed the ladder as best she could, though it was awkward holding on to the pipe. She didn't want to let it go now.

The light grew brighter; the air a little warmer. Her relief at climbing to the open street, at the base of a streetlight, lasted only till she found that she was in the park square at the center of town, till she realized the warmth was coming from great, sky-licking fires consuming the entire block. She stumbled across the treeless, torn earth of the park, through rolling gusts of smoke. She saw the piles of bodies in the very center of the park and the other bodies being dragged there by the milky-eyed mob, by the shambling, giggling victims of the undiluted, aerial Dirvane 17 spraying that had taken place yesterday and today.

Till she saw that something squatted in the center of the pile of bodies . . .

Till she saw the demon.

7

Bald Peak Observatory

"This time, Stephen, you must believe in what you see," Winderson was saying, his voice reverberating from the observatory's walls, its metal ceiling. "You won't be able to go where we want you to go unless you *know* it's all real. Your will won't be forceful enough; it'll be compromised. It's all about *will*, in that place."

Stephen shook his head. "I can't believe in it, not that way. . . ."

They were sitting together on the metal steps that led up to the telescope. Part of the room was brightly lit, part in deep shadow. They were drinking coffee. Stephen was only pretending to drink his; he was afraid it might be drugged. If they drugged him, he'd lose all judgment of what was real.

But what Winderson wanted him to believe in . . . no. It

was as outrageous as believing that Christ had been resurrected, that "the Buddhas are everywhere, trying to help us, though they are long dead."

Because if the world Winderson wanted him to visit was real, was more than a sort of psychic shadow, then the demons might've been real.

"He must be shown," Latilla said, crossing the big, echoing room.

She must've opened the door, Stephen thought, but he hadn't seen her come in.

"I don't want to ruin him—" Winderson glanced at Stephen, modified the demurral "—pile on too much too soon. He's got the gift, but he's fragile."

"The alignment is tonight. The sacrifice has been made. We have only till exactly ten P.M. He is our only retriever."

As Latilla came toward them, crossing the canvas tarp that someone had laid over the floor, Stephen saw she was strangely dressed. She wore a robe of some kind—black, with white symbols sewn on it. Runes, maybe. And she was barefoot. She wore a silver circlet, like a metallic headband with a pentagram, pointing downward at the front. Within the pentagram was that familiar rune.

Then another figure came from the shadows—a man in the uniform of a U.S. Army general. But he, too, wore a circlet like Latilla's around his head. He was barefoot, too. A military uniform, with braid and brass—but he was barefoot. It looked ludicrous, really.

These people, Stephen decided, *are a little crazy. Definitely, don't drink the coffee.*

"Stephen, this is General Maseck," Winderson said, taking off his shoes. "General, Stephen Isquerat."

The general nodded brusquely. He was a gangly man, with a neck slightly too long, a pronounced Adam's apple, a red mouth so pinched it seemed buttoned shut, a sharp nose, and angry blue eyes that stared at Stephen as if to challenge him to laugh at his bare feet. Stephen noticed they were pale, bony feet.

"We lost touch with Dickinham," Maseck said, going to a coffee urn set up on a table near the bottom of the stairs.

"He's dead," Latilla said blandly. She went to the coffee urn but didn't take a cup. Instead she took a handful of sugar packets, tore them open with her teeth, and dumped the sugar in her mouth.

Stephen watched her, fascinated. She looked back, he thought, like a snake watching a mouse.

What had she said about Dickinham? He's dead? She hadn't said, He was killed in a car accident. Or whatever. She just said that he was dead. As if it weren't particularly unexpected.

Stephen glanced at the door, wondering if he was so caught up in this thing now that he couldn't get out.

But there was Jonquil to think of. She was counting on him.

Barefoot now, Winderson stood up, looking at Latilla. "Are you sure Dickinham is dead, mistress?"

"Yes. I have been so informed. He rather carelessly fell afoul of some of the general's pets. You must all work harder on internal communication."

Mistress? Stephen thought. Her whole manner of speaking had changed. The odd, affected character she'd played earlier seemed to have vanished. She seemed imperious now—despite eating handfuls of sugar—and very much in charge, as if she had dropped some kind of pretense. She was a sorceress and a queen.

Maseck's scowl deepened. "They are not my pets. . . ." He hesitated, seemed to realize he was speaking out of turn. "Mistress, they are a valid experiment."

"General," Winderson said. He caught Maseck's eye.

Maseck glanced at Stephen and shrugged, then sipped his coffee. "What is it, then, we're going to attempt tonight?"

"There will be no attempt," Latilla said, swallowing sugar. "There will be a *doing*. This will be accomplished."

"Yes," Winderson said.

"Yes," the general said.

"Uh . . . is—is my assistant around?" Stephen asked. "Glyneth?" He craved someone he could relate to.

"Why do you ask about her?" Latilla said, her tone very careful, as she watched him.

She was still an old woman in an unflattering hairdo, but Stephen found he couldn't think of her as an old woman anymore. "Um—well she *is*, after all, my assistant," Stephen said, not understanding why he had to defend his question.

"Yes, so she is," Winderson said, smiling at him. "But, uh . . . we're all the assistant you'll need tonight, Stephen. And remember—Jonquil is counting on you. Now, if you'll come over here."

"Has the circle been consecrated properly?" Latilla asked, her voice harsh.

"Yes, mistress," Maseck said gruffly, as he drew the tarp back, exposing a huge pentagram recently inlaid into the floor in copper strips. The figure was about forty feet across. There were black runes within each point, and in the center was the hook-bottomed cross Stephen had seen before.

"Oh, Jesus," Stephen murmured under his breath.

Latilla shot him a look that made him think of a reptile spitting poison. "Say no names, for whatever reason, that will interfere with the summoning." Her voice had become almost a croak.

Stephen found himself staring at the door. Winderson noticed and, all avuncular, took Stephen's arm. "Right over here . . .

DEMONS

stand at this point, Stevie. Oh, and take off your shoes. Helps the energies pass through."

Stephen hesitated. He *felt* Latilla looking at him. It was as if she were leaning against him with all her physical weight, though she was thirty feet away. "Take them off," she echoed. Her voice had changed again; lower now, more guttural.

Stephen felt weak in the knees and sank to the floor, began taking off his shoes, though he hadn't made up his mind to do it.

There was a pressure in his head, a *squeezing*.

H. D. came in, then, taking off his shoes at the door. He was wearing a business suit; and he stripped off the gray jacket as he came, tossing it to one side. Barefoot in an Armani suit, he crossed to one of the points.

Five people for five points.

Stephen felt a *wrongness* that couldn't be defined or quantified.

"He's not in the proper state," Latilla said, glowering at him. Her voice was an inhuman squawk now—the sound of a hinge being torn off with a crowbar.

"Stephen," Winderson said gently, "just relax. We're here to help humanity. To set an example—make everyone stronger, more efficient. Open up the world to a new kind of power. It's just the latest innovation, that's all it is."

Looking at the pentagram, Stephen thought: *No—this has to be something ancient.*

"You're going to feel terrific in a moment. You're going to feel right. You'll *know* you're right! Remember, Stephen—the big picture. Something you see from the top of the ladder. It may seem a strange ladder, but this really is the secret of climbing it. Trust me, Stephen. And don't forget—it's going to save Jonquil."

Stephen took a deep breath.

See the big picture.

Help Jonquil.

He nodded. "Let's do it. I'll do what I need to do, to help Jonquil. Whatever you need me to do."

Though Latilla was evidently some kind of priestess, seeming more than ever in charge, it was Winderson who began to chant in some language Stephen had never heard before. It had a strangely familiar ring to it, though. As if he'd heard it sometime, and had forgotten it. And yet . . .

Latilla seemed to be *doing* something. Something he'd never seen anyone do before. She was standing within her point of the pentagram, her arms crossed over her chest, and her head was rolling in a slow circle on her neck. Her whole body was going rigid, veins standing out on her forehead, her neck. The others were watching her, but not Winderson. She shuddered and made a long slow hissing sound.

Then something began to form in the air over the pentagram. Something tenebrous, agitated within itself like a swarm of flies. Something that looked hungrily out at them.

Rostov, Russia

On the other side of the world . . .

Nine of them: holding hands at each point of the nine-pointed figure in the floor of the chamber, the grotto carved into naked rock, under the unknowing city. The smell of burning incense cloyed the room; candles guttered and blew in the niches; a charged breeze stirred Ira's hair, though there should have been no wind here.

Ira felt as if he were only now waking up from the nightmare. The humiliation, the beatings in a cold cubicle under a searing lightbulb, had been the culmination of a dark journey he'd been on without knowing it. Now in this dim, rocky chamber, in meditative communion with the others, he felt a connection to something that set him above all doubts, all misgivings. He had opened, inside himself, in a way he had never opened before, opened a door he hadn't known was there, because he had nothing to lose. He'd already lost everything in the torture chamber. He didn't care what he risked, now, by opening himself utterly to this higher vibration. He understood what had happened to Marcus, and it was all right.

Now, he realized, they were all once more *in place*; he was where he should be. He was doing the appropriate step in the dance of life, and the music was sweet within him. He felt the bottled-up rage clearing away, like something dank and noisome drying under a sudden ray of sunlight.

This cell of the circle had tried more than once; Marcus had had some trouble connecting, even though he was more than Marcus now. Melissa, too, had been distracted, her anger and uncertainty tormenting her: inner torturers. But Marcus had gone into a deep trance of some kind. Now, he had really connected with the higher, and with the white-bearded old priest and Araha and Yanan, as if to help them cross some gap, some interval.

With Melissa and Marcus and Ira at last just where they should be, the darkness lifted.

The walls began to shine. And something began to appear over the figure on the floor. Summoned, sustained there, by all of them. A living community of light: the Gold in the Urn. And then a man—conveyed by the Gold from the far side of Death.

Bald Peak Observatory

Stephen felt a tugging from Latilla. She stood opposite him, and she was looking at him, her head skewed so far to one side it looked as if she had broken her neck. She made a come-here gesture, and he found himself walking toward her, into the face in the center of the pentagram.

Into ecstasy.

A dark ecstasy, a nightmarish glory that seemed to lift him into the air with sheer rushing delight. It was sexual, and more than sexual: rapture and a thundering cascade of megalomania. He felt as if the rush were lifting him off the floor. It was like his charged blood was itself straining toward the ceiling and carrying him up with it.

"Ahhhh. . . . *Jonquilll*," he heard himself say quite uncontrollably.

He saw her then—Jonquil floating before him, naked, arms open, lips parted, labia parted, breasts in a slow-motion weightless dance. "Stephen!"

The two of them were floating—and he realized with a cracked joy that he was staring down at the others, that he was levitating ten feet above the center of the pentagram. Some part of his mind registered distantly that not one of those watching him seemed in the least surprised.

He reached for her, but the swarming in the air around him thickened and he could see nothing but a tornado of black dots, each one embodying some intense earthly desire squeezed into a throbbing mote.

He was hoisted to an unknown center point, felt himself locked to some kind of axis through the engine of energies lifting him. He could feel that axis—almost as an axle, a long rod connected to the infinite fires of all chaos—going right through him, penetrating him under the sternum, pinning him in space. He could feel it rotating inside him, a spike of energy that burned as bright and hot as an acetylene torch.

It was unbearable. He screamed—but it was a scream that expressed joy as much as horror, changing from one to the other from split second to split second.

His whole body shook with waves radiating outward from that central axis, like seismic waves rippling flesh and bone, cracking joints. Then he felt the now-familiar wrenching and wailed to know he was being pulled out of himself.

Crashing down—and up—through the surface of the sea of energy again, flying through living symbols, membranes of molten metal, then finding himself in the meta-landscape he'd seen before, with more of the mountain peaks like the one he'd traversed: a mountain range of interlocked preconceived ideas that here became solids.

The sky was restlessly busy with those detached, impossibly whirling airplane propellers that were spinning symbols— were they spinning or just in more than one place at the same time?—iron crosses or reverse swastikas or shifting geometrical shapes, each with its own feeling axis.

He realized he had come here through one of the living symbols, as if it were a portal. He felt himself drawn to another, unable to hold back from it. Once he drew close, there was an inexorable suction that pulled him in . . .

. . . so that he passed into yet another subplane that extended from the previous one. It was a sunless world without ground; there was nothing but sky—no reference for up or down—and an infinite field of what looked at first like luminous, violently contending leafless uprooted trees, their branches and roots constantly whipping at one another, wrestling, intertwining to seek a grip. Never in cooperation, only in contest; tearing, their movements whippingly frantic so that they appeared to fast-forward in the cinema of his mind's eye. They weren't plants; they weren't organisms. They were more like enormous thrashing branchworks of sentient, discrete energy, closer to sustained lightning than to creatures of matter, and they filled a world that was otherwise a blue, seething mist, a world without ground, empty except for these contending organisms of pure will.

A relentless natural selection held sway here, so that some grew while others diminished; and one in particular was overtaking the others around it, using the energy of each overwhelmed enemy to take on two more.

Stephen understood somehow that these were living beings of his own universe, seen as if through a metaphysical X-ray device, exposing their hidden psyches.

He found himself drawn to the largest of these, and one of its seeking tendrils seemed to sense him. It lashed out, entwined him, and pulled him screaming soundlessly into its crackling core.

And he became one with it. He *was* it—and he understood it from within. Understood all these beings: They were egos, their minds primitive, their desires exquisite and always uppermost. Their substance was defined by desire. Each branch was a desire, sustained for a moment, satisfying itself as best it could, receding for another moment, so that each raking branch of desire appeared and vanished in a flicker, reaching out, grabbing, taking, sinking back—all happening so fast that the afterimage of one lingered while the next appeared. Thus the tree effect: the distorted, hungry, bushiness of raging forks of energy.

Now in the midst of the growing creature he felt a terrible, shattering exaltation that nearly consumed his identity as he grew with stolen life. Suddenly he *was* overwhelmed and lost himself in the life force, the ego of the thing he was occupying. And he felt the raging crackle of its yearnings as his own, as distinct wants, each reaching for an orgasmic culmination in the human scenes that rushed flashing by. He felt sex become rape and ejaculation; he felt hunger becoming theft and gorging; he felt the domination of others and then their destruction; he felt anger becoming violence; he flashed on himself fulfilling all of this in the human world, in people: a young man in a gang rape of a thirteen-year-old girl, ravaging her sleeping innocence; a fat man at his overladen table; a neurotic teacher screaming at a young child, "You're a moron!"; an angry girl gangster shooting another girl in the head. He was all of them! He was fucking! He was biting down! He was crushing! He was *killing*!

But there was another, growing sensation. That he—the being he had become—was itself being consumed. Was itself about to be swallowed by something else from some other place. His pure desire had made it just the right flavor, the perfect sustenance for That Certain One.

So the thing Stephen had become was itself swallowed and blasted within this other something. Propelled, like a nutrient in a man's bloodstream used for some specific purpose, into a subdimensional bowel . . . into yet another vessel.

Now he was in the human world again, but he wasn't there as a human. He had entered a far more powerful vessel. But he had entered the continuum for traveling they called a *street*. Someplace Stephen vaguely recollected—but who was Stephen?

To one side were rows of big boxes, used for storing goods to be bartered for a currency—they called them *shops*. There were vehicles parked in the street—combustion-powered vehicles on black wheels. The name "Ash Valley" came into his mind. There was an open space around him, what they called a *park*. Now it was occupied by hundreds of wretched, poison-maddened souls, capering with milky eyes and flailing arms around a mound of their own dead. And squatting within it was . . .

Stephen.

Or—whoever he was. Hadn't he been Stephen? They were dancing around him as he sat on a throne contrived of a shattered, burnt-out car among the heaps of tangled, torn corpses, like a guru sitting amid offerings of flowers. The bodies had gone all purplish and green and red like flowers; little fires burned here and there among them. How gorgeous! What thunderous music he heard in the contemplation of it!

"HA-HA-*HAAAAAA!*"

He laughed, rocking with delight, slapping his knees with his leathery hands.

Hands! Great, dark, clawed hands! Yes, now he had a body! Humanoid but four-armed, with serrated teeth in great snapping jaws, human eyes, twice the size of any of these little creatures capering around him . . . what was it they called his kind? A Gnasher? Nonsense—he was a spirit prince! A prince in the court of That Certain One, a great power, a reigning principality. See how the spark-vessels danced around him!

He leapt to his taloned feet and danced, himself, kicking the heads from corpses in his unbridled delight—a dance of triumph, victory over these underlings, with a world of his own to rule! They had given him this world in exchange for the power that would eat them alive. Ho, their excellent mistake, the delicious jest: thinking that they would consume *it* while *it* consumed *them*!

And now he was here, and it all belonged to him!

Then he saw one of them who was not one of his servants. He sensed that her mind was free from the poison and from That Certain One. She wore a mask to protect her from the toxins that his allies had spread over these others to inflame their worst instincts and destroy their higher reasoning. The substance that soon would coat, would transform, the entire world. She had protected herself from it!

In a rage of frustration, he bounded toward her . . . saw her stumble back and raise her arms over her head in protective reflex and despair.

In some flickering back room of his mind, another small frightened self shouted weakly, *No! That's Glyneth! Don't hurt her!*

But it was a small distant voice, lost in his roar of murderous delight.

———

Glyneth had twice tried to escape from the riotous square, the shattered park, the demon presiding over this Hell on Earth— and twice the armed men in gas masks, blocking the side streets with their vans, had driven her back, pointing their military-issue .45 automatics.

She'd had to continue moving to keep from being borne down by the teeming, milky-eyed victims of D17 who shambled through the park. Some were like people in the throes of a nervous breakdown, walking around wailing, pounding their heads. Others were like people who'd flipped into a killing rage, stalking through a house or business, shooting anyone in sight. Still others were dull, robotic, as they dragged the dead to the heap in the center of the carved-up park.

Thirty feet in front of her, a man was raping the body of another man; then he collapsed, a corpse himself, atop the first. Other men were copulating with living and dead women in the reeking, pallid heap of disarrayed bodies.

She looked around now for a house she might break into— a place where she might find shelter—or for a way out past the men in the gas masks, the men carrying electronic clipboards and digital video cams. But the houses were all burning or loud with screaming, smashing people. Then a big Indian guy came staggering toward her. She turned to run—and saw the demon coming toward her. The Indian stopped in his tracks, seeming to listen to some inner voice, then he began to drag a dead body toward the great heap in the park.

Till now the demon had remained still, as if it were meditating; it had taken no notice of her. She had walked around under its baleful gaze like a rabbit creeping past a dozing hawk.

But suddenly the demon woke from the strange stupor that had held it, leapt to its feet, and capered about—and then it spotted her. It took a step toward her.

She knew there was no running from it. She fell to her knees and began the inward prayer.

Then she felt a hand on her shoulder and looked up to see a man standing at her side. His face was unseeable: His head was caught up in a globe of fire.

After a moment she realized that he wore a bubble-shaped helmet and that the fire was the reflection of the burning buildings.

She turned and saw that the demon was hesitating.

She heard an amplified voice booming from the man's bubble helmet. "Every hour has been the hour of Judgment; every day has always been Judgment Day! And now the day shows itself for what it is! I am here to witness, Lord the Christ! In the name of the Annointed, I witness!" She recognized his voice: the street preacher she'd seen that day in the park.

"You, sir! It is you, who stays the demon's hand now!" Reverend Anthony boomed. "The man within the shell! Let the actual man rise up! Let him take command of the demon as a horseman rides a horse! I call on Christ and his apostles to give him the strength! I give him my life, Lord—to witness thy truth!"

———

What had stopped him? Stephen—the semi-Stephen, the demi-demon—wrestled inwardly with the aversion, the sudden visceral need to recoil from the solemnity in the shape of the man standing behind the woman he'd intended to kill and eat.

He took another step toward this peculiar, shouting little man, but when the figure in the bubble helmet blocked his way, babbling his eccentric invocations, Stephen found himself rooted to the spot as if part of him were recoiling, another part pulling forward, each part canceling the other so he couldn't move at all.

The frustration built volcanically inside him till he tore free, erupting into motion.

Lunging at the man, he gripped him by the throat, smashing his helmet with his free hand, making glass fly—then blood as he squeezed the man's throat till his head exploded—the little man praying all the while.

And it was as if dying was this human's greatest weapon against the thing Stephen had become. Stephen felt a kind of back-blast from that death; it ripped into him: a sudden freeing of pure spirit. Stephen/not Stephen recoiled in horror. Spirit was what the demon kind craved, yet they could tolerate only the sparks, and even those they could consume only briefly. But this—it was like expecting a small flame and getting an all-consuming fireball.

Stephen recoiled within the demon more with each second, withdrawing from it even as it leapt over the girl's head, forgetting her in its anguish, clawing at itself, running toward the men in gas masks—the men standing by their vans in the side streets. It charged, roaring into them, ripping and tearing. Surely the fire could be put out with the blood of mortals. Three of them fell, and still the demon felt no better: Their blood could not cool its misery.

Panicking, it turned and ran on all fours like a loping wolf back to the great stinking heap of corpses, to climb and burrow into it. Then the demon was hidden, curled up like a fetus, and Stephen at last was able to wrench himself free.

He found himself falling upward through a crackle of energy, to emerge from a whirling portal into the world of floating mountains and sentient mist.

————

Seeing Reverend Anthony killed, crushed in the demon's hands, Glyneth fell to her knees to pray for him and for forgiveness. She had allowed the evangelist to sacrifice himself for her. Her gas mask was saturated and she coughed as a billow of greasy smoke drifted over her. The demon, seeming on fire from within, had leapt over her to the military intelligence men blocking the side street. She had looked away from what the demon did to them—but she looked again when the demon ran back to the mound of corpses, to burrow itself away.

Gagging and coughing, she got up and sprinted toward the side street. She had to jump over dying people as she went — ordinary people, hairdressers and policemen and teenagers and grocers and nurses, all succumbing to the final effects of Dirvane 17.

The event had onionskin layers: an experiment with pesticides was actually a military intelligence experiment; the military experiment was actually the first stage of a mass human sacrifice; another kind of summoning.

From a Professor Shephard, Paymenz had learned that certain members of military intelligence were also members of the Undercurrent: survivors of those who'd summoned the demons nine years before.

And here was the fruit of it: men, women, and children crawling, clawing like rabid animals, dying.

She ran past one of the men who'd perpetrated this—himself dying, torn in half.

She mouthed, *I'm sorry,* because not even such a man should die that way, and, slipping on his blood, she fell, whimpering. And breathing hard—her filter was almost used up. In a minute or two she'd be breathing D17.

Oh, God, she could become one of *those people*: the white-eyed shamblers. Ex-people. Pitiful and murderous.

She got up and ran full tilt, dodged a clutching hand that thrust from the cab of an overturned fire truck, just glimpsing the milky-eyed giggling face that went with it.

She ran, hearing her own breath coming harder and harsher in the gas mask, the goggles steaming up, blurring . . . and then she saw the van. A silver-gray van, seemingly deserted.

It was intact, with a door standing open. Cautiously, she looked inside. No one there. And no other gas masks. But the keys were in it!

Chest tightening with hot wires as the gas mask's overtaxed filter began to shut down, she climbed in, closed the doors, made sure the windows were shut, turned on the engine—and spotted a switch on an unfamiliar cylindrical dash mechanism labeled INTERNAL AIR CLEANSE.

She nodded to herself. This van belonged to the Pentagon experimental team; they'd have that kind of accessory. But it'd take time to work.

She hit the switch, coughing as the air came thinner and thinner through her mask, and put the car in gear, roared off down the road.

Ahead, in the center of the street, a round-faced middle-aged woman in a yellow knit pantsuit—the top of it torn half away, exposing her bloodied breasts—was weaving along, tearing out handfuls of her hair as she went, her eyes flat white, her lips foaming red. Alone in the midst of the street, in profound distress and beyond help, she seemed to represent all Ash Valley's victims. *She was probably someone's mother,* Glyneth thought, and tears began to flow. She had to suppress an impulse to run the woman down just to end her misery. Instead she veered the van around her and kept on toward the edge of town.

A double beep came from the mechanism on the dash, and a green light flashed. She pulled off the gas mask and gratefully inhaled clean air.

As she drove, her soft weeping became wracking sobs as Glyneth for the first time had a moment to think about more than survival.

"We failed," she said aloud. "*I* failed."

The circle had wanted her to confirm Winderson's part in what was being planned, had wanted to confirm their suspicions about Latilla. Who was she, really? They were sure about George Deane; they assumed H. D was part of it. Winderson, a master of public image, had covered his involvement well. He hadn't been one of the active invokers nine years before. They'd held a group of Saturnian adepts back, in case they failed, a group called the Undercurrent.

Winderson had been closely associated with Deane, and with the network of companies who'd promulgated the invasion . . . the invasion she remembered clearly, unlike so many around her. She'd seen Grindums and Spiders and Dishrags ravaging through a mountain community where she'd been doing work for the Sierra Club. Most of her friends had died that day.

Driven half mad by what she'd seen, Glyneth had looked for an explanation, for understanding. Through a certain Dominican in Snow Mass, Colorado, she was introduced to Yanan and Paymenz, and service to the Conscious Circle. And it was they who told her how the invasion had come about and what

big industry's part in it had been. She began an obsessive can-
vassing of corporate America—looking for patterns, connections to That Certain One. Then she heard about psychonomics
from a disgruntled former trainee, and she began to look
closely at West Wind. She used a fictitious academic background to get into the company . . . and Yanan pointed her to
Stephen.

When it became clear just how deadly Dirvane 17 was—
and equally clear from the e-mails she'd intercepted how many
state officials had been paid off about what was happening in
Ash Valley—she tried to convince Paymenz to do something
sooner, to alert the more sympathetic newspapers, the EPA, the
CDC, the U.N., *someone*, for God's sake.

Paymenz had begged her to hold back. "The circle says not
yet. They say that it's important for reasons I don't really understand that Stephen Isquerat turn the tide himself. It's no accident, his role in this—he possesses a gift, and that's why the
Undercurrent wants to twist it to their own use. But that gift can
work against them. If we simply report them, they'll cover up,
make excuses. They have to be stopped permanently. We could
lose some people in Ash Valley, but it might save millions later."

"No, goddamnit." She sobbed, now. The van fishtailed on
the road; she was having difficulty seeing through her own
tears. Thick clouds were gathering. A rainstorm, soon.

Up ahead, a group of cars was burning in the center of the
highway. She had to drive on the shoulder to get around them.

"No . . ." No, they should have done something—*anything*—
to stop this. That kind of logic—let a town die to save others
later? That was like West Wind's logic.

No!

They had failed. The mass sacrifice in Ash Valley happened
too soon. The intervention would come too late.

It was all just plain too fucking late.

———

"What's happened?" Latilla's harsh voice, heard from some distant corner of the sky. "Have we lost him?"

"There was interference." Harrison Deane's voice. "They are dogging us, somehow."

"I feel them; it's making me sick to my stomach."

Wasn't that Jonquil's voice? Was it possible? Stephen wondered vaguely. Could she be here or with them?

Where was *here*?

He was walking along one of those floating mountain peaks made of assumptions, another mountain whose base was its peak. If he looked closely at the ground beneath his feet, he could see it shifting within itself, as if constantly reaffirming its stony substance.

He couldn't bear looking at the nervous streamers of mist between the whirling symmetries in the sky. The faces that formed, when he looked at the mist, seemed so *afraid*.

Stephen felt wrung out, numb, and deeply afraid. He felt that for the first time he understood the expression *hanging by a thread*.

If he didn't hang on to that thread of identity within himself, he would shatter into a thousand Stephens, each to be sucked into one of those whirling symbols in the sky, each to be consumed by one of the living vanities who'd ruled that other world. He'd be annihilated by a thousand outlandish appetites.

The ecstasy he'd felt—he'd do almost anything to get back to it. Maybe . . . anything.

But the last part of the journey . . . had it been a dream, that vision of Ash Valley, of Glyneth? It had to have been. To become a demon, squatting in a great mound of corpses . . . maddened, dying people in a masque of death, dancing and murdering all around him . . .

The Reverend Anthony. Had he really killed him?

"He's beginning to—"

"Silence, idiot. You have forgotten our connection to his consciousness, here."

They had, after all, told him that what he was to experience was real. So that . . . was real? All those dead people—really dead?

"Stephen . . ." Jonquil. She was here! He could see her!

She was lying a few yards away, in a sort of girl-shaped groove cut into the ground, wearing only the nightgown she'd worn at the hospital. He hurried to her, knelt beside her, taking her warm hand in his. He couldn't see his own hand—but he could feel it touching hers.

She seemed to see him anyway, looking right at where his eyes should be.

"Stephen—it's getting worse. My sickness. I need the Black Pearl. It's the only thing that can stop them."

"Who, Jonquil? Who're our enemies?"

"An ancient circle of magicians, Stephen. This struggle of magicians has always gone on, but they have lately disguised themselves as *good* people. They attack us because they know we're creating a new and better world. They made you see what they wanted you to see—they made it seem that the god form you inhabited was something evil. They made you see dead people where there were living ones. They made you see depravity in Ash Valley, where there was only strength and goodness!"

"So it was them—they made it seem that way?"

She looked at him and drew him close, as if she saw his skepticism and blotted it out by encircling him—what there was of him here—in her arms.

"What can I give you, Stephen?" she breathed into his ears. The entire universe became suffused with the scent of gardenias.

"I . . . want you, Jonquil. And . . . I want . . . I want that feeling I had, that first rush that I felt, that feeling of ecstasy—like I never had to be scared of anything. I was the ruler of a universe of pleasure. . . . Oh God, oh fuck! I want that again. I want to be there with you! I saw you there—and I love you, Jonquil!"

"And I love you, Stephen. But I'm going to die unless you bring the Black Pearl to me. The rest of us don't have the gift of *going* like you do. You have an amazing gift for astral travel."

"But you're here . . ."

"I can only go so far. But you—why do you think you can travel in these places without going mad? No one else could go so far as you have and keep his sanity—not a human being. It's part of your gift. And you can go where the Black Pearl is. You have the gift of carrying its substance within you."

He could no longer hold himself back. He tried to lift her, to gather her in his arms—to mingle himself with her. But his hands plunged into warm mush—which became a syrupy mire, her entire body liquefying and running across the shifting stones under his knees.

"Jonquil!"

He stood up, and watched as her liquid remains, her rippling face, sank into the stone of the mountain, like water into loose sand. Gone.

"Help me . . . go to the Black Pearl. You must go of your own free will, because it is your will that takes you there. Find the Black Pearl. Take it to the god you inhabited before. His strength will become mine and I will survive! And I promise you, we will find the ecstasy of the dark glory, Stephen!"

With hands he couldn't see, he reached out to the sky. "Tell me, then! Tell me where to go to save her!"

He found himself moving toward one of the whirling symbols, the symbol of Saturn.

And through it—through an inversion, an inside-out of

himself that was becoming almost familiar, feeling he would explode but clinging to that inner thread as he fell through the sea of energy and emerged . . .

. . . in the sunless world of struggling egos, the thrashing groundless trees of energy wrestling with wires of desire. A landscape without land, an infinity of crackling loci, each trying to consume the next.

But one had grown bigger than all the others. It was like the tree Yggdrasil compared to the rest, overshadowing them all like a giant among midgets. Over an eon this tree had grown a single dark fruit, a dark globe that throbbed within the twisting, ever-restless branches of shoots, just above the incandescently pumping central trunk. Was it indeed black, this fruit, this Pearl? It was as silver as it was black, as iridescent as it was silver. It was as absolutely its own spherical shape as the cosmic egg had been before the Big Bang, yet it was quivering within itself with the concentrated electricities of undiluted will.

He knew this with the gnosis of the astral world—with the knowledge of sheer perception: He knew it for a certainty. The Black Pearl was an accretion of pure, selfish will. It was the movement toward the fulfillment of desire from a thousand, thousand egos, swallowed up by this great ego and stored here like a million lightning storms of electricity contained in a single battery.

Stephen saw it now, and he understood. The quantum uncertainty at the root of matter bent itself to will. Normally will was too weak to bend it much, but *this* will was imponderably concentrated, powerful enough to transmute reality. To give power to those who tapped into it—and that would include the power to cure Jonquil and to give him and Jonquil life in that continuum of ecstasy he'd all too briefly experienced.

"YES!" he shouted without a mouth, and plunged in spiritual flight toward the great Yggdrasil of this world, the Black Pearl at its center.

But this being was all senses—more senses than mind—and it sensed him coming. It thrashed its limbs to stop him, clawing at him with its crackling, sentient tendrils; the murderous, sentient whips snapping all about him. He flew betwixt them—just barely.

"Medusa!" *Was that Jonquil's voice?* But he couldn't let anything distract him.

Never before had he felt so vibrantly present as at that moment when he dove and spun and veered and wove like a swift through a hurricane-lashed forest, using every erg of his mental focus to avoid the trapping lashes of the ego giant's limbs.

Then he was approaching the Black Pearl.

"Medusa!"

"Jonquil?"

The message from Jonquil came to him compressed into a thousandth of a second:

"Don't look into the Pearl. Turn your perception away. But open your arms and envision yourself growing big. Imagine swallowing it. Do not look into it—it's like looking at Medusa."

He was plunging toward the Black Pearl. It was bigger than his arms could contain.

But he did as she said, envisioned himself growing gigantic, plunging into the ego tree, swallowing the Black Pearl, taking it like a pill.

He felt it enter him—and he shrieked with agony. It burned. It was like swallowing a sun whose fire was pure hatred.

And then he was sinking into the trunk of the ego tree, sucked into it, letting it digest him, and flying to . . . the world of men. Ash Valley, California.

———

How quickly the rain clouds had gathered, Glyneth thought, as she tossed the cell phone in the back and turned the van around. The rain came tentatively at first, pattering down on the windshield, then lashing it so she had to turn the wipers on high. Her heart felt like a hard, dead lump inside her. She felt cold and very, very lonely. Because she had chosen to die.

She couldn't turn her back on these people. She knew it was a waste of time to go back to Ash Valley, but she was going anyway. Because it was partly her fault this had all happened. That boy she had smashed with a length of pipe, that woman tearing her hair in the street. Dead people piled like some sick celebration of the Holocaust: She had failed them, and she should die with them. Maybe she could help someone, somehow.

She had been on the van's cell phone for some minutes. The highway patrol had heard about the disaster in Ash Valley, but no one wanted to hear that it had been orchestrated on purpose.

I just don't deserve to survive, she thought. *I could've saved those people somehow.*

The rain fell so hard the road was hidden by a sheet of water.

The rain! she thought, with a rush of realization. *And the wind!*

Together they would wash the D17 from the air. Maybe some who had taken shelter, out of the open air, might survive. She could help a few of them escape the demon, the butchering lunatics who stalked the ruins of Ash Valley. But those sons of bitches in the other vans might well make sure they didn't make it. The demon hadn't killed them all.

She looked in the glove compartment, and found what she'd hoped to find. A loaded .45 automatic.

———

Stephen cackled with joy as he felt the power begin to seethe out from the Black Pearl burning at the core of his being.

He sat up on his wrecked-car throne and raised his fists into the downpour, calling down lightning and dancing with it as it struck to ignite fires in the methane of the rotting corpses piled around him.

The rain hissed into the smoldering remains of the burning houses; it churned the exposed dirt of the Ash Valley park into mud. It cleansed the air of the poison—but the toxin had done its job. It had killed hundreds of the humans, had sacrificed their life energies in order to bring him here, and it would make it possible to bring the others: a second, greater swarm, an invasion of the seven clans that would dwarf the first. But they would turn men into gods, not demons. The sacrifice had laid the groundwork, had opened the gate wide enough . . . and now it was up to him, to it, to her, to the god and goddess he had become, to give birth to a new world.

————

The rain eased off and Glyneth was a little surprised at the way the vans were racing out of Ash Valley. Were they rushing to get out ahead of the authorities? She glimpsed only one of the driver's faces. It was etched with naked fear.

What could they've seen that was worse than what had already happened?

But then she saw it herself as she got within a few blocks of the park. A giant.

She slowed the van to a crawl, craning to look up at it.

The demon had grown, fed by the sacrifices. It was about six stories high, she guessed. Now seven, now eight.

There was something else. Something almost astronomically repulsive about it.

It was pregnant. Male or female or both, it didn't matter: It was obviously, gruesomely pregnant. Its glowing middle was swollen, and, through skin stretched to transparency, she could see many thousands of small figures squirming like sperm

DEMONS

under a microscope, like maggots in a boil—but she could see their silhouettes, now and then, when they became briefly disentangled from one another: Gnashers, Grindums, Spiders, Dishrags, Bugsys, Sharkadians, Tailpipes. All writhing in the translucent sac of the demon's belly.

How soon before it gave birth? Did Winderson and his friends know?

Probably not, she guessed. That Certain One deceived its followers.

She could just make out, behind the demon's features, a faint semblance of Stephen's. He had helped them bring this about somehow. Something in him had completed the magical circuit.

She drove onto the side street that led into the park. There was a single van there, half blocking the road, and three men stood beside it, arguing. They had their gas masks down around their necks—the air must be safe, now. Two of them were pointing at the giant a block away, standing up to its ankles in corpses, the skyscraping, swag-bellied demon shaking a stiff dead man at the sky like an insane queen threatening with its scepter.

She slowed her van, looking for a way around them. The taller man, the one she'd seen talking to Dickinham near the park that day, spotted her and seemed to recognize her. Probably the guy from the trailer, too. He stalked toward her, cocking his .45. She snorted at his overblown confidence. She powered the window down, leaned out, and said, "Peace, asshole." Then she shot him through the throat.

He fell, clutching his spurting neck. She fired at one of the other men; he fell. The third ran from her and then screamed as the demon took a single step, picked him up, and threw him whirling into the sky.

He never did come down.

She hesitated, wondering if she should crash the van into the giant's legs. *Useless. Try to find some of the local people, get them out to safety.*

Then the demon spotted her—and it bent down, smashed the van with its fist, crumpling the roof and sending it rolling into the ditch.

———

Stephen—and the demon—shook the world with a roar of rage.

There she was again, mocking him! This time she wouldn't scurry away into the night! He could feel the children! And the seeds of the new world inside him roared in gleeful agreement, squirming in a wash of dark energy.

The Stephen thing reached down for her.

"Hiya, boy kid."

Stephen felt himself shriveling up, going somewhere else, somewhere within . . .

He looked around. Where was he now?

He was in a big empty room made out of leather. He sat on the floor, panting, shaking from the sudden disengagement.

It was a round room with irregularly curved walls, two high windows shaped like eyes, a sort of grate shaped like a partly opened, fanged mouth. The light came from the eyes and mouth, falling from those three sources across the man sitting on the floor, opposite him, leaning back against the leathery wall with a sad smile on his face.

Boy kid.

Something his father had always called him.

His father: wearing the clothes he'd worn when he'd taken his son fishing: the same old flak jacket and jeans and hip boots. His father with the sagging face, the humorous brown eyes, the tousle of receding, curly gray hair.

"Dad?"

"Yep. It's me."

Stephen looked down at himself. He could see his hands now, his body. He was naked but embodied. And it was the body of a boy. "Where are we? How'd you get here?"

"We're not where we seem to be. What you see is a construction that represents reality somewhat symbolically. Our spirits have been transported to a neutral bubble in astral space. Amateurish cartooning on my part, really. I created it. I can't sustain it long. The Circle has called me. Somewhere in Russia, those who could get together called me. They pulled me from where I wandered, contacted me through the Gold in the Urn. Those who've gone on before, and who try to help us as they might, managed to pull together enough power to bring me here to talk to you, to give you a choice."

"But this place . . ." Then, looking around, it struck Stephen: He was inside a big, hollowed-out head. And he recognized the shape: It was the head of the demon.

"Yes, the demon you've inhabited."

"He is a *god*!" Stephen shouted, springing to his feet.

"So they tell you. It's the apotheosis of irony, really, to call that ludicrous, bloated, murderous demon a god. And they're telling you that the carnage you have seen all around him is just an illusion—and if you won't believe that, then next they'll lead you to believe the carnage is justified. You're not in a rational state—you haven't been since that girl took you into her bed. You were seduced, by her and Winderson both. Do you know, Stephen, how Winderson came to be indebted to me?"

"What?" Stephen felt drunk. "How?" Stoned and dizzy and half numb. His mind, he supposed, was shutting down. He'd had to deal with far too much.

"I'll tell you: He'd date-raped a girl when we were in college. He drugged her with that date-rape drug they had back then. He drugged her and he raped her and then, in his drunkenness, he called in two of his friends and he let *them* rape her. Well, the girl told a confused story about the whole thing. He was arrested—and he had a lot to lose. He would've gone to jail. He was my roommate and he could be very likable. At the time he made it sound as if he'd just gone a little wrong, and it was going to ruin his life.

"I didn't have some great destiny ahead of me as a leader of my father's corporation. I had no other friends, but I had a weakness, a need to sacrifice myself, so that others would like me. So I said I'd take the rap. I'd say I drugged her as a prank— and that he hadn't known she was drugged. That he left, didn't know the others took her, later. All lies. And I got a suspended sentence—the Windersons pulled some strings. But the university threw me out, naturally.

"I got into another school—again, with the Windersons' help—and eventually I became a schoolteacher.

"But *he* did it, Stephen. He did those things to that girl— not me. What sort of person would do that, hm? Ask yourself that, boy kid. Dale Winderson's that cold, and more. He's sacrificed a town full of people because he believes the power generated here will give him immortality and his own little cosmos to play around in. It's their fantasy, foisted on them by the dark puppeteer who squats on his Saturnian throne."

"I . . . you aren't really my father. This is some kind of test."

"I really am your father. I'm a spirit, now, Stephen—but just as real as I was in material life. I had the chance to develop my being, once dead, in a certain place I cannot describe, and the circle brought me here to reason with you. To tell you that if you struggle to control the demon, you *can* succeed. If you refuse to identify with his desires, his lusts, you *can* control him . . . but it means reaching in and taking the Pearl out—that node of pure will. Sacrificing it—the *real* sacrifice that should be made. Show the Pearl to them, Stephen. The four members of the Undercurrent you know—they arranged this so they wouldn't have to see it directly. Funny how here, the men possess demons and not vice versa. But that's always been the secret."

The father stood up, walked over to his son, and put his hands on the boy's shoulders. "You're going to have to give up a great deal. You'll have to accept the pain of knowing what you've done. It's going to hurt. But it'll be worth it."

Stephen felt like a little boy, again—sobbing out an explanation to his father. Here, he was only the small person at the center of himself—the undeveloped essence of himself . . . still a child. "But Jonquil—I have to save her!"

"Uh-huh. Son, you know inside somewhere that the hospital was a setup. It's a real hospital, but everything you saw there was theater. The nurse was an actor. That girl isn't sick, Stephen. Right now she's joining the others in the observatory. Why do you think you've been hearing her, seeing her? She's well, she's strong—and she's a monster, Stephen.

"They're using you. They want to feed on the whole world. Their kind have been feeding on the world like parasites for a long time now. They want to swallow it whole. Like they've swallowed you."

"Dad, I haven't got the strength to fight it!"

"Yes, you do," Stephen's father said, taking his son in his arms. "Yes, you do. Just be willing to sacrifice everything. The truth is, you have nothing to lose. Jump that abyss, son. Faith will carry you over it."

"I don't have any goddamn faith!"

"Do you trust me? You sometimes did when I was alive."

Stephen wept onto his father's shoulder. He knew it was really him. He could feel it: This was really, authentically, palpably his father. "Yes . . . yes I do."

"Then trust me in this. You can take command. . . ."

Stephen's father hesitated, looking at the light coming through the windows. He cocked his head as if listening. Then he nodded. "It seems I have to go now. We've used up all that we've paid for—all the grace we had, to hold your mind in this place. We got you here between two blinks of an eye, Stephen. When I let you go back, you'll be on your way to kill someone. And you don't *have* to kill her, Stephen. In less than a minute the great antibirth will happen—and those living appetites will burst into the world, through you. All at once, they'll explode out of the demon.

"But try to remember. Remember yourself, remember me— and you *will* be able to choose. In order to choose, you must see that you are inside a monster—and you must *wake up* inside it.

"Good-bye, son. See you again sometime." His father kissed his cheek.

"Don't go!"

But he was gone, and the place dissolved around Stephen, becoming fibrous, rotting away like an old jack-o'-lantern. Dissolving . . .

Stephen was again standing up to his ankles in corpses, towering over the ruins of a small town, shaking his fists at the sky—and bending to tear a young female human from the little gray vehicle.

———

The van rolled onto its roof. Glyneth crawled out through the half-crumpled window frame, not caring that edges of broken glass were raking her sides, carving strips of skin away. The van was on fire, and she could feel the pressure of an imminent explosion building inside it. She could smell the gas fumes. She didn't want to burn to death here. Better to let the monster tear her apart.

She managed to squirm clear, got to her feet, and took a

few steps—when the explosion smashed her down again. The wind knocked out of her, she lay shaking in the mud beside the road. Flames danced along the frame of a small red-painted tricycle lying on its side nearby. She could see the crumpled child who went with the tricycle lying in the yard, facedown in mud, quite obviously dead.

She began to pray again, feeling as if she were praying into a void because God seemed absent from all creation.

"Great Organizer, Christ and Buddha, forgive me my surrender to despair . . . lift me up. . . ."

She looked up to see the demon squatting, about to take her into his claws. It was squatting carefully, out of deference to the great obscene hemisphere of its swarming belly. Just a dozen yards from her, that swollen sac—and through its translucent skin she could see faces leering at her in sickening delight.

"Stephen!" she shouted at it, though she knew it was useless. "Stephen, wake up!"

The great taloned leather hand reached for her. She thought absurdly of King Kong and Fay Wray, and laughed harshly at the death that she was going to have.

But—was it toying with her?—the demon hesitated.

She saw a sort of *clearing* in its eyes—it seemed to *see* her, as if for the first time. To recognize her.

She heard a voice rumble from deep inside it.

"Glyneth . . . pray . . . for me . . ."

She knelt, closed her eyes, and prayed—with all her being. She had nothing to lose.

———

Stephen struggled to hold himself back. Watching Glyneth, he could *see* the prayer as a kind of emanation, a living energy.

And then something carried by the prayer, like water carried in cupped hands, washed over him, and he knew with a crystallized inner certainty: Winderson and Jonquil *had* been lying to him.

And he had been lying to himself. He had killed a good man—the Reverend Anthony—with his own hands. And he had helped them do all this to Ash Valley. He saw himself, then, as he was, within the demon—the ragged, mewling face at the other end of the mountain he'd glimpsed that day.

No. That wasn't going to be the way of it. He didn't have to do any of this.

But a thousand roars of fury shook him—he felt *them* boiling up inside. They sensed his change of heart; *they* would overtake him. The demonic offspring would burst free—

He straightened up, and very deliberately, using his claws, tore into his own middle, just above the belly, and wrenched the Black Pearl free.

Its energies removed, that which kept the demonic colony in this world collapsed.

———

Glyneth felt something change, felt it in the air. There was a sense of unseen rejoicing. The Gold was rejoicing, somewhere.

She stood, in time to see the demon stumbling backward, falling to its knees, swaying there, one hand holding the strobing black light of the Pearl, the other clutching at the wound in its belly.

From which thousands of demons now erupted. Birthed into the world.

We failed—the Circle failed! she thought, despairing.

The giant demon hitched itself backward and leaned on a house that creaked and cracked under its weight, as the Black Pearl vanished from its talons. And it looked with confused fascination as the mass birthing rippled and roared over the ravaged park. Demons hopping, leaping, slashing, whirling— demons birthed but lost without the Black Pearl.

The newborn demons surged outward in a wet squirming gray-green mass, almost like a swarm of bees, but each one big as a man, or bigger. The two-story-high mass writhed as the demons clawed at whatever was nearest . . . and then focused their frustrated attention on the giant who'd birthed them. Thousands of demons turned, as one, against the giant demon, coming at it in ravenous waves, like the charge of an army. The giant squealed in rage as they attacked it like piranha, all of them at once, so that its shredded flesh sprayed into the air from their thousands of gnashing jaws, slashing claws. When it was reduced to a shell, a smoking miasma, they hesitated, blinking.

And turned on one another.

Without the correct completion of the ritual—without the Pearl's energies that would have disseminated into each of them—they had no power to attack the world of men. They turned in murderous wrath on each other, demon consuming demon.

Glyneth watched in frozen revulsion as the seething dia- bolic swarm began to implode, each vanishing into the other.

Until the army of demons seemed to drain away into itself, the squealing mass shrinking as if it were falling from a great height, to vanish to a great depth. They were completing— through rage and carnage—the vast abortion of a thousand, thousand demons . . . who were sucked one into another and then into the hole in space from which they'd come, drawn away into the rift in probability with the sound of a sudden gi- gantic indrawn breath. And a single collective wail of despair.

Where, though . . .

Where was Stephen?

Bald Peak Observatory

Jonquil walked out of the shadows toward the group arranged around the pentagram. She was drawn there in spite of herself. She knew she should run. She couldn't.

In the center of the room, the throng of black nodes had coalesced around Stephen and compressed into his hands.

Latilla screamed. In Stephen's hands lay the Black Pearl.

"No—not here! In the god! It must be inside the god! It must feed the young!" she cried out, backpedaling frantically away from him.

The onyx sphere in his hands was exactly as big as the Gold in the Urn had been when first released—but it was the Gold's opposite. Its black light seemed to summon every gaze in the room. It demanded their attention. They felt themselves drawn to stare into it.

Jonquil walked toward the Black Pearl. So did Winderson, Harrison Deane, and the general and Latilla. They tried not to, but they couldn't help themselves. They moved like sleepwalkers.

As awareness returned to him, Stephen didn't look at the object he held in his hands. He felt a guidance from somewhere, and he knew what to do. He stared over their heads. He was particularly careful not to look at Jonquil, especially when she begged, "Stephen—take it away!"

He shook his head firmly, and he waited.

Waited.

Medusa.

They stared into the Black Pearl . . . and saw themselves in it. Saw themselves reflected in it. It was a spherical black mirror.

In it, they saw themselves as they really were; they saw their naked souls.

They screamed.

Still, they were drawn to approach it, and, one by one, they put their hands on it.

Then they were gone.

Their bodies fell to the floor—Winderson, H. D., Latilla, the General, Jonquil—staring, breathing . . . empty. Their minds, their essences, what shreds of soul they had, had all been drawn into the Black Pearl.

Out of the corner of his eye, Stephen saw their faces writhing in fish-eye distortion *within* the Pearl. He felt himself tugged to look closer . . . and forced himself to look at the ceiling.

The telescope.

He heard a gentle whispering from within himself. He walked to the metal stairs, and up the clanking flights to the telescope. Still looking away, using only his peripheral vision, he pressed the Black Pearl against the lens of the modified telescope. It was sucked up, like a bubble going backward into a bubble pipe, vanishing into it. There was a burst of dark energy at the other end of the telescope as a screaming, living substance blasted away into space. He looked to see where the telescope was pointed: the moon.

He shuddered, suddenly so weak he was near collapse. He wanted to get away from here.

But first he climbed down to the bodies lying around the pentagram. They were alive but truly empty. Comatose. Vegetative. They would live out their lives, silently decaying in a mental hospital.

He looked around and found a tool closet. In it were a hammer and chisel, and he took them back to the stairs. He carried the tools up to the telescope, and smashed it as well as he might.

"What the hell are you doing? What's happened to the boss?"

Stephen looked down to see Crocker gaping up at him.

"The experiment here is over," Stephen told him. "If you don't want to be arrested in the fallout from what's gone down in Ash Valley, you'd better leave. Tell everyone."

"But what'd you do to the boss? He's like staring into space—and Jonquil and . . ."

"Yes—they're comatose. For good, it seems to me. You see the pentagram thing on the floor? Do you know what it is?"

"Fuck, no! And I don't want to know!"

"It's the reason they're the way they are. You really don't want me to tell you. Get away from here or surrender to the police. They can't keep their backs turned forever. They'll say it was all the chemicals, you know. And your laboratory."

Crocker gaped even more widely—and turned, ran from the room without another glance at the bodies.

Stephen smashed another lens. Then he tossed the tools aside, went out to make some calls and find a car.

Portland, Oregon

Ira let it wash over him. Just being home with family. Being safe and fed and warm and knowing something, at least, had been accomplished. Not perfectly accomplished. Too many had died. But it hadn't been for nothing.

Professor Paymenz laughed and shook his head. "Marcus, I am *not* going to play poker with you for Oreos. Last time you got all the cookies, I got the humiliation, you got the bellyache, and your mother got mad at me."

Ira sat on the sofa, with books piled on either side of him; he was watching a lava lamp. The absurd goo stretched up, buckled, globuled, rose, rearranged . . . all in a pretty, artificially rosy light.

They were in the living room of Paymenz's apartment, cluttered with lava lamps, malodorous with cat boxes, coated with cat fur, crowded with bookshelves. It was an hour after the simple dinner Melissa had made for them. Ira had picked at his food as usual; Yanan had gone home shortly after dinner, apologizing that there was work he must do.

"Come onnn," Marcus pleaded with Paymenz. "Be my homie dog, Granddad. One hand. Just one hand."

"Oh, go on," Melissa said, her eyes misting, "play him for cookies. He's been through a lot."

"We don't have any Oreos."

"I got some for him. They're in the cabinet over the fridge."

"You were ready to spoil him."

"Just a little."

Paymenz sighed. He reached up to tug his beard—but it wasn't there, and he scratched his chin instead. He went to the kitchen with Marcus, they got the cards and cookies, and began to play at the kitchen table.

"Yo-whoa!" Marcus said. Just exactly like the Marcus of old. "I get to shuffle, not you!"

"I'm your granddad, you know, have some respect. Okay, you shuffle. Paranoid kid. What a generation of vipers."

Melissa came to sit by Ira. She had to move a stack of her father's books to the floor before she could sit down. She took his hand.

He looked down at it a little self-consciously: The bones had mostly healed straight. His hand had been only slightly broken. One of his cheekbones had healed a tad crooked, he knew.

Ira started to say something about the dead in Ash Valley. About Glyneth, sick in a hospital, only a few blocks away. About the price they had paid.

But he decided against it. Not so long ago, he'd have said it. He'd have hammered on the dark side; he'd have railed about the night and brought everyone with him into the darkness.

Now it was different. Now he had died. Now he was something new. He was the same and he was different.

So he said nothing, and he simply held her hand.

And he thought, looking around the room, that each little lamp, each light source cast a shadow—and without the lamps and the window, the room would be *completely* dark. And Melissa sat in a dim part of the room; her face illuminated mostly from the window, the moon and stars and the city's light. The light on her face, in that moment, was like the light you saw on the Earth in photos taken from space. In a way, they were always in the dark. As the whole Earth was always floating in the perpetual dark of interplanetary space— but for the Sun. There was only a vast darkness broken by individual light sources. And each source added its light to the whole.

"I'm just incredibly, amazingly relieved that Marcus is himself again," Melissa was saying. "I know it wasn't possession— I know Mendel *was* Marcus—and Marcus was Mendel, but it just wasn't natural. There was a Marcus that was particularly him, that child. That was lost . . ."

"He's back now. Mendel's gone to sleep. Our boy is well and happy."

She smiled at him. "Funny how you seem more optimistic— after something so terrible happened to you."

He shrugged and kissed her.

The doorbell rang. Melissa swore, then got up to answer. It was the old shaikh, Araha, and a man Ira didn't recognize. But he guessed who it was, and went to shake his hand.

"Stephen Isquerat," said the young man.

"Hi, I'm Ira. This is Melissa."

Stephen was looking around. He seemed bemused.

Melissa chuckled. "Not what you expected, right? So—how's Glyneth?"

"Responding to treatment. The cancer isn't . . . too advanced. It was so sudden . . . but I think she'll be all right. I'm going back to the hospital in a couple of hours. They're doing some more tests now."

"Our faithful young Stephen has set up a cot beside her," Araha said. "How is the boy?"

Melissa beamed. "He's great. His old self."

"Have you no coffee, nothing for an old man?"

"I'll get it—coffee and cookies. You guys push whatever needs pushing onto the floor and find a seat," Melissa said, bustling into the kitchen.

Stephen went and sat down, across the room, looking abstractedly into a golden lava lamp.

Marcus shouted, "You cheater! No way you got a straight!" from the kitchen.

Ira smiled. Araha looked gravely at him. "She believes?"

Ira nodded. "More or less. Anyway—I'm very grateful to Mendel."

"Well—he's not precisely acting. He has found that he can go to a playful, innocent place in himself, and be the boy. He is, after all, the boy. It took some time for him to find it. He will be the boy for her, for as long as she needs it."

Ira glanced at the kitchen. He could hear Melissa chattering with them; she hadn't heard Araha. It was all right. She was no fool, but Mendel's performance was seamless. And she wanted to believe.

"Come," Araha said. They went to sit with Stephen.

Stephen smiled at them, but Ira saw that he had tears in his eyes and his hand shook on the arm of the sofa. Ira could see that he had to make a perpetual effort at seeming well, seeming okay with himself, and that he was just propped up, somehow.

"What is it?" Ira asked gently.

"I . . . helped what happened . . . to happen. I was part of it. The dead . . . children . . . all the suffering . . ."

"Yes. We all failed. But you succeeded, too. You did something great. And the harm you did was really just humanity's fallen state showing itself once again. It was everyone's sin."

Araha nodded approvingly. "You take care of Glyneth . . . but they tell me you're a volunteer with other cancer patients."

"It's what I want to do—to help heal people."

"You will. You see, we all fail. But we go on, and we redeem ourselves where we can, Stephen. Simply . . . wherever we can."

JOURNAL OF STEPHEN ISQUERAT, JUNE 2

Glyneth and I will be married next month. God bless her.

But the joy is a little blighted today by a government announcement. The lies and cover-ups about Ash Valley have come to a culmination: chemically induced insanity, hallucinations. Only a few people at West Wind are being prosecuted. Payments are being made. West Wind's stockholders have voted to make an enormous settlement with survivors and relatives of victims, and yet West Wind's stock has gone up. . . . It's higher than it was before.

I have to let it go. Just let it go.

It's not so hard, now, to let it go. Since the day of the Black Pearl, I've never quite shaken the feeling of the unreality—or limited reality—of the material world. It comes and goes. For a while I could feel nothing but remorse. But now . . . when I've accepted my part in things, the ghostly feeling comes back: the feeling that everything is spirit. People are just spirits, waves on the sea of spirit, surfacing in this world for a while, then sinking back.

Before, it frightened me—that sense that mind and spirit underlie all physical reality. That, despite appearances, it's all just . . . spirit.

But now, it's a comfort to feel it. Because that truth is what redeems existence itself.

The waking have one world in common;
sleepers have each a private world of his own.

—HERACLITUS